THE HAWK
and the JEWEL

Lori Wick

HARVEST HOUSE PUBLISHERS
Eugene, Oregon 97402

All Scripture quotations in this book are taken from the King James Version of the Bible.

THE HAWK AND THE JEWEL

Copyright © 1993 by Lori Wick
Published by Harvest House Publishers
Eugene, OR 97402

Library of Congress Cataloging-in-Publication Data
Wick, Lori.
  The hawk and the jewel / Lori Wick.
    p.   cm. — (The Kensington chronicles ; bk. 1)
  ISBN 1-56507-101-8
  1. Man-woman relationships—England—Fiction.   I. Title.   II. Series:
Wick, Lori. Kensington chronicles ; bk. 1.
PS3573.I237H3   1993
813'.54—dc20   93-18835
                                                                          CIP

Printed in the United States of America.

To my father- and mother-in-law,
John and Helen Wick.
You welcomed me into your family with open arms.
You give of yourselves time and again,
and I am often the recipient.
Your life has been an example to me on
many occasions, and I thank you
for your love and strength.

THE AUTHOR

LORI WICK is the author of seven Christian novels including *Whatever Tomorrow Brings*, *As Time Goes By*, *A Song for Silas*, and *A Place Called Home*. She writes from her home in Wisconsin, where she lives with her husband, Bob, and their three children. In this new series, Lori expands her artistic horizons, taking readers across the sea to the sceptered British Isles.

Other Books by Lori Wick—

A Place Called Home Series
- A Place Called Home
- A Song for Silas
- The Long Road Home
- A Gathering of Memories

The Californians
- Whatever Tomorrow Brings
- As Time Goes By
- Sean Donovan

The Kensington Chronicles
- The Hawk and the Jewel

The Kensington Chronicles

DURING THE NINETEENTH CENTURY, the palace at Kensington repre-
sented the noble heritage of Britain's young queen and the simple
elegance of a never-to-be-forgotten era. The Victorian Age was the
pinnacle of England's dreams, a time of sweeping adventure and gentle
love. It is during this time, when hope was bright with promise, that
this series is set.

Prologue

LONDON 1832

THE CASKET DIPPED PRECARIOUSLY in the hands of the sailors as it was carried toward the docks. Lord Randolph Gallagher, Marquess of Woodburn, watched their progress and found himself flinching with pain, even though his wife felt nothing. The ship on which he had just sailed from the Arabian Sea, a ship he had felt anxious to leave for weeks, now held a type of solace. His eyes followed the men's descent down the gangway, but he was somehow hesitant to follow.

A massive coach pulled up behind the waiting hearse, and Lord Gallagher recognized it immediately. Still he did not move from his place on the deck of the *Katherine Ann*. Not until the small, white, strained face of his mother appeared in the window did his feet propel him forward.

He came to a halt just outside her window, the height of the coach as well as his own putting their faces at eye level.

"Is it true? Is it true what your message said?"

"It's true; Katherine is dead."

"And Sunny?" she whispered.

Randolph only shook his head. "There was no trace of her."

The older woman, small as she was, seemed to shrink before his eyes. "I can't believe it, Rand. If she were gone, I know I would feel it within me. I just can't believe she's dead too."

Randolph's eyes were filled with compassion. He'd had weeks on the voyage home to come to grips with the deaths of his wife and young daughter, but for his family the news was just hours old. With another check on the hearse, Randolph joined his mother in the coach. He listened to her whisper, again telling herself it just could not be.

Randolph stayed silent, praying that his mother would soon accept the death of her tiny namesake. He knew that until she did, she would give her heart no chance to heal.

His thoughts were drawn away from his mother as the coach lurched into motion. His mind moved to the faces of his three other children. They would have to be told, and swiftly, that their mother and sister were dead.

Part One

Shani

One

THE EMIR'S WARD PEEKED OUT OF THE SHADOWY DOORWAY into the empty courtyard beyond. The way seemed clear, but she knew well that looks could be deceiving. When she was certain that all would be safe, Shani crossed on silent feet.

The guards, standing unnoticed in their respective places, let her pass. She'd been sneaking across the outer courtyard since before her fifth year. Even though they were supposed to stop her, they never did—for Shani was their ruler's favorite. Nevertheless, before she reached the emir's chambers, her actions had been reported.

Ahmad Khan, ruler of Darhabar, dismissed the young slave girl attending him with only a brief move of his head. Ali, his chief advisor, had appeared in the entryway of his private chambers. There was a need to speak privately. The two men, long-time friends, settled themselves comfortably on the pillows and spoke in low tones.

"She will be here momentarily," Ali told his sovereign ruler.

"I understand she came across the courtyard."

"That is why I'm here," Ali went on. "It's a sign that she's feeling restless again. She will no doubt wish to speak of England."

11

Ahmad nodded thoughtfully. Nearly 13 years ago, a child and her mother had been brought to the palace. The child, whom they guessed to be past her second birthday, was clinging to the mother who, after nearly drowning, was on the brink of death.

Ahmad could see that she was a beautiful woman. Even in her injured state that was obvious. He would have kept her for himself, if she had survived. Within days of her death the father had come looking for them, but by then Ahmad was so taken with the beautiful child that he had lied about ever seeing her.

The grieving husband was taken to his wife's body. Katherine Gallagher was beautifully prepared, wrapped in cloth that had been dipped in rich spices. Without delay she was taken aboard her husband's vessel, and without the slightest twinge of guilt the emir had gone to the tower and watched them sail away.

From that point, discreet inquiries were made in England as to the child's home and the rest of her family. But before word returned to the palace, Ahmad had named her Shani. Her name meant "wondrous," and indeed she was wondrous in his eyes. She had a head full of chestnut-colored curls and violet eyes. Never had he seen eyes of such a color.

She was the delight of his world as she grew. There was never a day that she was not allowed entrance into his chambers. If one of his wives or concubines had joined him for the night, Shani was kept away, but if he was in the palace, she was allowed to seek him out. He was closer to her than all but two other members of his entire household: his chief advisor, Ali, and his favorite wife, Indira.

Indira had never given him a daughter. She had blessed him with five healthy sons, the oldest of whom was the heir to the throne, but never a girl. Shani became Indira's girl as well as his own. Indira loved her as her own child, and there was never a jealous moment between them. This could not be said of Ahmad's other wives, concubines, and children. However, no harm ever befell Shani since the entire palace kept her in their eye. Her status as his favorite brought much protection; it also brought her privileges she should not have had.

"She will be here shortly, my prince," Ali said, reverting to the name he'd called the emir through the years his father had been on the throne.

Ahmad nodded decisively. "Stay within hearing this day. If you are right, and she does want to talk of her home, we will take it as a sign. You know what to do."

Ali stood and bowed low. He slipped behind a semitransparent screen just as Shani's presence was announced.

"I think, little one, that your mind is not on our game today."

Shani lay back against the pillows and stared broodingly at the chessboard. "I was in the tower yesterday," she admitted softly, since it was strictly forbidden.

"And at the stables the day before that, and in the courtyard today," Ahmad added dryly. "Somehow I do not think your mind is on your sins."

Shani shook her head in agreement, but then she leaned forward, her youth showing in the clear, guileless depths of her eyes. "There was an English ship in the harbor. I couldn't see very well, but there appeared to be two women on board. They wore long dresses and scarves on their heads, but their faces were bare."

Ahmad's heart sank, although his face gave nothing away. He'd expected as much, but his suspicions didn't make what was about to commence easier. He had thought through the next few years carefully, and knew what must be done. Over Shani's shoulder, he watched Ali rise and move silently from the chamber.

"And you wish," Ahmad once again gave the girl his full attention, "that you could be on board the ship too."

"Oh, please, Poppy," she used her baby name for him. "I promise to stay out of the courtyard and the stables for an entire moon."

Ahmad shook his head indulgently. "We shall see."

It was the closest he'd ever come to agreeing, and Shani threw her arms around his neck. His other children never approached him without permission, but he had always allowed spontaneity with his Shani.

Shani was no better an opponent after hearing the good news; if anything, she was more preoccupied than before. So when another ten minutes passed, and she asked to be excused, Ahmad granted her wish without hesitation.

Ali entered the chamber a moment later, watching his master's face for emotion. At first glance Ahmad's look was guarded, but upon closer inspection, grief showed within his eyes.

"Have you taken care of the matter, Ali?"

"I have."

"So now we wait," Ahmad said, and his eyes filled with pain. Ali, upon seeing that pain, sensed his ruler's need to be alone.

Two

SHANI MADE HER WAY QUIETLY THROUGH THE PALACE and back to her own chambers. She slipped out of the short lavender vest she wore and kicked off the silky purple pants that hung just below her navel and were banded at the ankles.

She studied her naked reflection in the mirror for long minutes before slipping quietly out the door and into the bathing chamber. No one ever used the pools at this time of the afternoon, and Shani, beginning to feel self-conscious over her lack of curves, preferred to bathe alone.

"Fourteen years old," she said miserably as she swam in lazy circles, "with no breasts, no hips, and legs as long and straight as a boy's. Poppy will have to pay someone to take me to wife."

"Talking to yourself, Shani?"

Shani laughed softly as Indira, the only mother she'd ever known, came and sat at the edge of the pool.

"You do not bathe with us in the mornings any longer, little one. Why is that?"

Shani deliberately dove beneath the surface of the water, but Indira, not to be put off so easily, was sitting just as she had been when Shani surfaced. Her dark eyes were serious, yet loving; questioning, yet patient.

"I am restless," Shani admitted. "Not 30 minutes ago I was talking with Poppy. Now I'm swimming alone and pouting about the shape of my body. Nothing satisfies me anymore. It is as Poppy has always said; I'm the most spoiled child in the palace."

"What is wrong with the shape of your body?"

"It is shape*less*; that is what is wrong."

"You are young."

"Kadeem is younger and already with child," Shani pointed out logically. She was referring to another of Ahmad's daughters, one who had come into womanhood two years ago and was already married and expecting.

"I am 14," Shani pointed out, as though Indira might have forgotten.

What Shani didn't know was that Indira could not get her age from her mind. Shani's height and verbal skills had fooled them 13 years ago, but it was now quite evident that their Shani was not 14.

She also knew that to inform her of this now would crush her young heart, not because it would upset her to be a year younger—that would be a relief—but because it would mean admitting to other lies they had told her all the years she'd lived with them. Even if Ahmad had not forbidden her to speak of it, Indira would never have had the heart. It would instantly put Shani at ease over her lack of development, but it would also open such a world of pain and confusion for her that she might never be their Shani again.

"You are not concerned, are you?" Shani asked from the edge of the pool where she now dried herself. Indira was the only person she allowed to see her naked.

"No. You are not Indira, and you are not Kadeem. You are Shani, and you will become a woman when it is Shani's time to do so."

Mother and daughter walked into Shani's chambers together. Shani slipped into a short robe and then joined her mother on the pillows. Indira immediately began to brush Shani's hair. It was something she'd done just before Shani's bedtime from the first days Shani was in the palace. It was not bedtime on this occasion, but Indira sensed Shani's need for her tender touch.

As she'd done so many times in the past, Indira's mind wandered to what Shani's real mother must have been like. She had not seen the half-dead woman who had been rescued from the sea and brought to the palace, but she'd heard that she was a woman of beauty. To that time Indira believed that all English women were colorless, both in looks and temperament, but Shani's mother, if not Shani herself, had proven otherwise.

Shani's eyes were so blue they were purple, astonishingly rare in their small country. Even though Indira had no proof, she believed they would also be quite remarkable in England. It was more than Shani's unique appearance that changed Indira's opinion about English women; it was also her personality.

Indira had watched her march into Ahmad's chambers on many occasions, head held high even though punishment awaited her. Rarely had Shani admitted she was wrong or said she regretted an act, only that she was sorry to be caught. Indira, even knowing she was the emir's favorite wife, would never have been so insolent.

"Poppy said today that I could visit an English ship." Shani spoke suddenly, and Indira's hand faltered with the comb. "Well, not exactly. He said we would see."

"Well then," Indira said, effectively hiding the fear in her voice, "you have something to hope for now, something to put your restless mind to work."

Indira's arms came about her then, and even though this wasn't an uncommon occurrence, Shani felt she held her a little tighter than usual.

The evening ended well for Shani, as she was the only child to dine with both Indira and Ahmad. They laughed and supped until Shani grew sleepy.

When a palace eunuch escorted Shani back to her chambers, Indira joined Ahmad in his bedroom. They talked for hours before spending the night together. It was not a night of passion, but one of Ahmad holding Indira in his arms as she cried herself to sleep.

Three

August 17, 1844

"BUT WHY DOES POPPY WANT ME?" Shani questioned for the fifth time.

"Be patient, my child." Ali's voice was calm as they walked the halls of the palace toward the emir's chambers.

"I've not been near the stable *or* the tower, and only through the courtyard twice." She sounded so logical, certain that she was in trouble. Ali smiled but did not answer.

Shani hesitated on the threshold of Ahmad's chambers. She had never before feared him, even when she should have, but things in the palace had been different for a number of weeks. Shani was not certain she could explain the changes, but she felt them nevertheless.

"Come in, little one," Ahmad called to her upon witnessing her hesitancy. Shani, after bowing low, saw his smile and immediately relaxed.

"Ali has been very mysterious this day," she commented with her usual spontaneity, but as she came forward into the large salon, some of her apprehension returned. Standing beyond the emir was a woman she'd never seen before. The woman's dress was odd; her expression anxious. It was obvious that she was waiting for instructions.

"Again you hesitate," Ahmad teased her. "For years now you have begged me to board an English ship, and now that I have provided a way, you look at me with fear."

"A ship? This woman can take me to a ship?" Shani's voice was breathless with anticipation and disbelief.

"No. She cannot take you to a ship, but she can make you a suitable English costume to wear. The tower will watch for such a ship, and at such a time as I deem correct, I will arrange a tour."

Shani was so stunned she did not at first react. She looked to Ali, whose mouth lifted in a small smile, and then back to her Poppy. A second later she was leaping about the salon and screeching like a wounded animal.

"Shani," Ahmad's voice was sharp. Such displays were not offensive to him but they had a guest, and Shani's behavior had to be above reproach.

Shani, having been trained in control and the art of hiding one's emotions from the time she was a child, immediately quieted, her gaze dropping submissively to the floor.

"That is better," Ahmad told her, his voice still stern. "You will remain here with Ali and do all that he tells you."

Ahmad crossed to the door, and Shani's head turned to follow his progress. His disappointment with her was like a knife in her side, and she anxiously watched his retreating back.

As though sensing her gaze, Ahmad stopped short of exiting. He looked back and their eyes locked, only this time his were twinkling with suppressed laughter. Shani had to fight her own mirth when she saw those eyes, but at least she had the knowledge that she was back in his good graces.

Two weeks later Shani summoned Rashad, her personal eunuch, to her chambers. She gave him a message to deliver to Indira, and then she waited for a reply with ill-concealed impatience. There was never a time she wasn't welcome in her mother's rooms, but on this occasion Shani wanted privacy.

As she waited, she told herself to stay away from the mirror, but found it couldn't be done. A huge smile broke across her face as she beheld her image for at least the tenth time that day.

Her dress was made of red wool. The sleeves were long and narrow and the neckline high and stiff. Shani had never worn clothing that covered so much of her person. She lifted the front of the skirt and nearly giggled at the pale linen pantaloons and woolen stockings that covered her legs. Shani was still amazed at the amount of clothing she'd had to don. There had been pantaloons, a camisole, a shift, the stockings, and a petticoat. All of this was *before* the dress. She was literally swathed in clothing, but Shani was having such fun she didn't care.

She continued to study herself, turning to the side to see her profile and smiling with satisfaction. What she loved most about her new outfit was the way it disguised her body. She was still as straight up and down as a reed, but no one would be the wiser with the full skirt of the dress she now wore.

"What is so urgent," Indira's amused voice pulled Shani from the mirror, "that I must dismiss my maids from their duties and come to your chambers?"

Shani knew she was not angry over the disturbance. She stood waiting for her mother's inspection and verdict. Shani turned in a full circle when Indira directed her with a wave of her hand. She tried to stay silent, but it was impossible.

"Just look underneath," Shani chattered with the enthusiasm of a girl. She lifted the front of her dress to show Indira a network of underclothing. Indira's eyes widened as she took in shift, petticoat, and bloomers.

"So much?"

"That is what Calla said," Shani told her, referring to the woman who'd been brought from the north border to sew for the emir's young ward.

"Maybe the day you visit this ship will be cool, and you will be glad for much cloth."

"Indira," Shani said, suddenly very serious, "do you know what day I'm to go?"

"No, little one. Poppy has not spoken of this to me."

"Indira," Shani questioned again, her voice now a little frightened. "Is Poppy angry with me?"

"No, little one." Indira's voice was gentleness itself, knowing they had not hidden their emotions as well as they had believed. "Much is happening in the palace," she explained.

"Rashad tells me the centennial approaches."

"And so it does, but Poppy's mind is full of many things, one of which is your happiness. Always understand, Shani, his only wish is to see you happy."

Shani's mind was put to rest and she turned back to the glass. She studied her reflection again for long moments, not even aware of her mother taking leave of her chambers.

Four

September 5, 1844

CAPTAIN BRANDON HAWKESBURY STOOD ON THE DECK of the *Flying Surprise*, his eyes intent on the shoreline beyond. Flynn, his first mate, had come up beside him, but a longboat had left shore, and the captain did not turn or even acknowledge him.

An older man by several years, Flynn allowed the captain his silence. Only when he saw that the smaller vessel was drawing near, did he disturb his long-time friend, knowing the question could wait no longer.

"How many of the crew do you want on deck, Hawk?"

Brandon never took his eyes from the approaching longboat. "I really don't expect trouble." The younger man's voice was deep and calm. "Just tell the men to act normally, and to be courteous if spoken to."

The mate left him then, and Brandon went back to his thoughts, the first and foremost of which was that she would be on board in a matter of minutes.

Shani's excitement mounted as they drew closer to the tall frigate that rested easily in the water. Of all the English ships she had spotted, this was the largest. The *Flying Surprise* was a proud ship,

Shani determined, her mind running after a daydream of being the captain of such a fine craft.

As the longboat neared, her eyes grew round with wonder. The ship that had looked so small from the tower, and then bigger from shore, now loomed before her. Her mouth opened in unfeminine surprise for just a moment before she caught herself.

The boat pulled alongside, and in a moment Shani was swept into Rashad's massive arms. With Shani's arms around his neck and one arm behind her knees, he used his free hand to steady them on the ladder that led up to the deck. Shani held on with all the trust of a tiny child. Determined not to miss a thing, her head turned in every direction.

The moment her feet touched the deck, Shani felt a thrill race through her. She had finally made it onto the deck of an English ship. Why it had been such a cherished dream she wasn't certain, but it was so special to her, so unlike anything she'd ever imagined. She was for the moment, speechless.

She knew her father had been a little upset this morning. He had seen her new dress, kissed her goodbye, and told her not to disgrace him. She hoped she hadn't pushed too hard in an effort to get her way. Indira had said he had a lot on his mind lately, but Shani was not entirely sure that this was the problem. She decided to speak to him the moment they returned to the palace.

"Captain Hawkesbury," Shani heard Ali say, "we appreciate your kind hospitality in this matter. Please meet Ahmad Khan's ward." Shani came forward at these words and gave a small curtsy, just as Calla had shown her.

"This is Shani. Shani, this is our host, Captain Hawkesbury."

Brandon extended his hand and smiled at the small brunette with the huge amethyst eyes. Had Shani known him better, she would have seen that behind the smile was some very real worry over Ali's introduction. To this moment, Brandon had been led to believe his coming to get her had been the girl's idea, but now he was having serious doubts. Her first words to him only confirmed this doubt.

"I've wanted to see an English ship for the longest time," she said in softly accented English. "I can't thank you enough for your kindness."

She was so sweet, her manner so innocent and genuinely appreciative, that Brandon found he had to suddenly clear his throat. "The pleasure is all mine," he told her gently.

A moment later they began a tour of the ship. The crew, a hand-picked group of experienced sailors, knew exactly who the girl was. They were extremely polite when their young guest came across their paths.

The tour was detailed, with Shani's enthusiasm pushing them through every nook and cranny of the large vessel. They went below decks as far down as the hold and also saw the crew's quarters. They moved over every inch of the deck and took in the wheelhouse, the galley, and a small dining room used mainly by the captain and his officers.

They ended their excursion in the captain's cabin, and Shani was surprised to see that his cabin had a dining table also. Not as large as the other, but more than sufficient. She was taking in the warm, almost plush room, which, unlike the crew's quarters with mere hammocks, sported a real bed, writing desk, two large chairs, and a bathtub that seemed to be bolted to the floor, when Ali spoke.

"I took the liberty of bringing aboard some refreshment," Ali commented placidly. Shani had moved to study the maps over Brandon's desk and gave him little heed. In fact, she'd heard almost nothing since she came aboard, so thrilled was she with all there was to see.

Her host was very surprised at Ali's words, but Shani took no notice. Brandon was glad of her preoccupation for the first time, as he tried to figure out how he could politely refuse. As cups were filled by one of the two servants who had accompanied them, his mind was still searching for why Ali's actions disturbed him. Ali passed one to Brandon, took one for himself, and gave the last to Shani. Ali had correctly read the look on the captain's face, and when Shani's attention was once again diverted, he spoke for Brandon's ears alone.

"Drink without fear, Captain."

Brandon looked sharply at the smaller man, but did as he'd been instructed. Shani drank also as she stood on tiptoe to see out the window.

"Oh," Shani exclaimed suddenly. She took a stumbling step away from the window and sat down hard on the bed. "The ship must have rocked."

Brandon, observing her intently, did not mention the ship had only rocked slightly in the waves. He watched as she put one hand to her forehead, and he reached for her glass as it began to slip from her suddenly limp fingers.

"I must not be a very good sailor, Ali." Shani's voice had gone very weak. "I don't feel well at all." The last words were whispered, and Brandon watched in stunned fascination as she fell back on the bed. The entire episode happened so swiftly that he'd not even been able to react.

"There is no need for the worry I read in your face, Captain Hawkesbury. She will sleep but a few hours."

"You drugged her?" It was more of an accusation than a question. Ali nodded serenely.

Brandon was furious at this deception.

"I assure you it was necessary," Ali told him sedately before speaking a few words in his native tongue to the servants. Both men left the cabin, and Ali proceeded smoothly.

"Shani believed this tour was our granting of her wish to visit one of your English ships."

"Then she doesn't know who I am?" Brandon was astounded.

"She knows nothing. Again, I assure you my actions were necessary. Shani is of a strong nature. She would never have agreed to leave Darhabar on her own."

"But she will never believe I haven't kidnapped her," Brandon went on, his mind racing for a possible solution. It concerned him greatly that this man was so calm about something that was about to turn a young girl's world upside down.

Ali removed a folded document from the pocket of his cloak. "This will explain all to her."

Brandon took the paper and would have said more, but the servants returned, each carrying a large, ornate trunk. They placed the trunks out of the way and then returned to stand by the door. Brandon noticed that one man, the larger of the two, hesitated next to the bed for a moment, his eyes on the face of the sleeping girl. His expression gave no hint of his thoughts.

When Brandon's attention returned to Ali, he noticed the older man had produced a simple but beautiful jewelry box. Where it had come from, Brandon could only guess, but then guessing was all he'd done since these visitors had come aboard.

Ali held it out to him and spoke. "She will not be ready for this when she awakens. When she is calm enough to keep from throwing it overboard, please give this to her. It is a gift from his highness, Ahmad Khan."

They left then, and Brandon, having finally come to grips with the fact that no part of this affair had been left to chance, followed them up onto the deck. He watched from the railing as they again entered the longboat and the oarsmen rowed for shore.

He stood for long moments and watched as they worked their way through the surf. When he turned, it was to find his first mate waiting for orders. Brandon's first thought was of the girl below. Asleep or not, he felt he needed to be near her. After only a few instructions, he went below decks of the *Flying Surprise*, leaving Flynn in charge as they set sail for home.

Five

SHANI MOANED SOFTLY AS SHE WOKE after just 20 minutes of sleep. Though she hadn't had enough tea to experience its full effects, her head felt as though she'd been held under water too long. It didn't really ache, but everything was fuzzy to her eyes. When her vision cleared somewhat, she found that she was still in the captain's quarters. The first question on her mind was the whereabouts of Ali.

She stood, thinking to open the door and call to him, but the ship lurched suddenly, and Shani felt panicked as fear welled within her. She ran to the window, squinted out, and tried desperately to clear her vision. What she saw made her wish she hadn't looked. They were moving!

Shani, still slightly dizzy, made a dash for the door. She wrenched the portal open, only to collide with the hard expanse of Captain Hawkesbury's chest. She tried to move past him, but as surprised as he was to find her awake, Brandon was not about to let her escape.

"I've got to find Ali," Shani spoke breathlessly. "The ship is moving, and I've got to see him."

Brandon's heart wrenched at the anguish in her voice, but he knew he couldn't hide the truth from her. "The ship is moving; however, Ali has returned to Darhabar."

Shani finally looked up, full into his face. Tears had puddled in those captivating eyes, and Brandon eased her backward into the chamber and shut the door.

"You must not do this," Shani spoke in desperation, suddenly afraid to be alone with this man.

"Your leaving was planned by the emir," Brandon told her softly.

Even as he said the words, Shani knew he was telling the truth. Still she shook her head and tried to deny them.

Brandon reached for the document on his desk. "He left this for you. Ali said it would explain everything."

Shani took the offered paper with a shaking hand. She sat on the edge of the bed and read the first line. "It is because of my love for you that I have taken this action." The words were written in the language of Shani's adopted homeland, and even though she kept her head bent over the paper, she was not reading. Her mind was moving furiously, very aware of the way the captain watched her.

Years of living on the threshold of a harem, in a land where women were to be seen and not heard, had taught Shani how to hide her emotions well. Carefully schooling her features, she looked at the captain.

"I am sorry if my behavior was rude earlier, and I hope you will not find me rude now, but I wish to be alone."

Brandon felt it was the worst thing for her, but he could see no alternative. "All right. I'll check on you shortly." He rose reluctantly and left the cabin.

For the space of several heartbeats Shani sat still. In that brief time she convinced herself that her Poppy had made a mistake, and that if she could only speak with him, she could change his mind. Her eyes cast miserably around the room and fell upon the wardrobe. With a glance at the door and one at the buttons on the front of her dress, Shani went to work.

"I can see you'd rather be below, Hawk," Flynn commented. "You've only been up here a few minutes, and you're already pacing the deck."

"She said she wanted to be alone," Brandon commented as though trying to convince himself of that fact.

"You said as much, but if you feel it's not best, go back down. Remember, you're the authority where that little girl is concerned, and maybe the sooner she realizes it, the better off she'll be."

Brandon silently agreed with him, and after giving him a swift pat on the shoulder, moved to go back below deck.

Shani had no more closed the cabin door than she heard footsteps approaching in the passageway. She stepped back into the shadows, hoping she would be able to quiet her breathing before she gave herself away. She was dressed in her bloomers and a pair of pants she'd found in the wardrobe, along with a gigantic shirt. She was in danger of losing the pants, but if that was the price she had to pay to get home, she would gladly pay it.

The footsteps drew nearer. Shani nearly gasped when they stopped not five feet from her and the captain's door was opened. Shani knew she had only seconds before her disappearance was reported, but they were seconds she planned to use to her own advantage.

On silent, bare feet she moved toward the steps that led upward to the deck. When her foot was on the first step, the captain's door crashed behind her. No longer bothering to stay silent, Shani scrambled up the stairs in a panic. She heard the captain's shout behind her, but there was no hesitation as she gained the deck and ran for the stern of the ship.

Like a wild animal on the run, Shani rounded the wheelhouse, leaping over riggings, barrels, ropes, and other obstacles that stood in the way of her home. Even as she ran, her eyes caught glimpses of the shoreline on the horizon. It was shrinking at a rapid rate, but Shani had no doubt she could swim the distance.

The ship was in pandemonium in her wake. Brandon had come topside, shouting orders as he charged after the young girl. He'd finally got her in his sight, but wasn't close enough to stop the inevitable. He watched her dive without a moment's hesitation, reaching the railing in time to see her land in the water with perfect form. He tore his boots off, watched her surface, and then joined her in the sea.

The water, although not cold, was still something of a shock to Shani. She came up gasping for air and struggling to pull up the pants she was losing under the water. She realized she was going to have to let them go if she was going to swim the distance. After wrapping them around the back of her neck, Shani started toward shore with strong, sure strokes.

She hadn't gone 40 feet when Brandon laid hands on her. She'd still been removing the pants when his body hit the surface, and since the waters of the Arabian Sea were choppy, she had no warning of his presence.

Brandon thought he had a full-grown shark on his hands when Shani realized who held her captive. She fought him with every ounce of strength. Later Brandon wondered how long he could have held her if one of the longboats had not reached them so swiftly.

He passed Shani up to the waiting arms of a crewman, and then hoisted himself in behind her. She was still fighting, so as soon as he was aboard, he took her back into his arms. The men knew what to do and rowed immediately for the ship. Shani took no notice of them.

Brandon tried to subdue her without hurting her, but because she was bent on escape, this was no small task. At one point he secured her flailing arms and legs, only to have her bite him on the forearm. They were still struggling furiously when the boat pulled alongside the ladder.

Without ceremony Brandon slung her across his shoulder. He mounted the ladder so swiftly that Shani had scarcely taken a breath before she was back aboard the ship. Although she heard the orders he spoke as they moved across the deck, she didn't understand them. Shani was still over his shoulder when they entered his cabin. He shut the door and placed her on her feet.

A piece of toweling flew in her direction, and Shani grabbed it automatically. She didn't dry herself, but held it to her chest and looked at the tall man across from her. Why had she not noticed his size before? Shani shrank back, sure she was about to receive the beating of her life, but all Brandon did was look at her, the expression in his dark eyes unreadable.

Shani would have said something, but the door opened after a brief knock and a wiry, gray-haired man entered carrying two steaming buckets. He disappeared behind the screened-off corner of the room Shani had noticed earlier. Another man entered, more buckets in hand, and by the time the two had finished behind the screen and exited the room, Shani was shivering uncontrollably.

Brandon pointed to the partition. "Get behind that screen and into the tub."

Shani nodded, and even though Brandon hated the fear he saw in her eyes, he was too spent to reassure her. His only objective at the moment was to move swiftly out of these waters and take his young charge as far from these shores as he could possibly get her.

Six

As soon as Brandon was certain Shani was well ensconced behind the screen, he stripped out of his own wet attire and slipped into dry pants and a robe. A crewman entered bearing two steaming mugs, and Brandon accepted his with a grateful word.

Once again alone, Brandon sat at his desk and sipped the tea. Nothing had been as he had expected. He was under the impression that he would be going ashore for the girl, and that she was anticipating his arrival. Brandon sat quietly and tried to take it all in.

None of this is a surprise to You, Lord, he prayed silently, *so please help me to trust You in this. I praise You for her return and pray that I'll be able to handle the task before me. They're all so excited at home, Lord. Please keep us safe for this journey.*

He sat for many minutes committing the journey and all involved to God's care. After some time he reached for his Bible. He read a few chapters in the Psalms, but since his mind was so centered on the girl behind the screen, he closed his Bible after just a few more verses and prayed for her again.

Shani took a deep breath and tried to calm the frantic beating of her heart. She was shivering so violently she could hardly remove her sodden clothes. Her face burned, and shame threatened to choke her when she saw how bare her body had been in the wet bloomers, knowing that the captain and many of the crew had seen her nakedness.

Fearful that the captain would check on her, Shani hurried into the water as soon as she was undressed. She barely stifled a gasp at the change in temperature. Her skin had become so chilled that the water seemed to scald her.

Some minutes passed before she was able to unclench her jaw against the chattering of her teeth, and lay back in the water. She let her body sink low in the tub and closed her eyes as the water washed over her shoulders.

This cannot be real, she thought bleakly. *I'm going to wake and find that I have fallen asleep while Indira brushed my hair.* But even as the thought entered her head, Shani knew it would never be true. She was on this ship, and probably headed to England.

How many times had she wondered about her homeland and questioned Indira over her past? Indira had always answered as best she could, and Shani had oftentimes dreamed of going to England, but never once had she imagined being sent away from the only family she had ever known. Why would they do it? Indira had assured her many times that her entire family was dead. Who would take care of her in England?

"Oh, Poppy," tears gathered in her throat, and Shani tried hard to draw breath.

"Are you all right?" Brandon's deep voice spoke suddenly from the other side of the screen.

Shani didn't answer.

"Please answer me, or I'll be forced to come back and check on you."

"I am well," Shani answered stiffly, horrified at the thought of this strange man invading her privacy.

Shani heard nothing for some minutes after that, so she started violently when a dry towel was laid over the top of the screen. Joining this were two garments. From her place in the tub, Shani thought they appeared to be her underclothing; in reality, they were a robe and nightgown.

When a dress was not added to the lot, Shani wondered about the implications of such an action. She forced herself not to think about what might happen this night. Had the captain not called to her to finish and come out, she would have stayed in the water until she was once again chilled to the bone.

"I do not wish to come out," Shani called, wondering at her boldness.

"Supper is here, and you need to eat something. Get done now and into the nightgown and robe."

He did not sound angry with her, but something in his voice propelled her into action. Five minutes later she slipped around the partition and stood very still. She'd dried her hair as best she could, but she knew it hung in a riotous mass around her head.

"Warmer?" Brandon called the moment he spotted her.

Shani could only nod. Her hands clutched the front of her robe and were white with strain. At home her gown for sleeping was short, but in front of this man, Shani found herself thankful for this covering.

"Come," Brandon bid her, "have a seat."

Shani, afraid of angering him, did as she was told, taking a place at the small dining table that sat against one wall. Brandon immediately placed food before her, and while Shani stared at the strange fare, he sat across from her. Shani's eyes flew to his, and then to his empty place setting.

"You do not eat," she commented, although she didn't know why.

"I'll eat later," he told her. "For now I'd like you to eat and listen to what I have to say."

Shani opened her mouth to say she was not hungry, but her stomach growled as if on cue. Ignoring her utensils, she picked up a strange-looking piece of bread and nibbled on the edge.

"I'm not sure what you've been told about yourself, so I'd like to clear a few things up for you." Brandon paused to make sure she was listening before going on.

"First of all, I was not aware of the fact that my coming would be a surprise. Until Ali introduced you as—" Brandon hesitated over the name, having heard it only twice.

"Shani," she supplied softly, but with great pride.

Brandon nodded. "I guess the first thing I should have told you was your real name."

Shani's mouth opened, and her eyes widened. Brandon wondered what the next few hours would bring if she didn't even realize her name had been changed.... The thought hung in his mind.

In the moments that Brandon was silent, Shani searched her own mind for some way of gaining the upper hand. Her chin rose slightly when she felt sure of herself.

"I do not know for what purpose you have stolen me, but I am sure if you return me to Ahmad Khan, you will be rewarded handsomely." It was a bluff on Shani's part, but she was suddenly terrified of what he might tell her. Surely Poppy would take her back, if only she could make this man believe he wanted her.

Brandon shook his head slowly, not wanting to crush her, but knowing he could not condone her denial of the situation. His heart turned over with compassion for her, but he also felt some anger at the cowardly way the emir had handled this whole affair.

"Your name is Sunny Gallagher, and you were born in England," Brandon began softly and continued when he saw curiosity flame in her eyes. "Ali sent word and asked for someone to come for you. Until now they believed you were dead."

"Who thought I was dead?" Shani whispered, her brow knit with confusion.

"Your family."

She shook her head and came out of her chair, searching the room as though she would run. Brandon stood also, keeping himself between her and the door. It was now dark outside, and they were many miles from shore. Were she to escape again, they would never recover her.

"I'm sorry," Brandon said as he took in her panic. "I didn't know how else to tell you."

"You lie," Shani whispered, her eyes begging him to admit it.

"No, Sunny, I don't." His eyes begged her to believe him.

"I am Shani!" she lashed out in a last defense.

"No," Brandon's voice became very firm. "Your name is Sunny, and that is how I will address you. I think this has been too much for you," he went on in an unyielding tone. "I want you to go to bed and get some sleep."

Shani, nearly out of her head with confusion, voiced the first thought that came to mind. "You will not order me to bed as you would a child. I am nearly 15."

This time it was Brandon's turn to be surprised. All Shani's movements came to a complete halt on seeing his raised brow.

"It's true that your birthday is near," he said softly as he watched her eyes grow round again. "But you're going to be 14, not 15." Brandon's voice was at its gentlest, but this announcement was still more than Shani could handle.

Her mind screamed that this man was lying to her, but in her heart she knew the truth; she knew who had done the lying. Ahmad, Indira, Ali, Rashad, all of them—for years they had lived a lie. For years a family she had never known had grieved her death.

Shani tried to take it all in, tried to make herself understand, but it was too much. Black spots danced before her eyes, and she heard harsh sobs coming from someone's throat. It would be morning before Shani would understand the sobs were her own, and that Brandon had caught her just before she hit the floor.

Part Two

SUNNY GALLAGHER

Seven

SUNNY OPENED HER EYES but did not immediately move. Her temples ached, and her eyes felt gritty when she blinked. It was a relief to let her eyes slide shut again, but as soon as she did, yesterday—all of yesterday—came sharply to mind.

The faces of Ali and Rashad swam before her mind's eye, and the pain Sunny felt was like a knife in the side. *I have a family in England, and rather than tell me the truth, I am drugged and taken away by a stranger.*

Her mind ran through the events of the last weeks. The distance Ahmad had placed between them and the clinging way Indira had acted at the oddest times washed over her with fresh understanding. And Rashad, always kind to her, had begun to treat her as a rare bird. Calla had not only sewn her clothing, but in ways most subtle told her of England, what she would see and how she must act.

Sunny had taken all of Calla's words to heart, so no one aboard this English ship would be offended by her behavior, but never did she imagine she would need such knowledge for other reasons. Sunny suddenly remembered her age. While sleeping, her robe and gown had twisted around her, so she rose slowly from the bed and adjusted the heavy fabric.

Almost reverently she let her hands slide over her flat breasts and stomach. *I am just 13*, the words sounded with wonder inside her mind. *For so long, I am different, but now, now I am just young, and in this there is no sin.* Sunny allowed herself a brief time of joy over this truth, and indeed it was brief. All too soon she remembered that this was the only thing she had to be happy about.

Her eyes cast about the room, little more than a closet. In doing so, she caught sight of her two trunks, which now sat opposite her bed. She approached them with a heavy feeling of grief settling around the region of her heart.

They plotted against me well, she told herself as she approached the trunks quietly. Kneeling, she lifted the lid of the first one and felt tears sting her eyes. It was filled with clothing similar to the outfit she had worn on board. She'd been so upset by the day's events that she hadn't even stopped to wonder why the captain had night raiment to fit her. Calla must have made her an entire wardrobe.

"Sunny?"

The calling of her name brought her to her feet. By the time Brandon opened the door, she had backed up until her legs hit her bunk.

Brandon stopped as soon as he saw her. The morning light was dim, but not so low that he missed the single tear and the wet trail it left on her cheek.

"I suppose by now you'd hoped to wake up and find that all of this was a bad dream."

His deep, gentle voice was almost her undoing. The tight rein she had on her emotions nearly crumbled in the face of his kindness.

"When you're ready, I'll send for breakfast." Brandon waited for her nod, shut her door, and left her alone. As soon as he had exited, Sunny began to wonder where he had come from. She followed him to the door, opened it, and found herself on the threshold of his cabin.

Sunny was surprised at herself. On the tour yesterday, she had completely missed this door and the small room off his cabin. Sunny glanced back to her own room, searching for yet another door. She found none and realized that the only way out was through the captain's cabin.

Brandon had gone to his desk, but noticed Sunny the moment he was seated. He watched her take in the cabin with new eyes, but couldn't quite tell what she was thinking. His neatly made bed was the last place she looked before turning her direct gaze on him.

"Are you a eunuch?"

Brandon's thoughts had wandered far in an attempt to guess her thoughts, but never in his wildest dreams would this question have entered his mind. He swiftly reminded himself where she had spent the last 12 years of her life and tried to answer calmly.

"No, I'm not."

"Then I cannot sleep in this room with you."

"You don't sleep in this room," Brandon replied, hoping she would be reasonable. "You sleep in your own room."

"But there is no lock on this door, no way to stop your passage to my bed."

Brandon could see that he would have to grow accustomed to her bluntness. "Sunny," Brandon's voice was very gentle, "you have nothing to fear from me."

"I do not know you. I cannot take your words as truth." Sunny began to wonder if there was anyone left on this earth whom she could trust.

They were both silent a moment while Brandon debated what to say next, but Sunny was the first to speak.

"I need another room." She tried to sound authoritative, as if she would not take no for an answer.

"That is out of the question." Brandon's voice, although kind, was unyielding. "You are under my care for the space of this voyage, and I will see you back to England safely."

"And who will have my care when we—" Sunny didn't finish the question, completely forgetting for the moment about her sleeping arrangements. Brandon, in all fairness, knew it was time to tell her everything.

"Why don't you get dressed and have some breakfast? While you eat, I'll explain how you've come to be here."

Remembering that they had not settled the sleeping arrangements, Sunny hesitated. She was suspicious of this captain, kind though he was, and wondered if breakfast was just a distraction on his part.

Of course, she told herself, *had he intended to harm me, he might have done so by now.* Without further word Sunny turned and entered her room, shutting the door firmly behind in order to dress for the day.

Having watched her face, Brandon felt vaguely dissatisfied with how little her eyes gave way to her thoughts.

꙳   ꙳   ꙳

Sunny was quite hungry by the time she had struggled into her dress. What had seemed like such fun the day before was a lot of work today. She couldn't remember everything she was supposed to put on, so she left most of her undergarments off, but that didn't solve her newest problem. The dress she had picked out buttoned down the back. Sunny bent her arms until they ached but still could not reach all the buttons.

Nearly 45 minutes had slipped away, and Brandon, not wanting to rush her, hesitated outside her door. He'd heard a tremendous rustling and shuffling for a long time, and then silence. If he didn't know better, he would have guessed she was no longer in her room.

"Sunny, are you ready?"

The angry brunette didn't answer.

"May I come in?" Brandon called to her, and when she again remained silent, he opened the door a shade and peeked around the corner.

The small room was a disaster. The trunks were empty. The bunk and floor were strewn with dresses, shoes, and feminine apparel of every type. Sunny's face was flushed, and she looked ready to kill. Brandon had to arrest the amused smile that threatened.

"My dress is not ready," Sunny stated tightly.

"Does it button in the back?" Brandon, the brother of one sister, easily deduced the cause of this hurricane.

The clenching of Sunny's jaw was all the answer he received, and with a move of his hand, Brandon motioned for her to join him in the main cabin.

She stood with rigid posture as he fastened the five small buttons that she could not have possibly reached, also taking note of her bare back, and wondering how he was going to explain feminine attire to her. Not wanting to deal with it at the moment, he immediately, and with all the aplomb of a servant seating the queen, seated Sunny at the table. He heard her small sigh, and with quiet efficiency he uncovered the bowls of food on the table so she could eat.

She did eat—with her hands. Brandon, well aware of Eastern customs, had suspected she would do so, but had also decided to let Sunny's family tackle this problem. It wasn't that she spilled food all over herself and the cabin; in fact, she was very neat. Using pieces of bread to scoop or soak up her entire meal, however, would make her a humorous oddity in London.

What Sunny's host didn't realize was how proud she was of herself. Calla had talked as she'd fitted and measured Sunny, and the young girl had learned some interesting facts about life in England. Never once had Calla mentioned the use of a spoon or fork, but Sunny did know that napkins were used instead of finger bowls.

When Sunny had her fill, she loftily used her napkin to wipe her mouth and hands, even though she didn't feel at all clean when she was done. She also realized, as she laid her napkin down and folded her hands in her lap, how bland the food had seemed. Too hungry to notice earlier, Sunny now felt a vague dissatisfaction over what certainly must be English food.

"Did you have enough?" Brandon asked her suddenly.

"Thank you" was all Sunny replied, reminding herself just in time that to comment on the food would be disrespectful.

Brandon opened his mouth to begin his story, but Sunny had begun to think of England.

"Did my mother and father send you here?"

"Not exactly," Brandon answered carefully, not caring for the direction this conversation was heading. He had wanted to start the story by telling her how much she was missed, and about the joy all who had known her had been given to know she was alive and returning to them.

His hesitancy made Sunny so sure that something was wrong, she stood. "I do not know you." Her small hands were balled into fists at her sides, so great was her frustration. "I do not know if your words are truth."

"Sunny, please sit back down." Brandon saw her panic and kept his voice even. "You have nothing to fear from me."

"But how can I know this?"

"Because in a way I'm like family," he assured her gently. "Your brother is married to my sister."

Sunny was instantly captivated, and with trancelike movements sat down and stared at Brandon.

"I have a brother?"

Eight

"WHEN YOU WERE 15 MONTHS OLD, your parents decided to take a trip. They left England on a ship headed for various parts of the world. You were with them," Brandon began quietly.

"Off the coast of Darhabar there was a storm. They were close enough to port that the ship's captain thought they could drop the longboats and go to shore for safety. But the storm was unpredictable, and as the boat carrying you and your parents was rowed toward shore, a huge wave hit. Your parents lost track of each other in this wall of water, and when your father could see again, you and your mother had been washed overboard.

"In the storm your father could do nothing but pray. So as soon as the waters stilled he began his search. For days he combed the waters and ports in search of some sign of you. When he visited Ahmad Khan's palace, he was shown to a private chamber where they had prepared your mother's body. Your father was so grief-stricken, that when they said they had not seen you, he didn't suspect a thing. You were so small; it wasn't at all hard to believe you'd been lost to the sea.

"Your father returned to England with your mother's body and tried to put his life back together. Sunny Gallagher, your grandmother and the woman you were named after, never believed you were dead. I wish now that she had lived to see how right she was."

"So my father sent you?" Trying to grasp all that was significant, Sunny's head was spinning over this news even as her young heart told her it was true.

"No, he didn't send me. Ali contacted your oldest brother, who is married to my sister. We're all very close because of that tie, your siblings and my family, and with my ship and sailing experience, they asked me to come."

"Is my father dead too?" Sunny suddenly asked, already knowing the answer.

Brandon nodded regretfully. "About four years ago. His heart suddenly stopped. He was gone before a doctor could be summoned." Brandon fell silent then, not wishing to overwhelm her.

"What are these 'siblings' you speak of—sisters?"

"Siblings are brothers and sisters," Brandon told her and reminded himself to watch his choice of words. "You have two brothers and one sister. They are all a good deal older, each married with children.

"I'm a person who enjoys maps and charts, so on the voyage over, I took the liberty of drawing up a family tree so you would understand our family ties." Brandon rose and fetched a roll of paper from his desk. "As you'll see, you're an aunt eight times over."

Sunny accepted the paper offered to her, and like a person in a dream rolled it open on the table. Brandon, never taking his eyes from her face, helped her hold the edges down as she read. After a moment he began to point and explain.

Gallagher Family Tree

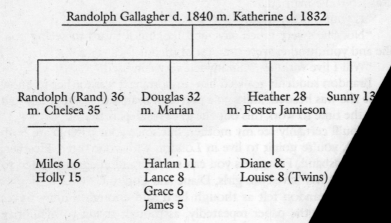

Randolph Gallagher d. 1840 m. Katherine d. 1832

Randolph (Rand) 36 m. Chelsea 35	Douglas 32 m. Marian	Heather 28 m. Foster Jamieson	Sunny 13
Miles 16 Holly 15	Harlan 11 Lance 8 Grace 6 James 5	Diane & Louise 8 (Twins)	

"This is your father and mother, and here is your oldest brother, named after your father. We call him Rand. He married my sister, Chelsea. I wrote down everyone's ages, so as you can see, you actually have a niece and a nephew a few years older than yourself.

Hawkesbury Family Tree

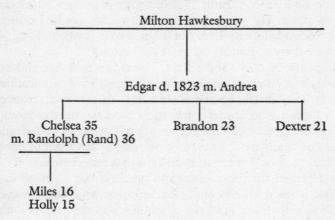

"My family is on this side," he went on. "You see here under my folks are my sister Chelsea, me, and then my brother, Dexter. Dex is engaged to be married."

"Is your mother dead?"

"No. She's very much alive and looking forward to seeing you. ...r mother were the best of friends."

...with her?" Sunny felt very confused.

...ly realized how important it was for her to know ...nd said a prayer of thanks that her family had ...ut ahead of his departure.

...ther, but since your parents are both ...ndon with your sister, Heather, ..." Brandon again pointed to Louise."

...said enough. Sunny's eyes ...s though trying to memorize

...did you come for me?"

Brandon had already told her this but patiently answered again. "When Rand was contacted we all sat down, your family and some members of my own, and discussed the matter. When all was said and done, my position and sailing experience made me the rather obvious choice."

Sunny remembered then that he had said this was his ship and agreed that he was the logical person to sail for her. But she did not realize there was more behind the word "position" than she realized. She didn't feel disappointed that no one else had come, just curious over what they might be like.

"How long will I stay?"

Brandon stared at her, completely nonplussed. That she would not understand the permanence of this arrangement had never occurred to him. He felt a bit cowardly, but decided to throw the answer back at Ahmad's feet.

"Ali said that the letter he left would explain everything." Brandon could only hope that after these words, the letter actually would fulfill that promise.

"Oh," Sunny looked stunned. "I did not read all the words, and I do not know—" she hesitated when Brandon rose and retrieved yet another paper from the desk.

"You must have dropped it in your hurry to leave." Brandon's voice was a bit amused, but it was lost on Sunny as she opened the letter.

"It is because of my love for you," she began again, "that I have taken this action. You will be angry, but I know what is best. The family you have in England has position, power, and money. You will be welcome and have care. Indira will miss you. Think of us when you open the jewel box. It comes with my love, Poppy."

A single tear escaped the corner of Sunny's eye as she looked up at Brandon. "I am not to go back." It was a statement, not a question, but Brandon still nodded in agreement, knowing the sooner she accepted the fact, the easier it would be.

"What is this jewel box?" Sunny tried to distract her own tortured thoughts.

"Something Ali left for you. Did you want to see it?"

"I would cast it into the sea, were it in my hands," she whispered, knowing she hadn't diverted her thoughts at all. She felt so betrayed and angry that she wanted to scream.

Brandon's brows rose as he thought how well Ali had known

what her reaction would be. He also saw the anger building in those stunning purple eyes. Brandon asked himself if he should sidetrack her or let the anger come. He decided on the latter and stayed quiet as she crumpled the paper in her hands.

"He had no right," she suddenly spat furiously.

Brandon was certain she referred to Ahmad's method of sending her away.

"He had no right to lie all these years! All this time I am not his, I am not given to him by an English man whose wife had died. I am not the daughter of a man who trusts me to Ahmad's care, wanting the best for me. He *lied*—all these years he lied!" More tears had gathered in her eyes, and Brandon could see they were tears of fury, tears of the betrayed.

As she stormed the cabin floor, her hands were clenched and her hair, not having seen a brush recently, swirled around her shoulders.

"I was safe. I was happy. Now I have only lies." She stopped and buried her face in her hands. Brandon stayed in his seat for a few moments and then rose to put his arms around her. He knew very well that she would push him away, but on the slim chance she would welcome a shoulder to cry on, he approached.

Tears in the palace were not something the emir had enjoyed, and he only allowed shows of emotion on rare occasions. Not even Rashad, in deference to his ruler's preference, had comforted her when she cried. Sunny had never had a man hold her when she was upset, and at this moment, when her world had been torn in pieces, nothing was of more comfort than the feel of his strong arms surrounding her or the smell of his shirt as she buried her face against his chest and wept.

Brandon said nothing to stop her tears or avert her from this grief. She had, in a sense, experienced the death of a loved one—an entire family of loved ones. Brandon believed her tears, grief, and anger were all healthy ways of handling the hurt.

When the worst of the storm had passed and Brandon had handed her a handkerchief, he asked if she wanted to talk a little more. Her head shook in the negative, and Brandon knew that now was the time for a little diversion.

"Let's head back into your room for a little while."

Sunny, having come to realize that he meant her no harm, told him she did not need to sleep.

"I'm not suggesting that you do. You have a bed to make and two trunks to repack."

His planned diversion worked like a charm. Sunny's chin rose with indignation, and her eyes flashed purple fire. Brandon thought she looked like a young princess. She also sounded like she was addressing a servant.

"I have never made my bed or picked up my clothing. Why," she sputtered angrily, "I do not even know how!" She sounded almost proud of the fact.

Brandon wanted to smile, but knew better. He also decided not to mention that she obviously didn't know how to use a hairbrush either. Her thick tresses hung in unruly strands around her face, back, and shoulders.

Brandon calmly turned her around and propelled her in the direction of her bedroom. "Then I think it's high time you learn."

Nine

"YOU ARE HURTING ME!" Sunny told the captain angrily.

"That," Brandon's voice was as calm as ever, "is why you must do this every day."

Sunny let out a disgusted sigh but said nothing.

Brandon had let another two days pass before mentioning Sunny's hair. At his suggestion that she brush it out herself, she had stared at him as if he'd taken leave of his senses.

So now they sat together in a sheltered spot on the deck, and Brandon tirelessly ran the brush through her hair, or at least made the attempt. Some strands were so tangled he feared he would need to cut them.

At one point, when he had one side brushed smooth, he made Sunny brush for a while. But it was clear that her heart wasn't in it. She grew distracted easily and ended up with nearly as many snarls as when she started. Brandon tolerantly retrieved the brush and went back to work.

"I hope you realize that I'm not on this trip to play maid to you," he told her suddenly, although his voice held no rebuke.

"Why did you not bring a maid for me?" Sunny asked the first question that came to mind, thinking what an excellent idea it was.

Brandon could only shake his head. She was so clearly accustomed to being waited on hand and foot. He had been raised in a home of considerable wealth, and even now, in part because of that wealth, was considered one of London's most sought-after bachelors.

In his home, however, money had never been an excuse for acting helpless or being unwilling to learn new skills. Sunny obviously believed that if she didn't know something by now, especially something that didn't interest her, then she didn't need to learn.

"What is my sister like?" Sunny turned suddenly, and Brandon saw the spark of curiosity in her eyes.

"Like a grown-up version of yourself. You look like you might be taller someday, but other than your eye color, your faces are very much alike."

"Did my mother have my eyes?"

"No, you have your grandmother Gallagher's. I believe that is why you were named for her."

"And she is dead?"

"Yes, about seven years ago now."

Sunny turned back so Brandon could finish her hair. His sister would certainly laugh at the job he was doing, but it looked better than before.

Brandon was lost in thought for the next few minutes. His mind raced from how hard it could sometimes be to read Sunny's face to the fact that he could no longer tolerate watching her eat with her hands.

He hated to invite a battle, and he was learning fast that with Sunny a battle was easy to come by, but it was time she learned to eat with a fork. Lunch was less than an hour away, and Brandon had determined to talk with her before the meal. He knew the customs in the East were vastly different from those in England, but England was where they were headed, and Sunny was going to need to learn to conform.

"Put it in my left hand?"

Brandon was again telling himself not to laugh. "Sunny," he spoke with the utmost patience, "in order to cut your meat, you put your fork in your left hand and the knife in your right. When the meat is cut, the knife goes at the edge of your plate and the fork goes back into your right hand, so you can continue eating."

It was the second time he had explained all of this, and he told himself if it took the rest of the day, she would do it correctly. Sunny scowled fiercely at him, but Brandon's voice and face remained calm.

"Give it a try now," he ordered softly.

"To eat with my left hand is barbaric." The words were said with lofty disdain, but Sunny's eyes belied her words. Not haughty, they were following Brandon's progress through his meal. Throughout the verbal explanation, he'd calmly eaten, using his knife and fork in perfect form to show his young charge how it was done. He told her she could no longer use her hands and fingers, and it was understandable that she was growing hungry. He kept up the scheme until she at last gave it a try.

The meat was very tasty, but Brandon watched a look of loathing cross her face after she had painstakingly cut the meat and placed it in her mouth. He watched as Sunny held the fork out in front of her and stared at it.

"I do not like the taste of steel in my mouth."

"I guess that will take a little getting used to. In no time at all, you won't even notice it."

Sunny put the fork and knife down. "I will starve."

"Not on my ship, you won't." Brandon put another forkful of food in his mouth and chewed imperturbably. "If I have to truss you up and feed you like a baby, I will."

"Why do you treat me as a child?" Sunny's voice was high-pitched with frustration.

"Sunny," Brandon's voice was totally logical, "you are a child."

She had no argument for that. "What is 'truss'?" she asked suddenly.

"It means to tie," Brandon said briefly and concentrated on his food. He didn't look her way again, but did say a prayer of thanks when she picked up her fork and made a valiant attempt at her meal.

"Everything is so strange," Sunny whispered when she climbed into bed that night. "My clothes, the food, the eating—all so strange. I will never understand. I will never be truly English."

Sunny was on her way toward depression, but then she realized something inside her had changed. Some of the restlessness had abated. For over a year now there had been an unsettled feeling within her. Every day she had felt the discontent rise up, and on most days she learned to fight the feeling by doing something she was not allowed, certain this would drive the feeling away. Whether she went to the tower, the kitchens, the stables, or across the court-yard, the restlessness stayed with her.

When she'd had special times with Indira or Ahmad, there was little or no restlessness. But Sunny found that whenever she was left with her own thoughts, her mind would stray and become unsettled. Her attitude would result in a certain type of fidgeting, and Sunny would act on impluse, even though she knew better.

Just thinking of it made her feel fidgety. She rustled about in the bedcovers for some time before sleep came to claim her. Brandon, waiting for just that, sat at his desk and listened to the sound of her silence when it finally came.

After the first day when she had jumped ship, he had not let her out of his sight. Any 13-year-old who would jump from the deck of a fast-sailing ship, intent on swimming home, was not to be trusted. She had shown no other signs of running, but Brandon was not con-vinced that she was as settled as she appeared. This was the reason he was getting ready to take his bath at 10:00 at night.

Each evening he waited for her to sleep before climbing into the tub. Although the tub was too small for his 6'3" frame, he enjoyed these evening baths. They allowed him to relax and dwell on all of the things for which he was thankful.

When he completed his studies at Oxford three years ago, at the age of 20, and was commissioned onto his first ship, his mother warned him that at times his duties and responsibilities would threaten to overwhelm him. Her advice after this had been simple.

"Stay in God's Word, Brandon. Read your Bible every day and enjoy God. You may not enjoy all you see going on around you, especially when there is hurt and suffering, but you can enjoy God. Dwell on Him, His promises, and His love for all people. He will see you beyond every sunset."

Her words and those of the psalmist came to him now as steam rose around him, clearing his mind of the day's events. He meditated on Psalm 147: "He healeth the broken in heart, and bindeth up their wounds. He telleth the number of the stars; he calleth them all by their names. Great is our Lord, and of great power; his understand-ing is infinite. The Lord lifteth up the meek; he casteth the wicked down to the ground. Sing unto the Lord with thanksgiving; sing praise upon the harp unto our God."

"I know, Lord," Brandon prayed quietly then, "that in Your

love You have brought Sunny back into our lives with a purpose. Thank You for Your power and infinite understanding. Use me especially now, and the family once we're in England, to bring Sunny to Your Son, Jesus Christ."

Ten

SUNNY STARED AT THE HAIRBRUSH IN BRANDON'S HAND and then at the man himself. He was smiling at her, but those dark, raised brows told her he was waiting with his usual persistence for her response.

It didn't bother her all that much to take care of her hair; it was just that she could never remember to brush it. Being reminded made her feel like a child. She was one, of course, but didn't care to admit it, even to herself.

She finally took the brush and plopped down on Brandon's bed as though she'd lived in this cabin all her life. Six weeks had passed since they had set sail, and Sunny was feeling as much at ease with Captain Brandon Hawkesbury as she had with Rashad or Indira. He was overbearing at times, but family ties and traditions in her land were taken very seriously, and the fact that his sister was married to her brother afforded the captain a tremendous amount of respect.

While Sunny brushed her hair, Brandon worked over the ship's log at the desk. She noticed he wrote something every day.

"What are you writing in, Brandon?" Already she was losing some of her accent.

"It's the ship's log. I record where we've been, the weather conditions, and anything outstanding that happened on board."

"Do the pages have dates?"

"I date them."

"What's today's date?" Sunny's voice had dropped, and Brandon turned to look at her.

"It's October 19. Why do you ask?"

"My birthday was yesterday," she whispered. "I had forgotten how the days were passing." She looked absolutely bereft, and Brandon came away from the desk and joined her on the edge of the bunk.

"Sunny, look at me," he commanded softly, and spoke again when she brought her eyes to his. "You're forgetting how you came to be at the palace."

Sunny looked completely confused, so Brandon explained.

"As with most things, Ahmad Khan did not know your birth date either. You were born on November 11, 1830, which is still over three weeks away."

Bewildered, Sunny blinked at him. Would the surprises ever stop? Would she ever really know who she was and where she belonged? After just a few short weeks at sea, Sunny already found her mind to be a confused mixture of Darhabar and England. The wind on the deck was always cool, and she was thankful for the heavy cloth used for her clothing. But there were never mounds of pillows for her to lounge upon, and though she tried sitting cross-legged on her bunk, it was not the same.

She had finally grown accustomed to sitting in a chair and eating with silverware and using both hands in the process, but some of the food was so tasteless Sunny wondered at times why she even bothered.

"Are you all right?" Brandon asked when she just sat staring at him.

"I do not know myself," she admitted softly. "You do not like who I am, and you want me to change. I do not know what *I* want."

Brandon's heart turned over. "I love you, Sunny," he told her sincerely, "just the way you are, but you're going to live in England, and even if Darhabar and England were exactly alike, that would mean adjustment. The fact that they're not at all alike is going to make things even more difficult for you.

"You will not be waited on constantly at your sister's home, nor do I really believe you would care to be. There may be someone to help you with your hair, but you also need to know how to care for it on your own.

"My pushing you to make your bunk, do your hair, eat with a fork, and put on the proper clothing is not my way of saying I dislike who you are. I love you," Brandon repeated, "and I want your adjustment in going home to be as smooth as possible."

Brandon slipped his arm around her, and Sunny let her head fall against his shoulder.

"Did I tell you about the first time I ever saw you?" Brandon asked, knowing he was the only real thing in her life right now. He wanted her to understand just how English she really was, and to see that she was going home to a family who waited eagerly to see her.

"You've never told me," Sunny replied, her face turned with interest.

"Our homes are close together, and word was sent to my mother that Katherine, your mother, had safely delivered you," Brandon began. "I was ten years old at the time and thought that babies were rather bothersome creatures, but I was curious too.

"When mother went, she allowed me to accompany her. You were so tiny," Brandon smiled. "While my mother held you, I put my finger in your hand. You clutched onto it with a surprising grip. I had a new appreciation for babies after that. I couldn't see enough of you. It was awfully fun to watch you grow that first year. I missed you terribly when you went away; we all did."

Sunny smiled at him, loving the mental pictures he painted. Brandon gave her a little squeeze, kissed her brow, and went back to his desk, leaving Sunny to finish her hair. He did so hoping she felt a little easier about who she was and where she was headed.

Brandon noticed that Sunny regained more control of her emotions with the passing of each new day. He knew that the family would love her no matter what she was like, but Brandon still wondered if any of them would ever see her eyes pool with tears, or if anyone would see the frightened, vulnerable face he'd seen when Sunny realized she had been underhandedly sent away by the only father she'd ever known.

Brandon had a sense that by the time they came into port, these feelings and many more would be well hidden from any and all seeking eyes. He had seen them all and praised God for this fact. They had given him a love and tenderness for this girl that he couldn't have put into words if he had tried.

"Sometimes I hate him all day, and sometimes I wish I could wake up in my bed in the palace," Sunny said softly one night.

"Did it help to reread his letter?" Brandon asked, having seen her doing so just that morning.

"No," she told him flatly. "He said I am loved, but then I am sent away." Sunny, who was sitting across the cabin from Brandon, looked into his eyes. "This is not love."

"I don't know about that," Brandon told her thoughtfully. "When I think of the loving family that awaits you in England, and how hard it must have been to send you away, I think he might love you deeply."

Not having considered this, Sunny frowned, but a moment later the hardness returned to her eyes. She was not ready to be so understanding. Brandon sighed mentally. If she was not careful, the bitterness would eat her alive.

Brandon believed that if anyone had reason to be bitter, it was the family who had been lied to and robbed of her company for so many years. As it was, no one felt that way. They certainly didn't condone the emir's actions, but they praised God for the return of Sunny, and were determined not to let bitterness ruin that praise.

Sunny, now able to spend time away from Brandon, left the cabin just after breakfast the next morning. As had become her routine in the past week, she headed for the galley. Connie, the ship's cook, was standing over a large pot, and Sunny knew that lunch was on the stove.

"Good day to you, lass. Did you sleep well?"

"Yes," Sunny told him with wide-eyed innocence. It was beyond her why people asked such a thing. In her youth, she had yet to experience a poor night's sleep.

"What are you cooking, Connie?"

"Bean soup." The rotund cook raised his ladle so Sunny could see his fare. She smiled at his obvious pride, and they talked about the ingredients for some minutes until Sunny heard Brandon's voice in the companionway.

"We'll be in port in the morning. I'll be going ashore and can take care of it then."

Sunny left the galley in a hurry, and Connie, having heard the captain's voice and knowing why she left, smiled after her departure.

"We are to be in England tomorrow?" Sunny was out of breath at the prospect.

"No, Sunny," Brandon explained. "We're docking in Freeport, Sierra Leone, for water and supplies."

"You will go on land?"

"Yes, I'll be going ashore, but only briefly. I will not—" Brandon continued swiftly when he saw that Sunny was about to speak, "be taking you with me. I must leave early and will probably return before you're awake."

Sunny was crushed. Brandon saw the disappointment in her eyes, but knew it was best to leave well-enough alone.

"You will not pout over this," he told her softly and watched as her expression turned from anger to pride.

In a way that was all too familiar, her chin came into the air. He turned away to hide his smile, for he knew she hated any reference to her youth.

Sunny was more disappointed than she believed she had let on, and turned away from Brandon's back to go up on deck. Once at the railing, the wind tugging at her hair and clothing, she made a promise to herself about the next day.

I may not be allowed off this ship, but I will be here, on the deck, seeing all I can of this Sierra Leone.

Eleven

SUNNY AWOKE TO AN ODD SOUND and lay for a moment, trying to place what was wrong. It took some seconds for her to remember they were docking. She realized then that it was the ship's lack of motion that had awakened her. She flew out of the bed, but just as Brandon had predicted, he was gone. Sunny tore out of her nightgown and dressed as swiftly as she was able. Ignoring the brush because she was headed out into the wind, she reached for the door of her little room and ran across Brandon's cabin. With a smile on her face, she placed her hand on the latch and pulled.

Sunny found it locked. She stood in stunned silence for a moment and tried the door again. It didn't budge. With a determined yank, she made yet another attempt. Frustration rose within her, and she pulled until her hands hurt, but the door remained firmly shut.

"How could you?" Sunny's voice sounded in the empty room. Hurt feelings quickly gave way to anger. By the time Brandon arrived nearly an hour later, she was in a fury.

Brandon came aboard ship with a feeling of contentment. He had accomplished all he had set out to do, _and_ found a close friend of his at home. He had said nothing to Sunny for fear of raising her hopes and then having to dash them, but now that he knew John was home, he planned to take Sunny onshore. They were expected

60

for lunch. It wouldn't be a long visit; the *Flying Surprise* would sail with tonight's tide, but it would break up the tedium of the ship and give Sunny contact with a few other believers.

"Any sounds from my cabin?" Brandon asked Flynn.

"I've checked a few times—all is quiet."

"Good. We'll be going ashore in a few hours, and she'll be well rested. We're going to John and Cheryl's, and I have some jobs for Angus and Billy. Tell them to accompany us."

"You'd like a carriage?"

"If Angus can arrange it, yes. I'll be in my cabin."

Flynn nodded, and Brandon moved toward the companionway. Once at his cabin door, he lifted the lock and used his key. He had regretted such an action, but it had given him peace of mind while off the ship. On opening the door, however, any and all peace of mind was shattered, along with a heavy ceramic mug that hit the wall near his head.

"How could you?" The words were spat in fury, and a hairbrush came through the air.

"I trusted you!"

Brandon ducked his way into the door as a book came crashing somewhere above his head.

"That's enough, Sunny," Brandon spoke firmly, but not loudly enough, since another book was picked up and hurled. Her aim was far off, and Brandon was headed in Sunny's direction when she grabbed something off his desk and raised it high.

"Stop!" Brandon's voice thundered in the small room, and Sunny, so shocked over hearing his raised voice, slowly lowered her hand. "Put that on the desk." Brandon's voice was softer now, but no less angry.

Sunny complied, and then backed away when Brandon started toward her. She stopped when she saw that he was headed to the desk. Sunny watched in fascination as he picked up the item she had been ready to throw, and gave it a good going over. His voice was now gentle as he turned to her and explained.

"This is a sextant; I can't navigate this ship without it. Since we're not out to sea, it wouldn't have been a complete disaster. If you had broken it, I would have been left searching for a replacement, but none that would match the caliber of this one."

Sunny's eyes were huge in her face over what her anger had caused her to do. She had been warned as a child that her anger was going to land her in trouble someday, but other than the emir administering a hard slap across her face when she'd been nine years old, Sunny had yet to regret her wrathful outbursts. She felt ashamed for the first time, and it was not a feeling she enjoyed.

"Are you going to punish me?" Sunny's calm voice belied the turmoil within.

Brandon looked at her, regret knifing through him. *She's not sorry, just worried about my punishing her.* The thought was deeply disturbing to him.

"If you mean, am I going to physically punish you, no, I'm not. But I did have plans for us to go ashore, and now I'm not sure if we should."

Sunny looked utterly crestfallen. Brandon continued to watch her, wishing that he could know her thoughts. As it was, he received his wish.

"I have a temper, and I've been in trouble before because of it."

Brandon nodded. "I'm glad you're aware of that, Sunny, but I don't want you worried about your punishment alone and not sorry over your actions."

This was clearly a new thought for the fiery brunette. "I don't know what you mean."

"I mean..." Brandon hesitated, not certain how to explain.

"I am sorry," Sunny filled the breach with an apology.

"And I thank you for that apology," Brandon told her, still not certain that Sunny's heart was in the right place, but knowing that for the moment he would have to be satisfied.

"We'll be leaving here in two hours." Brandon's gaze pinned her to the floor as he took in her appearance, starting with her bare feet and ending with the mass of curls around her head. "In that time you will clean the mess you've made in this cabin, find a clean dress, and brush your hair. *And* you need to wear shoes."

His eyes then lit with humor as all remorse vanished from her face. Sunny hated to be reminded about her hair and clothes, and in a moment it was as if the earlier incident had never happened.

"Are the people of Freeport so above me that I must dress to please them?" Her chin was nearly in the air, and her eyes were flashing purple fire.

"We have been invited to lunch," Brandon told her calmly. "A friend of mine lives here. He and his wife are expecting us at 10:30."

"Are they English?" The "princess" was gone, and Sunny was 13 once again. She was also breathless with excitement.

"John is. Cheryl is half French."

Brandon's frame shook with silent laughter as he watched her run for her room, her hands already tearing at the buttons of her dress.

Billy drove the carriage through the streets of Freeport, and Sunny never drew her face from the window. Brandon spent the short ride talking to the back of her head.

"How long are we staying?" Sunny asked.

"We sail with the evening tide."

"Oh!" Sunny exclaimed as though she hadn't heard him. "What is that building?"

Brandon couldn't answer because she was blocking his view, but she didn't seem to notice.

"Are we staying the night?" she asked next, and Brandon decided it was best not to answer. She had been a perfect angel since she had appeared in the middle of his now-clean cabin. Her dress was fresh, there were shoes *and* stockings on her feet, and her hair was brushed smooth, though hanging loose. Brandon helped her with a few pins, and after a bit of work the effect was darling. He'd pulled the sides back away from her face, which only served to accentuate her eyes and high cheekbones even more.

They were pulling up in front of John and Cheryl's house when Sunny suddenly turned to Brandon with a worried frown.

"Will I be all right with your friends?"

"Of course, but there's no need to worry. I'm not leaving you with them."

"No, no," Sunny frowned at not making herself understood. "Will I say the right things?"

"I'm sure you will," Brandon spoke with complete confidence. "Are you worried about whether or not they will like you?"

"Yes, and my English."

Brandon's brows rose on this, until he realized he'd never told her how excellent her command of the English language was. He was about to do so when Angus opened the door and held his hand out for Sunny to alight. Brandon followed, realizing as he did that Sunny's doubts had raised a few of his own. As they moved up the steps of a lovely home, he prayed that all would go well in the next few hours.

Twelve

"YOUR ENGLISH IS BEAUTIFUL."

Sunny beamed over the compliment and fell just a little more in love with her hostess. Cheryl Cosgrove was petite, dark, vivacious, and seven months pregnant. She was only seven years older than Sunny, and her sister, Judith Brompton, was engaged to marry Brandon's brother, Dexter. Cheryl had taken to Sunny with her hesitant smile and soft speech the moment she walked in. Until that moment Sunny did not realize how much she had missed female companionship.

The four of them lunched together, and it was a lovely affair with mouth-watering dishes of every sort. Sunny found herself wishing she didn't have to go on to England, where she believed the food to be as bland as that which was served on the ship. She also preferred her hostess' dress to her own, with its puffed sleeves, full bodice, and rounded neckline. The beautiful forest-green satin fabric contrasted sharply with the heavy brown wool of her own.

"Cheryl is right, Sunny," John commented now. "Your English is nearly flawless. How is it that after living so many years in Darhabar, your English is so polished?"

Sunny's chin rose in a way that was becoming familiar to all in her company. "It was my father's wish that I be well versed in all things English." Her pride for the moment caused her to forget the emir's betrayal.

"So you've known all along where you were from?" This came from Cheryl.

"Since I was five. It was then I noticed the differences between my sisters and me. Indira was given permission to tell me when I asked her, and a few weeks later, my English lessons began. We studied for two hours every day, right up to my tenth birthday."

"Who taught you?"

Some of Sunny's confidence deserted her, and she went on in a hushed, troubled voice. "He was an Englishman. Until I came onto Brandon's ship, I thought the man was my Uncle Graham, brother of my dead father. I realize now that this couldn't be."

John and Cheryl looked to Brandon for some sort of explanation, and he quietly told them Sunny's story of how she was found after the storm and taken to the emir as an infant. An uncomfortable silence fell over the room until Cheryl broke it with a gentle question.

"You said that you were versed in all things English, Sunny. Please tell us about the rest."

Sunny took the offered lifeline, effectively pushing from her mind the bearded English face of her so-called uncle.

"I am familiar with all of your religious beliefs. They are of great interest to me, as I am more accustomed to everyone having the same beliefs. I am also trained in your history. England has warred with many nations. I do not like war. Darhabar is a peaceful country." The pride was back in her voice, and she smiled at her hosts.

Listening intently, Brandon realized how much Sunny had told about herself in the last minutes. He had wanted to question her at times, but was reluctant to make her feel as though she were being interrogated. He knew that was the last thing she needed from him.

Brandon praised God for Cheryl's gentle way of talking to her and the way Sunny seemed to blossom under the attention. Not many minutes passed before Cheryl was taking Sunny from the room to show her the baby's nursery. Breathing a sigh of relief after her exit, Brandon was ready for a break from his young charge.

"Tell me, Hawk, how are things going?" John's question was as sensitive as the man himself, and even though they were alone, his voice was low.

"I think they're well, but a few things bother me. I'm not sure if I should be checking into them or putting them behind me, content that Sunny is going home."

"Were you able to gain any clues as to why they let the girl go?"

"No, and that's one of my biggest concerns. I had no time alone with the man who delivered her to me, and at the time I was hesitant to cause a scene. You see, Sunny knew nothing of my arrival."

"Are you serious?" John's voice spoke of his surprise.

"She was told she could tour an English ship when it came into port. She was introduced to me as though I was just any captain on the sea. After her tour they gave her something to drink; the drink was drugged."

John continued to stare at his friend as Brandon related the entire story. John's eyes grew large as his surprise turned to astonishment on hearing that Sunny had jumped overboard.

"By the time I got her back in the cabin, all I wanted was to move out of those waters and take her as far from Darhabar as possible. I knew if I stayed, she would only attempt another escape, and after all these years, I was not about to lose her again. Before I met Sunny I felt more reasonable. I viewed her coming home with a certain amount of detachment. But after meeting her, my emotions took over. After I'd seen her, all I cared about was her comfort and safety."

John nodded in complete understanding. There was something very vulnerable about Sunny Gallagher. She was a proud beauty and seemingly in control of every move, but if one watched long enough, one could see the tiny cracks in her armor, cracks that gave away the fact that she was little more than a frightened child.

"She doesn't care to be reminded that she's still a child." Brandon voiced his friend's thoughts. "But she is, and I am committed to seeing her home and safely into the arms of her family."

"We're praying for both you and Sunny, but I think you know that, Hawk."

"Yes, I do, and I thank you, John." A brief silence ensued while both men digested events of the day. Brandon shifted, seeking more comfort in his chair, and asked, "How is the mission work going?"

John, always willing to talk about the way God was using him and Cheryl, began to share about his work. Cheryl and Sunny were still not back, but for the moment the men didn't notice. They might have been surprised to know that there was an equally intense conversation going on upstairs.

"If you are English, why do you live here?"

Cheryl hesitated over her answer, reluctant to use the word "missions" or "missionaries." "John and I love Freeport, not just the country itself, but the people. We have something we believe in very strongly, and feel a burden to share it with others."

"What do you share?"

"We share our belief that the Bible is God's Word, and that His Son, Jesus Christ, is the Savior of the world."

Sunny looked thoughtful. "I wonder what Brandon believes. He reads often, and when I asked him about the book, he said it was his Bible. Do you and Brandon believe the same Bible?"

"Yes, Sunny, we do. What do you believe, Sunny?" The question was put very gently, and the young girl responded to the warmth in Cheryl's voice.

"I believe as Indira does."

"Indira?"

"My mother in Darhabar. She believes that we have no control over anything on this earth. All things are ordered, and what is to be will be. The emir believes that we control our own destiny, but of course he would feel that way, seeing as he's a man."

Her voice carried a note of cynicism, and Cheryl asked carefully, "What does his being a man have to do with it?"

"Men control everything in this world," Sunny told her logically, and with complete assurance. "You must realize that since you're married. John's word is everything, yes?"

The word "no" sprang to Cheryl's tongue, but she quickly stifled it. How in the world could she deal with such a dictatorial belief without making a mockery of God's perfect plan for husbands and wives?

"John and I have a partnership, Sunny," Cheryl began. "He is the head of our home, yet he's also a servant."

Cheryl stopped when she saw a look of total confusion cross Sunny's face; she'd said it all wrong. If only Sunny were staying longer in their home, they would have a chance to show her what their marriage was like. Cheryl opened her mouth to try and repair the damage, but John chose that time to call her from downstairs.

"Come on, Sunny, the men are looking for us. Maybe we can talk later."

Sunny didn't seem at all put out by the interruption and moved down the stairs with a carefree step. Cheryl would have been alarmed to learn that responding as soon as her husband called only proved to Sunny that her belief was correct—Freeport, England, Darhabar; they were the same. Men ruled all, especially the women.

"How many horses do you have?" Sunny's face shone with enthusiasm, and John smiled.

"Why don't we head out, and I'll show you."

Sunny was out of her chair so fast the adults laughed. All rose to accompany her, and when they reached the back door, Cheryl spoke.

"Go ahead with John, Sunny. I'll be along in just a moment."

The two did as she bade, and when Brandon would have followed, Cheryl stopped him with a hand to his arm. He glanced at his hostess and then at Sunny and John before quietly shutting the door again.

"If you were able to stay longer," Cheryl began, "I would not interrupt you right now, but I think you should know about the conversation Sunny and I had upstairs."

Brandon listened quietly, his face serious, while Cheryl relayed nearly every word of the exchange she'd shared with Sunny. "I don't think I handled it very well, Hawk, but she's cynical, and rather resigned to the way she believes life is. I'm sorry if the things I said have only made the situation harder."

Brandon's hands came to her shoulders, and he bent and kissed her cheek. "There is no reason to be sorry. Sunny adores you, and it's done her a world of good to be in your company. Hopefully she'll feel free to question me about the Bible now. I've been hesitant to say too much, hoping that the first questions would come from her."

"In Sunny alone you're going to be dealing with what John and I encounter every day—a distorted view of God. The first thing Sunny needs to understand is that God does not view women as second-class citizens."

They were walking toward the stables now, and Brandon thought, not for the first time, what a gem John had for a wife. Brandon voiced his sentiments.

"I hope John knows what a find you are. It's too bad I didn't meet you first," Brandon teased.

Cheryl laughed. "Well, there's Judith, but Dex has snapped her up."

"I could wait for Lynn," Brandon teased, referring to Cheryl's youngest sister.

"She's only nine," Cheryl laughed.

"True," Brandon said with a charming smile. "But I'm not ready to tie the knot just yet. At least with your father's money I'd know she wasn't marrying me for my own."

There was something in his tone that caused Cheryl to stop just outside the stable door. "Is it as bad as all that?"

Brandon shrugged, but his eyes were pained. "That, and the title I'm in line to inherit, seem to make me quite a catch." Brandon's voice turned sad. "No one seems to be interested in finding out that I prefer tea to coffee, that I love walking in the rain, or anything else about me as a man. I certainly don't want a wife who dotes on my every whim, but I'd sure like a woman who would love me even if I were penniless or without a title to my name."

Cheryl touched his arm but remained silent. There wasn't anything to say. They were close enough, however, that there really was no need.

Thirteen

THE WIND CAUGHT AT SUNNY'S HAIR and tugged at the skirt of her dress. Her bare feet were cold on the deck, but she took little notice. Today she was 14. She smiled into the wind for just an instant.

Brandon had been out of the cabin early so she had dressed slowly. She now took careful inventory of her body. Her chest was still as flat as it had been ten weeks ago when she stepped aboard the ship, and there was still no definition between her waist and hips.

It was now so clear why Indira had wanted her to accept herself as she was. She knew the truth. Sunny tried to accept that fact herself, but it was hard. She took a moment and thought about the fact that looks and body shapes could run in families. If only she knew what her mother looked like.

"If only I could see her, just for an instant, I might know some rest."

"See who?"

Brandon was suddenly at her side, her shoes in his hand. She shot a long-suffering look in his direction and then bent to put them on.

He watched as she slipped into them, then smiled into the flushed face she had raised to his. She didn't blush often, and he wondered over the thoughts he had obviously interrupted.

"Would you like to be alone?" he asked with his normal sensitivity.

"Not really," she spoke as the embarrassment faded. "I was just thinking about my mother."

Brandon nodded. "Anything in particular?"

"I was wondering what she looked like," she told him softly, looking younger than her 14 years.

"She was a beautiful woman, with hair the color of yours. Her eyes were dark blue, and people said she had the warmest smile in all of England."

Sunny smiled at the image, but her eyes were troubled. He had said nothing of her frame. She looked out to sea as her heart ran with ways of asking what was sure to be an inappropriate question.

In Darhabar, or rather in the emir's palace, a person's body was considered a thing of beauty. Sunny was starting to see that this was not so in England, at least not on this ship. Whenever she came from her bedroom in just her underclothes, Brandon would tell her to get dressed. Her underclothes alone covered more of her body than any of her clothes in Darhabar, but to this English sea captain, it was not enough.

And she had never seen Brandon's unclothed body; not that she particularly wanted to. But he seemed to go out of his way to protect her from seeing something with which she was all too familiar. Almost from the day she had arrived in the palace, she had been wandering in and out of the servants' rooms or Poppy's bedroom.

Then of course she had lived on the edge of the harem, where nudity was not only commonplace, but expected. Most of the women were very proud of their bodies and would have been highly amused at the English way of covering oneself.

"Something is troubling you," Brandon commented softly. "Can you tell me what it is?" He'd been studying her profile closely and wishing, as he did often, that he could read her mind.

"I want to ask you a question, but I'm afraid you'll be angry with me."

Brandon's brows rose on this. "I'm sure you would agree that I don't anger easily."

"That's true," Sunny agreed with a wry smile, thinking of how many times he should have beaten her. "But this is personal. This is not something the English talk about, and I know you want me to be English."

"You *are* English, Sunny, and you're going to be living in England, but I'm not trying to wipe away every moment of your past. If there is something I can tell you, I will."

Sunny looked out to sea again and then turned back to Brandon.

He watched as she crossed her arms over her chest as though trying to protect herself.

"I want to know about my mother's body." These words were uttered in a great rush, as though she were afraid of not getting them out.

Brandon's face gave nothing away, but he was calling himself every type of fool for not reading her worry over her own figure much sooner. Until that moment he'd completely forgotten how she had been led to believe she was older. His voice was calm and gentle as he answered her question.

"Your mother was fairly tall and her figure was lovely. She carried herself with grace and confidence."

Sunny's disappointment with this description was more than evident. She turned back to the sea, and Brandon hesitated, not wanting to embarrass either of them but knowing she needed to know more.

"Your mother had womanly curves, Sunny, but she was not heavy," he tried this time.

Sunny's head turned back immediately, her eyes alight with yearning. "You mean she was not fat?"

"Yes, I do, but I also mean that she was not overly endowed."

Brandon saw in an instant that he had lost her, and found himself wishing that Chelsea were here. He knew that if Sunny wanted him to be much more specific, he would be blushing like a little girl.

"What is this 'endowed'?"

Brandon saw no hope for it; he would have to be more candid. "What I mean is that she was not large-breasted or full-hipped."

To his credit, he did not blush, and Sunny's face cleared as though a heavy load had been lifted from her mind. Such simple words, but they were enough to put her mind at ease. With her questions answered, she looked out over the waves.

"Indira was heavily...endowed." She struggled with the word for a moment and then proceeded. "She had very full breasts and hips," Sunny went on without looking at Brandon. "Were you to see her, you would see that it was not at all hard for Poppy to marry her."

Suddenly all Brandon's embarrassment evaporated. "God's perfect plan is for husbands and wives to enjoy each other in every way, but how a woman looks is not as important as what's on the inside."

"That may be the case in England, but in Darhabar, a man wants beautiful daughters so he can find husbands for them."

"How do the women feel about that?"

"It doesn't matter how they feel," Sunny stated in a surprised voice. "They have no choice. No woman has money of her own, and without a man, she cannot survive." Sunny sighed on this note. "I find myself wishing I had money."

"Why?" Brandon asked, although he was quite sure he knew the answer.

"So I can stay single. I never want to be controlled by a man."

Brandon found himself mentally thanking Cheryl for clueing him in on Sunny's view of marriage. "You don't think you'll find a man who will cherish you and love you enough *not* to dominate you?"

Sunny shrugged. "He would still have the money, and thus, the power."

Brandon debated over telling Sunny what was on his mind, and swiftly reasoned that she would be told soon in any event.

"You have money of your own."

Sunny turned slowly away from the railing and took a step closer to Brandon. Her hands took hold of the front of his cloak. She searched his face for signs that he was teasing and found none. Brandon went on in a soft voice.

"I believe I told you that your Grandmama Sunny never believed the news of your death. She never changed her will, and left you more than half of her wealth. If you're careful, you have enough to live comfortably for the rest of your life."

Brandon had no trouble interpreting Sunny's thoughts now. Her eyes had slid shut, and her whole body had slumped with relief. The smile she sported was one of quiet rapture.

"Do you have a birthday gift for me, Brandon?" she asked softly, having opened her eyes.

"Yes."

"I won't need it," she told him in a fervent whisper. "You've just given me the last gift I'll ever need—freedom. Now my body needn't be a worry." She met his eyes for just a moment before once again going to the rail.

Brandon left her then. He was somewhat pleased by the peace he saw in her eyes, a peace he'd had yet to witness, but as he went below and settled at his desk, his prayer was that the peace would not last.

"Don't let the money be enough, Lord. Give her a special restlessness until she searches for You and learns what true freedom can be."

Fourteen

SUNNY'S BIRTHDAY SUPPER THAT EVENING was to be in the large dining room that Brandon shared with his officers on other voyages. First Mate Flynn and the ship's bos'n, Kyle, were to join them. Decked out in their finest togs, both men arrived as Brandon stood critically eyeing the room with its dark mahogany furniture. He wanted everything to be perfect before going to claim his young charge.

Neither man spoke as Brandon shifted a chair here and moved a candlestick there. He was on his way out the door before he even seemed to notice them. His dark eyes pinned them in place as he assessed their clothing. Upon the inspection and after a brief nod, Brandon moved into the companionway and toward his cabin. He would have laughed at his own seriousness had he seen the grins on the men's faces at his departure.

Sunny peered into the mirror in her room and reached for her hairbrush for at least the tenth time. The feathery strands of hair over her forehead would simply not behave. She fussed a bit more and then heard the cabin door open. After a quick look down the front of her dress, she moved to the doorway of her room.

Brandon, looking taller than ever and resplendent in all black save a snowy white shirt and cravat, was waiting patiently for her appearance. He smiled with genuine pleasure at the sight of her in a dark burgundy velvet gown. The collar and cuffs were pink satin, and Brandon thought she looked adorable.

Sunny didn't feel adorable at the moment; she was confused. Why had she never noticed before how good-looking Brandon was? She realized suddenly that he'd been dressed this way the first time they met, but she'd been too taken with the ship to give much notice. Suddenly Brandon's deep voice broke into her thoughts.

"I realize you don't want any presents," he teased her, "but I hope you will still do me the honor of having dinner with me and a couple of my men."

Sunny's eyes widened in surprise over both comments, making her forget her previous thoughts. They had never eaten with anyone else, and she abruptly realized how rude she must have sounded earlier that day.

"Brandon, I'm so sorry—" she began with true remorse, but broke off when he moved toward her.

Sunny's eyes closed, and Brandon's arms came around her small frame. His hugs always had a way of making her feel like the most cherished girl on earth. He held her close, and then pressed a soft kiss to her forehead.

"I'm only teasing you," he spoke as he now held her at arm's length. "You will of course receive your gift as soon as we eat."

Sunny's smile was brilliant as Brandon moved away from her, stood at attention, and then offered her his arm, using his best court manners to escort her to supper.

She caught her breath when she saw the captain's dining room. A cream-colored tablecloth was spread on the large table, and the room fairly sparkled from the china and crystalware at each place setting. Candles burned in the center of the table, and the lanterns were turned high.

Kyle was the first to approach, and he came over to Sunny with a grave face. She watched as he produced a star, made from fine white rope, knotted so intricately that it was only three inches across. He handed it to her, pointed to the center, and spoke. "Happy birthday, my lady. I tried to get 15 knots in the center here, seeing as you're 15, but only 14 would fit."

"But I *am* 14," Sunny told him with a wide-eyed innocence.

Kyle's own eyes widened with just the right amount of conviction.

"I thought you were 15. You look 15."

Sunny beamed up at the man as she uttered a soft word of thanks and thought she'd never met anyone so kind. Kyle was forced to turn away swiftly. She so reminded him of his own Mary, who had turned 14 just last month. She felt just as Sunny did, that growing up couldn't happen fast enough. For this father, who was away most of the time, it came all too swiftly.

Flynn's gift came next. He gave Sunny a slim volume of poetry. She reacted as though she'd never had a gift so treasured. So effusive was her thanks, the older man went away feeling as though she'd given *him* a gift.

Billy entered the room at that moment with the first course. Sunny was growing more accustomed to the fare, and the meal was eaten with pleasure. All three men did their best to entertain the birthday girl, and Sunny was a marvelous audience as they told stories of previous sailing days.

Brandon had been to sea for only three years, but both Flynn and Kyle had more than their share of tales and kept up their constant verbal sparring. One hated for the other to have the upper hand, and it was always impossible to know who would have the last line.

Connie had gone out of his way in the galley with both the meal and dessert, and when all had their fill, Brandon produced his own gifts for Sunny. The first thing he handed her was a slim book, looking much like the poetry book from Flynn. He spoke as Sunny looked inside.

"The pages are blank, because it's a journal. I only wish you'd had it from the first part of the voyage, so you could have recorded everything. Somehow, though, I think you'll remember."

"Thank you," Sunny murmured as Brandon paused and reached into his pocket. It was obvious that he had something in his closed hand, but he spoke without showing it to her.

"Your family had little time to gather their wits when they first heard you were alive. I'm sure by now they all wish they'd have sent birthday gifts, but for now all I have is this."

Brandon opened his hand. Lying in the center of his palm was a gold ring set with a large amethyst stone. He held it out to Sunny, and she took it reverently.

"It belonged to your Grandmama Sunny, and she always wanted you to have it. Heather remembered it just before I left."

All three men watched as she slipped the beautiful stone onto the ring finger of her right hand. The ring was much too large for her tiny finger, and her shoulders slumped a little until she looked to Brandon again. His hand was extended once more, only this time a fine gold chain hung from his fingertips.

"I thought that might still be a bit large for you, so I picked this up in Freeport. Maybe you could wear the ring around your neck until it fits your hand."

Sunny had said nothing during any of this. She watched while Brandon retrieved the ring, slid it expertly onto the chain, and then rose to fasten it around her neck. The ring dropped below the collar of her throat, and Sunny immediately reached for it. She held it up, now nearly cross-eyed trying to see it, and gazed at it for many minutes.

"Thank you, Brandon," she replied finally, and he could see she was fighting her emotions. The men were quiet for the next few moments in an effort to give her privacy, and then Flynn tactfully moved the subject to their return home.

"Another month, I'd say, and we'll be in London."

"I'm thinking we're closer to three weeks," Kyle told him.

"Now what would you be knowing, Kyle? A baby to the seas is what you are."

"That's true if I'm comparing myself to your 70-some years."

Flynn, a man in his fifties, snorted with indignation and the two were off again, much to Sunny's delight. She was drooping in her chair by the time Brandon called a halt to the festivities. He sent her to the cabin ahead of him, and then had a few words with each man.

Kyle was the last to see Brandon to the door, and he thanked his captain for including him in the party.

"Sunny likes you," Brandon replied. "I knew it would do both of you a world of good, seeing as how you miss your own family."

"Indeed I do, and as a father of some years, may I give you a bit of advice?" the older man asked as his mind's eye pictured Sunny's dark hair, perfect complexion, and nearly hypnotic eyes. "Keep an eye on that young lady, Cap'n. Lovely as she is now, someday she'll be a priceless jewel. When that day comes, you mark my words, she's going to lead some poor chap on a long, merry chase, and she won't even need to try."

Fifteen

IT WAS THE TENTH OF DECEMBER when Sunny stood on deck of the *Flying Surprise* and gained her first view of London. They had come late in the day and hit high tide, enabling them to move up the Thames without delay. Sunny had little time to mentally adjust to the changes about to overtake her.

It had begun to drizzle, and even though Sunny had heard Brandon call to her to put on her cloak, she didn't seem able to move. The town of Freeport had been a surprise to her, but London was a shock. The city was huge. Buildings such as she had never imagined rose above her, and Sunny fought back the panic rising within.

Not having noticed that Brandon had stopped calling to her, she nearly jumped from her skin when he appeared at her side. He had been on the verge of scolding her for standing in the rain, but as he slipped the cloak about her and took in her pale features and wide, frightened eyes, he said nothing. With deft movements, and without taking his eyes from her face, he fastened the satin frogs at her throat and drew the hood over her damp, curling hair.

He had to call her name twice before she dragged her eyes from the passing landscape to look at him. When she did, his heart nearly melted over how young and vulnerable she appeared.

"You're going to be fine," he told her softly. "In no time at all we'll be at your sister's, and you can get settled in your room."

"Does she live on the water?" Sunny's attention was again on the shore.

"No, she lives in town. We'll be docking and then taking a carriage to her home." Brandon finished what he wanted to say, but he could see that he had lost her. As he went back to his duties he prayed that he and everyone else would be sensitive to her needs in the hours and days to come.

Just past an hour later Sunny watched a couple come on board ship. Brandon greeted them with obvious delight and familiarity, and Sunny suddenly wanted to run and hide. What if they were her brother and sister? What if they didn't like her? Sunny forced herself to look away from the small group, out over the docks and the busy activity below. She took a deep breath and tried to calm the frantic beating of her heart.

It took some mental scolding, but she succeeded. By the time Brandon called to her, her face was composed and her manner serene. He approached her with a smile and took her arm to lead her to the waiting couple by the gangplank.

"Sunny, this is my brother, Dexter, and this is his fiancée, Judith Brompton. Judith is Cheryl's sister."

The resemblance was apparent in both families, and Sunny immediately relaxed. Dexter was nearly as tall as Brandon and sported the same dark good looks. Judith was much like Cheryl, a few years younger perhaps, but the warmth in her smile was the same.

Without an invitation Judith stepped forward and hugged Sunny. The young girl responded much like she did in Freeport, and before she realized what was happening, Judith was chatting away and leading her down the gangplank to a waiting carriage.

The men followed and, speaking in a low tone, Dexter filled Brandon in on the last four months. Brandon praised God over the news that his grandfather, the Duke of Briscoe, was still alive. He had said his goodbyes before he left, but it had been his deepest hope that the old man would be there when he returned. Both families were well, Sunny's and his own, and everyone was looking forward to being at Bracken, the duke's home, for Christmas.

Sunny, completely unaware of anything but Judith, was listening attentively and doing her best to answer the questions asked of her. The carriage was in motion for some minutes before the conversation shifted, and for a short while the adults in the carriage conversed alone. In those few moments Sunny let her eyes roam over Judith's beautiful cloak, hat, and dress.

Not wanting to be caught staring, she shifted her eyes to the window, thinking as she did, that both Cheryl and Judith had wonderful taste in clothing. Compared with their outfits, Sunny's cloak and dresses were dowdy. Her attention was then caught by some women who were on the street as the carriage passed. They too were dressed in stylish cloaks with matching hats in gorgeous colors. With sudden and disheartening knowledge, Sunny knew her clothes were all wrong.

Her face burned as questions ran through her mind. Had Calla really been here? Why hadn't Brandon said anything about her clothes being wrong? What would her sister say when she saw her?

"Sunny?" Brandon called her name for the second time, and she turned, just barely remembering to compose her features.

"Yes?"

"Are you all right?"

"I'm fine," she lied smoothly. "Are we nearly there?" Sunny asked the first question that came to mind, anything to keep from dwelling on the way she felt, which was absolutely miserable and on the verge of hysteria.

Brandon glanced out the window. "Another ten minutes. What do you think of the city?"

"Wonderful." Again she lied, but this time Brandon caught it. Wishing they were alone so he could question her further, Brandon smiled gently at her before she turned to look out the window once again.

Heather Jamieson, Sunny's sister, stood in the doorway of what was to be Sunny's room. It was a nice room, functional actually, but Heather didn't want nice or functional, she wanted special. Foster had talked her out of doing any remodeling until Sunny arrived, and now she regretted it. First impressions were so important, and this room had always been a bit dark and masculine.

Foster had reasoned that Sunny would want to have a say in the decorating, thinking that would make her feel more at home. As she took in the dark brown draperies, and equally dark carpets and bed hangings, Heather wondered if maybe they hadn't made a mistake.

A moment later, a maid was sent to tell Heather that his lordship and Sunny had arrived. Knowing it was too late to change a thing, Heather took a last glance at the room and told herself not to run as she hurried down the stairs to meet her sister.

Sunny's head tilted back as she took in the four-storied gray-stone mansion that belonged to her sister. With only two other mansions in sight, the street itself was not busy, but the noise of the city streets just a block away could still be heard.

Sunny was rooted to the spot until she felt Brandon's hand on her back. She preceded him up the wide steps. Once at the top the front door opened, seemingly by itself. Dexter and Judith caught sight of Sunny's serene features as she entered her sister's home for the first time and were very impressed by how well she seemed to be doing.

Brandon, on the other hand, was not fooled a bit. He knew just how well Sunny could hide her thoughts and found himself wishing that Judith and Dexter had not met the ship so they could have had more time to talk. But as with Heather and the bedroom, Brandon also knew that it was too late to change a thing.

Sunny told herself not to look around as her cloak was taken and she moved through the entryway and into a large parlor at the prompting of Brandon's hand. She determined not to think of her dress, cry, or to let herself feel how cold she was. Sunny moved a step closer to the fire for warmth and looked as composed as the queen herself.

Only a moment passed before Sunny saw a woman enter and come toward her. She was taller than Sunny, but the resemblance to her own features was marked. Brandon did not make introductions this time; in fact, he couldn't speak at all after seeing the look on Heather's face. He was sure he must have looked the same when Sunny stepped aboard ship four months ago.

Sunny was still looking like a statue as Heather moved to stand within two feet of her. She smiled into the face that was a younger version of their grandmother. As for Sunny, all she could do was stare.

"Hello, Sunny," her sister said softly. "I'm Heather."

"Hello, Heather," Sunny managed.

Heather could not stay away from her for another moment. She moved then and took Sunny in her arms. Her eyes closed against a rush of tears, and Heather scolded herself over crying.

Sunny was also fighting tears, but of a different nature. The ship had felt so safe, and the air at sea so clean, unlike London, which smelled of sewage. Until they had docked, it had all just seemed like a long, wonderful dream. She'd had all of Brandon's attention, and the reaction of her family was only a thought in her mind. Now she was also having to share Brandon. Since she was now meeting her family in person, imagining them was no longer a game.

What if, after a few months, they feel that my coming here has been a mistake? What if they decide I'd be better off back in Darhabar, and I'm sent away once again? These were the last thoughts that ran through Sunny's mind before Heather released her. Sunny hadn't really hugged her older sister in return, but didn't realize this until Heather held her at arm's length.

None of her disappointment over Sunny's poor response showed on Heather's face. She stood looking into the composed face of her sister, praying for the right words to express her joy over Sunny's return. In an instantaneous decision, she decided to say nothing personal.

"Supper is in 30 minutes. Would you like to see your room or stay here and warm yourself by the fire?"

Sunny knew that Brandon would not be in her room, and wanting to be near him, she opted to stay by the fire. With this decision out of the way, everyone took a seat. It was as if everyone in the room had been holding his breath while Heather and Sunny met, and now the conversation flowed around the youngest member of the family with a familiar ease.

Much to her relief, no questions were directed at Sunny, and it wasn't many minutes before her attention began to wander about the room. Moving nothing more than her eyes, she studied the elaborate fireplace and the portrait hung over the mantel. Her gaze also took in the rich furniture and ornate rugs.

Heather, some feet away from her, could not drag her eyes from her sister's face. Dexter and Judith were talking easily, and Sunny never realized Heather's scrutiny or thoughts. *She's so young to hide her fear behind a mask of composure. Do I really have a chance of getting close to this sister who was raised in such a foreign way?* Heather's thoughts made her feel as though she could cry all over again.

Her eyes shifted from Sunny, and she found Brandon's gaze upon her. His look was compassionate, but the small shake of his head told her she couldn't cry right now. Heather sat and prayed. She asked God to rescue her until she could be alone, and rescue her He did. His help came in the form of her twin daughters, Diane and Louise. Heather had never been so glad to see them.

Sixteen

"YOU LIVED IN A PALACE, Aunt Sunny?" Diane wanted to know.

"Yes," Sunny answered softly and watched both girls' eyes grow wide.

"Then she must have been a princess," Louise breathed after a moment, and the two identical faces turned to each other for just an instant, their young minds filled with grandiose dreams.

"I was not a princess," Sunny told them. "But I was the ruler's daughter."

The question-and-answer session had gone on for some minutes now, but Heather did nothing to interrupt. Sunny seemed a bit more relaxed since the girls' nanny had delivered them, and Heather had to remind herself that even though Sunny was in her generation, she was only six years older than her eight-year-old nieces.

Supper was announced a few minutes later, and Sunny was surprised when the twins bid her goodnight. She too was having a hard time figuring out in which part of this family she belonged and was surprised that the little girls were not eating with them.

Dexter and Judith had been invited to stay for the meal, and even though the food was the best served to her since her journey had begun, the delicious tastes were lost to Sunny's troubled young heart. Her mind ran the gamut from wondering what had become of her trunks to hoping she would never have to look at her clothes again.

When Sunny wasn't thinking about her clothing, she fretted about eating properly. She watched everyone closely in an effort not to humiliate herself, something no one at the table missed. In fact, her scrutiny of the others was so keen that she bumped her water glass at one point and filled her plate with liquid.

The decision to run and hide was cut short by the arrival of Foster, Heather's husband. He was late and made his apologies as he moved toward Sunny. He stood looking down at her for just an instant before he spoke.

"Welcome home, Sunny. I'm Foster, and I hope you'll be very happy with us." He bent and kissed her cheek before taking his seat at the head of the table, his kind blue eyes sparkling with pleasure.

Sunny's eyes followed him, and she decided in an instant that she liked what she saw. He was tall and lean and his face was open with kindness. Sunny watched as Foster and Heather smiled at each other. Unknown to them, their action did more for her heart than anything else she had seen or heard since arriving.

The evening progressed, and beyond a comment here or there, no attempt was made to draw Sunny into the conversation. Wanting very much to be left alone, Sunny did not complain. Not long after they'd moved into the drawing room, Brandon suggested that she might want to turn in early.

Sunny's features were as composed as ever as she thanked him and bid everyone goodnight. She was pleasantly surprised over not being handed over to a servant at that point. Both Brandon and Heather escorted her upstairs to her room.

"I'm in the room next door if you need something, Sunny," Brandon told her as soon as they were inside.

"And I'm across the hall and two doors down," Heather added. A maid had pulled the bedcovers down and laid out a nightgown. Heather called her over and introduced her to Sunny. Her name was Sally. Thinking that she might not have understood, Heather told Sunny once again where her room was.

"It doesn't matter what time it is, just come and get me if you need something," Heather added.

"I'm sure I'll be fine," Sunny told her easily. "Thank you for everything."

It was clear that she wanted to be left alone. Heather wasn't sure what to do, so she took Brandon's cue and bid her sister goodnight. Shutting the door behind them, Brandon told Heather he would talk to her and Foster in the library in ten minutes' time.

❦ ❦ ❦

Sunny turned slowly and took a long look around her dark, rather depressing bedroom. Thinking she was alone, she nearly jumped from her skin when she turned to find Sally near the door.

"Can I help you with your dress, Lady Sunny?"

Sunny was about to decline, but then remembered the row of tiny buttons down the back of her dress. She turned obediently for Sally's assistance, but just as soon as the maid had the dress unbuttoned, Sunny stepped away from her.

"I can manage now, thank you."

Sally, an experienced servant of many years, did not let her surprise show. She bid her mistress goodnight and left the room on silent feet.

Brandon, just coming out of his room, was surprised to see Sally in the hall. He knew she hadn't had enough time to settle Sunny for the night, and he almost questioned her. She curtsied to him as she passed, but Brandon stayed silent. He stood in the hall for some moments, indecision riding him. Sunny wanted to be alone, and he knew how she felt after being cooped up on ship. But with everything she'd seen and heard today, should she be left to herself?

He decided not to step in right then and moved toward the stairway. Halfway to the library, however, he changed his mind. He went ahead to tell Foster and Heather that he was going to be delayed. He honestly hoped he would find Sunny sound asleep, but either way he was not going to do another thing until he checked on her.

The windowpane was cold against Sunny's cheek, but she was glad. *You almost broke down,* she castigated herself and knew she deserved much worse than to shiver on the window seat. The bed looked so inviting, but she was not in command of her emotions just yet. She knew the feel of that mattress and the softness of the pillow would destroy her control.

She glanced over at the fireplace where the flames danced invitingly, making the window seat even colder. She began to shiver then, but not just with the cold. Never had she felt so frightened and alone. London was so huge, and she was living in a houseful of strangers. So deep in her misery, Sunny did not hear the knock or the opening of her door.

When a shadow fell across her face, she started and looked up to see Brandon standing beside her. He reached for her, but she shrank away from him like a wounded animal. If he touched her, she knew she'd be lost.

Brandon, his face in the shadows, could hardly deal with the emotions running through him at the sight of her. That he had actually considered leaving her alone was now abhorrent to him. As he studied her trembling form, she fought desperately for control.

"Stand up, Sunny," he told her suddenly, using a voice he would employ aboard ship.

Sunny did as she was told, standing straight as a line, her chin raised with effort.

Brandon glanced around him and saw Sunny's nightgown on the bed. He went to the bed, scooped it up and took it to the dressing screen. After tossing it across the top, he turned back to Sunny and leveled her with a look.

"Get behind the screen and get into your nightgown." It was a command and Sunny obeyed without hesitation.

Some minutes passed, and Brandon heard the rustle of clothing as Sunny worked. Heather came to the door, a questioning look on her face. Brandon did not speak to her but motioned her to a chair by the door, one that sat in the shadows. Heather no more than sat down when Sunny appeared, her hair down and her nightgown in place.

"Now, would you like Sally to come in and brush your hair?"

"No," she told him emphatically.

"Would you like me to brush your hair?"

Sunny shook her head. The now-tender tone in his voice made it impossible for her to answer.

Brandon sighed mentally. "Sunny," he began. "You've had a long day, and you must be feeling frightened and alone. Let yourself have a good cry; it's what you need."

"I don't need to cry," she told him, her voice wooden.

Brandon saw no help for it. He stepped close to her and before she could guess his intentions, he reached for her forearm and pinched a small piece of skin with enough force to leave a bruise.

Sunny's mouth dropped open with surprise and pain. Tears flooded her eyes.

"You hurt me," she accused him, sounding much like a small child. A torrent of weeping followed, and Sunny buried her face in her hands.

Brandon immediately lifted her into his arms and laid her in the bed. Heather, so wanting to be of help, could only stare as her sister curled into a ball and sobbed harshly into her pillow. Brandon sat beside her, one arm around her, and one hand smoothing the hair from her face. He told himself he was going to stay here all night if she needed him. He didn't speak, and neither did she, but Sunny knew that if Brandon moved from her she would cling to him with all her strength.

Heather, still sitting by the door, suddenly felt Foster's presence by her side and, turning her own face into his waistcoat, let her own tears flow.

Nearly half an hour passed before the sobs abated and the last shudder ran over Sunny's frame. Brandon rose and adjusted the bed-clothes around her before blowing out the lantern. Sally, not needing to be asked, came in with her knitting and settled next to the fire. Brandon and the Jamiesons made their way from the room.

It was a silent threesome that entered the library moments later. Foster had called for tea, and when everyone had refreshed themselves, Brandon began to talk. He told of his first meeting with Sunny and progressed through the story, sparing no detail. Dexter had seen Judith home, but he'd come back in time for tea and was now listening to the story with Heather and Foster.

"You can't mean," Heather stopped Brandon at one point, "that Sunny literally jumped overboard and began to swim."

Brandon didn't reply; his serious look of regret told her it was all too true. Heather looked at her husband, her eyes wide and unsure. Foster wanted to offer some words of reassurance, but found he had none.

"I can see I've shocked you, but if you stop and think about some of the stunts that Chelsea's pulled over the years, it might help."

"Not to mention Grandmama Sunny," Dex inserted, and everyone smiled.

All the grandchildren knew the first Sunny Gallagher as a wonderful, caring grandmother, and all of them missed her even now. But whenever she had talked of her past, it was evident to all listening that she had been as independent and adventurous as any girl could be.

Brandon finished his story about the voyage, making a point of telling everyone how different Sunny had become from the first part of the voyage to the last. Both Foster and Heather looked greatly relieved when he was finished. Before Dexter left for the night, the four adults spent some time in prayer. They petitioned God for wisdom in dealing with Sunny and the chance to build a relationship with her, one that was filled with love and trust.

Seventeen

WHEN SUNNY WAS STILL ASLEEP at 9:00 the next morning, Heather decided to wake her. She entered the room quietly, and with Sally's help, opened the heavy drapes on all the windows.

The girls had been nearly frantic at breakfast to see her, but Heather had told them their Aunt Sunny needed her sleep. She promised they would all have lunch together. But before then, Heather had much to talk over, and do, with her sister.

Her sister. How long had she wished for a sister? It was true that she and Chelsea were very close, but Heather had always missed having a sister of her own. Of course, there were 14 years between them. As Heather settled onto the edge of the bed, she prayed that this would make no difference to Sunny.

Sunny woke up when she heard her name called and squinted against the light in the room. She blinked at the person sitting on the edge of her bed and then saw that it was Heather—Heather garbed in a beautiful dress.

"Good morning," the older woman greeted her.

"Good morning," Sunny returned, feeling like a new person after her night of sleep. "Your dress is beautiful," she commented softly as she looked at the pale green day dress.

Heather beamed. "Would you like one of your own?"

This question brought Sunny bolt upright in bed. "You have another one?"

"Not one that would fit you, but the dressmaker will be here in an hour, and we can tell her you like this fabric."

"I'm to have a new dress?"

"Many new dresses."

Sunny looked very pleased, but then uncertain. "Brandon told me I have money to take care of myself, but I don't know where—"

"Your wardrobe is a birthday gift from Foster and me. He told me at breakfast you were to have a complete winter wardrobe. He's coming home for lunch and will certainly want to know what you picked out, so we'd best get started."

Heather crossed to the first wardrobe and opened both doors. Sunny's eyes widened to see that all of her clothing had been hung within.

"I think this one will do for the day. The others are not quite your coloring."

Heather had pulled out the dark velvet with the satin collar and cuffs Sunny had worn on her birthday. Sally was laying out her underclothes and clucking under her breath over missing items.

"Did some things get left aboard Brandon's ship?" Heather asked her.

"I don't think so," Sunny answered as she climbed from the bed.

"Well, no matter, we'll order as much as you need. Get dressed now, and I'll send Martha in with your breakfast." She was at the door and paused. "After lunch, Sunny, we'll decide how we're going to redecorate this room."

Sunny was left in the middle of the room, gawking at the closed door. If Sally hadn't been on hand to prompt her, she wouldn't have been dressed before noon.

Never in her life had Sunny seen so many fabrics. The clothes she'd worn in Darhabar had been colorful, but most were sheer silks and some satin.

An hour ago, Sunny had barely finished her breakfast when she'd been hustled down the hall to Heather's room, sent behind the screen, and told to strip down to her underclothes. Minutes later a parade of women had entered. Under the direction of a petite woman with a beautiful head of gray hair, the fitting began. Sunny was introduced to Madam Angelica, London's premier dress designer. Madam Angelica, although pleasant, was all business. She directed the proceedings expertly and with a majestic air.

Heavy wools to the sheerest of linens were brought forth and considered. Still in her underclothes, Sunny was measured and then directed to sit on a stool. Bolt after bolt of fabric was placed beneath her chin. She understood most of what went on, but was confused by Madam Angelica, who came repeatedly to stand before her. She would gaze into Sunny's eyes and then say something in a language Sunny did not understand.

Sunny looked to Heather each time it happened, but her sister only smiled at her. By the time they all left, Sunny was feeling hungry and a little cold. Heather buttoned the back of her dress and just as she was finishing, Madam Angelica returned. She had forgotten something and was bustling her way out the door when she spied Sunny in the velvet dress.

Her hands rose to heaven as though supplicating someone above, and then she moved toward her.

"The color is good, but the fabric and style are much too old. She is but 14," Madam Angelica stated as if this explained everything. "Tonight," she spoke dramatically as she went out the door, "tonight she will wear her first Madam Angelica creation." She looked at Sunny again, repeated the foreign words one last time, and went out the door.

"What did she say, Heather?"

Heather's smile was very amused, which only added to Sunny's confusion.

"I won't translate word for word, but Madam Angelica is quite taken with your eyes."

"My eyes?" Sunny asked, still uncertain. Heather smiled at her lack of artifice.

"They're quite an unusual color, and she's looking forward to dressing you."

Sunny nodded, still not sure what all the fuss was about. They were just eyes, like anyone else's. She had moved to the fire to warm her hands when she remembered she hadn't seen Brandon all morning.

"Where is Brandon?"

"He had some pressing matters to attend to this morning, but he left you this." Heather retrieved a folded note from her writing desk and handed it to Sunny.

Dear Sunny,

I'm sorry I missed you this morning
but trust you slept well. I hope to
return for supper, but if I'm delayed,
will you please go riding with me at
10:00 tomorrow morning?

Until then,
Hawk

"He signed it Hawk. I never call him that."

"I think it's habit. What did the note say? Will he be here for supper?"

"He's not sure. He asked me to go riding with him in the morning, though."

"Oh, we'll have to come up with a riding habit for you between now and then." Heather eyed her critically. "I think I know just the person."

In keeping with the pace of the whole morning, Sunny found herself scurrying down the hall behind her sister. Questions ran through her mind, and her head moved from side to side in an attempt to see things she'd only had time to glance at, but she kept up with her sister, thinking she'd never had such a busy morning in her whole life.

"I took your advice," Heather whispered to her husband, catching him before they were joined by the rest of the family. "I've kept her so busy she hasn't had time to think. I wish you could have seen her face when Madam Angelica was here; her eyes looked like moons."

Foster smiled and kissed her. "Has she missed Brandon?"

"She asked about him, but he left a note. He asked her to go riding with him in the morning. I sent word to Margaret Arenas just an hour ago to see if Sunny could borrow one of Katie's habits."

Husband and wife, still as much in love as they were the day they were married, would have stood and talked all afternoon, but they knew their daughters and Sunny were waiting. They moved into the dining room for a delightful meal with the newest addition to their family.

That afternoon Heather included the twins when she and Sunny talked about redecorating the bedroom. The girls were full of ideas, all a bit young, but Heather easily steered the conversation back to Sunny's tastes. Before long, and with a little coaxing on Heather's part, they had some ideas.

Sunny had been hesitant at first, but the more time she spent with her family, the more she saw that they were people like everyone else. It also looked like they were going to keep her. If they were going to send her away, why would they buy her clothes and spend money on her room?

In the late afternoon, the twins were allowed to see more of their aunt, and the three of them played a game on the nursery room floor. Diane and Louise loved this aunt because she was young and got right down on the floor to play with them.

Sunny was growing more relaxed as the day progressed, her only nagging worry being Brandon. He was still the most solid person in her world, and not having seen him for hours bothered her whenever she thought of it. She was also angry with him and decided she had a bone to pick with the man. Despite her anger, she very much wanted to see him again.

At the moment Brandon was in the same frame of mind. He had seen his mother and grandfather and was now rushing back to London so he could see Sunny. She'd been on his heart most of the day, and it had been a revelation to him how attached he'd become to her. Sunny and the girls were still on the floor when he walked into the nursery and quietly took a seat without their notice.

Sunny, in her best dress, was sprawled on the floor in a most undignified manner. Her shoes had been kicked off and were two feet away from her, and strands of hair were falling in her face as she bent over the game. She looked like she was having a wonderful time.

Diane was the first to spot her uncle, and she jumped up from the game to greet him. Louise was fast on her heels, but Sunny, after pushing to a sitting position, stayed on the floor. Upon sighting him she broke into a huge grin, but then she reminded herself that she was annoyed with the man, and the smile disappeared.

The girls' nanny, Miss Charlotte, interrupted them just after Brandon arrived, and after the game had been put away, took the girls to wash for supper. Sunny left the nursery without speaking to Brandon and headed toward the library for a book on English history, one that Heather had mentioned to her. Brandon followed slowly, Sunny's shoes in his hand.

Sunny was scanning the rows of shelves in the library when she heard the door open and close behind her. She knew exactly who it was, and other than a brief pause, decided to ignore him. Brandon took all of this in stride and settled himself onto the davenport, his long legs stretched nonchalantly out before him. After a moment he spoke.

"Angry with me, Sunny?" His voice was soft.

Sunny turned to him immediately, her chin raised indignantly. She glared in his direction and then yanked at the fabric of her sleeve. The small bruise on her bare arm was revealed for just a moment before she adjusted the sleeve and flounced toward the door in a huff.

Brandon stayed in repose until Sunny was just past him. His arm shot out and caught her around the waist. Before Sunny could draw a breath she was deposited neatly beside him. She turned on the seat in outrage, ready to burn his ears with angry words, but stopped at the look of regret on his face.

"I'm sorry it left a mark." Brandon's voice was deep with intensity. "You have more control than some adults I know, but there is a time for crying. Last night you were nearly ill for holding in your emotions. I knew that nothing I said would have the slightest effect. I am sorry I had to pinch you, but I'm not sorry that you cried."

"I didn't want to cry," Sunny admitted.

"Can you tell me why?"

Sunny's chin rose, and she looked away from him. "Crying is a sign of weakness. I'm not a weak person."

That's true, Brandon thought, but said, "I've seen grown men cry."

He didn't miss the look of revulsion that crossed her face, but he continued, "In fact, I've cried myself."

Sunny's head turned back to him, her eyes searching his face. She had such admiration for this man and considered him one of the strongest, most honorable men she had ever met. Where she had grown up, however, crying was considered shameful, especially for a man.

"Where were you today?" Sunny neatly changed the subject; Brandon decided to let her.

"I went to see my mother and grandfather."

Sunny was surprised. She had assumed that when he went to see them, she would accompany him. Brandon correctly read the look on her face and quietly continued.

"I'd like to tell you about them when we go riding in the morning. And then, if Heather has no other plans, my mother is expecting us for lunch the day after."

Sunny was so pleased that she didn't say anything for a moment. Her face gave none of her thoughts away.

"Is there some reason you'd rather not go?"

"Oh, no!" Sunny was horrified at the very thought. "I *want* to meet your mother; I want to meet her very much."

Brandon smiled. She had gone from being practically expressionless to a state of near panic at not being understood. Brandon thought wryly, *There's never a dull moment when you're with this girl.*

Eighteen

SUNNY'S FIRST MADAM ANGELICA was indeed a feast for the eyes. Perfectly suited for a girl of 14, the pink silk creation with puffed sleeves, a simple lace bodice, and full skirt was presented to Sunny with a flourish. Unfortunately, Sunny was too upset over her underclothes to take much notice. She had already surprised Sally into retreat by refusing to wear all that was required of her, and now she stood facing her sister.

"Why do I need this other petticoat when I have a shift?" Sunny was standing in bloomers and a camisole, a linen shift dangling from her fingers.

"Sunny," Heather's voice was calm, but just barely. Didn't her sister realize the work involved for her to have a complete ensemble in one afternoon? Heather took a deep breath. "You can't go around half-naked beneath your clothes." This might have been an exaggeration, but Heather meant to have her way on this. "You need a petticoat that goes to the floor. It gives proper fullness to your skirt and keeps you warm and well covered."

"But Heather," Sunny too was running out of patience, "I'm nearly suffocating in what I have to wear now." These words had barely escaped Sunny's mouth when there was a knock on the door. Heather went and found Brandon in the hall. She told him with the move of her eyes that it was not going well.

Heather would have been surprised to find that Brandon was pleased with such news. That Sunny was not walking around like a perfect statue, as she had been just 24 hours previously, was good news indeed. Heather handed Sunny her robe and allowed Brandon entrance.

"You never said my underclothes were wrong." Sunny wasted no time in accusing him. "Heather wants me to wear this," Sunny held out the shift, "plus that thing." She pointed in disdain to the bed where Heather had placed the voluminous petticoat.

Brandon made himself comfortable by the fire and spoke calmly. "You need to bow to Heather's judgment on this. Not being married, I'm not familiar with everything you need to wear. Heather wouldn't ask you to put those things on unless it was necessary."

This was clearly not what Sunny wanted to hear. She looked between the two adults and then spoke to Brandon.

"What if I refuse?"

Brandon silently applauded Heather when she answered for him. "I'm hoping that you won't, but if you do, you'll not come downstairs for supper. I'll not allow you to be out of your bedroom unless you're properly dressed."

This was all stated very calmly, but Heather was trembling inside. Sunny looked back to Brandon, but he didn't so much as blink. He would make himself walk from the room before he would do anything to undermine Heather's authority.

Sunny, clearly angry with both of them, retrieved the petticoat and disappeared behind the screen.

"It's all very well and good for you to tell me *I* have to dress this way, when you can sit there in simple pants and coat."

Brandon didn't acknowledge the caustic remark that came from behind the screen, but he did give Heather an encouraging smile. He would have to meet with her again and tell her that this was yet another good sign. An angry, *talking* Sunny was infinitely better than a quiet one. With a quiet Sunny, you never knew where you stood or what damage she was doing to her own emotional state by bottling everything inside.

Brandon let himself out of the room before Sunny emerged from behind the screen. He was in the drawing room with Foster when the women appeared. Sally had gone to work on Sunny's hair the moment she was dressed. The simple style, pulled back at the sides and left long down her back, along with the lovely gown she wore, made Sunny look as she should—like a young lady on the threshold of womanhood.

Brandon rose when Heather and Sunny entered and went directly to Sunny. He lifted her hand within his own, bent low, and kissed it ever so softly. Still holding her hand, he lifted his eyes to hers.

"You look enchanting this evening."

Sunny couldn't help but smile. Brandon's eyes were brimming with merriment, and after grinning at him Sunny almost giggled.

"You're not angry with me?" she asked suddenly.

"No, I'm not. But as you can see, Heather's word is law around here, and you had better get used to it."

Looking very resigned, Sunny nodded reluctantly. Brandon's heart turned over, but he said nothing. The sooner she became accustomed to obeying Heather and dressing like an English girl, the better for all concerned.

"Do you really like the dress?" Sunny's question cut into his thoughts as she looked down and inspected herself for the tenth time.

"Very much."

Sunny smiled again, looking very pleased. "Foster and Heather are buying me new dresses for my birthday." As had become Sunny's habit when she was lost for words, she lifted her grandmother's ring on its chain and fingered it for a moment. Brandon smiled at the act.

Just moments later supper was announced. Feeling tired but peaceful, and sitting at the end of the table opposite her husband, Heather felt a bit awed over the fact that Sunny had only been with them for one day. It had not been the easiest of days, but she praised God for all that was accomplished and for His will in the days to come.

"But I thought you'd be here," Sunny told Brandon as he made his goodbyes that evening.

"I'll be back in the morning for our ride, but I have a town house here in London, and that's where I'll be tonight. If you need something, Foster and Heather are right here, and if you must see me, Heather can send word."

The words did not completely comfort Sunny. She knew that Brandon was not going to be around forever, but she had somehow envisioned his presence for some time to come. She reminded herself then that he wasn't going away for good, and that she was acting like an infant. Brandon watched her shoulders straighten and her chin raise before she bid him goodnight. He bent close and spoke into her now-composed features.

"Do I need to pinch you again?"

Sunny's shoulders slumped, and she shook her head. There was no fooling this man. Brandon bid his host and hostess goodnight before slipping his arm around Sunny's shoulders.

"Walk me to the door," he bade her.

Sunny did walk with him to the front door and found she felt better. Brandon kissed her cheek before he left and reminded her that he would be there promptly at 10:00. Sunny had almost forgotten about their ride in the park. She went to bed nearly singing with anticipation.

Nineteen

BRANDON AND SUNNY HAD BEEN ON THEIR RIDE for only ten minutes, when Sunny blurted out what was on her mind.

"Is this animal ill?"

Brandon kept his face averted until he stopped laughing and was able to control his features. He knew when the groom helped her into the saddle that she'd been disappointed. She watched Nick, his own high-spirited gelding, with envy as they rode from the Jamiesons' toward the park.

Sunny had told him that she was used to horses, but Brandon had not been willing to take a risk without first seeing how she handled one. As they now rode side by side, he could see that he had underestimated her. She commanded her mount with a skill far beyond her years. His own sister, Chelsea, preferred a spirited mount and had the skill to handle one. On the other hand, Chelsea's daughter Holly was afraid of horses, and she was a year older than Sunny.

"Brandon," Sunny was not going to let the matter drop. "Why was I given a horse that's still asleep?"

"Because your telling me you had spent time around horses did not tell me you really knew how to ride."

Sunny scowled at him, but anything she might have said was cut short by the approach of another rider. The other rider, whose mount was lathered with exertion, was Lord Lindley, Duke of Colton. He'd been a friend of Brandon's father for years before his death.

"Good morning, Hawk," the older man greeted him.

"Good morning, sir," Brandon returned. "Lord Lindley, I'd like you to meet Lady Sunny Gallagher. Sunny, this is Lord Lindley; he's been a friend of the family for years."

Brandon watched the older man's eyes light with admiration and amusement when Sunny nodded to him like a queen on the throne and then spoke as though addressing a lowly subject.

"You've ridden this animal hard. It is to be hoped that you had a good reason."

It was obvious that Sunny did not expect an answer since she heeled her mount forward, leaving the duke nearly laughing and Brandon ready to wring her slim neck.

Brandon opened his mouth to apologize, but the duke stopped him.

"It's all right, Hawk. You forget I knew her grandmother. She is just as I'd expected her to be—beautiful and nobody's fool."

Brandon relaxed visibly. "Thank you, sir. You're very understanding."

"Not at all. She amuses me, and at my age," the older man went on good-naturedly, "I find little that does."

The duke, having had his say, moved on, and Brandon heeled his horse to Sunny's side. He was ready to launch into an hour's lecture on manners, but Sunny stopped him with the first question out of her mouth.

"Brandon, why did you introduce me as Lady Sunny Gallagher? And why do Sally and Martha call me 'Lady Sunny' or 'my lady'?"

Brandon reined Nick to an abrupt halt. Sunny had never questioned her title, so Brandon had assumed she understood. It was a cold morning but not raining, and Brandon made an instantaneous decision to explain things right then. He swung off Nick's back and approached Sunny's horse.

"I realize we haven't gone far, but I'd like to walk while I answer your question."

Sunny looked a bit surprised but didn't resist when Brandon reached for her waist. After walking a short distance, they turned off onto a side trail and Brandon began.

"How much do you know about our royalty, Sunny?"

"I've been taught all about England. You have a queen now, Queen Victoria, and she's married to Albert, who is the Duke of Saxony."

"That's right, but below our royal ranks, England has other titles. Dukes, marquesses, earls, barons—have you heard of those?"

Sunny looked incredibly pleased. That very morning she had been reading in an English history book and had seen titles of this type everywhere. Duke was the highest title; in fact, there were less than 40 dukes in all of England, and Sunny could see that this rank was of considerable importance. After duke came marquess, then earl, viscount, and baron. She explained what she had read to Brandon, who looked relieved over her understanding.

"But Brandon," she went on before he could, "I still don't know what that has to do with me."

"Your father was the Marquess of Woodburn," he explained, "and your mother, as his wife, was the Marchioness. Thus, as his daughter, you are Lady Sunny."

Sunny's eyes widened at this, but Brandon kept talking.

"The oldest male in the family inherits the title, so your brother Randolph is now the marquess. His son will have the title someday, but for the time being, Miles is an earl."

Sunny's eyes continued to grow, and Brandon found himself uncomfortable. He didn't want to sound like a braggart when he came to his own position, but he wanted to clear all of this up immediately.

"Your brother Douglas is also an earl and so is Foster. An earl's wife is a countess, so your sister is the Countess of Penbrook.

"I am a marquess, but as oldest male, when my grandfather dies, I will assume his title of duke."

Sunny suddenly looked shocked, and Brandon was more uncomfortable than ever. "Lord Lindley," she whispered. "The man you introduced to me. Is he a duke?"

"Yes," Brandon answered with great relief, seeing he had been too full of himself to think that she was going to be the least bit impressed with his title.

"I told him he had been too hard on his horse. That was rude, wasn't it?"

"Yes, it was." Brandon's voice was gentle, but he was also tempted to laugh. "His horse was quite blown, but it *is* his animal and none of our business. I've also known him for years, and he's a very decent chap."

"Did I embarrass you?"

Brandon shook his head. "He was most understanding, but next time you might not get off so easily. You're going to need to learn to keep your opinions to yourself, especially where your elders are concerned.

"You're in an unusual position, Sunny, because your age and generation don't really go together. At times you're going to find yourself surrounded by your brothers and sisters, but feeling like their child instead of their sibling. For the time being, just keep quiet unless you're spoken to, and you'll get along fine."

Sunny was still taking all of this in as they finished their ride and headed back to the house. Lunch was being served and as was the pattern, the twins joined them. The meal was just ending when a messenger arrived looking for Brandon.

The news was not good. Brandon's grandfather had taken a turn for the worse, and Brandon's presence was requested immediately. He left with just the briefest of thanks, and Sunny was left feeling nearly bereft. She was back in her room, feeling very much at loose ends, when she finally realized what Brandon had said about his own title. His grandfather was a duke and he would inherit the title. Brandon would be a duke someday!

Then Sunny thought about the fact that someone you love must die in order for that to happen. It was the same in Darhabar. Ahmad Khan would need to die before his oldest son could take the throne. The thought gave Sunny mixed emotions. A feeling of despondency stole upon her and lingered for most of the afternoon.

Twenty

BRANDON WATCHED THE MOTIONLESS FACE of his grandfather and thought of the precious years he had known him. He let his mind retrace the years to his first remembrance of this man. Brandon had been four at the time, lively and precocious, a trial to nurse and nanny alike. He'd just escaped his nanny, making a clean getaway from the nursery only to charge into the hall and run directly into the long, darkly clad legs of the man now lying in the bed.

Brandon remembered looking up into his face, expecting to see anger and seeing only unspeakable delight. Brandon's face mirrored the joy when he was then scooped up into his grandfather's great arms and carried into the library.

An hour of pure bliss followed as Brandon was able to ask all the questions he wanted and touch everything within his reach. But the memories he savored most from that hour so many years ago were his grandfather's eyes and the love he had seen there.

Those eyes still held love when they looked at Brandon, but now Brandon couldn't see them. Three days had passed since Brandon had been summoned to Bracken, his grandfather's home—three days of not seeing the love in his grandfather's eyes. The sudden thought of never seeing those loving eyes again was so painful that Brandon felt tears fill his own. Brandon prayed as the pain squeezed around his heart.

Your timing is perfect, Lord, and if You're taking him today, You'll give me strength. I thank You for the years we've had and that he knows You. Give each of us the comfort we need to face the days and hours ahead.

Brandon finished his prayer by petitioning God on his mother's behalf. His mother, Lady Andrea, was in a chair by the window. She was closer to the duke than anyone else on earth, and losing him was going to affect her deeply. As she stared out the second story window at the winterscape below, her eyes were dry but sober at the thought of losing this man who had been more like a father to her than a father-in-law.

With his chin resting on his steepled fingers, Brandon let his gaze roam the room. It was a beautiful suite, not depressing like so many masculine rooms, but manly nonetheless with its heavy, carved furniture and deep green decor. Brandon's eyes had just taken in the white marble fireplace when something made him look back at his grandfather. The old man was staring at him, his eyes tired but filled with the unwavering love that Brandon had missed so desperately. When Brandon could speak, he did so softly.

"Welcome back."

"Thank you, Hawk." The elderly voice was low.

Brandon looked at him for a moment, and then asked the question he knew would be understood.

"Are you slipping away from us, Papa?"

Milton Hawkesbury moved his head on the pillow. "I don't think so. I don't feel the pain as much now, and in fact I'd like some water."

Having heard the voices, Brandon's mother joined them. She bent low over the bed to assist her father-in-law with a cup. A few more words were exchanged, and then the old man slept again. After he'd dropped off, Brandon and his mother recognized their need for a rest from his bedside. They left him in the care of his nurse and went downstairs for lunch.

Dexter was just getting in from a trip to the north and wanted to go straight to the sickroom.

"I think he might pull through." This came from Brandon as the three stood close and spoke softly.

"I'd like to see him."

"I think that's a good idea," his mother said. "He just went back to sleep, but as Brandon said, he'll probably come through, and you'll be there when he wakes."

"Right. I'll sit with him for a while. Has Chelsea been here?"

"Yesterday," his brother answered. "Both she and Holly."

Dexter nodded before turning for the stairs and taking the flight two steps at a time. After his departure his mother had a lunch tray sent up to him in the duke's room.

Two days later the duke was sitting in a chair by the window. He was still very weak, and shouldn't have been out of bed, but his color was good and his eyes sparkled with humor as he teased his great-granddaughter.

"What do you mean you're not married?"

"But Grandpa," Holly told him, her eyes wide with pleasure and suppressed laughter, "I'm only 15."

"I'll bet you've got a string of young men chasing you. She has, hasn't she, Chelsea?"

"Not quite a string, but she is rarely without companionship." Chelsea watched her daughter dimple on these words.

"Just as I thought," the old man stated, his loving eyes on Holly's smiling face.

Brandon caught a look of fatigue at that moment and suggested his grandfather return to bed.

This earned him a scowl, but the duke's voice was not angry, just matter-of-fact. "I am a bit tired, but if I go to bed, you'll all leave."

"I'll stay and talk with you," Andrea offered, and Brandon, Chelsea, Dexter, and Holly exited the room.

"Everyone is going to be at Rand and Chelsea's for Christmas this year and then here for Boxing Day. You'll probably have more company than you'll know what to do with."

Andrea made light conversation until the eldest Hawkesbury was settled once again under the bedclothes, halfway hoping he wouldn't remember that everyone had originally planned to spend Christmas there. He looked drained, but his color was still good and his eyes alert. Andrea desperately wanted to see him improve.

"I've got to get better so Hawk can leave."

"I'm sure he's in no hurry to be away." Andrea's voice was gentle as she adjusted the pillows.

"Maybe not, but I won't see his son if he doesn't marry soon."

"I wouldn't be too sure about that. This is the fourth scare you've given us this year, and here you are, as sassy as the day you were born."

The old man ignored the impertinent remark. "And what about you, Andrea? Were you not tied here, you could marry again."

Andrea regarded him soberly from her chair by the bed. "I've buried two husbands, Milton. I'm not sure I could do it again."

The duke reached for her hand, their understanding going deeper than words. They sat together without talking until the old man fell asleep.

$\mathscr{Twenty\text{-}One}$

SUNNY SAT ON HER BED, looking into the wardrobes in her room. Her clothes had been delivered, and even though her face showed disinterest, her mind raced. Never in her wildest dreams had she imagined such a wardrobe. As the emir's daughter, she had everything her heart could desire, but this, *this* was more than she could fathom.

Madam Angelica had produced dozens of sketches for examination, but Sunny never understood that she was to have so many things. There were at least three dozen dresses, five riding habits, more than a half-dozen evening gowns, four fur-trimmed cloaks, and underclothes. More than Sunny cared to have in a lifetime.

The clothes she'd had on ship, the ones she had been so proud of before they landed, had vanished. Only the burgundy velvet with the pink satin collar and cuffs remained. Sunny had been wearing it when Sally cleared away her other clothes that morning to make room for the new arrivals. The twins had come in after the new wardrobe was delivered and insisted she put on something new.

Sunny looked at her closed bedroom door and then slid off the bed and onto the floor to lie on her stomach. She reached beneath the bed and pulled the hidden dress toward her. She hated herself for the tears, brought on from just the feel of the fabric.

Could it really be just a few weeks past that she'd worn this dress to her birthday celebration with Brandon? At the moment it all seemed like a long-ago dream. With the dress held under her arm she

110

went to her high dresser and pulled out the star Kyle had made her. She was fingering the delicate rope with sweet remembrance when someone knocked on the door. Before Sunny could stop her, Sally entered and spotted her with the dress.

"I came to fix your hair for supper, my lady, but I see I've missed one of your dresses. Would you like me to take it now?" Sally had started to move toward her, but stopped abruptly when Sunny's chin rose in what Sally affectionately thought of as Sunny's princess stance.

"I wish to keep this dress." Sunny's voice matched her pose.

"I think that's very smart, my lady," said the wise Sally. "Here, let me hang it at the end of your wardrobe." Sally's smile was genuine, but Sunny hesitated.

"No one will touch it without your permission," Sally told her softly, and Sunny relinquished her hold.

A few moments later Sunny was seated before the large mirror that hung above the dressing table, and Sally was drawing the brush through her glorious chestnut hair. Sally loved doing Sunny's hair because the girl was not so self-absorbed that she never took her eyes from her own reflection.

This evening Sunny was reading her history book. It was not an easy task while having her hair brushed, but the young woman was captivated. She looked up only when someone else knocked on her door. Heather entered without waiting for an answer, and behind her was a footman carrying a large trunk.

"If there's anything special you want packed, Sunny, be sure to tell Sally."

Sunny only stared at her sister.

"Sunny," Heather spoke with uncertainty. "You did realize we're leaving for Rand and Chelsea's in the morning?"

"I thought we were going for Christmas."

"Christmas is three days away, Sunny. Today is the twenty-second."

Heather did not linger, and Sunny was glad. She laid her history book down, and for the first time since Sally started her hair, she stared at herself in the mirror.

The drive to Willows' End, as Rand and Chelsea's home was called, was a complete surprise to Sunny. After leaving the busy

London streets, the carriage soon moved out into the country. The land was somewhat barren in the winter months; still, Sunny found it beautiful and very tranquil. The countryside rolled and dipped with hollows and hills, and everywhere she looked the land was criss-crossed with low stone walls.

Cattle and sheep grazed contentedly, and the twins could not stop talking or pointing them out. They carried on about their Uncle Rand's lands and stables, the main house, cottages, and carriage house. Sunny listened with only half an ear. She was going to meet Randolph and his family. What would they be like? Would they like her?

Up to this time, the news that she had a niece and nephew older than herself had made little difference to her. Suddenly she was nervous over the fact. And what about Rand himself? He was her brother. Heather had been glad to see her, but what if she was just a nuisance to Rand? He hadn't come to see her when she was in London. She was, after all, young enough to be his daughter. Perhaps he would just as soon she had stayed in Darhabar.

The thought was so unsettling that Sunny did not hear Foster addressing her. He stopped when he realized her mind was elsewhere, and after exchanging a glance with Heather, left her to her thoughts for the remainder of the journey.

Randolph Gallagher, Marquess of Woodburn, stood at the library window and let his eyes study the long, willow-lined drive. It had been wet lately, and he wondered if his family had been delayed by the roads or a late departure from London. When the door opened behind him, he glanced over his shoulder and saw that Chelsea had entered. With an outstretched hand, he welcomed her into the curve of his arm.

"Are you wishing them here?" Chelsea asked.

"I think maybe I am. I fear she won't understand why I didn't come to London as soon as she arrived."

"You can explain it to her."

"True," Rand said. His mind was already back on his youngest sister and what she must be like. He'd talked to Brandon at length, and where most people would be shocked at Sunny's independent behavior on ship, Rand had admired her courage and spunk. She sounded a lot like his own dear wife, and Rand couldn't imagine life without her. His arm tightened around Chelsea for just a minute, and then they both spotted it—the Jamieson coach was coming up the drive.

"What are you doing in here?" Miles asked his sister Holly when he found her practically hiding in the upstairs salon.

"Nothing," she said a bit defensively.

"Didn't you hear Binks say that Heather and Foster are here?"

"I heard," the young woman said softly, and Miles came in and shut the door. Holly went on just as softly after Miles sat down across from her.

"Doesn't it bother you a little bit that she's our aunt, but we're older?"

Miles shrugged, clearly not at all concerned. "I guess it might seem a little funny, but I assumed we'd act more like cousins to each other, since she's just 14 to our 15 and 16. I don't really think there's going to be a problem."

"What if none of us likes the other?"

Again Miles shrugged. "There's probably nothing to like or dislike one way or the other. And if there is, then we'll all be thankful she's just here for Christmas."

Miles was so logical that Holly nodded reluctantly and rose when he did. He led her to the door and then held it with gentlemanly ease so she could precede him into the hall.

Sunny stared into the fire that danced merrily in one of the vast fireplaces in Rand and Chelsea's large parlor. She felt so cold she wished she could crawl in with the flames. The coldness, the same type she had experienced when she met Heather, was now seeping into her bones as she waited for her brother to arrive. The twins had been ushered away by their mother, and now she and Foster waited alone.

"Why don't you sit down, Sunny," Foster suggested.

She tried to smile at him. He was always so kind, but at the moment she didn't think she could move to do as he'd suggested.

"They're not going to bite you," he remarked with a teasing glint in his eye. This did wring a slight smile from Sunny, but just then the door opened. Without delay the smile and all traces of strain left Sunny's features, and as composed as ever, she turned with stately ease to meet her family.

Rand was not sure what he had been expecting, but this slim, beautiful girl who stood looking more poised than many adult women he had known was decidedly not it. He sent up a prayer of silent thanks that Brandon had warned him of her self-control. She was indeed hard to gauge with her collected features and proper stance.

"Sunny," Foster said, wanting to break the ice and start things on the right foot. "This is Rand and his wife, Chelsea."

"Hello," Sunny said, nodding her head just slightly but not smiling or showing warmth of any kind.

Rand and Chelsea both greeted her, but the strain in the room was evident. Rand felt miserable, but he didn't have a clue as to how to help the situation. Chelsea, usually able to jump in and save the most awkward situation, was clearly at a loss also.

Sunny was so *perfect*. She had just traveled by coach for hours, but every hair was in place and her dress was flawless. She had done no developing of any kind in her 14 years, so her manners did not fit the young body clothed by the dark blue traveling suit, but Rand's heart turned over at how unsure she must be feeling inside, and he decided to act as normally as he could.

"Please, Sunny, sit down. We're glad to have you here at Willows' End. If there's anything you need, just ask."

"Thank you," Sunny told him and sat like a statue on the edge of the settee.

"How was the trip?" Chelsea interjected as she also sat.

"Fine, thank you." Sunny had decided that these people were not going to like her, so she was going to be on her best behavior until she could leave this place. She actually preferred what she had seen of Willows' End over Heather's house in London, but she was certain she must be an intruder here, so she told herself not to relax.

The strained silence that followed those few words was broken by Binks, who was head of housekeeping in this vast home. Nearly all the servants answered to him. His wife, Mrs. Binks, was the Gallaghers' cook.

"Lady Heather is asking for you, my lord," he said to Foster. "Shall I tell her you are indisposed?"

"No, Binks, I'll come. Tell her I'll be right there." He turned to Sunny and smiled. "I'll see you later," he told her kindly and left, thinking this might be the best thing to have happened.

Chelsea was thinking the same thing and stood with Foster. "I can't think what has become of Miles and Holly. I'll see what's keeping them." Sunny watched her leave and began to feel so cold again she rose and went back to the fire.

Rand watched as she held her hands to the flames, and knew an ache to put his arms around her so deep that he thought he wouldn't be able to restrain himself. Sunny turned to find him watching her and, for just a moment, couldn't take her eyes from his. Sunny decided to tell him that she knew she wasn't welcome in his home.

"I'm sure it's not very easy for me to come here like this, but I'll not be any bother to you while I'm here, and Heather tells me we'll be gone in a few days' time."

"Is that what you think, Sunny?" Rand's voice was deep. "That I don't want you here; that you're going to be an inconvenience?"

Sunny's chin rose. Rand saw this move and knew that there was way too much space between them. He rose and came to stand next to her by the fire. When she didn't turn to face him, but instead turned back to look at the fire, he took her by the shoulders and turned her toward him.

"The day you were born I already had two children of my own. You would have thought it was my wife and not my mother who'd had a baby, so great was my joy. I first saw you when you were six hours old. On that day when I first held you, I watched as you opened your eyes and in so doing, walked straight into my heart.

"You left here with Mother and Father when you were just a year old, and it was like having one of my own children taken away. Some time passed before we heard that you had been lost, and I ached for months over the thought that I couldn't hold you and play with you again.

"And now after being separated from me for nearly 13 years, you're here in my own home. If you expect me to keep my distance, you're going to be disappointed. I've been forced to be separated from you for all these years, but no longer."

All of this said, Rand wrapped his little sister in his powerful arms. He could tell he had shocked her speechless, but at the moment he didn't care. It took over half a minute for her to relax in his arms, but Rand was patient. The trembling had left her frame, and her arms were now hugging him back. He lowered his head so his cheek could rest on the top of her head. Tears clogged his throat. He tightened his grasp slightly and spoke softly.

"I wanted to come to London as soon as you arrived, but I couldn't get away."

Sunny shifted and tipped her head back to see his face.

"Do you mean that?"

"Every word," he told her fervently. "The only thing that kept me from dropping everything here and rushing to see you was knowing you'd be coming today."

Sunny smiled then, a smile that started in her heart and worked its way right up to her mouth. Her brother loved her. Sunny couldn't think of anything more wonderful.

In the next few moments brother and sister were talking like old friends. Sunny learned all about the land Rand owned, managed by men from the village. He also owned and operated several woolen mills. Sunny was captivated.

She shared with him about her trip with Brandon and a few facts about her life in Darhabar. They probably would have continued talking for hours, Rand telling more about his work and Sunny about her life in London, but Binks opened the door. Chelsea entered. She was followed by Miles and Holly.

≈ Twenty-Two ≈

HOLLY GALLAGHER WAS SHORT, with a full figure, a lovely face, and a fun-loving personality. At the sight of her aunt, all previous fears melted away, and she smiled at Sunny as if she were a long-lost friend. The other people in the room, including her brother, were forgotten as Sunny found herself smiling shyly in return.

Introductions were made, but it was some moments before Sunny really turned to look at Miles. He was a picture of his handsome father in face and build, and unlike Holly, he was not smiling. He was staring at Sunny as if he had never seen a young woman before. Sunny, not sure what to think of his scrutiny, nodded in his direction and let herself be drawn into a conversation with Chelsea and Holly.

"Did Rand tell you how badly he had wanted to come to London?" Chelsea asked her sister-in-law.

"Yes," Sunny said with an understanding smile. "He said he was very busy."

"I'm so glad you're here now," Holly broke in and smiled once again. Sunny found herself liking her more than ever.

"Mum," Holly went on, "May Sunny and I go to my room? Oh," the older girl stopped suddenly. "I can call you Sunny, can't I?"

"What else would you call me?" the younger girl asked, completely forgetting their relationship.

"Aunt Sunny," Chelsea supplied kindly and then turned to Holly. "If Sunny doesn't mind, it's fine with me."

117

"Diane and Louise call me Aunt Sunny," she said softly, obviously considering this for the first time. "But they're younger than I am."

Holly beamed again. "It's all settled then. We'll see you later," Holly called to the room in general, and then took Sunny by the arm and nearly dragged her from the room.

Rand and Chelsea exchanged grins and spoke quietly for a moment. Neither mother nor father noticed how quiet Miles had been during the entire exchange.

Holly's bedroom so fit her personality that Sunny felt like she knew her better just by walking over the threshold. It had begun to rain outside, but with pale pink draperies and bed hangings, the room was cheerful despite the lack of sun coming through the glass. The background of the wallpaper was pristine white with pink, green, and blue flowers and umbrellas.

Holly's bed sat in grand style on one wall, and two tall wardrobes sat opposite. A lovely white writing desk with a matching chair sat in the alcove of one window. A settee was angled into one corner, and in front of it sat a low table sporting a brass candle-holder.

Holly's dressing table was a monstrous affair with a huge mirror hanging above. She also had a full-length freestanding mirror in dark wood, which contrasted sharply with the lighter furniture but was all the more striking because of it.

"Is that Grandmama Sunny's ring?" Holly asked, breaking Sunny out of her inspection of the room. Holly took her hand once again, and Sunny answered after she and Holly were settled on the bed.

Sunny's hand automatically went to her chain. "Yes. Brandon told me Heather sent it. He gave me the chain and the ring on my birthday."

This was simply the first of many questions Holly was to ask. As the time moved on Sunny answered each one, but there the conversation stopped. Sunny was so taken with her niece she hardly knew what to say. Holly didn't seem at all put out by the silences that cropped up when she ran out of questions, but Sunny, so wanting to be liked, felt strained each and every time.

"What kinds of things did you do in Darhabar? I mean, how did you spend your days?"

A curious look flitted over Sunny's face, and Holly felt alarmed.

"I'm sorry. Perhaps you'd rather not talk about it. I should have been more sensitive."

Sunny looked surprised. "It doesn't bother me to speak of it, but until you asked me I'd never given it much thought. I spent much of my time sneaking into the kitchens or the stables or the tower."

"Why did you have to sneak?"

"I was not to be in those areas. They were not as protected, and as the emir's daughter, I was in more danger. But I loved the kitchens and being with the horses, so I went anyway."

"Were you ever caught?"

"Of course," Sunny said matter-of-factly. "Punished also, but it was always worth it."

For the first time it was Holly's turn to be out of words. She stared at her aunt, seeing just how different they were. Holly hated to get into trouble and almost never made the same mistake twice. And the horses! The thought made her shudder.

"What do you usually do to keep busy?" Sunny asked, feeling very pleased with herself because she had just realized that she could send Holly's questions right back to her.

"Oh," Holly seemed pleased to be asked. "I love to paint, and I love to play the piano. Mother says I'm quite good, and my instructor comes two days a week in the wintertime. Oh," Holly went on, now warming to her subject. "I'm working on the most beautiful tapestry. Would you like to see it?"

"Yes."

With that small word, Holly took Sunny down the hallway, up one more flight of stairs, and into the upstairs salon. The room was empty, and Sunny's head was spinning with what she had seen of the mansion as she rushed along behind her niece.

"This is it," Holly spoke proudly as she displayed a beautiful tapestry for Sunny's inspection. Sunny took in the field scene with the perfect little trees bordering on the edge and a stream flowing through the middle. She bent low to look at the tiny handwork and turned to Holly.

"You're doing this with your own hands?"

"Of course. Haven't you ever done a tapestry, Sunny?"

Sunny could only shake her head as she turned back to the beautiful work square. Holly was showing Sunny some of her mother's work when Binks came to the door.

"You have visitors, Lady Holly. Lord Kemp and Lord Taylor are in the blue parlor."

"Thank you, Binks," Holly spoke sedately, but nearly squealed when Binks shut the door.

"Did you hear that, Sunny? Brice Kemp and Victor Taylor are here." Again she had Sunny's hand and was taking her to the door and back along the hall and down the stairs. "We've got to freshen up and get down there to see them."

"Who are they?" Sunny finally asked as Holly shut her bedroom door behind them.

"Brice is *19*," Holly replied, as though this explained everything, "and the best-looking fellow you'll ever hope to see. He was rather homely a few years ago, but he's been away and when he came back, oh my! Vic is cute too, but he is Miles' age," she finished dismissively.

Sunny still didn't understand what the fuss was about, but suddenly found herself under Holly's scrutiny. Holly came forward and fixed a stray curl at the back of Sunny's head and then put her hands on Sunny's face. She gave each cheek a little pinch.

"There, that will put a little color in your face. Other than that, you look great. I, on the other hand, must change this dress. Will you undo the back?"

Holly turned and Sunny obediently unhooked her. It seemed like hours before they left the room, and Sunny was certain that whoever had been here would now be gone. She couldn't have been more wrong. The two young men waiting for her stood when Holly walked into the blue salon and looked as though the answer to their every prayer had come true.

Sunny felt self-conscious when their eyes fell on her for the introductions, but it lasted only a moment before they were both once again looking at Holly. Indeed, she was wonderful to see. She had changed into a beautiful festive gown of green and gold, and had her hair artfully piled on top of her head. Little ringlets hung around her face, making her large lovely eyes all the more catching.

But it wasn't her looks that really held Sunny's attention; it was her manner with the boys. It was obvious that she knew them well, and even though Holly never intended to exclude Sunny, she did.

Sunny sat back and watched as Holly teased and laughed with the young men as though they had been friends for years. And as Sunny thought about it, she realized they probably had.

She found herself wishing she could be alone, but she didn't know how to leave. Nearly 30 minutes later Miles joined them, and Holly impulsively decided they needed to play a game. Before Sunny knew what was happening, she was at the round table by the window with seven cards in front of her.

Holly gave her quick instructions on the game, and they started playing. Sunny didn't have the foggiest notion of what she was doing. If she had been more aware, she would have noticed certain eyes on her. Brice studied her face and found himself wishing she were older. Vic's thoughts were that she was a bit dense because she had said so little all day and was taking forever to play her hand. Miles was fascinated by her beauty and poise, and after witnessing a brief look of confusion in her eyes, he was filled with compassion. Holly, who hadn't yet understood how well Sunny could hide her feelings, thought she was having a wonderful time.

The torturous game had not gone on very long when the door to the parlor opened. Sunny didn't look behind her even when the others greeted Brandon. She felt his presence behind her, but still didn't move, even when his hand came over her shoulder and he played her next card. When the hand ended, he pulled her chair out, and spoke in smooth tones.

"Since you have four, I'm sure you'll forgive my stealing Sunny for a while."

Sunny nodded to the table in general as she stood, and Brandon saw her to the door. With a hand on her arm he took her to the door of the library. He started to knock, but Binks spotted them and spoke.

"Allow me, my lord." The servant opened the door, and after asking if they desired refreshment, left them in peace.

Sunny had not been in this room before, and for just a moment she let her gaze roam. It was twice as large as Foster's library, holding more books than Sunny had ever seen. It would be a wonderful place to explore, but right now Sunny was hurting inside, feeling like an outsider and a fool. She told herself she was selfish as well and turned to Brandon.

"How is your grandfather?"

"Holding his own very nicely. Thank you for asking. How is Sunny?"

The question, asked so lovingly, made Sunny want to cry. She did not immediately answer. It seemed that all she did lately was weep, and even the risk of being pinched did not stop her from taking time to compose herself.

"I want to go home."

"To Heather's?"

"No," Sunny answered before she thought.

She had never intended to say that to anyone, and even though Brandon said nothing, she regretted her words. It had nothing to do with him or the rest of her family, but she didn't fit in and was certain her staying would never work. She was comfortable with her siblings, but she was the age of her niece. Brandon had warned her that it would not always be easy, but Sunny never dreamed it would be so painful.

Brandon had thought they would sit and talk, but Sunny began to meander about the room. He realized now that he had been selling her short. He had half-expected her to rail at him for his long absence, but it seemed she understood about his grandfather.

What hadn't occurred to him was that she wouldn't immediately fit in with Holly and Miles. He could tell the moment he'd walked in the room that she was having a miserable time with the game, and it was all too easy to guess that her time spent with Holly's friends had been a bit of a strain. From her earlier comment she had clearly convinced herself that she was never going to adjust.

Sunny was still walking around the room, not seeing much of anything, when Brandon retrieved something out of the cabinet on the wall and pulled two chairs up to a library table.

"Come here, Sunny," he said after he had taken a seat and begun to shuffle a deck of cards. Sunny approached but didn't sit down.

"Have a seat; I'm going to teach you the game of whist."

"Why?"

Brandon leveled her with a look. "So next time you'll know how to play."

Sunny looked back at him. *So this is the way it's to be—no talk of going home.* Sunny sat down slowly and picked up her hand. *No matter,* she told herself. *You knew he wouldn't have let you go anyway.*

Twenty~Three

THE ENTIRE HOUSE STIRRED EARLY ON CHRISTMAS MORNING. Sunny would have slept for several more hours, but Holly came bursting into her room wanting to know why she was still in bed. Sunny squinted at the dark beyond the window.

"It's dark out."

"I know. That's part of the fun."

Sunny stared at her niece. "You're not dressed."

"That's part of the fun too. See, I've got your dressing gown." Holly held up a pink satin garment. "Now put this on and let's get downstairs before we miss all the fun."

Still very fuzzy around the edges, Sunny did as she was bade, but as she slipped into her dressing gown and Holly tied her hair back with a ribbon, she was still trying to understand all the excitement. She knew the history behind the holiday but had always had the impression it was a time for children. Holly acted as though she thought she herself was getting gifts.

Holly hurried Sunny down the stairs and into the large salon. All vestiges of sleep evaporated when Sunny stepped over the threshold. This had been the first room she had seen in this mansion, but it looked nothing at all like she had originally seen it. A Christmas tree, over 20 feet in height, towered over them on one corner of the rug. The furniture had been rearranged to accommodate it and was also set up for a perfect view of the lavishly decorated tree.

Gifts, seemingly hundreds of them, flowed out from under the tree like water from an overflowing brook. Nearly all the family had gathered, talking and drinking coffee or tea, and those not yet there were arriving fast.

Rand, Chelsea, Brandon, Foster, Heather, Dexter, Miles, Diane, and Louise were all waiting within. Sunny's brother Douglas, his wife, Marian, and their four children, Harlan, Lance, Grace, and James had arrived late the night before and were just coming in behind Sunny and Holly.

Douglas had fallen in love with his little sister as quickly as his other siblings, and he was the first one to hug Sunny and wish her a happy Christmas. She was ushered along in some confusion and wonder until she found herself next to Rand and Miles. A cup of hot cocoa was pressed into her hands. As Sunny sipped it, she let her eyes take in the wonderful scene as her mouth tasted the delicious, sweet liquid.

To add to the festive air, evergreen garlands were hung around the mantel and over all the doors and windows. A fire crackled in both hearths, and the glossy fabric of the chairs and settees reflected the lights of the many lamps set about the room. Holly had been right; part of the fun was the dark outside.

Sunny sipped from her cup and snuggled back into the davenport, her eyes taking in tree decorations that ranged from cut-glass baubles to carved wooden animals.

Sunny suddenly noticed that everyone seemed to know where they belonged. As if by magic, seats were taken and quiet descended. Rand rose from Sunny's side and went to stand before the group.

"It's a pleasure to stand before you each year and give thanks for all that God has given us, but I think you'll all agree that *this* Christmas far outweighs anything this family has ever experienced."

Sunny immediately found herself the center of attention. Eyes turned to her and everyone was smiling; Sunny even saw some tears. Rand went on to speak of other things for which they were thankful, but after the attention shifted from her, Sunny didn't hear most of what he said.

Rand's departure from the davenport left her sitting alone with Miles, and as usual he made her nervous. She was certain he didn't like her. He would stare at her, but then turn away the moment she looked at him. He hadn't said more than ten words to her since she arrived, and she decided he thought of her as an intruder. Holly had told her that Miles was home for only a week at Christmas before he had to be back at school. He obviously didn't care for her being here, encroaching on his time with his family.

Sunny was not left to brood on this for very long because Rand was now finished speaking and Foster was taking his place. Foster was evidently the official gift-giver, and suddenly Sunny knew why Holly had been so excited. It was a thrill to watch the younger children, from 11-year-old Harlan to five-year-old James, go up en masse to receive their gifts with many squeals of delight, hugs, and thanks.

Things were just settling down when a gift was pressed into Sunny's hands, and then another, and another. She stared at her lap as if in a trance and then around the room to see that all the adults were receiving gifts. Rand had been watching her carefully, completely prepared for her reaction. She turned to him, her face very composed, and spoke softly.

"I don't have gifts for anyone."

"Of course you don't," he spoke easily. "You didn't have time to shop. But what you must understand, my sweet little sister, is that *you* are your gift to us." Rand paused to let her take this in.

"There isn't anything more precious to us than your presence this year. Next year, you'll know us better and have time to shop."

His words were just what she needed to hear, and a tremendous weight lifted from her heart. She glanced down at the packages in her lap and then at Miles. That he had been listening to every word was quite clear, and some of Sunny's joy deserted her as she steeled herself for some angry remark or glare.

To her surprise and Miles' credit, he smiled at her, a sincere smile that carried a good deal of tenderness. Sunny returned the smile, thinking that it would be nice to be friends with Miles and wondering if there just might be a chance.

Rand's thoughts ran along the same vein. He had noticed very soon after Sunny's arrival that Miles was taken with his aunt. He couldn't blame him. Sunny was lovely, and Miles was at an age where females were one of the most fascinating things in his world. The fact that he saw only boys at school only added to the attraction.

He was close to his mother and his sister, so for the most part Miles was relaxed around women and girls, but he had obviously never come across someone with whom his heart did battle. The fact that she was his aunt did not, at least for the moment, seem to make any difference. Miles, with his good looks and fun-loving personality, was quite popular. Sunny didn't look at him with calf's eyes, and this probably added to the fascination.

"You haven't opened a single gift." Brandon's voice broke into both Rand's and Sunny's thoughts.

"Oh, I guess I haven't," Sunny spoke with surprise. Miles shifted over, and Brandon joined the three of them on the long davenport.

Sunny's fingers shook a little as she opened the first gift. It was a tiny cologne bottle from Douglas and family. Sunny was so taken with it she forgot the rest of her gifts. Not until Rand urged her to finish did she again notice the other presents.

Rand and family gave her a lovely broach and a ring to match. The ring was a perfect fit, and Sunny slid it onto her small finger with tremendous delight. From Brandon she received a riding crop, and from Dexter and Judith a beautiful pair of calfskin gloves.

Foster and Heather gave Sunny a book. It was again on English history, but different from the one she had in London. They also gave her a miniature of her mother. Sunny was so captivated by the tiny portrait she said nothing for many minutes. The family that had gathered around her moved away, giving her a moment to herself.

When it was just Sunny and Brandon, Sunny turned to speak with him quietly. "Where is your mother?"

"She opted to stay with grandfather today. Normally we would be there with her, or she would come here to Willows' End, but when grandfather took that turn, plans were changed. They're expecting us tomorrow."

"Whom are they expecting?" Sunny had to ask, afraid to assume she was included when she might not be.

"The entire family will be over there for a few hours, but you and I are going early."

Sunny did not look pleased, but Brandon, knowing her well, did not assume she wasn't.

In truth, Sunny was neither pleased nor displeased; merely curious. Lady Andrea, her mother's best friend, had been a preoccupation for her through the entire voyage, and after *not* meeting her the last time, she had put the woman out of her mind. Now, however, it seemed she actually would be meeting Brandon's mother. She seemed such an important link to the past for Sunny, and Sunny desperately wanted to know her. Sunny fretted about it until her stomach came to the rescue.

"Breakfast is in one hour," Chelsea's voice rang through the room. "You all have until 8:30 to dress and be in the large dining room." Everyone cheered at this announcement, and the room slowly emptied.

Sally was waiting when Sunny got to her room. After a brief bath, Sunny was buttoned into a beautiful rose-colored day dress. The fabric was a lightweight wool, with long sleeves and a high neckline. Sally pulled the front of Sunny's hair away from her face, securing it in a gold clasp at the crown of her head. The rest was brushed until it shone and left hanging down her back.

Holly's maid had been equally as busy with her hair and dress, and when Holly stopped by Sunny's room to collect her, Sunny told her how pretty she looked.

"We always have callers on Christmas day," Holly told her. "I want to look my best."

Immediately conjuring up images of Brice Kemp and Vic Taylor, Sunny fervently hoped she would be elsewhere if Holly had callers.

The girls had just stepped into the hall when Louise rushed past them, six-year-old Grace in tow. Both girls stopped suddenly and came back to give great attention to the older girls' dresses. Never uttering a sound, Grace reached out a tentative hand and reverently touched the full skirt of Sunny's dress. Sunny was catching a glimmer of how eye-catching her clothing was, but she was still a long way from understanding the effect her looks had on most people.

"A forage?" Sunny asked in confusion.

"Yes," Holly explained patiently. "Mother always plans one when all the nieces and nephews are here. We break into teams of two or three, and off we go."

It was midmorning and breakfast was over. The adults, parents and nannies alike, were having some time of their own, and Chelsea was entertaining the children. Holly was called across the room before Sunny was able to ask exactly what it was they did on a forage.

"Okay," Chelsea called to the group gathered in the library. "Sunny, Holly, and Harlan are team captains. You must listen to your team captain and return here together as a team."

This said, Sunny found a list pushed into her hand. Before she knew it, the room had emptied, or nearly emptied. Sunny was raising the list to her eyes when she realized both James and Grace were standing at her feet. She looked down into their expectant faces and wondered what she was supposed to do. It hadn't happened often, but her family sometimes forgot how foreign English customs were to her. After searching their faces, Sunny read the list, hoping she would understand.

> ~ red ribbon
> ~ blue shoe
> ~ feather quill
> ~ book of poetry
> ~ lace handkerchief
> ~ sheet of music
> ~ kitchen spoon
> ~ large pot
> ~ thimble

The list was no help to Sunny at all, but Miles, who had told his mother he was too old for such things, had come into the library in time to hear Grace's question.

"What do we look for first, Aunt Sunny?"

"Are we supposed to look for these things, Grace?" Sunny asked right back.

"It's a forage," the little girl explained logically.

"A fowage," James added, whose r's all sounded like w's.

Miles had come forward and carefully taken the list from Sunny's grasp. She watched in confusion as he walked directly to the books and plucked a thin volume from the shelf.

"A forage is a race where you run around and collect the items on your list. The first team back with their list complete wins. Now this is the poetry book you need. Go to the kitchen and get the pot. You can collect all the other things on the list and put them in the pot." This said, Miles turned to go.

"Grace," Sunny whispered, "do you know where the kitchen is?"

Miles stopped before he reached the door, his hand coming to the back of his neck in a long-suffering move. If he didn't get out of here, he was going to start staring at Sunny again, but the sound of her puzzled whisper and the confusion he saw in her eyes stopped him in his tracks.

"I'll show you," he heard himself saying, and the next thing he knew he had the four of them rushing through the house toward the kitchen. The other teams had been ahead of them, but as the object of the game fully dawned on Sunny, the look of delight on her face was worth the loss.

They came away from the kitchen with both the pot and spoon, and were rushing toward Miles' room for a feather quill when Sunny realized that Grace had a red ribbon in her hair and James was wearing blue shoes.

They went to Sunny's room for the lace handkerchief. Miles shot into the music room for the sheet music, while he sent Sunny and the little ones to the upstairs salon for the thimble. They were still searching when he returned because only Grace knew what it looked like.

"Here it is." Miles produced it in record time and threw it in the pot. Racing back downstairs, they just beat Harlan and Lance to come in second place behind Holly and the twins. There was much laughter and fun as the items were checked. Some moments passed before Chelsea realized that Miles had aided Sunny's team. She pulled him aside as the rest of the group filed out to replace their treasures.

"How fair was that, Miles, with you and Sunny working together?"

"Quite fair," he told her wryly, "considering Sunny hadn't the faintest idea what a forage was."

Chelsea's hand came to her mouth. "Is she all right?"

"I think so," he answered softly.

Chelsea smiled at his understanding and raised up on tiptoe to kiss her son's cheek.

"Are you all right?" Chelsea wanted to know now.

"I will be," he admitted.

"Thank you, Miles."

He smiled by way of acknowledgment, but it was a smile so strained that when he told her he was going to visit his best friend, Jordan, she did nothing to detain him.

Twenty-Four

THE DAY AFTER CHRISTMAS WAS BOXING DAY. Started in 1833, the first workday after Christmas was declared a legal English holiday. The tradition at the Gallagher household was to spend as much of the day outside as possible to give the staff their own chance to celebrate Christmas.

Douglas, Marian, and the children had left first thing that morning, but the remainder of the family was planning to ride up to the hunting lodge to picnic and fend for themselves for most of the afternoon. From there they would ride to Bracken for a brief visit and exchange of gifts with the duke.

Brandon and Sunny were the only ones not included in the plans. They would be leaving for Bracken right after breakfast and joining everyone at the lodge for lunch. Brandon had told Sunny how to prepare, and when she appeared in the downstairs foyer to meet him, she had already given her satchel to Binks. It held her riding habit, boots, and needed toiletries for the day.

They took Brandon's large coach to Bracken, and after they were on the road, Brandon explained that they would take horses from his grandfather's stables for the ride to the hunting lodge. Most of the animals there were his own, and he was looking forward to seeing Sunny's face when he gave her a spirited horse for the day.

"How long is the ride?" Sunny asked just moments after they had begun.

"Little more than half an hour in good weather, but it's been rainy, so it could stretch to an hour."

Fully content at finally having Brandon to herself, Sunny settled back against the squabs and shocked him with the next words out of her mouth.

"Brandon, where is my money?"

Sunny's finances had been the furthest thing from Brandon's mind, so he was quite taken aback at her query. As he took a moment to ponder, however, he saw that it was logical she would be concerned. He and Rand had discussed the talk Rand had with her during the gift-opening, and he should have known this question would not be long in coming. He was also the logical person to ask, as she still seemed more at home with him than anyone else.

"Not everything is in liquid assets, but your cash is—"

"Liquid assets?"

"Cash," Brandon supplied, and Sunny nodded before he went on.

"Your money is in banks; three banks and several accounts to be exact. Was there a particular reason you asked?"

"Well, I can't expect Foster to pay for everything, and I rather like the idea of having money of my own."

"Freedom," Brandon guessed quietly.

"Yes," Sunny admitted, with a slight raise of her chin.

Brandon understood how she felt. She had lived in a world of domination and subserviency, and even though Brandon believed God's perfect plan was for the man to be the head of the home, he knew well that God's plan did not include tyranny or making a chattel of one's wife. But this was exactly how Sunny had grown up.

"When the holidays are over, I would be more than happy to escort you to the bank and explain everything to you." Brandon did not tell her that by the family's vote, he had been chosen to govern her spending and financial freedom over the next few years. Why he was hesitant to explain this, he wasn't sure himself.

"Your Grace." Williams, the duke's personal valet, spoke to the duke in a soft voice as he approached the old man's chair. The duke woke but didn't move.

"Your grandson and Lady Sunny have arrived. Would you like to see them now?"

The duke realized then that he had fallen asleep while reading his Bible and hadn't even had breakfast. He had not slept much in the night, and he was sure this was the reason for drifting off while reading.

"I'd like to have an hour or so, I think. Brandon will understand."

"Shall I ask Parks to tell them Lady Andrea is in the conservatory?"

"Yes, do that," the duke replied before rising to shave for breakfast.

Sunny liked Heather's home in London and thought that Willows' End was beautiful, but nothing could have prepared her for the magnificent beauty of Bracken.

Hundreds of years old, Bracken was an almost poetical use of wood and stone. The main portion of the old mansion, which seemed more like a castle to Sunny's eyes, was three stories high and seemed to stretch in all directions. Sunny's head tipped way back as Brandon took her through the extraordinary front door. It towered many feet over Brandon's head and was elaborately carved, with huge iron rings for door handles.

Sunny stepped over the threshold at Bracken, her mind lingering on what she had seen already. It took her a moment to reckon with what her eyes now beheld. She had thought the palace at Darhabar was grand, but this was magnificent.

A huge staircase rose before her, some 30 feet across and branching at the second level to head into two separate wings. A chandelier hung directly over Sunny's head nearly 25 feet up and sparkling with beveled glass and brass.

Sunny heard Brandon's voice, along with that of another man, but she took no notice as her eyes swept over spotless, dusky blue tiles. The carpet on the stairs was another shade of blue, and the walls were light peach. Behind the stairs Sunny spotted what appeared to be a gallery of paintings. She saw what must have been portraits of Brandon's ancestors, elaborately framed and looking very important.

Sunny was barely aware of the way Brandon took her arm and

moved her toward the door. As they exited, her last thought was to wonder where all the many doors she had seen led.

"Those are the east rose gardens," Brandon pointed to a terraced portion of land some distance from the house as they followed Parks' instructions to find Lady Andrea. "You can't really appreciate it now, but the gardens are a riot of colors in the spring."

"Where did Parks say your mother was?" Sunny asked as they moved on down the path.

"In the conservatory, which was built in 1786. It's my mother's joy in the winter."

Not knowing what a conservatory was, Sunny asked, "What does she do there?" Just as Sunny asked, the building came into view. Brandon watched her face as she took in the five huge windows at the front. Each was multipaned with a rounded top and stood some 15 feet high on the front of the graystone building. As they approached the middle window, Sunny could see the glass door where they would enter. Even through the foggy glass she could also see the most wonderful display of foliage she had ever beheld.

Warmth enveloped them as they stepped through the door. The ceiling was at least 20 feet high, and some of the trees inside looked fully grown. Sunny was tipping her head back, trying to take in the expansive room all at once, when she heard a feminine voice.

"Happy Christmas, Brandon."

Sunny watched as a tall, beautiful woman came forward to hug and kiss her son. Andrea smiled into his eyes before turning to face Sunny. Andrea was not a woman easily given to tears, but the sight of Sunny Gallagher, Katherine's daughter, was a sore test of her emotions.

"Hello, Sunny," she finally spoke, her voice huskier than normal, her face open to every emotion she felt. Sunny felt tears sting her eyes over the love she saw there.

"I've wanted to meet you," Sunny whispered, quite taken with Andrea's quiet, gentle manner. "Brandon has told me that you knew my parents for years, and I've wanted very much to know about my mother."

Andrea's heart broke at how young and vulnerable she sounded. Her arms went out, and Sunny walked into them. Brandon took a slow stroll around the conservatory to give them a moment's time. When he returned, Andrea had decided they needed to go back to the house and have a lengthy chat.

"I somehow had the impression you had a young lady with you."

Brandon rose from the chair in his grandfather's study and went to embrace the man. They both took chairs then, and the old man's eyes twinkled as he spoke again.

"How are you going to court this girl if you can't keep track of her long enough to introduce her to me?"

Brandon smiled in return. "I think you're forgetting she's only 14."

"Fourteen?" The duke was truly surprised. Why had he thought Sunny Gallagher was nearing 17? "Is she really that young?"

"Indeed she is, but aside from that, she's also like a sister to me."

"She's no more your sister than Andrea is mine," the duke informed him.

"That's quite true, but it doesn't change a thing."

"Meaning what?"

"Meaning," Brandon spoke good-naturedly, "I've no feelings for her beyond that of a beloved baby sister."

"Hmm, I suppose that's true," the duke reluctantly conceded. "So when are you going to quit roaming the seas and look for a wife? I want to see my great-grandson."

Brandon shrugged but didn't reply. It was a longstanding exchange between them, and even though his grandfather was serious about wanting to see the future Duke of Briscoe, Brandon also knew that the older man would never want him to rush into a hasty union just to see the family line continue. They proceeded to talk for the next hour, giving Brandon's mother and Sunny plenty of time alone.

"This is Thomas Brent. We were married for four years when he suffered a collapse. The doctors said it was his heart and that they could do nothing. He was with me only another six months."

"Why did Brandon never mention him to me?"

"I'm sure it was an innocent oversight on his part. You've had so many people to meet, and Thomas had no family. He and I never had children. Brandon was probably trying to keep things simple for you."

Sunny studied the man in the painting, very pleased that Lady Andrea had shown her the portrait of her second husband. He had hair the color of new straw, and even though his mouth was in a straight line, laughter seemed to lurk behind his eyes. Sunny thought he must have been a joyful man. She turned to say as much to Andrea but found her staring at her late husband's picture, a wistful expression in her eyes.

"I've been very blessed by God," she said softly. "I've loved and been loved twice in my life."

"Thomas Brent *and* Brandon's father," Sunny stated quietly.

Andrea turned back to her as though just remembering her presence. "Yes. Brandon's father." She led the way out of her sitting room into the hall and down four doors to a very masculine bedroom. Over the mantel hung a portrait of Edgar Hawkesbury. This time it was Sunny's turn to stare.

He was an older version of Brandon in nearly every way. His hair was dark but peppered with gray, and his eyes were penetrating. His features were nearly identical with Brandon's aquiline nose and strong, almost stubborn jaw.

"I've been told we look alike," a masculine voice said from the doorway, "so you be careful with your comments on that portrait."

Andrea turned with a huge smile, but Sunny's look was hesitant. So this was Brandon's grandfather, the man who had been near death not six days ago. He was unsmiling now, and Sunny was unsure of what to make of him.

"You mustn't tease this girl, Milton," Andrea admonished him, her own voice teasing. "She won't want to come back."

The old man's eyes, probing now, studied Sunny until her chin rose ever so slightly. The duke chuckled. "I think she's made of sterner stuff than that, Andrea."

"You're probably right," the lovely widow agreed with a grin. "Sunny, allow me to introduce you to my father-in-law, the Duke of Briscoe. Milton, this is Lady Sunny Gallagher."

"You've the look of your grandmother," the old man stated as he took her hand. "She was a woman I greatly admired."

Sunny wasn't sure how to reply to this, but she was saved from embarrassment when Brandon appeared behind his grandfather. Andrea saw the look of relief on Sunny's face, and was struck with how hard all of this must be for her. She was so good at hiding her feelings that Andrea, in just an hour's time, had completely forgotten that Sunny was English only by birth.

As the four made their way downstairs for tea, Andrea meditated on how much the right hairstyle and clothing could do for a person. To look at Sunny, one would think she was English born *and* bred. Andrea felt terrible over not having fully grasped this before. Brandon had described their journey in great detail, but not until she had seen the young look of uncertainty on her face did Andrea stop and think how it might feel to be *introduced* to one's family. It gave her pause, and although she was talkative during tea, her heart was very prayerful.

The Lord saw to Andrea's prayers just an hour later when she found herself alone with Sunny once again. When they had come from the conservatory earlier, Sunny had been so taken with the rooms of Bracken that it had seemed an awkward time to try to discuss her mother, but suddenly Sunny was ready. In fact she opened the conversation.

"Why are there no children between Heather and me? Fourteen years is a long time."

"You're right, it is," the older woman agreed. "When Katherine learned you were on the way, she was quite amazed. Her pregnancy and delivery with Heather were very difficult, and the doctor said there would be no more babies. God must have had other plans, however. Whatever the problem was, it healed, and news of your coming was greeted with great surprise."

"Did they want me?"

"Oh, Sunny," Andrea's voice grew tender. "I'm sorry if I made it sound otherwise. Your parents were thrilled, as were your siblings. Your nursery was next to your parents' room, and your mother and I spent hours in that room talking and planning."

"What kind of plans?" Sunny was fascinated with this glimpse of the past.

"Your name, for instance. She and your father never had a single cross word over it. A boy was to be Evan, and a girl was to be Sunny."

"Who was Evan? Grandmama Sunny's husband?"

"That's right. He died years before you were born, but he was a wonderful family man with a godly spirit and a true love for all near him."

"My father wanted me too?" Sunny had to know.

"Oh, my," Andrea spoke warmly. "You should have seen his face after you arrived. He couldn't take his eyes from you. He exclaimed over and over how much you forget about babies once your children grow older. Willows' End, always a place of joy, rang with laughter and delight upon your arrival."

There wasn't anything Andrea could have said that would have affected Sunny more. Her parents loved her, and she had been born at Willows' End. She was suddenly filled with a full, warm rush of feelings.

Just looking at her, Andrea could tell nothing, but progress was being made. Sunny was slowly accepting her new life and coming to truly believe that England was her home and that her family loved her dearly.

Twenty-Five

THE FAMILY LOUNGED AROUND THE HUNTING LODGE as though they lived there day in and day out. Holly had the twins in the loft, but Heather, Foster, Rand, Chelsea, and Miles were in the great room sipping cups of strong tea. The topic of conversation had roamed greatly, but at the moment Sunny was on everyone's mind.

"Are you worried about the future?" Rand asked his brother-in-law.

"A little," Foster admitted. "We've gone nonstop from the moment she arrived, and now that we're heading home tomorrow, I wonder how she'll adjust to routine."

"Holly and I talked briefly," Chelsea interjected. "She told me Sunny seemed most impressed with her stitchwork. Maybe after you go she'll be ready to settle down and learn some of the gentler arts. Has she shown any interest in music?"

"Not that I'm aware of." Heather spoke now. "We're going to redecorate her room, but that won't take more than a month. She seems to genuinely enjoy the twins, but I realize we're a young home for her."

They fell silent and then Rand spoke, measuring his words with care. "I have something I'd like to share with you, and I think you know me well enough to realize this is no criticism on my part. Chelsea and I talked about it, and I want you to know how much I would love for Sunny to live with us. This is no reflection on your parenting skills; you understand that, don't you, Heather?"

"Of course."

Rand nodded with satisfaction and went on. "I'm not really sure when it hit me, but since Sunny is the age of my own two, I've always felt like she *was* one of my own. I'm praying you'll all be very happy and that she will settle in and be most content in London. But please know that if the time ever comes when you think she would do better at Willows' End, you don't even need to ask."

"Thank you, Rand," Foster responded in all sincerity. "We hope that she will love London and our home as well, but we also have discussed this between us and with Brandon, and we want what's best for Sunny."

They talked on for some time, all four adults freely sharing their thoughts. Miles sat quietly, not expected to add to the conversation—something for which he was most thankful. When it came to his Aunt Sunny, he couldn't seem to think straight.

The gift exchange with the duke was a quiet affair, everyone intent on not tiring him. Milton was not unaware of his grandchildren's effort on his behalf, and since he did tend to tire in the late afternoon, he was all too happy to keep the festivities brief.

Sunny and Brandon had not gotten away early enough to join the family at the hunting lodge, but they rode back from Bracken to Willows' End with everyone who was going on horseback. In the best of spirits, Foster drove a two-horse buggy with his own girls and Holly, since the latter was none too keen on horses and his girls were too young to take the saddle for such a long ride.

Everyone else rode on horseback. Sunny felt as though she'd been set free as Brandon boosted her onto the back of a lovely little spirited mare. Her name was Pepper, and with the way she tossed her fine head she clearly showed how she liked the light load on her back.

The group set off, and within moments Sunny and Chelsea were in a race to the footbridge up the trail. Chelsea's horse, a large gelding, won easily, but Sunny didn't care. It felt so good to gallop as she had in Darhabar, and this time with permission. Since she was not to be anywhere near the stables in Darhabar, she had always "borrowed" a horse against her father's wishes.

"So what do you think of her?" Brandon called to Sunny as he came abreast of the two women.

"She's wonderful," Sunny told him with sparkling eyes. "I could go for hours."

Chelsea laughed and looked at her brother with mischief in her eyes. "You really should let Sunny ride the Captain, Hawk. She's quite experienced, and it would give her a great thrill."

"Oh, Brandon, could I?" Sunny immediately loved the idea, but Brandon was scowling at his grinning sister.

Most members of his family were completely without fear when it came to horses, and were in fact excellent horsemen. But Brandon was of the old school that believed a woman was to be coddled. You did not put a woman on the back of a horse like Captain, or Rand's stallion, Jackson.

"It's out of the question, Sunny," Brandon told her and shot another reproving look at his sister. "Chelsea can goad me all she wants, but I think this animal is too much for a woman, or even for a small man."

Chelsea did not look the least bit repentant, and she deliberately moved her horse into Brandon's path to cut him off. He reined in sharply before catching onto her trick. Chelsea had dug her heels into the flanks of her own horse and shot off like a bullet. Brandon rose to the challenge, and Sunny, knowing she hadn't a chance of catching them, heeled her mount to give chase.

Most of the ride back to Willows' End was made in short races with much laughter. A few miles from home everyone slowed to walk their horses. Sunny couldn't remember when she'd had such fun.

The servants evidently had a wonderful time themselves, for they were also in high spirits as the family returned. Sunny, as did the rest of the household, had a bath before dinner and, possibly because it was the last night, had the best evening of her entire visit.

"Your mother says your brother is coming to London for a time."

"Cecil or Marcus?" Foster wanted to know.

"Cecil."

Sunny heard their conversation but paid little attention. They had been home from Rand's for nearly three weeks, and Sunny was intent on learning to sew like Holly. Heather had mentioned the possibility when they had become resettled, and Sunny had jumped at the idea. Heather would have been surprised to find that Sunny had not done so out of genuine interest but because she so wanted to fit in and to please her sister.

So far, the skill had eluded her. She was forever stabbing herself in the hand or finger, and she was always in too much of a hurry. More often than not, her thread was in a mass of knots and her colors all ran together like a painting in the rain.

"Having trouble?" Heather asked when she heard Sunny say something under her breath. Sunny was careful to compose her features before answering.

"Just the usual; my thread is all tangled."

Heather came over and sat by her, and in the space of a few moments had Sunny on the right track again. She went back to her own sewing while Foster continued to read the letter from his mother.

"It says he has business here," Foster commented. "Do you want to ask him to stay with us?"

"You didn't finish the letter," Heather replied. "It says that he's rented a town house on the east side."

"Oh, well, that will be easier, I guess. I'm sure he'll come by when he's settled."

Husband and wife exchanged a glance. Cecil was a kind young man in his early twenties, but he had always been a bit of a dreamer. Foster's family was quite well-to-do, so there was no need for Cecil to work, but it might have been better if he had, as he always seemed a little at loose ends.

He had left school without apparent reason a month before Christmas, and his coming to London on business was something entirely new. He had never even attempted to make something of himself, and one could only imagine what he might be up to now.

Before Cecil made an appearance at the Jamiesons', Brandon came for a visit. Sunny had seen him only once since Christmas, and that had been for their visit to the bank. Now when he came the following week, the serious look on his face caused Sunny to know that her fears about his going back to sea had come true.

"You're going back out on your ship, aren't you?" Sunny wasted no time in coming to the point.

"Yes, it's time. My grandfather is doing well, and I've some shipments that must be arranged."

Sunny was glad they were alone. She did nothing to fight the tears that flooded her eyes. Brandon moved close to her on the library davenport and slipped an arm around her shoulders. For more reasons than she could name, she sobbed against him. He was such a solid comfort in her world, and whenever something happened, good or bad, he was the first person she wanted to tell.

Brandon let her cry. He knew his leaving was going to break her heart, but he had no choice. When she began to calm he started to speak, knowing she wouldn't catch every word but needing to assure her of his feelings.

"Whenever I hear of a ship coming to London, I'll send a letter to you. I'll miss you and pray for you every day. There is so much you haven't seen of London, and I hope that you will make this your home in every way. I know Heather and Foster want you to be happy. They will take care of your every need. No matter how far away I am, I'll always love my little Sunny."

His words nearly started her tears afresh. Sunny hiccuped. Thinking how much he was going to miss her, Brandon fell silent. A moment passed, and he rose to retrieve something from the table in the hallway.

Sunny watched him return with a deceptively plain box in his hand. When he handed it to Sunny, she saw that it was actually a very beautiful box, overlaid with brushed gold and latched with a solid gold clasp. It didn't look like anything she had ever seen in Darhabar; in fact, the design was very English. Sunny, having already remembered who the box was from, felt somewhat disappointed.

"Ali gave this to me after he drugged you. Do you remember my mentioning it?"

Sunny nodded.

"At the time you wanted nothing to do with it. How do you feel now?"

Sunny hesitated. The rejected feeling from that day, a feeling she hadn't experienced in weeks, suddenly flooded through her.

"You don't have to take it. I can keep it and bring it to you when I return, or even give it to Heather to hold for you."

"No," Sunny said finally. "I'll keep it."

She lapsed into silence, and Brandon was hesitant to press her.

He let the matter drop but gave her one more word of comfort.

"I have to leave right after dinner, but if you write to me, you might feel better. There won't be any way to send the letters, but you might feel as though you've actually spoken with me. That might help if you're feeling low."

Sunny thanked him with a smile, and soon after they went in to dine. The time passed all too quickly, and Sunny was reminded of Willows' End and the look of pain on Rand's face as he had said goodbye to her. Sunny was beginning to think she couldn't win. First she was sick with anxiety over meeting all of her family, and now she was sick with grief over having to say goodbye.

The *Flying Surprise* sailed with the morning tide, and both Dexter and Sunny were on the dock. They had arrived too late to speak with Brandon but alighted from the carriage in time to watch as his ship crept away from the mooring. Just when it seemed that he would be too far to notice them, Brandon spotted his brother and Sunny.

He raised an arm, and Dexter waved in reply. When Sunny stayed motionless, Brandon put a hand to his lips and threw her a kiss with a gentle move of his hand. Sunny, tears running down her cheeks, returned the gesture. She and Dex watched until the ship was out of sight.

Knowing Sunny was already missing Brandon, Dexter did not try to engage her in conversation as they returned to the house. Thankful for his consideration, Sunny stared out the carriage window. She sought the shelter of her room as soon as she could. When the door was shut she lay on the bed and stared at the gold box on her bedside table. She had yet to open it.

The box was such an odd link to the past as well as to the present. Until now Brandon had kept the box, so in some ways it was a link to him. On the other hand, it was from the emir, delivered by Ali, and that made it a definite link to Darhabar.

Sunny sat up slowly on her bed and reached for the box. She moved the catch that served as a lock and raised the lid. Her eyes were round with wonder as she emptied the contents on her bed. There appeared to be three completely different sets of jewelry.

The first set was a necklace, ring, and bracelet in silver, all smooth as glass, with no design whatever. They were so polished that Sunny could see her face in the silver of the ring. The second set was gold, etched and ornate, and included two bracelets, a necklace with three strands of chain, and another ring. The last set held some of the most beautiful pieces Sunny had ever seen. A broach, bracelet, and ring, all set with perfect sapphires and diamonds.

Sunny fingered each piece in turn before reaching for her grandmother's ring at her throat. As beautiful as it was, none of the jewelry from the box had given her as much pleasure as her grandmother's ring and Brandon's chain.

"I can't think why he would give them to me," Sunny spoke aloud to the empty room as she began to speculate on why the emir had given her these jewels. "He never tried to buy me before."

"Why?" Sunny whispered now. "Why must I have been sent away in order to know my family? I was happy. I knew who I was. Did he not think my heart was big enough to hold everyone?" Suddenly she was angry all over again. "He had no right to choose for me."

With an angry sweep of her arm, Sunny sent the jewelry flying across the bed. She cried then, and cried hard, anger continuing to boil within her. Anger toward the emir, anger toward Brandon for leaving, and anger toward herself for giving in to her tears. She cried for several minutes and was just gaining control when the door opened. Sunny turned with surprise; there had been no knock.

"I'm sorry, my lady," said Tina, a new chambermaid, softly. She had a load of linens in her arms. "I didn't realize you were in here."

"It's all right," Sunny told her, and wondered not for the first time about Tina's oddly accented English. Sunny turned back to the jewels on her bed and slowly gathered each article into the box. In her preoccupation with the jewels, she failed to notice how slowly Tina closed the door, or how intently she studied Sunny and the strewn contents on the bed.

Twenty-Six

HEATHER STUDIED SUNNY'S PALE FEATURES across the breakfast table and wondered if she should call a doctor. It was quite typical to experience a midwinter slump, but Sunny's ailment, if it could be called that, ran much deeper. It was nearly March, and in the weeks following Brandon's departure Sunny had run from one activity to the next.

When she couldn't seem to master the stitching project she had started, she took up reading. Not just reading for pleasure but *insatiable* reading. Never without a book, Sunny even came to meals with her nose in a book and only laid it aside when she was asked.

The passion for reading lasted only two weeks. After that came the horseback riding. No less than twice, and sometimes as many as five times a day, Sunny went for a ride in the park. A groom always accompanied her, and rain or shine, she went off riding most of the day.

All of this had come to a halt ten days earlier when she had come down with a cold and Heather insisted that she stay indoors. In just a matter of days she was herself again, but now she was no longer interested in riding. She sat around the house looking bored or playing with the girls when they were not having lessons.

She was so despondent that she did not even seem to notice the changes that were happening in her body. Foster and Heather both noticed that Sunny seemed to fill out a little more with each passing week, but Sunny paid no attention. Heather knew it was only a matter of time before she began her monthly cycles. Sunny had understood every aspect of the life cycle when Heather talked with her, but even after they had discussed it, Sunny seemed as uninterested in that as she was with everything else.

The only person who was able to spark *any* emotions in her was Cecil, only it wasn't a pleasant emotion. Heather debated for only a minute and knew she must give Sunny the bad news.

"Cecil and his friend Smitty are coming this afternoon and staying for dinner."

Sunny pulled a face. "Must I come down to dinner, Heather?"

"Yes, I think you should."

Sunny let out a long-suffering sigh, and Heather smiled to herself. She and Foster had discussed the problem, and seeing that Cecil had been very proper in his infatuation, they had decided Sunny was not going to hide in her room whenever she didn't like someone.

"He writes me poems," Sunny said with obvious disgust.

Heather hid another smile. "He likes you."

"He called my eyes 'purple coronets.' Now isn't that the most ridiculous thing you've ever heard?" Sunny rolled her eyes in frustration and Heather could not hold her smile; in fact, she let out a small laugh.

"It's not funny, Heather. He stares at me all the time, and I can't think why."

Heather grew very serious. "He likes you."

"So you said."

"No, Sunny, I mean he really cares for you. I think he hopes that someday you'll care for him. After all, he is only five years older than you are."

"You mean," Sunny spoke as light dawned, "that he's thinking of marriage?"

"I believe so."

Sunny looked thunderstruck. "But Heather, I'm not going to marry, not *ever*."

"I know how you feel, but I'm sure Cecil hopes to change your mind."

Sunny let out another gusty sigh. She played with the handle of her fork for a moment and then continued softly, still staring at the utensil in her hand.

"I would never marry a man like Cecil, even if I did change my mind. He's nice enough, but he's not like Foster or Brandon. Cecil told me that the bank gave him too much money the last time he was in. He was thrilled because it was at the bank's expense."

Sunny looked her sister in the eye. "You or Foster or Brandon would never do that, because it would be stealing. I think it has something to do with the way you feel about the Bible. I don't agree with the Bible, but I like your honesty."

Heather's heart thundered within her. For weeks now she had hoped that Sunny would see a difference in her life and feel free to question her. She'd prayed much over it, and had to admit that she had begun to despair of its ever happening. Now she confessed her lack of faith, thanked God for this opportunity, and smiled gently at her sister.

"We do take honesty very seriously, and it is because of the Bible, but not just the Bible, Sunny. Jesus Christ of the Bible—*He* has made us the people that we are."

"You think He is God, don't you?"

"Yes, I do. The Bible says He is, and I believe the Bible to be God's true Word."

"I don't think He was God," Sunny admitted without heat or argument. "I think He was a great teacher and a good man, but not God."

Heather shook her head slowly. "If He isn't God, Sunny, then there is nothing good about Him."

Sunny looked stunned, but Heather went on.

"If Jesus Christ isn't God, Sunny, than He was the biggest liar that ever existed. Think about His life and the way He proclaimed to be God, right up to the point of death on a cross. Think of all of the people who fell for His lies and followed Him—and not just followed Him but fashioned their very lives to emulate His own.

"Like I said, Sunny, if Jesus Christ is not God, then there is nothing good about Him. Foster, Brandon, and I all believe with our whole hearts that He is God's Son, and the Savior of the world."

Sunny had no reply to this, but Heather could see that she was thinking. Heather was struck anew over how faithless she'd been. She asked God to help her believe that He loved Sunny enough to tenderly bring down the wall she had built around her heart. For the first time she prayed, believing that her beloved baby sister would someday know God in a truly personal way.

Cecil Jamieson watched Sunny across the table and tried to think of something clever to say. He glanced at his partner to see his response to Sunny's beauty, and just as he had hoped, Smitty was as taken with her looks as he was.

It had been most disappointing that Sunny had not made an appearance downstairs until dinner was ready, but Cecil knew they had the rest of the evening to see her. He also knew that most of his friends would have laughed over his love of a 14-year-old girl, but they had never seen Sunny.

She was a jewel among women. He knew she was young, but he could wait. In fact, Cecil tried not to think how beautiful she would be in a few years' time, knowing how long he would have to wait to declare himself. He recognized that she was only now on the threshold of womanhood, but with her flawless skin, marvelous eyes, and breathtaking profile, it was all too easy to see that she was going to grow to be the most beautiful creature in all of London.

Cecil noticed that she looked a bit unhappy tonight, and that concerned him. He hoped it had nothing to do with Smitty's coming to dinner, and dismissed that idea as foolish. Cecil knew he could cheer her, if only he could talk to her privately and read her his latest sonnet. *It's all about her hair,* Cecil thought to himself. *Her glorious chestnut hair, that falls in shining waves about her shoulders slim.*

"As if it wasn't enough to have Cecil staring at me, now he's brought his friend along and they stare together!"

Sunny and Heather had not yet joined the men in the parlor, and Sunny was speaking in a furious whisper so as not to be overheard.

"It's because I'm getting breasts, isn't it, Heather? I've always wanted breasts, but if this is the way it's going to be, I'm going to hide in my room!"

Sunny had turned away to stomp around the empty dining room, and Heather turned away also, her shoulders shaking with silent laughter. She was sorry that Sunny was so uncomfortable and that Cecil had to make such a fool of himself, but it was so good to see some color in Sunny's face.

Heather turned back to find Sunny watching her suspiciously.

"Yes, I was laughing," she admitted, "because you're such fun, even when you're mad."

Sunny looked crestfallen, and Heather, seeing just how miserable her sister was, knew she needed to be taking this seriously.

"I'm sorry, Sunny," she spoke earnestly. "I'll have a word with Foster, and he can talk with Cecil. For tonight, I'll help out as best I can, and you do your best to be kind."

"All right," Sunny agreed, and the women went in to join the men.

In the following two hours Sunny did her best to be kind to Cecil, but she did *not* like the ingratiating Smitty, and made no secret of it. Heather watched with fascination on two occasions when Sunny put Smitty in his place with just one chilling glance. Heather knew that Sally secretly called her the Princess, but tonight Heather wondered if maybe she shouldn't be called the Queen.

"It's almost as if Rand knew this would happen," Heather said to Foster four days later as they climbed into their bed for the night. "She's so despondent and quiet, and I think she might be losing weight."

"I don't think he knew this would happen, but he does have a teenage girl of his own who has already passed through some of the changes Sunny is going through. Maybe he suspected that she would grow restless—not that Holly is anything like Sunny," Foster added dryly.

"I'm glad she's not!" Heather defended her sister. "I love Holly, but Sunny is special, and I wouldn't want her to be like anyone else!"

"Heather, Heather," her husband crooned softly when he saw how worked up she was becoming. "I love Sunny too, and you're right, she is wonderful. I was just commenting on Rand's perception."

"I'm sorry," whispered Heather, who now cried on her husband's chest. "I just want her to be happy. I really believe she needs to go to Willows' End, but I already miss her and she's not even gone."

"I know how you feel," Foster told her tenderly. "But it's not as hard for you to get away as it is for Rand. You and the girls can go and see Sunny whenever you like."

Foster smoothed his wife's hair away from her face and held her until she slept. He was not looking forward to Sunny's departure any more than his wife was, but what he really dreaded was telling Cecil that she would be leaving London and that he was *not* to visit her at Willows' End.

"Come to Willows' End? You mean for a visit?"

"A long visit," Rand told his youngest sister. "For the spring and through the summer and longer if you like."

Sunny looked to Foster, who smiled at her, and then to Heather, who was sitting next to her on the davenport.

"You're sending me away?"

Heather's heart broke, and her resolve not to cry nearly crumbled. "No, love," she spoke as she stroked Sunny's hair with a tender hand. "We would never send you away, but you're not happy here in London. We all think some time at Willows' End would do you a world of good. The countryside will be dotted with lambs by now, and the terrain is perfect for riding; not to mention Holly's being there. She's so much closer to your age."

"You can return here anytime you want or stay on as long as you like," Foster interjected.

Sunny looked thoughtful and then spoke softly, "Does Chelsea want me to come?"

Rand smiled. "Chelsea and Holly can't wait to see you, and I'm sure to have tearful women on my hands if I return without you."

Sunny nodded. "What about the twins?"

"They'll miss you," Heather told her. "But they'll love an excuse to go to Willows' End for a visit."

"You'll come and see me?" Sunny seemed surprised.

"Of course," Heather laughed. "And like Foster said, if you want to come back, you need only ask."

Sunny looked uncertain for only a moment longer before she smiled and agreed. Everyone hugged her, and five minutes later she ran upstairs to tell Sally she needed to pack her things. Her heart nearly sang with joy as she reached her room. She was going to Willows' End.

"Sunny is coming for an indefinite stay at Willows' End."

"What was that?"

Miles turned to his roommate, unaware that he had spoken out loud.

"Nothing," Miles said. "I was just reading a letter from my mother."

"When do you go home?"

"The first of June."

"Oh. That's only a month away."

"Right" was all Miles said, but his thoughts were quite different. *You have one month to settle your emotions—and not make a fool of yourself this time.*

Twenty ~ Seven

"Is this the way, Holly?" Sunny called to her niece as she eagerly climbed to the very top steps.

"Yes, this is the place," Holly answered reluctantly, brushing webs from her face. The door to the attic creaked, and Holly saw dust fly as Sunny plunged her way into the room.

"Oh, Holly," Sunny exclaimed. "I can't believe you never come up here!"

Holly stood brushing her hands together as she watched Sunny rush to the window she had spotted from the ground.

"Look at this view," Sunny breathed. "I can see miles beyond the stables."

Unwillingly Holly joined her, stepping over aging artifacts from generations of Gallaghers. They were standing by the one dusty window in the topmost room in the south tower, a tower that was more ornate than useful.

"And what do you two think you're up to?"

The stern voice of Mrs. Boots sounded in the doorway, and Holly jumped as though she'd been caught stealing something. In a faltering voice she began to explain, but Sunny cut her off.

"Oh, Boots dear, come see the view from this window. It's simply glorious."

Mrs. Boots gave a good-natured shake of her head, and Holly stared at her in wonder. The only person to ever get away with calling Mrs. Boots "Boots dear" was her father, at least until Sunny had arrived. Mrs. Boots had been with the Gallagher family since before Heather was born, and her word among the servants was law.

Both Miles and Holly adored her, and were adored in return, but they toed the line when it came to matters of the household. Chelsea was forever telling Mrs. Boots that she was indispensable, and Rand, even though he thought the world of her, had her neatly wrapped around his little finger.

Sunny had only been at Willows' End for a week before she had emulated Rand's way with her. Mrs. Boots, remembering the day Sunny was born and then the day her father returned from his voyage without her, could not find the heart to deny her a thing.

"What made you come up here, love?" Mrs. Boots asked as she joined the girls by the window.

"I saw this window from the stables and wondered about this part of the house," Sunny answered, but she was preoccupied, already spotting something else that caught her interest.

"All right," Mrs. Boots caught Holly's distressed look over being in the attic. "Out with both of you. You're already dusty, and I don't want a bit of this dirty stuff dragged through the house."

Holly gladly exited the room, but Sunny followed more slowly, taking a last look around as she went. The view from the window had been so captivating that she realized how she missed the chance to do some great exploring. As she moved down the dark staircase, she promised herself that she would get back up to look in those trunks before the month was out.

Mrs. Boots saw her to her room with orders to clean up for lunch, but Sunny's mind was still on what she had seen from the window. When Holly, freshly turned out, came to collect her for lunch, Sunny was still in her underclothes.

Holly flopped on the bed. "We're going to be late if you don't hurry."

"Oh, I know, but I was thinking about something." Sunny moved with a pronounced lack of urgency, and when she looked up it was to find Holly's eyes on her.

"What's the matter?" Sunny wanted to know.

"Nothing," Holly smiled. "I was just thinking how much you've changed since Christmas, and how pretty your figure is becoming."

Sunny looked down at her small breasts and slim hips and then at her voluptuous niece. "I won't ever have your figure," she said resignedly.

"That doesn't matter," Holly told her honestly. "You'll probably look like Aunt Heather, and she looks lovely in everything she wears. Like my mother always says, a smaller figure is easier to work with."

Sunny thought of Chelsea, who was tall and very full-busted, and nodded, seeing for the first time that Holly was probably right. Chelsea and Holly were able to wear very few rounded necklines, and when they did wear them, the necklines were very high in order to be modest. There wasn't a style that Sunny couldn't wear, and she suddenly found herself hoping she would have Heather's nice shape.

Thoughts of figures and fashion seemed to be on everyone's mind that day, including Chelsea's. Immediately following lunch, she told the girls they were to have new summer wardrobes. Holly reacted with girlish delight, but Sunny was not thrilled. Chelsea immediately noticed her lack of enthusiasm, and when Holly left the room Chelsea questioned her.

"You're not excited," the older woman commented softly.

"I was just fitted for a wardrobe before Christmas," Sunny returned with true chagrin.

Chelsea hid her smile. Most girls would have reacted as Holly had, but Chelsea was swiftly learning that although Sunny was more than predictable in some areas, she was a complete surprise in others. It was always a shock to Chelsea when Sunny displayed indifference toward her looks and clothing. The only reason she was ever well-turned out was because her maid, Christie, went to such efforts.

"I know you'd rather forego the fitting, but you'll thank me when you have a closetful of lightweight dresses to wear this summer."

"All right, Chelsea. Thanks," Sunny acquiesced, but after only a moment she looked troubled once again.

"Now what's wrong?" Rand wanted to know.

"I don't want to spend money on a wardrobe; I want to buy something else."

"I'm covering the cost of your wardrobe, so you needn't worry about that. What did you want to buy?"

"A horse!" Sunny's eyes lit with excitement.

Rand and Chelsea stared at her.

"What horse?" Chelsea wanted to know.

"Townsend's stallion, King's Ride," Sunny spoke enthusiastically. "Not King, of course, but when we were at the Townsends' last week, one of the hands told me that Dandy just had a filly." Sunny paused to catch her breath, she was so excited. "The sire is King. The groom let me peek in the stable, and Rand, you won't believe how lovely she is, a roan with the proudest head I've ever seen. She was standing by Dandy, and I—"

Rand and Chelsea listened quietly to this recital, feeling a bit stunned. If this had been their child, they would have already told her no, but this was Rand's sister, and a decidedly affluent sister at that. They didn't know exactly what Brandon had told Sunny about her finances, but if she was worrying about affording the horse *and* a summer wardrobe, he had obviously not divulged to her just how well off she was.

They were also running into another problem, one they had talked over but not faced—that of Sunny's being a sibling, and therefore more independent than a child. To this point, all Holly's rules had applied to Sunny, rules governing such activites as bedtimes, study hours, and outings.

As Sunny prattled on, Rand realized the very reason that she knew about the filly was because she was his sibling and not his child. Both she and Holly had gone with him to the Townsends', and since Holly had never visited the stables before, Rand had felt no need to mention his desire that the girls stay away. He was a little alarmed at the moment to think that Sunny had visited the stables and he hadn't even known it.

There wasn't a servant within miles of Willows' End who didn't know exactly who Sunny Gallagher was, and it was not as if their positions allowed them to report Sunny's actions to her brother. That, along with the confident way she carried herself, must have made everyone feel she was a law unto herself. Rand realized that they wouldn't have turned her away from the stables for any reason, even though there was some breeding going on in one of the outside corrals. This was exactly where he had been, while assuming his sister and daughter were visiting inside with the ladies of the house.

"Are you angry with me, Rand?" Sunny's soft voice cut into his thoughts.

"Not with you, Sunny, but I am a bit perturbed with myself." Sunny looked totally confused before Rand continued.

"You see, sweetheart, Holly is not the least bit interested in horses; it never once occurred to me that you would come to the stables."

Sunny looked utterly crestfallen, thinking back to Darhabar. "You don't want me in the stables?"

"Not when there is breeding going on," Rand told her bluntly.

Sunny's features immediately cleared. "Oh, that. I've seen horses bred many times."

"That is beside the point," Rand told her sternly, wondering not for the first time what manner of man had raised his sister. "It is totally out of the question for you to be present at such times. It's an embarrassment to the attendants, and I will not allow it."

Sunny's look turned to one of disgust. "Now you sound like Ahmad Khan."

"I do?" Rand was thoroughly surprised.

"Yes."

"So you were not allowed in the stables during breeding?" Rand was still coming to grips with being compared to the emir.

"I was not allowed in the stable *at all.*"

"So how do you know—"

"I snuck in," Sunny interrupted, offering her reply with a shrug.

It was all so matter-of-fact on Sunny's part that Chelsea felt laughter bubbling inside of her. She was careful to keep this well hidden, but it was really fun to watch a younger version of herself. No wonder Rand had wanted Sunny to live with them. As much as he would have denied it, he loved women who were unconventional.

"Well, you're not going to sneak into stables while you're living with me," Rand began, but Chelsea cut in with a gentle word.

"I'm sure you wouldn't, would you, Sunny? Rand has no problem with your going to the stables when the horses aren't breeding. And from what I can see, you're only interested in riding the animals. Am I right?"

Sunny nodded with relief over Chelsea's understanding and looked up to see her brother coming toward her.

He came to Sunny and took her in his arms. "I'm sorry I flew off at you."

Sunny hugged him back, thinking as she had many times in the past weeks how nice it would be if he were her father and not her brother.

"Chelsea and I were going to surprise you," Rand said when he had released her, "and buy you a horse later this summer. But if you've got your heart set on this one, I'll ask if it's for sale."

Sunny gave no answer to this wonderful news, but simply threw her arms back around his neck and gave him a mighty squeeze.

Chelsea was next, and Sunny stood for long moments next to Chelsea's chair and let herself be held. Chelsea, smiling at Rand over Sunny's shoulder, wondered anew at this young sister, this enigma that had come to live with them. Sometimes such a child in need of a mother's touch, and other times a woman, levelheaded and sure.

While Chelsea and Sunny were still embracing, the door to the dining room opened, and Miles stepped in. They hadn't seen him since Christmas, and the physical changes in him were marked. He was taller, more filled out, and if possible, even more handsome.

Mother and father both rushed to greet him. Chelsea prayed as she went that he had also changed emotionally, at least enough to handle having Sunny as a permanent resident of the house.

Twenty~Eight

SUNNY STARED OUT HER BEDROOM WINDOW, wanting to go to the stables but knowing she would encounter Miles if she did. She let the lace curtain fall back into place and sat on the edge of her bed. He was almost as bad as Cecil, the way he stared at her without speaking and hung around outside the door when he knew she was planning to head for the library or salon.

He wasn't going to be here all summer, but it looked to Sunny as though the weeks he was staying were going to be long. She wondered if maybe she should go back to London, but then Cecil's face popped into her mind, and Sunny despaired. Would she ever find a place to be happy?

There was a knock on the door. Sunny, wanting to be left alone, remained quiet. The ploy didn't work. The door opened, and Holly's head came in.

"Sunny?" she said softly. "May I come in?"

"I don't feel very well, Holly," the younger girl told her niece, but Holly came in anyway and carefully shut the door.

Sunny watched her quietly as she retrieved the desk chair and brought it close to the bed. Holly sat, and this time it was her turn to stare. Sunny had begun to look thin and pale in the last few days, and today there was something more; today there was profound regret in her eyes. Holly knew that her mother had tried to talk with Sunny and gotten nowhere.

"You don't feel well?" Holly asked now, her voice tentative.

"I'm not sick," Sunny said.

"But there is something wrong, Sunny, isn't there? Are you having your monthly flux?"

"No," Sunny responded as she wrapped her arms around her waist, turning her head to look out the window.

"Have I done something?" Holly sounded near to tears.

"No," Sunny said with surprise. "It's not you, Holly. I'm just feeling like I might need to go back to London."

"But why?" Holly nearly wailed. "Why would you want to leave when we're having such a good time?"

Sunny didn't say anything for some moments. Miles was her brother, and Sunny knew Holly loved him unreservedly. She also knew that no one else in the house was aware of the problem. It had taken her contact with Cecil for Sunny to understand why Miles had stared at her at Christmastime. Now as she looked back, she strongly suspected that his parents had been aware of what was going on because he had made an effort to keep his distance.

This time was different. Miles was very careful about when he stole his glances. Sunny was sure if she explained things to Holly, Holly would tell her it was all in her imagination.

"I'm not leaving this room, Sunny," Holly said abruptly, in a rare show of sternness. "Not until you tell me what's going on."

Sunny sighed, thinking she was probably leaving Willows' End anyway, so what would it matter if Holly knew the truth?

"Did I ever tell you about Cecil?"

"Cecil? You mean Foster's brother Cecil?"

"Yes, he's the one. He moved to London not long after Christmas. I had never met him before, but well, he liked me quite a bit."

"Oh," Holly said in understanding. "You miss him. Well, Sunny, why didn't you say so? Mummy and Papa would love for him to visit. He could—"

Holly stopped chattering when she saw the look of absolute despair on Sunny's face.

"You don't miss him?"

"No."

Holly was silent for a moment. "I'm sorry I interrupted you, Sunny. Please go on."

She did so in a quiet voice. "I didn't like him the way he liked me. I mean, he was very kind, but Heather thought he might have marriage in mind, and," Sunny gave a small shudder, "I didn't care for him in that way at all.

"I think I could have stood it, but he was always looking at me, writing poems for me, and trying to talk to me when I wanted to be alone. I could take just about everything but the staring. I just hate it when people stare at me like I've got an extra eye or something."

Sunny's voice had become quite heated, and Holly, who never minded suitable male attention, knew that now was not the time to tell Sunny she was stared at because she was beautiful.

"Well, anyway," Sunny went on, her voice now sounding reconciled, "it is happening all over again, only it's worse this time. At least Cecil didn't live with us."

"Sunny," Holly began, "I really want to understand, but I'm afraid I don't."

Sunny saw no hope for it. "I know you love your brother, Holly, but I can't take his constant staring at me."

Holly looked uncomprehending, and Sunny felt quite suddenly incensed.

"It's Miles!" she nearly spat at her niece. "Miles gawks at me, and I can't stand it!"

As quickly as the anger had kindled, it cooled, and Sunny felt defeated and as tired as a well-used rag. Holly's brow furrowed, and Sunny waited for the wrath that was sure to be directed toward her.

"He does stare at you, doesn't he?" Holly said the words almost to herself. "I've never given any thought to it, but he does; I've seen him." Holly's own anger began to mount, but Sunny finally recognized that it was not directed at herself. "And if he continues to stare at you, you're going to want to leave." Holly paused before saying, "Let's go!"

"Go where?"

"Come on," Holly strode to Sunny's wardrobe. "Get changed into your oldest dress. Then we'll go to my room, and I'll change."

"But why?" Sunny asked as Holly unbuttoned the back of her dress.

"Why? I'll tell you why. We're going to have a little talk with my brother."

Miles walked from the stables, his steps dragging just a bit. He'd waited over an hour for Sunny to make an appearance, but she had not come. It seemed he couldn't see enough of her. He had thought her beautiful at Christmas, but with the changes in her figure, she was downright distracting. His disappointment over her failure to appear was keen.

The stables at Willows' End were to the rear of the property, and the closest way to enter the house was through the kitchen in the back, but Miles liked to go in the front door. He took the path slowly, enjoying the walk around the house. Everything was beautiful in June.

His mother loved evergreen bushes, and they grew in huge clusters at all corners of the mansion. Miles was passing the bush that sat at the corner of the library when he suddenly found himself set upon by bandits, their weight hurling him face first to the ground. Miles was so surprised by this charge against his person that at first he didn't react. He shook his head over the incongruity of an attack during daylight, but when he tried to rise up, a hand pushed the side of his face to the ground.

There had been a flurry of bodies and clothing with much scuffling and grunting, and now someone was calmly sitting on his back. This someone had his arm twisted high up behind him, so high he felt as if he could touch his own neck. Even at that he felt sure he could overtake whoever it was. He was on the verge of putting up a fight when his sister's cologne wafted through the air and hit his nostrils.

"Can you hear me, Miles?" she said.

"I can hear you," he said in sudden anger over this ridiculous assault, thinking Holly was too old for such nonsense. "What are you playing at, Holly?"

"I want you to listen to what Sunny has to say." She twisted his arm up higher, and Miles grunted in real pain. "Are you listening?"

"Yes!" he barked at her, hurt and embarrassed to his soul over the fact that Sunny was not only witnessing this, but was a part of it. Not until Holly had said Sunny's name did he realize that the weight on his back felt so heavy because it was both his sister and his aunt.

His anger, now as full-blown as the girls', caused him to move without thinking. He rose and twisted violently at the same time, sending the girls flying. He spun on the balls of his feet, crouched low, and readied himself for another of their attacks. No attack came.

Holly had fallen free and unharmed. Sunny, on the other hand, had gone back against the base of a tall stone statue. She was in the process of righting herself, but her hand had gone to the back of her head. Miles saw immediately that she had hurt herself.

His anger instantly drained from him, and as he watched her, remorse over how violent he had been ran deep within him. It drove deeper still when he saw tears standing in her eyes.

"I shouldn't have jumped on you. This is your home, Miles. I promise I'll be gone before the week is out, even if I have to walk back to London." This said, Sunny stumbled to her feet and ran for the house.

Miles dropped to his seat and then heard his sister crying. Not quite so tolerant of her tears, he turned, ready to hush her, but even Holly's eyes were too much for him.

"Please," she pleaded softly, her gaze holding his own. "She hates it when you stare at her, Miles. Please stop. I don't want her to leave. She's like a sister, and I've never had a sister. I want her to stay more than I've ever wanted anything."

Holly did not wait for him to answer, but pushed slowly to her feet and followed Sunny to the house.

The ground was damp, but Miles stayed seated. He was furious with Holly and Sunny both, but mostly with himself. He had determined not to make a fool of himself, but that's exactly what he had done. He didn't know how long he sat there, probably no more than a few minutes, before he heard steps behind him. Not caring if his sister was still bent on destruction, he stayed his ground. Surprisingly, his father stepped off the path and around him to sit on the pedestal of the statue where Sunny had fallen.

"The girls attacked me," Miles began, hoping for some sympathy.

"So I saw."

Miles stared at his father before hanging his head in pure humiliation. He found he was no longer angry with anyone. He had acted like a child, and now his aunt had been hurt both emotionally and physically and his father had witnessed the whole affair.

"It means a lot for me to have my baby sister here, but you're my son and I love you."

Miles raised his head.

"Unlike Christmas, I had no idea you were struggling with your feelings for Sunny this summer. I wish you had come to me. I love you, Miles," he repeated, "and if Sunny's presence here is that much of a burden, I'll return her to London in the morning. I must admit to you, I want it all. I want you both here. However, if you're going to make me choose, I choose you."

Miles' agony increased. There was no reason for Sunny to leave, if only he could get a hold of himself.

"I feel like I love her," the younger man admitted painfully.

"I'm sure you do" was his father's understanding reply. "And unless I miss my guess, you've decided you'll be miserable without her. I would also guess that you've not gone to your heavenly Father for help. He can see you through this. He will give you strength to control your feelings for a girl you can never have.

"Sunny is a lovely person, and I think you would enjoy having her as a friend. If you continue as you are, however, she won't know how to deal with you, and to protect herself you'll know only animosity from her."

Miles stood then, and Rand put his arm around his son's shoulders. Both men headed for the house and into Rand's study. Rand had been correct in his guess, Miles had not prayed about his feelings. The men did so now. There were no miracles as they turned to God with this need, but Miles rose from his knees many minutes later knowing that he could fight this feeling, and would. With a new resolve he went to his room to freshen up and then to find Sunny. It was time to apologize for the way he had acted.

≈ Twenty-Nine ≈

As JUNE GAVE WAY TO JULY, Rand struck a bargain on Sunny's behalf with James Townsend for the sale of the roan filly. The moment he had seen the young horse, he had agreed with her estimation of the animal. London Lady was a beauty. It was agreed that Lady, as Sunny called her, would be sold to her that summer and would come to live at Willows' End within six months' time, the proper time for weaning.

In the meantime, Sunny rode Miles' horse, Windsor. He was Miles' favorite mount, but Miles had gladly given the fine gelding over to her as a type of peace offering after they had talked. And it had worked. Miles and Sunny had grown very close in the days to follow, and Miles learned how prophetic his father's words had been. Sunny was a wonderful friend. He also began to understand why Holly had so desperately wanted her to stay.

There weren't many people who were as entertaining as Sunny. She was bright and cheerful, and even though they tried to talk her out of some things, she always had a wild scheme cooking in her head that meant fun or excitement for all. Today was just such a day. Weeks ago, Sunny had spotted what looked to be a small pond while she was standing in the south tower. Now she had two blankets and a picnic lunch all packed and sitting in Holly's buggy. Miles was on Jolly, and with Sunny astride Windsor, they were off.

"Are you sure you know the way, Miles?" Holly worried as the horse pulled her single-seater trap across the meadow.

"I'm sure. What are you worried about?"

"I'm worried about what happened the last time. I refuse to ride on the back of your horse again. If this buggy can't get through, I'm turning back."

Sunny laughed and called back to her. "You were white as the moon while on the back of that horse."

"It's all well and good for you to be laughing, Sunny Gallagher, but taking us into the swamp was all your fault."

"I know," the younger girl said, an unrepentant grin on her face.

Holly shook her head much like her mother would. Sunny's grin was infectious, and even though Holly had been livid at the time, she was very much over it now and found herself grinning in return.

"There it is," Sunny cried as they topped a small rise and saw a perfectly round pond sitting off to the west. The sun glistened off the surface, causing Sunny to heel Windsor into an easy lope and urge him in the direction of the water. Miles, on the other hand, stayed by Holly's horse and buggy.

Many changes had taken place in Miles since his talk with his father. He was now 17, and without conscious thought, had become very protective of both Sunny and his sister. Not completely certain of the terrain, he was hesitant to leave Holly on her own. Sunny oftentimes seemed more rugged and sure of herself. For the first time in his life, Miles did not feel impatience with Holly's fear of horses, only compassion for her.

"Am I going to make it?" Holly asked as they progressed slowly.

"I think so. Father wouldn't have let us come if he had thought it was dangerous."

Miles had not thought of this until just then, but saying the words out loud made them both feel better. Miles looked ahead to see that Sunny had already dismounted and was walking by the water. As they followed in her path, he wondered if there was anything of which she was afraid.

"How deep do you suppose this water is?"

"*No!*" Miles and Holly shouted in unison, having learned the way Sunny's mind worked. Their aunt scowled at them.

"I didn't mean I'd go in right now, but I thought maybe I could come back—"

"It's over your head, Sunny." Miles cut her off with what he was sure would be the final word.

"What does that have to do with it?"

"You'll drown," Holly told her as if she'd taken leave of her senses.

Sunny shook her head with complete confidence. "I've been swimming since I was a baby."

"You have?" Holly was now captivated. "I didn't know that."

"It doesn't matter what you know," Miles interjected, wanting to nip this idea in the bud before Holly could unconsciously encourage it. "No matter how well you swim, Sunny, it's not safe to come here on your own. If something did happen, we might never find you."

This was all said so kindly, showing how much Miles really cared, that Sunny didn't have an argument. They laid out the lunch then and were just beginning to eat when two riders came into view and bore down on them.

"It's mother," Miles spoke when they were still far off.

"And Heather!" Sunny cried a moment later as she came to her feet. She met them a good ten yards away, where Heather reined in her horse, jumped to the ground, and took her sister in her arms.

"So how is school?"

"It's going well. I'll be glad to finish."

Miles looked at his best friend, Jordan Townsend, and wished he was as close to completion, but Jordan was more than a year older than Miles and had started school that much earlier.

They had been the best of friends since the time they were young, mainly because of the close proximity of their homes. Nothing had ever shaken the foundation of that friendship, but they were as different in appearance as any two friends could be. Both were handsome, but where Miles was broad and dark, Jordan was slim and blond. Miles' eyes were brown, Jordan's blue. Their friendship was cemented by their mutual love of horses, reading, discussing Jesus Christ and His life on the earth, and, when they had time, courting some of the local girls.

With conflicting schedules and serious studies, there was not much time for seeing each other or courting, but both boys were very interested in eventually finding wives. Because of their good looks, each enjoyed his fair share of female attention. They both attended all-male schools, but whenever they did venture into town, it was to the delight of many a young female heart.

Jordan, a bit more easygoing than Miles, would have laughed this off if mentioned to him, but Miles was quite aware of the fact that they took their looks for granted. This was why he decided to warn Jordan about Sunny. Since Jordan was his best friend, and he and Sunny were becoming closer all the time, it was important to him that the two hit it off. At the moment, they were both on horseback headed to Willows' End for lunch, and Miles knew that now was as good a time as any.

"Before we get to the Willows, Jordan, I need to warn you about my Aunt Sunny."

"I'd forgotten about her coming back. I thought you said she was living in London."

"She was, but now she lives at Willows' End."

"Oh." Jordan seemed rather uninterested. "What about her?"

"Well," Miles suddenly felt uncomfortable, as though revealing something about Sunny would be destroying her privacy. However, Miles knew the same girls Jordan did, and he also knew that Jordan had never met anyone quite like Sunny Gallagher.

"She's just a bit unusual," he spoke finally.

"Unusual how?" Jordan pressed him. "Does she have four ears?" he asked with a twinkle in his eye.

"No, it's not that type of unusual. She's unique, and very beautiful," Miles added softly.

"Honestly, Miles," Jordan snorted with laughter. "You're always falling for an older woman. What was it you said last time, about one of your mother's friends? 'She has the face of an angel.'"

Jordan's hand had come to his chest, and his voice had become highly dramatic. Miles laughed at being caught out, but that incident had occurred three years ago. He opened his mouth, ready to remind Jordan of that, but changed his mind.

Jordan could be altogether too sure of himself where girls were concerned. Miles decided to let him find out for himself that Sunny was not the age of his mother's friends.

"A forage?" Holly asked with great reservation. "But there are only four of us."

"I know, but at Christmastime when I was here for a forage, I didn't know what I was doing. Chelsea wrote the lists for me this morning, so you take Louise and I'll take Diane, and the first team back wins."

Sunny grinned in triumph, and Holly was very suddenly taken with the idea. The twins were nearly jumping with excitement at the older girls' sides, and in the next instant Holly snatched her list, along with Louise's hand, and ran for all parts of the house.

Following on their heels Sunny and Diane ran pell-mell, and all four of them hit the kitchen in a wave of feminine laughter. They were back out in record time, but when Holly and Louise headed for the stairs, Sunny dragged Diane outside.

"It says we need a flower."

"What color?" Diane thought she knew just the place.

"Any color but red," Sunny told her.

"I know where. Come on."

The girls ran from the front of the house, around the side, and smack into Jordan and Miles.

"Get the flower, Diane; I'll be right there," Sunny directed, thinking quickly.

"Miles," she went on, grabbing the front of his coat with both hands. "Give me your handkerchief."

"Sunny, what are you two doing?" he asked in amazement, taking in Sunny's flushed face and sparkling eyes.

"It's a forage, and if you don't give me the handkerchief, Holly and Louise are going to beat us back."

Miles began to search his pockets, but was sidetracked by the dumbfounded look on Jordan's face. He glanced at the other man's chest and spotted the handkerchief in his breast pocket.

"Here," he plucked it out with fast fingers. "Take Jordan's."

"Thank you," she said softly in her princess voice, scowling a bit since she'd just noticed Jordan's intense stare.

Sunny was on the verge of cutting him in two with a look and a few words, but Diane suddenly appeared at her side.

"I've got the flower."

"Good." Sunny forgot Miles and his rude companion. "Come on. We'll get the rock at the front door and finish up inside."

They left the men standing in the path, Jordan staring down at the place where Sunny had been standing and Miles grinning at his friend while doing his utmost not to laugh. When Jordan realized Miles was still there, he turned and spoke thoughtfully.

"You did try to warn me, didn't you?"

"Yes I did," said a well-pleased Miles.

Jordan shook his head very slowly, still wondering if he had dreamt her, or if there really had been a girl as lovely as he had ever seen.

"Next time, Miles, plant your fist alongside my jaw, do anything you have to do, but make sure I'm paying attention."

Miles' incorrigible laughter could be heard all the way to the stables.

"So who won?" Heather wanted to know as the girls approached both her and Chelsea as they sat in the music room upstairs.

"They did," Diane offered. "But we still had fun."

Sunny hugged her niece, thinking how wonderful it was to have them here.

"Do you really have to go in the morning?" Sunny asked.

"I'm afraid so, love. We've been here a week, and I miss Foster."

"You four had better clean up for lunch," Chelsea instructed.

They had all forgotten their stomachs in the thrill of the chase, and after the reminder, all were glad to file out and do as she bid.

While Christie was brushing her hair, Sunny remembered that Miles had brought someone with him, someone who had made her instantly uncomfortable. She thought Miles had called him Jordan. With this in mind, it was with measured tread that she went to the dining room, uncertain if he would still be there, and *most* certain she didn't want to see him if he was.

Much to her chagrin, Miles had her figured out. When she would have peeked in the door and backed quickly away, he had been watching for her and called her name. She had no choice but to enter, and when she did, the young blond man she had seen outside came to his feet in one graceful, confident move.

"Sunny," Miles began, his eyes sparkling with private amusement, "I'd like you to meet Jordan Townsend. Jordan, this is my aunt, Sunny Gallagher."

Jordan smiled most charmingly. Having very much liked what he had seen outside, he was determined to get better acquainted with the lovely Lady Sunny.

Upon seeing Miles' twinkling eyes, Sunny shot him a reproving look, one that was old beyond her years. Bowing politely, she greeted Jordan cordially, but her look and stance were frigid. As soon as propriety allowed she turned away from him in what could only be considered a deliberate snub. A moment later lunch was called.

"What did I do?" Jordan whispered to Miles as soon as the room emptied and the girls were out of earshot.

Miles eyed his friend and felt bad that only minutes ago, he had found the whole thing amusing. Jordan looked stricken.

"She doesn't like to be stared at," Miles told him, kindness now filling his voice.

"Are you serious?" Jordan had yet to meet a woman who didn't like to be noticed.

"Yes, I'm serious. And once she's concluded that she doesn't like you, she might take some time in forgiving you."

"She's already made up her mind not to like me?" Jordan was shocked all over again, and Miles thought how correct he'd been in thinking that Jordan took his "way with women" for granted.

"I might be wrong, but it looks to me as though she wants nothing to do with you."

"So what do I do?"

"You don't have to *do* anything if you don't want to." Miles had suddenly become very logical.

Jordan's hands came to his slim hips in a gesture of impatience. "Not do anything, Miles? You must be joking. I've offended your aunt, and I was rather hoping to know her better...much better. Now, will you please help me?"

Miles nodded. "Be kind to her, but don't make a big deal over her. If you do, she won't get anywhere near you."

"Should I apologize for staring?"

"No, hold off on that. Wait and see if she'll even look at you."

Jordan grinned and opened his mouth to assure Miles that this would not be a problem, but Binks' voice broke into their conversation.

"Lady Chelsea is waiting for you, Lord Miles."

"Thank you, Binks. We'll be right along."

Miles exchanged a last glance with the decisive-looking Jordan before leading the way to lunch.

Thirty

IT TOOK JORDAN EXACTLY FIVE MINUTES to see that he'd been a conceited fool where Sunny Gallagher was concerned. During the entire meal, she never once looked in his direction. He had even directed a question to her, which she answered in a monosyllabic reply while looking down at her plate.

He planned to speak with her as soon as the meal ended, but Sunny slipped away so swiftly that all he saw was the swing of her skirts as she disappeared out the door. Jordan hung around for the better part of the afternoon, talking with Miles and Holly, but there was no sign of Sunny. Knowing that his mother would be expecting him at home, he left before five, telling himself that he would be back tomorrow, and every day thereafter, until he had a chance to speak to that girl.

"You and I need to have a little talk," Chelsea said gently to her young sister-in-law just after Jordan left for the day.

Sunny didn't have a clue as to what Chelsea could want, and since she could think of no reason why she was in trouble, she agreed without compunction, flopping down on the bed as though she hadn't a care in the world.

"The Townsends have been our friends and neighbors for a long time, and I did not care for the way you treated Jordan today."

Sunny's carefree attitude evaporated. She sat up on the side of the bed and frowned intensely in Chelsea's direction. What she didn't know was that Chelsea was a kindred spirit, and Sunny's glare didn't daunt her in the least.

"Did Jordan say something to you that was offensive or that hurt your feelings?" the older woman wanted to know.

"No," Sunny had to admit.

"Did he touch you in some way, even casually, that bothered you?"

"No, Chelsea." Sunny was beginning to be confused.

"Then you were rude to him for no reason?"

"He stared at me," Sunny stated with haughty disdain.

"As I said," Chelsea went on, "you were rude to him for no reason. Hear me out!" Chelsea cut in, her hand raised in the air, when Sunny opened her mouth to protest.

Sunny settled back on the bed, and Chelsea continued.

"You're going to have to get over your aversion to being admired. You are a lovely young woman, and you're going to continue to grow more attractive as the years pass. Unless I miss my guess, the women in Darhabar were kept away from men, other than their husbands."

"That is correct."

"As you have noticed, it is quite different here in England. If you were drawing attention to yourself by wearing revealing clothing or throwing yourself at young men, then I would be talking to you about that. As it is, our culture is as you've witnessed. You must understand and begin to tolerate it when people admire you.

"Don't misunderstand me, Sunny; if someone is making improper advances, I want you to get away from him immediately and come to me or Rand. But where Jordan is concerned, well, he and Miles have been friends for so long that he is like my own son. He waited all afternoon for you to come down so he could make amends, but your feelings were hurt so you were up here pouting."

"I do not pout!"

"It certainly looks to everyone in the household as though you do. When you can't handle something, you just run away from it."

Sunny had never been called a coward or told that she pouted, and she didn't like it now. But Chelsea was right. She had run away from Cecil, then Miles, and now Jordan. She had even done it weeks ago with Brandon, when she was still living with Heather. Because she was angry, she had left the nursery and gone to the library without even speaking to him.

Sunny walked to the window and looked out, trying to deal with this newly revealed truth about herself. Each time it seemed that all was going well, someone or something appeared on the horizon, and her world became unhappy all over again.

Of course, Sunny had heard about Jordan Townsend, but no one had mentioned that he was extremely handsome and personable. Before meeting him, Sunny had hoped they could be friends, but the moment he gawked at her on the path, his mouth hanging open, her old anger reared up. This time, though, she had hidden behind that anger not only because of his rudeness but also to keep the fascination she felt for him at bay.

Sunny knew she wanted to see Jordan again, and in fact had felt tortured by her pride about staying in her room all afternoon, but now Chelsea had called her a coward, and that was something that had to be taken into hand first. She was not going to run away anymore.

"You want me to ignore people's stares?"

"Most times, yes, but not where Jordan is concerned, or when you have a situation like you did with Miles."

"What am I to do?"

"In your kindest voice and most gentle manner, say, 'Please do not stare at me,' or 'Is there some reason you're staring at me?'"

"What good will that do?"

"Most people probably don't know they're even doing it, so I believe it will do a lot of good. Sunny, I'm not saying that it's perfectly all right for people to stare and be rude, but it *is* going to happen, and you must not be rude in return. If you find you simply can't cope with someone, come to me on the spot. I believe Heather helped you in that way with Cecil, didn't she?"

Sunny nodded, glad the older women had spoken of it.

"I want you to come to me the same way. This is your home, and I want to do all I can to see you peaceful and content. That's why Rand and I are here."

Sunny felt as if a load had been lifted from her shoulders. She rose and kissed Chelsea's cheek, and the older woman stood in order to hold her close. Holly found them like this, and within moments had dragged Sunny to the upstairs salon to talk and work on their joint venture in tapestry. Sunny, feeling much like a caged animal, was more than happy to escape the prison she had made of her room, even if it meant she had to sew.

The next day dawned warm and beautiful, and Jordan, although busy at home through the morning, had plans for the afternoon. He was on the verge of telling his mother that he was headed to Willows' End until dinner, but before he could utter a word, he found his plans painfully dashed.

"Jordan dear," his mother began. "I'd like you to run some papers over to Bracken this afternoon. I could have the servants see to it, but they are your father's documents and are quite important. You haven't seen Lady Andrea or the duke for some months, and I know they'd enjoy your visit."

"Yes, of course, I'll take care of it directly after lunch." Jordan had hidden his disappointment in an effort to please the mother he adored, but his thoughts were torn as he rode toward Bracken. He did love visiting Bracken and the duke, but he had worked hard all morning, thinking to reward himself with a visit to Sunny.

After some moments of reckoning with the truth, and not a young man to brood, he rode from his father's stables, determined to enjoy the day and equally determined to see Sunny on the morrow.

"I would never have come here on my own, Grandmama, but Sunny would have. She wanted to come on horseback. When father heard her plans, he ordered a carriage to be brought around."

Holly's look was so comically exasperated that Andrea chuckled softly. Holly shrugged and smiled in return, and her grandmother hugged her again.

"How about your mother—couldn't she get away and come with you?"

"No, Mummy's having some ladies in; I can't recall the occasion. That, along with Aunt Heather and the twins leaving, is why Sunny wanted to come. It made their going easier. She did send you a letter, though." Holly could change the subject very easily. "She said you should look for her next week."

"Well, you and Sunny come back with her if you can."

"I'm sure Sunny will; she loves Bracken."

"Does she now?"

"She talked about it all the way over here, that and your conservatory and gardens."

"That must be where she's gone with Papa. Shall we join them?"

Andrea and Holly did just that, heading out through the huge glass doors on the east end of the parlor and around to the lush flower gardens of Bracken. They spotted Sunny and the duke from a good distance off. They appeared to be in deep conversation.

"I don't plan to marry," Sunny told him emphatically.

"Now why is that?" the duke, who always seemed to be matchmaking, asked her calmly.

"Well, I don't want someone having control over me. I don't think I could be happy like that."

"Doesn't Rand have the final word at Willows' End?"

"Yes, he does, but he's very kind about things, even when he says no."

The old man looked down into her trusting face, a face as exquisite as the flowers surrounding her, and thought that if she ever did marry, the word "no" would probably be the hardest thing her husband would ever have to say to her.

"I was happily married, and so was my wife," Milton told her then, his liberally seamed face smoothed into serene lines.

Sunny nodded. "Rand and Chelsea are happy, and so are Heather and Foster. But for those two happy marriages, there are many that aren't."

"Of whom are you thinking?"

Indira's face jumped into Sunny's mind, but she pushed it away. Indira was happy. However, Saleem, Rownay, and Keskeet, the emir's second, third, and fourth wives, were little more than possessions to be brought out several times a year.

"I guess I don't know anyone here in England, but that still won't change my mind."

"You must follow your heart, my dear," Milton told her seriously, "and I hope you will learn to follow after God's heart as well."

"Now that sounds like something Brandon would say," Sunny said affectionately.

"I can believe that. Our beliefs are quite similar. They match the beliefs of my father and grandfather—men who believed their faith needed to be handed down to each generation." He hesitated and then went on softly. "And you, Sunny, what do you believe?"

"I'm not sure I believe that you have to believe anything, but I know some things I don't believe. I don't believe that there is just one God. God comes in many forms, and each one of us must decide which God we want to worship, or possibly not believe in any God at all.

"I don't think any man has the right to tell someone else how to act or live. No one should have that type of authority."

"If no man has the right, my dear, then who does?"

Sunny looked at him in confusion, and then her face cleared. "Well, there have to be laws about murder and such, but not for other, more personal things."

"Does Rand have the right to tell Holly no?"

"Yes."

"Who gave him the right?"

"Well, he's her father."

"So what? That doesn't give him the right to deny her something unless he has an authority that backs up his position as her parent."

Again Sunny looked uncertain and then said softly. "You're talking about the Bible."

"Yes, I am. Even parental authority comes from God, and not just any God, but the one and only living, holy God of the Bible. Your not believing in the one true God doesn't change the fact that He exists."

His words were spoken in such tenderness that Sunny did not feel rebuked. She did feel somewhat confused. What if there really was just one God? Before this moment she had never let her mind even entertain such a belief. There was certainly more to the Bible than she had ever realized, if her family was to be believed.

"Don't take my word for it, Sunny," the duke went on, cutting into her intense thoughts. "When you get home, ask Chelsea for a Bible and read the first book. Genesis means beginnings, and I think you might enjoy reading about how perfectly God planned things."

Sunny nodded and smiled at him. The duke reached with a weathered hand and gently patted her cheek. A moment later they were joined by Andrea and Holly.

❧ ❧ ❧

"Young Lord Townsend is here, your Grace."

"Jordan?" Holly spoke with pleasure.

"Yes, my lady."

"He'll probably want to freshen up," Andrea interjected for the duke. "But please ask him to join us for tea, Parks, just as soon as he's able."

"Very well, my lady."

No one seemed to take notice, but Sunny suddenly had a piece of sandwich in her throat that did not want to go down. Jordan was here. What would she do? She recognized the fact that she wanted to see him again, but she had somehow believed she would have more time to prepare herself.

In truth, she had exactly five minutes before Jordan walked into the large salon, as tall and good-looking as he had been the day before. The duke rose and shook his hand. Then Jordan bent over Andrea's hand, smiling at his best friend's grandmother with familiar ease.

He went to Holly next, kissing her on the cheek before turning to Sunny.

"Jordan, have you met Sunny?"

"Yes, Lady Andrea, I have." He moved forward then and took Sunny's hand in his own. "It's nice to see you again, Sunny." The smile he gave her held just the right amount of warmth, and Jordan dearly hoped that no one had noticed how fast his heart was pounding. He'd ridden directly to the stables and had seen the Gallagher coach, but had not allowed himself to hope that Sunny was actually at Bracken.

Sunny had eventually swallowed the sandwich but not without great difficulty. She now spoke softly, feeling her cheeks grow warm under his warm, almost tender, gaze.

"It's nice to see you also, Jordan," she managed after a moment.

"Do sit down," Holly invited, passing him the platter of sandwiches as he took his chair. Andrea gave him his tea.

"Thank you," Jordan said sincerely and began to discuss his schooling when the duke questioned him. He was very aware of Sunny's discomfort and made an effort not to look at her or show excessive interest in any way. He found this no easy task, since she looked very fetching in a dark pink day dress, with a rounded lace neckline and deep hem, her hair pulled away from her face and falling in lovely waves down her neck and back.

The women of the room all listened or at least appeared to be listening as Jordan and the duke conversed. Sunny was actually concentrating on her manners. She had suddenly found herself all thumbs. Her plate tipped in her hand, nearly spilling its contents, and her cup clattered on the saucer each time she put it down. Placing both cup and plate on the tea table, she finally gave up and folded her hands neatly in her lap, telling them to stop trembling.

The duke, whose eyesight was not the least bit affected by his advanced years, had observed some interesting facts since Jordan's arrival, the first of which was Jordan's studied care not to look at Sunny. The second was Sunny's sudden attack of nerves.

Tea was finished without ceremony, and still the duke and Jordan talked. When Parks and a downstairs maid came to clear the tray, the duke suddenly had something he insisted Andrea and Holly see in the garden.

"Should Sunny come with us?" Holly asked in all innocence.

"I think not," the duke said after a moment. "She was just in the gardens with me this morning, and someone needs to stay and keep company with Jordan."

Sunny searched the faces in the room and noticed that no one thought this unusual, so she kept her seat as the three left, watching the door even after it closed on their departure. It took a moment for Sunny to realize that Jordan had reseated himself and was waiting for her to speak. She could feel his eyes on her, and after taking a deep breath, she turned and let her eyes meet his.

Thirty-One

"I'VE BEEN LOOKING FORWARD TO SEEING YOU AGAIN," Jordan said when Sunny's eyes finally rested on his.

"You were?" Sunny seemed surprised by this admission.

"Yes. I acted out of line when we met yesterday, and I'd like a chance to apologize."

This had been the last thing Sunny expected to hear from him, and for just an instant, she was speechless.

"Have I made things worse?" Jordan's already kind voice had become very tentative.

"No," she assured him quickly. "I was just thinking that I'd acted rudely to you, and I didn't expect you to—" Her voice trailed off in embarrassment, but Jordan smiled.

"Well then, we'll call it a draw, shall we?"

"A draw?" Sunny spoke with hesitation, but also interest.

"We'll leave it as it is. No more apologies needed, and we'll be on good speaking terms," Jordan amplified carefully, seeing how swiftly he had confused her.

Sunny suddenly forgot they had even been on awkward terms. "I thought to draw was to mark on canvas or paper."

"It is. But it's also to be even, as I just used the word, or to draw water from a well; that is, to bring it up in a bucket."

Sunny was on the edge of her chair with attention. "Are those all the meanings?"

"No, there are more. You can use the word 'draw' when you're trying to trap an animal. You might say, 'I put the food in the forest to draw the rabbit into the snare.' "

"Are there more?" Sunny's face was avid.

"Let me think," Jordan was silent a moment, thinking he had never had a conversation like this in his life. He was also having the most fun he'd had all week—this girl fascinated him. One minute she looked so proud as to appear almost arrogant, and the next she was admitting ignorance over a common word in the English language.

"You can draw money from a savings account, but that's much like getting water from a well. You can also draw interest on your money, which is more like the words 'gain' or 'accumulate.'" The conversation had continued in this vein for the better part of 20 minutes, when Sunny suddenly stopped short from asking one more question. The interest was gone from her face. She stared at Jordan, her expression unreadable.

"What are you thinking?"

Sunny's face did not change, even when she answered truthfully. "That you're as nice as Miles said you were."

Jordan smiled, and Sunny found herself smiling in return.

"I was hoping you would think so," Jordan admitted and again they shared an easy smile.

Holly was some feet away from her elders when Andrea spoke for the duke's ears alone.

"I'm so glad you took the time to show us flowers that I pointed out to you two days ago."

She spoke with just the right touch of humility in her voice, but the duke was not fooled. He turned his head and met her steady gaze. Only an instant passed before he grinned. He was completely unrepentant over the fact that she had seen through his matchmaking ways. Andrea shook her head and was on the verge of scolding him when Holly cried out.

"Uncle Dex is here."

The duke and Andrea followed in her hurried path and watched as she embraced her uncle. Dex still had his arm around Holly when the duke and Andrea arrived, talking in quiet tones.

"After seeing you I was rather hoping that Sunny would be here too."

"Oh, but she is here," Holly told him triumphantly. "She's in the house with Jordan."

"Is something wrong, dear?" Dexter's mother asked after he'd greeted her and kissed her cheek.

"Nothing that Sunny can't fix." He spoke with what his mother recognized as a hopeful expression. "Judith's sixth bridesmaid has eloped, and Judith wants Sunny to take her place," he explained. "We'd love to have her if she's willing."

"Of course she'll be willing," Holly exclaimed, having missed any undertones of doubt. "Any girl would be. May I tell her?"

Dexter had barely answered when Holly ran for the house, completely missing the look of uncertainty on each adult face.

"What do you mean, you can't?"

Holly stood in the middle of the room, arms akimbo, a look of total disbelief on her pretty round face. Just minutes earlier she'd arrived with what was certain to be the day's greatest news, but Holly was now stunned to see that Sunny was not excited in the least.

"I just don't think I could," Sunny answered helplessly. Until Chelsea and Holly had explained weddings to her some weeks ago, Sunny had never realized the pomp involved in an English ceremony. She was only to be a guest at the wedding, but even at that, the entire ritual had sounded a bit intimidating.

"You've told me there will be hundreds of people at that wedding. You and I were going to sit together and be together at the reception. I can't walk up the aisle of a vast cathedral by myself."

The duke had opted to retire to his room for a spell, but both Andrea and Dexter had entered the parlor in time to hear Sunny's last words.

Holly caught Jordan's eye just then and backed off entirely, allowing Dexter to approach Sunny. He stopped before her and smiled kindly into her eyes.

"Did Holly explain the situation to you?"

"She said one of the bridesmaids has eloped." Sunny did not go on to say that Holly had needed to define the word "elope."

"That's right, and the first person Judith asked to replace her was you. Now," he went on sounding so much like Brandon that

Sunny wanted to cry, "I won't force you to accept, but you'll see more of Judith. You'll also get to visit with Cheryl, who is coming with John and the baby just to be in the wedding."

"But I would have seen them anyway," Sunny reasoned softly.

"True," Dexter conceded. "But you'll see more of them if you're in the wedding party. And don't forget, Brandon will have returned, and as best man, he'll be a member of the wedding party as well."

Dexter could see she was vacillating and added, in a coaxing voice, what he thought would be the final push.

"You'll get to come to London and be fitted for a new dress."

"Oh, Uncle Dexter!" came Holly's distressed cry, having also seen that Sunny was coming around. "That's the last thing you should have said to her."

Dexter, after staring in surprise at his niece, turned to take in Sunny's chagrined face. He couldn't help but laugh. "And here I thought that would be the frosting on the cake," he spoke between chuckles.

Everyone laughed then, including Sunny. They talked for just ten minutes more, and hardly believing it was the sound of her own voice, Sunny impetuously heard herself agree.

"So how was London this trip?"

Sunny's nose wrinkled in distaste, and Jordan laughed.

"I can't think why anyone would choose to live there," she commented softly as her horse stepped lightly along the path.

"Oh, I don't know," Jordan countered as his own mount fell easily into line. "I rather like the noise and excitement."

"How do you feel about the smells?"

Jordan chuckled again. "It can be pretty bad in midsummer."

"It was bad in late summer," Sunny's voice was wry, thinking of the open sewers and the streets filled with filth and decay.

A month had passed since Dexter had found Sunny at Bracken and asked her to be in the wedding party. She had left the following day with Dexter and gone to London for a first fitting; Holly had gone along to keep her company. Then just a week ago she had returned for the final dress fitting, staying with Heather and Foster both times. Now the wedding was just three weeks away, scheduled for Saturday afternoon, September 13, 1845.

"Will you be at the wedding, Jordan?" Sunny suddenly wanted to know.

"Yes, ma'am," Jordan told her with friendly ease. "Will you save me a dance?"

"A dance?" Sunny spoke in surprise. "Will there be dancing?"

"Certainly," Jordan replied with some surprise. "At the reception."

Sunny looked horrified. Such a thought had never occurred to her. She didn't know how to dance and wasn't sure she wanted to learn. She worried about it all the way back to Willows' End. As soon as she and Jordan joined Chelsea and Holly for tea, Chelsea wanted to know what was bothering her.

"The dancing that's planned for the reception."

"Ah," Chelsea said, her tone understanding. "I don't think you need to worry on that end."

"Why is that?" Jordan wanted to know.

Chelsea grinned at him, feeling a bit sorry for what she had to say, but knowing he would take it well.

"You've forgotten Sunny's age, Jordan. Neither she nor Holly will be attending dances before they're 17."

Jordan was silent. He had forgotten that he was four years older than Sunny. His disappointment was acute, but in order not to make Sunny feel worse, he kept this to himself. Doing so was made all the more difficult when he noticed that Sunny looked relieved.

"We can make an appearance, though; isn't that right, Mummy?" Holly put in.

"Yes, just long enough to see the bride and groom and have a bite to eat. Then you're back to Heather's without a fuss."

"Who's putting up a fuss?" Miles wanted to know as he strode jauntily into the room.

"We're discussing the fact that the girls are too young to attend the wedding dance."

"That's right," Miles spoke as he tugged first on his sister's hair and then Sunny's. "You're both just babies."

This brought cries of outrage from both parties, but Miles refused to take the words back.

"You'd best not cross us, Miles," Sunny told him with a piqued glint in her eye, "or you might find yourself having to avoid all the evergreen bushes in the very near future."

Miles's hands immediately went into the air in a gesture of surrender. "I yield; I yield," he cried. "You're both very mature, and I'll call out any man who says otherwise."

Sunny's look was downright arrogant with this win, and the room exploded with merriment.

An hour before the wedding, Sunny's look was not so fun-filled. She could have cheerfully strangled herself for agreeing to be a part of this. Not even when she had met her family had she experienced such an awful attack of nerves. The other females in the wedding party, all a good deal older than herself, were having a wonderful time, laughing and talking like old friends.

Staring down at the courtyard below, Sunny stood alone at the window in a cavernous room at the rear of the church. There had been quite a commotion when the bride had come in some moments ago, and Sunny had turned from the window to smile at her. Judith, a vision in loveliness, was now in another, smaller room where she would stay until it was time to make that long walk down the aisle.

Another commotion started in the room, but this time Sunny did not turn. She knew it was not yet time to leave, and for the moment she just wanted to be left alone.

"Holding up?"

Sunny turned in surprise at the sound of Dexter's voice.

"What are you doing in here?"

"A little bird told me you were white with strain, so I thought I'd pop in and check on you."

Sunny managed a small smile and then asked the question she had been afraid to voice all day. "Did Brandon make it back?"

Dexter smiled, knowing he was about to relieve some of her anxiety. "Last night. I know he's eager to see you, but there just isn't time before the ceremony. They're sewing him into his pants right now."

It was the perfect thing to say. Sunny let out a small chuckle, and some of the color returned to her face in a rush. Dexter kissed her suddenly flushed cheek and took himself off. Sunny's jitters did not return until she was starting up the aisle.

Thirty~Two

SUNNY'S PERIPHERAL VISION TOLD HER that Brandon was across the church from her, right to the side of Dexter, but she was afraid to look at anyone save the clergyman, lest she miss her cue to go back up the aisle and make a fool of herself. She had refused to look to the left or right as she came down the aisle and did not even look into the face of the groomsman who met her halfway to the altar.

The vastness of the cathedral caught Sunny's attention for just an instant. Her eyes moved covertly over the walls that were covered with paintings and seemed to stretch for dozens of feet above her. She was studying the way the sun poured though a huge round stained-glass window above the bishop's head, when she suddenly remembered why she was there. With a jolt of fear that she might have missed something, she brought her eyes back to the service.

It was nearly over now, and although Sunny had heard some of it, she was vaguely aware of the fact that she had missed the wedding. No one watching her would have guessed the turmoil going on within as she stoically stood in a dress of pale blue silk, full in the skirt and fitted across the bodice. The sleeves were sheer and puffed at the shoulder. Gold and dark-blue braid lined the seams and bodice and trimmed the edge of the rounded neckline.

Sunny was as lovely to behold as the bride, but in truth, she was feeling something near to pain over having Brandon so close but not being able to talk with him. At the moment it felt as though he had been gone forever.

In the next minutes the ceremony ended, and Sunny, acting almost without thought, moved back up among the crowd on the arm of her groomsman. They were met at the back of the church by the crowd of guests that had not been able to fit into the cathedral. Sunny suddenly found herself separated from her companion and nearly lost in the crowd. The duke, Brandon, and Dexter, all so tall, swam into view from time to time, but the people pressing in around her were all so unfamiliar that Sunny knew a moment of panic.

She had been jostled from behind for the fourth time by the same rotund man when she felt a hand on her arm. Her first instinct was to pull away, but the sound of her brother's voice came to her ears.

Sunny allowed herself to be led away from the crush, out of the cathedral, and into a waiting carriage. Stuffed gently inside by Rand, she found both Miles and Jordan already occupying the coach. They each wanted to tell her how attractive she looked and how well she had done, but one look at her face silenced them. Sunny only glanced at them before turning her gaze toward the window. The carriage lurched into motion but moved only a few yards before stopping. This time Rand helped Chelsea and Holly in and climbed in beside them.

The ladies' skirts made the ride a bit cramped, but Holly was in such high spirits that no one really noticed. Her happy chatter worked its charm and effectively pulled Sunny from her pensive mood.

"Wasn't Aunt Judith a dream in that dress? Even her veil was heavenly. And Uncle Dex! He looked like a man who'd just been handed the moon when he kissed her."

Unmindful of the heat or cramped carriage, Holly chattered on for the entire ride to the banquet hall. Finding Sunny's eyes on her she grinned at the younger girl, and with a straight face, suddenly complimented her on how she'd made the walk up the aisle without tripping. Not able to help herself, Sunny laughed and the rest of the carriage joined in.

"I want to thank you girls for how well you're taking this," Chelsea told them as they moved up the huge stairway that led out of the banquet hall. Both girls were subdued and feeling a bit lonely over having to leave, but Chelsea was right; they were taking it very well. There were no complaints or pouting looks.

They were, however, trying to gain a last glimpse of the festivities below, so they missed the fact that Chelsea was not taking them to the cloak room. She turned this way and that along endless corridors and finally up another flight of stairs. The girls, speaking softly about their new aunt and sister-in-law, never noticed.

Chelsea opened a door and ushered the girls inside. Until she shut the door and the girls found themselves in semidarkness, they were still talking quietly. Chelsea said nothing, but waited for them to speak.

"Mum," Holly finally whispered. "Where are we?"

Both girls were looking at a huge empty floor, walled on three sides, but sporting a low, open railing on the fourth. From beyond that railing came the lights and music from the dance floor below.

"This is the balcony dance floor, and it won't be used tonight. You mustn't make a disturbance while you're up here. Talk in whispers. You may watch the dancing until 10:30."

Chelsea suddenly found herself thronged by soft young arms and fervently whispered thank-yous.

"You'll crush my dress," she admonished them, but there was a smile on her face. She stayed until both girls crept to the railing and knelt down to peek through the balustrade. She stood for a moment, looking at them in contentment. Just as she turned away, Sunny dropped to her stomach, kicked her wedding slippers off, and propped her chin on both hands to better see the floor below.

Chelsea walked away with a good-natured shake of her head. Both girls had been the picture of maturity during the reception, and now they lay on the floor like children, peeking out with envy on the adults below.

"I love Judith's dress," Heather breathed reverently.

"It looks heavy," Sunny stated logically.

Heather suppressed a giggle. "Leave it to you to think of that."

Sunny nodded and smiled in agreement. She leaned her head a little further through the rails. The scene below was like something out of a storybook. The well-wishers had been to supper and now the dance was in full swing. The orchestra had just finished with a minuet and had now struck up a waltz. Nearly hypnotized, the girls watched the women's skirts swirl and the gentlemen's courtly bows. It was all so lovely that Sunny found herself quite content to watch all night.

"I've got to go," Holly suddenly said.

"Is it 10:30 already?" Sunny's voice bespoke her disappointment.

"No, I'm going to the retiring room. Do you need to come?"

"No, I'll wait here," Sunny answered, so relieved that it wasn't yet time to go that she barely heard the rustle of Holly's skirts as she rose from her knees and quietly left.

Sunny was intent on Miles and his progress around the floor with the bride when the door to the upper dance floor opened. It was closed softly, and Sunny was just about to tell Holly to hurry or she'd miss Miles, but the person at the door spoke first.

"I've heard nothing save how grown-up you've become since I left, and here I find you with your shoes kicked off, and sprawled on the floor like a ragamuffin."

Sunny's eyes slid shut at the sound of that tender voice. She had begun to think she would never hear it again. With movements as smooth as a well-oiled wheel, Sunny rose. Her dress was horribly crushed, but Brandon took little notice and Sunny simply didn't care. To better see her face in the light, he joined her at the railing and found her upturned face smiling with the delight of a child.

"Hello, Sunny," Brandon said, a grin splitting his own features.

"Oh, Brandon" was all Sunny could manage before she threw her arms around his neck. They hugged for many moments, neither one able to speak.

"I missed you," Sunny finally said.

"And I missed you," Brandon added as he released her. "But I thought of you the whole time I was gone and prayed for you every day. I even brought you something."

Sunny watched as Brandon drew a thin gold bracelet from the pocket of his coat. He handed it to Sunny, knowing its full beauty would be hidden in the dim light.

"It's from the emir," he whispered. "He said to add it to the other treasures in your jewel box."

Sunny, who had been tenderly cradling the gift in the palm of her hand, froze. She slowly raised her face to Brandon, whose dark eyes had been watching her intently.

"You've been back to Darhabar?"

"Yes," he admitted softly. "I have never been comfortable with the way Ahmad Khan sent you away, and I wanted to confront him over it."

"Were you welcome?"

"Most welcome. He was quite interested to know how you were, and as I said, I was most determined to know why you were sent away so abruptly."

"What did you find out?"

"Very little. He said much the same as he had in his letter to you—that his love for you was great enough to give you back to your family. We spoke for the better part of an hour before I realized that if there was another reason or motive, the emir was not going to reveal it to me. I was given little choice but to take his words at face value. At least I tried, and I guess I really do believe that his actions, however abrupt, were out of love."

Sunny was silent for a moment.

"Have I upset you, Sunny?"

"No, I'm just surprised. I mean, you never told me what you'd planned to do, and I never—"

"If you'd known," Brandon interrupted, "and I'd been refused entrance to the palace, you would have waited all this time only to be met with disappointment. As it was, Darhabar was a closed book to you, and that left you free to settle here where you belong."

He paused and searched her face again. "And you have settled, haven't you, Sunny?"

Sunny's smile was thoughtful. "I think so. I still hate wearing shoes and what feels like 15 petticoats, but I'm getting there." Her smile turned very wry, and Brandon chuckled.

"I bought a horse," Sunny said, her mood changing swiftly. "I wrote you all about her, but of course I never mailed the letter." In the next minutes she told him all about London Lady, her face alight with excitement.

Holly joined them shortly thereafter, and Brandon gave her a warm hug and a big kiss. They talked for a few moments, and then Brandon informed them that as best man, he must return to the dance.

"Of course you must," Holly teased with a saucy smile, as she took in her uncle's splendid form in a black suit and snow white shirt and cravat. "I'm sure many a female heart was broken at your departure."

Brandon reached with a long finger and touched her cheek, his smile as teasing as her own. "You're an impertinent bit of baggage, Holly."

"When do you return to Willows' End?" Brandon, after earning a dimpled smile from Holly, had suddenly turned back to Sunny.

The younger girl shrugged. "I'm not sure. Are you leaving soon?" These last words were asked hesitantly.

"Not for a month at least," he told her easily. "But for the moment, I really must go."

He was gone with those words, and with him went Sunny's desire to watch any more of the dance. She was relieved when Rand appeared not 20 minutes later, their cloaks over his arm, to usher them downstairs to a waiting carriage.

Thirty-Three

FIVE WEEKS LATER BRANDON'S SHIP SAILED WITH THE TIDE. He remained on deck only until they were safely into the bay and then retired to his cabin to review his reports. Strangely enough, when he was finally settled at his desk, he found his mind straying far from his work.

Sunny and Holly had been at Bracken the day he had left. Brandon had been in an awful rush with last-minute details and had no time for socializing or even the briefest of conversations. He clearly remembered, however, the scene in the library at his departure. Sunny and his grandfather had been engaged in a fierce chess match, and Holly had been curled up on the oversized davenport, reading a book. It had all been so cozy and serene that now Brandon found himself momentarily preoccupied.

As he had left for London, he realized for the first time that the sea was losing its charm. How lovely it would have been to throw his coat over a chair and settle in next to Holly with a book of his own, or to bend his sharp mind to the task of letting his grandfather win at chess without his knowing.

"I want a wife and family," Brandon spoke softly in the empty cabin, and his mind, without permission, went to one of his dancing partners at Dexter's wedding reception—Dinah Hadley.

Dexter's status as grandson of a duke and Brandon's position as heir to the title had made the wedding a very newsworthy occasion in London society. Outside of family members, Brandon had made it

191

a point not to dance with the same woman twice.

London's tongue could be ruthless when it came to scandal and gossip, but Brandon wondered even now at how difficult it had been to dance with Dinah only once. Releasing her to another partner, when he was so fascinated by her conversation, had been very difficult indeed.

Dinah had grown up a good deal in the year since her coming out, and Brandon had teased her over not having been spoken for yet. He had been shocked speechless by her soft yet determined answer.

"I'm waiting for a man who puts the importance of his relationship with God over and above his title or his wealth." That she had shocked herself was quite clear when she turned a dull red and began to stammer.

"I beg your pardon, my lord. I was very rude just now, and I hope—"

"Don't apologize," Brandon had interjected, his voice kind. "Just answer one more question for me. Where do you put *your* relationship with God?"

"Above all else," she had told him sincerely. "And when He wants me to be married, I know that He'll provide a spouse who believes as I do."

The waltz changed to a minuet just after this, and Dinah was lost to Brandon for the rest of the evening. For her reputation as well as his own, he could not seek her out, and Brandon had found this one of the most difficult things he'd had to do. Unknowingly, Chelsea rescued him by telling him that Sunny was in the balcony. He had made his escape, however brief, and from then on the evening progressed smoothly.

Brandon sighed over his memories and massaged the back of his neck with a long-fingered hand. *And now I'm headed back to sea. I run the risk of never seeing Papa again every time I leave. This time it's more difficult; this time I don't want to go at all.*

Brandon suddenly remembered how well Sunny had taken his departure. She was adjusting very nicely, and Brandon thought how much he had to be truly thankful for. Allowing his accounts to wait, he took time to thank God for His tender care and to entrust Him with this journey and all the loved ones he had left behind.

Sunny's fifteenth birthday came and went, as did Christmas and New Year's. Almost a year to the date, Chelsea began to witness in Sunny the same listlessness that Heather had seen in London. She was pale and losing weight. Both Miles and Jordan were back at school, and neither Holly nor London Lady, nor any of her usual pursuits, seemed to cheer the quiet young woman.

"At some point we've got to stop turning tricks to amuse her," Rand said to Chelsea one evening after dismissing the maid for the night.

"If she's unhappy, she needs to face the problem and deal with it."

"I agree with you, Rand," Chelsea admitted. Turning away from the mirror at her dressing table, Chelsea gazed over at Rand sprawled on her bed. "Douglas and Marian have asked her to visit Portsmouth again and again. Maybe if we talk to her, we can make her understand."

"Understand what exactly?" Rand wanted to know.

"That this will be her last distraction. Although I'm not sure that, for Sunny, distraction is all that bad."

"Meaning?" Rand spoke patiently.

"Only that she's quite clever, and at some point she's going to see that all this running and searching is getting her nowhere. Someday she's going to see that Jesus Christ is the only person who can fill the void she's feeling. I don't know where or how or when, but I believe it with all my heart."

Rand stared at Chelsea for the space of a few heartbeats before he stood and held out his hand. Chelsea immediately rose and put her hand in his to be led through the adjoining door and into his bedroom. Rand still had not spoken when they climbed into bed and the darkness settled around them. Chelsea was nearly asleep when he spoke.

"I love you, Chels."

"Is that what you've been thinking of all this time?" she murmured sleepily.

"That and praying about what you said. I've finally decided that you're right. I'll take Sunny to Portsmouth myself. That will give us time to talk. Doug can bring her back in a few months.

"I will say this much, though—this will be the last time. She can visit anyone she likes for a week or two, but Willows' End is her home, and she's going to have to learn to be content right here."

Chelsea kissed Rand's jaw by way of agreement, and within minutes they were both asleep.

Sunny stood at the water's edge and remembered her brother's words to her some weeks ago: "You'll not find contentment by just running from one place to the next, not in Portsmouth or anywhere else, Sunny. You've got to make peace with who you are, and with God's Son."

Sunny had acted a bit cold to him for the remainder of the journey, but she now knew he had been right about finding contentment in Portsmouth. Not that she wasn't having a lovely time; she was, but something was missing.

She didn't see a lot of Doug, but Marian and the children were such fun. After getting to know her well, Sunny had quite simply fallen in love with little Grace. The boys were occupied with their school lessons most days, and Sunny had thought it wonderful that Grace actually knew less about stitching than she did. Sunny had to admit, however, that Grace was quickly approaching her level of skill.

Sunny heard her name on the wind and turned to see Marian approaching. The wind was somewhat cold, but both women loved the feel of it on their faces and hair. Sunny stayed where she was until her sister-in-law joined her.

"I know you love it out here, but we have a visitor."

"Who is it?" Sunny grinned at the sparkle in Marian's eyes.

"Aunt Lucy."

"Who is Aunt Lucy?"

Marian chuckled. "She's Brandon's grandfather's sister."

"The duke has a sister? I didn't know that. Why has no one ever spoken of her?"

"It's not because she's disliked; it's just that she hasn't been in England for five years, and she's simply dreadful when it comes to keeping in touch. We all have a tendency to forget she's alive."

"Where does she live?"

"Well, just now she has come from America, but before that she was several years in India."

Sunny's eyes had gone quite round, but she couldn't manage a reply. Marian tucked her arm into Sunny's and turned toward the house.

"I think you'll find she's quite a character, with a story for every day of the year." Marian paused a moment. "She says she's back in England to stay. She has purchased a home on the outskirts of London and is moving back because this is where she wants to be buried."

"What a horrid thing to say."

"Nevertheless, those were her words, and when you get to know her you'll find they're not all that unusual."

Before pushing her in the direction of the stairs, Marian laughed again at the look on Sunny's face and told her that she had only 15 minutes to get cleaned up for tea.

Lady Lucy Hawkesbury was indeed a character. In the first moments of meeting her, Sunny thought her something of a wonder, but in little time at all she noticed that her bright, dark eyes could be rather confused at times. Sunny had the impression that her mind was quite keen, but she really couldn't be bothered with the mundane details of life, such as keeping in touch with her brother or remembering that her spectacles were pinned to the lace bow that fell over her rather full bosom.

Aside from all of this, Sunny could see that she possessed a kind heart. Lucy loved Doug's children to distraction and was looking forward to seeing the rest of the family. She was thrilled when she learned that Doug would be returning Sunny to Willows' End the next week. Declaring in a no-nonsense voice that her own carriage would follow them, Lucy's smile beamed around the room as though the subject were settled.

"What if my house isn't ready?" the older woman wondered aloud, suddenly having second thoughts.

"Have you sent someone ahead to take care of it?" a very practical Harlan wanted to know.

"Well, I was going to, but somehow I think I forgot."

Sunny watched Marian's hand go to her mouth as she turned a laugh into a cough.

"Where is Tildy?" Lucy questioned.

"I'll find her for you," Lance offered.

"Who is Tildy?" Grace asked, but her question was never answered because Tildy, a woman who looked even older than her mistress, appeared in the door.

"Yes, my lady," she said with a kind reverence. Aunt Lucy blinked at her in some confusion.

"Your house in London," Marian prompted.

"Of course." Marian was gifted with the older woman's smile. "Tildy dear, have we done anything about the house in London? I mean, is it being prepared for our arrival?"

"Yes, my lady, but you had planned on visiting Bracken for a few weeks before moving in. You told your solicitor, Mr. Kent, that you wouldn't need it until the first of April."

"Oh, now I remember." The room watched as she suddenly went from relief to looking very unsure of herself.

"You're going home next week, aren't you, Sunny?"

"Yes, ma'am."

"I don't suppose my carriage could accompany yours?"

Sunny blinked in surprise. Why less then ten minutes ago, she had not asked Sunny but rather *told* her that she was going north with her. To Sunny's relief, Doug chose that moment to come in for tea, and the question was put to him.

He handled it with gentle aplomb, and in a few short moments the old girl had neatly maneuvered things to suit her. Sunny sat quietly and learned that she was to go home in two days' time, not the next week. She then watched in silence as Aunt Lucy remembered she had something for the children and ushered all of them out of the parlor and upstairs to her room.

The room was utterly quiet after her departure. Sunny sat staring at Lucy's vacant chair, but a muffled sound caught her attention. She looked to see that Marian had her hands over her face in an attempt to stifle her laughter. Doug and Sunny joined her, staring at each other in helpless surprise.

Sunny, when she thought about it, found she was not at all upset about going home, or even about having Lucy accompany them, but Lucy was far and away the most eccentric bundle of humanity she had encountered in her life.

Doug's words, spoken without malice before they were once again joined by the children, stayed with Sunny for the long ride home, as well as any time she occasioned to come into contact with Aunt Lucy.

"I dare say she's quite harmless, but I'll tell you, Aunt Lucy is a hen-wit if ever I've seen one."

Thirty-Four

THE CALENDAR READ MAY 3, 1846, when the *Flying Surprise* sailed up the Thames and into a London dock. Brandon had been off the shores of Morocco when he had felt such a need to return home that it nearly staggered him. Not a man given to flights of fancy, he tried to push the thought aside, but the feeling persisted. He started for London with a fraction of the ship's hold filled, his men thinking he'd taken leave of his senses. But Brandon had never felt this way in the past, and was not going to ignore the urging now.

After arriving and docking his ship, he headed straight for his town house, rousing his staff from their sleep to prepare his carriage. His staff was loyal to a fault, and in record time Brandon was bathed, fed, and headed out of London by 3:00 A.M. Two hours later the coach pulled into the courtyard in front of Bracken. The mansion was alight with candles, and Brandon, with a heavy heart, assumed he was too late. Parks met him at the door and put his fears to rest.

"You're in time, my lord," the trusted servant said softly. Brandon touched his shoulder by way of thanks and took the steps on swift, silent feet.

Brandon hesitated at the doorway of the duke's bedroom. His gaze quickly took in his mother, Dexter, Judith, Chelsea, and Rand before moving to the still form lying on the bed.

Andrea was the first of the group to spot him, and she rose and walked straight into his arms. The very sight of her oldest son was too much for her. So overcome with thankfulness that Brandon had made it in his grandfather's last hours, Andrea sobbed against his chest for long moments.

"I prayed, Brandon," she finally managed. "The doctor says he's probably headed into a coma now, but he's still with us, and I knew you would want—" She couldn't go on, but there was no need.

Keeping her hand within his own, Brandon approached the bed. He sat in the chair his mother had vacated and was vaguely aware of Rand sending the doctor, nurse, and servants from the room.

"I'm here, Papa," Brandon whispered. "I made it back to say goodbye." His voice broke on these words as he placed his hand into his grandfather's.

The old duke didn't stir, but it was enough for Brandon to touch his warm hand and see him again before he left this earthly life. Brandon continued to speak to him in low, loving tones, thanking him for the man that he had been, the spiritual leader, the kind Papa, the wise mentor.

Andrea and Chelsea wept as Brandon spoke, but their tears subsided when he finished his goodbye. The room was quite still when suddenly the duke's chest gave a great heave. Rand immediately went for the doctor, who waited in the hall, but after the briefest of checks, he informed the family that the duke was still with them.

He lingered for a better part of the morning, and only Brandon, Dexter, and Chelsea were with him when he quietly slipped into eternity.

The day of the old duke's funeral was hot and muggy. Still, over 300 mourners turned out for the service. There was no chance for the family to speak with each and every one, but the guests who crowded close were able to speak with the new duke and his family.

After what seemed to be hours the crowd began to thin. Brandon, beginning to feel his exhaustion, turned at one point to find Dinah Hadley standing hesitantly nearby. His fatigue suddenly fell away and he turned to her without hesitation, drawing close enough to see the tears standing in her eyes.

"Thank you for coming," Brandon sighed when he stood directly before her.

Dinah nodded. "I'm praying for you Brandon, for you and your entire family."

"Thank you," he said, feeling his words were grossly inadequate. He hadn't seen her since Dex's wedding, and her appearance here today, as well as her tears on his account, meant more to him than he could say. He wanted very much to reach for her hand, but knew it would be improper.

"I won't keep you," Dinah rescued him, her tears finally clearing and her heart showing in her beautiful eyes.

Brandon nodded, appreciating her thoughtfulness but reluctant to leave her. As he looked into her lovely face, he realized that she was the first person in three days who had taken his mind from his grandfather.

"May I call on you, Lady Dinah?" He asked softly, knowing that he couldn't just let her walk away.

"I would enjoy that, your Grace," she spoke sedately, but Brandon didn't miss the joyful smile that lit her eyes. Dinah turned then and moved toward the waiting carriages. Brandon watched her until he heard his sister calling his name. His heart was very full as he walked slowly back to his grandfather's graveside to stand with Chelsea and his mother.

"When I left on this last voyage, I wanted desperately to stay home," Brandon began. "In what seemed to be the blink of an eye, the sea lost its appeal for me."

Andrea shifted slightly to better see her son's face, but did not speak.

"I found myself daydreaming about how lovely it would be to stay home—in this home. And now, as ridiculous as this sounds, I feel like his death is my fault."

"Oh, Brandon, no."

"I know," he stopped her gently. "I know it was God's time, but the title has never meant more to me than Papa has, and I just wish he could still—" Brandon stopped as tears clogged his throat.

"Brandon," Rand said from his chair across the room, "don't forget that it was not only God's timing for your grandfather's death, it was also His perfect timing for you to inherit the title."

The younger man stared at him, and Rand went on.

"God knows very well that you are ready for this position. Your father died when you were very young. Dex was just a baby. Milton knew that you would be the next duke. As well as loving you to distraction, his every word and action when he was with you was to help prepare you for the title he knew would be yours someday."

"He's right, Brandon," Dex put in. "You're not as old as Father would have been, but there isn't one of us who doubts you're more than ready to take on the responsibilities of the Duke of Briscoe."

Part Three

The Duke of Briscoe

Thirty-Five

BRANDON LEANED BACK IN HIS DESK CHAIR and studied the document before him. Sunny was spending money like a drunken sailor. She'd always been very good about recording her purchases, and although Brandon was thankful she was being so honest, her spendthrift ways were becoming preposterous. Brandon gawked at one entry of a saddle that cost a hundred pounds.

"One hundred pounds," he whistled softly. "It must be lined with gold."

There was a knock at the door, and Brandon looked up as Parks, who had remained as head of the domestic staff at Bracken, slipped quietly into the room.

"Yes, Parks?"

"Will you be wanting a carriage for your appointment at Mowry, your Grace?"

"Yes, Parks. Thank you. Does my mother know I won't be here for tea?"

"I'll inform her myself, your lordship. I believe she plans to go home this evening."

"Tell her I'll be back before she leaves."

"Yes, my lord."

Brandon went back to his deskwork without another word. He opened a letter and saw that it was from Williams. The letter overflowed with praise for Brandon's generosity on his behalf. Williams had been with his grandfather from the time he had been a youth; in fact, Brandon thought the servant might have been older than his grandfather. He also knew it was long past time for him to be putting up his feet. Andrea had been sure that the suggestion of leaving Bracken would break the old servant's heart, but as Brandon had hoped, the man had been more than grateful.

"With all due respect, my lord," Williams had said, "Bracken is just not the same place without the old duke, and I—" He'd been unable to go on.

"I quite agree with you." Brandon rescued him and then continued, "Although I do hope to make this place feel like home again, I think it's time you had a home of your own."

As it was, Williams had a younger sister he had planned on living with someday. Brandon had not added to the inheritance his grandfather had lavished on this faithful servant, but had instead sent a swarm of workers to the home of Williams' sister with orders to paint and repair every crack and crevice.

Ironically the bills for the work arrived the same day as Williams' letter, and Brandon only shook his head at the small amount. It was little price to pay for the years of loving service he'd given this family. Brandon made a mental note to remember Williams and his sister with a huge hamper on Boxing Day.

Just an hour later, Brandon was in his carriage and headed in the direction of Mowry, the Hadley estate. It was a mid-July day, and rather pleasant. The sun shone brightly, but there was a nice breeze. Brandon thought he couldn't have picked a better day to see Dinah.

Dinah. Brandon finally allowed his mind to wander. He had been so busy in the last six weeks that he'd granted himself little time to think of her. Now he let his mind run to how lovely she was with her curly blonde hair and clear blue eyes. He wondered if he had ever encountered anyone gentler or sweeter. And she loved Christ.

Brandon's heart raised in prayerful thanksgiving for Dinah's faith. Two months ago he would have laughed at the idea of finding a Christian woman in his circle, but now he suddenly thought of how quietly the Hadleys lived and realized that if he hadn't seen her at the wedding, he would have never thought of her.

Lord L.C. Hadley, Dinah's father and fourth Earl of Mowry, was an older man, married for the second time—happily married, if the usual gossip could be trusted. Brandon's mind was drawn to Dinah again, and he wondered how young she had been when her mother died. He suddenly saw her as a small, hurting child, too young to understand where her mother had gone, and wondered at the sharp pain he felt around the region of his heart. He reminded himself that today she was a poised, lovely woman; someone must have had a kind, tender hand with her.

Brandon, riding with easy anticipation in his plush carriage, would have been surprised to learn that Dinah was not feeling the least bit poised at the moment. She scolded herself for acting like a giddy ten-year-old, but it did little good. She looked at her reflection for the fifth time, and then thought about changing her dress. It was a relief when someone knocked on her door and she was able to put her mind elsewhere.

"How are you?" Dinah's stepmother, Catherine, wanted to know.

Dinah was terribly relieved to see her and smiled gratefully at her appearance.

"You'd think he was coming to propose, the way I'm acting," Dinah admitted.

"As bad as all that?"

"Yes."

"Well, you look lovely."

"Thank you, Catherine."

The two women embraced, and Dinah thanked God, as she did so often, for this loving woman. Her stepmother was old enough to be her real mother, but she had always wanted Dinah to call her Catherine. There had never been a cross word between them.

Dinah shared the same loving relationship with her father, but he tended to be a mite forgetful. She found herself praying that he wouldn't look at Brandon with lowered brows because he'd forgotten the duke was coming to tea. Then she felt guilty for the thought—no girl could ask for a more loving father.

"You're worried about L.C., aren't you?" Catherine accurately interpreted the look.

Dinah gave a reluctant nod.

"You needn't be. I was just in his study, and he asked when the young man was due to arrive."

Dinah gave a great sigh, and Catherine chuckled. A moment later, a footman knocked and announced that Dinah's guest had indeed arrived.

Brandon let his gaze rest on Dinah's profile as she answered her father's question. She smiled lovingly at her elderly parent, and Brandon found himself warmed by the sight. When Dinah turned to find his eyes on her, she blushed but did not look away.

Catherine, observing the younger couple's fascination with each other, conveniently thought of a reason why both she and L.C. needed to leave the room. Her husband scowled at her, but this was the third time Brandon Hawkesbury had visited in nine days' time, and she was going to have her way on this one. Once outside the room, the earl turned to her with a frown.

"They shouldn't be in there alone."

"They won't be, at least not for very long, but I'm sure you've seen by now that Brandon's intentions toward Dinah are more than honorable."

Catherine, a good deal taller than her husband, suddenly leaned forward and kissed his balding head.

"Don't try your wheedling ways with me, Cat," he chided, his voice gruff.

Catherine's eyes became very wide. "But L.C.," she said, "they always work."

This brought a grudging smile to the old man's face, but before returning to his study he told his wife to keep an eye on that "young man."

"You look lovely today," Brandon uttered softly when the door shut.

"You said that last time you were here," Dinah teased.

"And the time before that," Brandon teased right back.

"Oh, now I know you're lying. I was terrified the first day you came."

"I know." Brandon chuckled. "I had come over here to talk with you, but you looked like you would leap from your skin if I said a word, so I had to content myself with just watching you. Not that I minded in the least," he added softly.

Dinah couldn't stop the blush that spread on her face, but unlike the first visit, she held his eyes lovingly with her own.

Brandon stood suddenly and moved toward a window. Dinah looked at his back in confusion.

"Brandon," she asked softly. "Is something wrong?"

"No," he replied with his back to her. "It's just that I—"

"What is it?" Dinah persisted when he hesitated.

Brandon turned from the window and held her eyes from across the room. "I know it's too soon to kiss you," he said softly.

Dinah's gaze, already tender with love, softened yet again. She stood and took a step toward him. Brandon, feeling like he had been granted his greatest wish, was moving to cover the distance between them when the door opened. A servant was bringing tea, and Catherine Hadley was just steps behind him.

Both Brandon and Dinah, from years of training, were able to cover the incident with ease, and no one seemed the wiser as tea was served. But even at that, there were occasional lulls in the conversation when Dinah would not hear her stepmother's question because her eyes were locked with those of the man she loved.

Thirty-Six

JORDAN'S HEART THUNDERED OVER SUNNY'S NEARNESS, but he worked at keeping his face an impassive mask. From where she stood directly in front of him, her head bent slightly, the faint fragrance of her hair intoxicated him. The desire to gently place his arms around her ran strong within him.

"There," Sunny stated with a triumphant smile and took a small step back. "That looks much better." She had been adjusting the neckline of his shirt and tie.

Jordan thanked her, his voice quiet with regret. Thankfully Sunny didn't notice. No other girl he knew would have stepped away from him so swiftly, but then there was no deceit in Sunny. She didn't feel romantic toward him, and she would never have flirted or pretended she did. Jordan was relieved to hear Holly calling them.

"We're all ready."

"Coming, Holly," Sunny called back, and tucked her hand in Jordan's arm. "I'm sorry you have to go back next week, but it's been a lovely summer, hasn't it?"

"Yes, it has." Jordan made a fast decision to not ruin these last days with sentimental dribble. "I'll miss you and your wild ideas."

Sunny laughed. "I'll miss you too, that is, until I get another wild idea, and then I'll enjoy the fact that you're not here to talk me out of it."

Jordan laughed with her as they rounded the house. The four of them—Sunny, Jordan, Miles, and Holly—were all headed to the

Cradwells'. Miles had some papers to deliver, and Sunny thought they should make an outing of it. Holly was in her trap, the picnic basket neatly stowed behind her, and everyone else was on horse-back. Because of Holly's buggy, they had a longer ride, so on the way home they would be stopping at the pond for lunch.

The young people made the journey in high spirits, and no one even noticed the warmth of the day. There was much laughter and talk, and before they knew it, they were riding into the stable area at the Cradwells'.

Both Miles and Jordan went directly to the house to see the elder Cradwell, but Jeremy Cradwell, a cocky youth of 18 years, was just coming out of the stable, so Holly and Sunny lingered. They had talked for just a few minutes when a beautiful white horse galloped through the paddock.

"Oh, my," Sunny exclaimed with admiration. "She's certainly a beauty."

Jeremy's chest swelled as though he himself had given birth to the fine animal.

"That she is," he said with pride. "You'll not find a faster animal in this part of the country. But then you wouldn't be used to seeing fine animals, not out of the Gallagher stables."

Holly felt Sunny stiffen beside her.

"You didn't really mean that, did you, Jeremy?" Holly asked hes-itantly. Her eyes begged Jeremy to take back his careless insult, but the young man didn't notice.

"Oh, I meant nothing personal in that," he went on expansively. "It's just that Rand is no horseman. His beasts are all right, I guess, but none are the caliber of Cradwell horses."

"Would you care to make a wager on that?" Sunny spoke with a calm that belied the feelings inside her.

"She didn't mean that," Holly cut in as she plucked at Sunny's arm and studied her calm features.

"I'm sure she didn't," Jeremy laughed. It was not a nice sound. "You'd think you were going to race me yourself, the way you talk." His smile had become patronizing, and Sunny's eyes narrowed into purple flints.

"And what were you thinking of riding?" Jeremy went on, his voice scoffing. "Certainly not London Lady. She's a nice mount, but she's no racer."

Jeremy turned then and really looked at Sunny, seeing for the first time that she was serious. She was watching him intently. Having been one of the many who had made advances toward her the first time he had seen her, only to be leveled by one of her looks, Jeremy didn't like her. The thought of putting her in her place did his heart a lot of good.

"So you'd like to race?" He was very serious now himself.

"Yes. Along the ridge in one hour's time."

"Why not now?"

"Because you're right; Lady is no racer."

"Done," Jeremy stated and held out his hand, not the least intimidated by any horse Sunny would bring from Willows' End.

Sunny shook his hand swiftly and moved into the stable. Within minutes she rode out again, this time at full speed, and headed for Willows' End, all to the accompaniment of Holly begging her to reconsider. When Sunny was out of earshot Holly turned her pleas to Jeremy, but he had already turned toward the stables, and she knew he wouldn't have listened in any case.

"Well, Hawk," his sister greeted him kindly. "We haven't seen you in a few weeks. How are you?"

Brandon kissed Chelsea's cheek and walked into the parlor with his arm around her shoulders.

"I'm well, and I was hoping to see Sunny. Is she around?"

"No, she's on an outing with Miles, Holly, and Jordan Townsend. I think they'll be back soon after lunch. Why don't you stay?"

"An excellent idea," Rand called from the doorway, taking in Brandon's serious look and the papers in his hand. "I've some things I need to discuss with you before you take my little sister apart piece by piece, as I suspect you're here to do."

All three adults laughed, and within minutes Rand and Brandon were closeted in the study.

Holly had barely been able to speak by the time Miles and Jordan had come from the house. Jeremy had already left, and it was some moments before she could make herself understood. Miles, thinking Jordan might have more pull where Sunny was concerned, asked him to ride ahead to the meeting place, so he could ride more slowly with his sister. As it was, all were there when Sunny came on the scene. Holly had to tell herself not to faint when she saw that her aunt was riding Jackson, her father's stallion.

"I don't want you to do this," Jordan finally cut in through clenched teeth after everything else he had said had fallen on deaf ears. Jackson sidestepped toward him suddenly, and he had to move away. At the same time, he knew he had been wasting his breath.

"I'll be fine," Sunny assured him smoothly, and they all watched as she scooped her hair up and stuffed it under the cap she had grabbed out of the stables.

Jackson danced to the side once again, and even though Miles was so angry he was seeing red, he had to admit that she handled the mount with ease. Even at that there was no way he would let Sunny leave without having his say. Knowing that to forbid her was the worst thing he could do, he directed his words to Jeremy.

"I'm holding you responsible, Jeremy." Miles' voice was low. "If Sunny gets hurt, I'll give you a thrashing you'll never forget."

Jeremy, who had more brawn than brains, only grinned. "It was her idea, Miles. I'm not forcing her."

Miles opened his mouth, but Sunny cut in.

"Well, let's get on with it. We'll race around the trees, onto the ridge, back along the pasture, around the other trees, and right back to this spot. First one back wins."

"And what exactly is the wager?" Jeremy wanted to know.

"If I win, you'll never again open your big mouth against Gallagher horses."

"And if I win?"

"I'll tell everyone that the Cradwells have the finest horses in the land."

"Done." Jeremy stuck his hand out and again they shook. Their three reluctant spectators refused to call the start, so Sunny let Jeremy do it. Within seconds they were off, leaving a cloud of dust behind them.

"What are you staring at?" Rand wanted to know, as Brandon stood at the study window that looked out over the ridge.

"Someone is racing along the ridge."

Rand joined him and spoke after a moment. "The white looks like it might be of the Cradwells' stables, and if it is, it's probably young Jeremy. He's got more nerve than sense."

"The other mount, the black, looks to be a fine piece of horse-flesh too. But whoever those riders are, they're foolish to be running along the ridge."

The men watched until the riders, moving neck and neck, were out of sight. Neither one had a clue as to who they were. Had they been able to view the horses for a few more yards, they would have seen one rider's cap fall, a cloud of chestnut hair flying out behind her.

"You don't have to come back with us, Jordan; my father is not going to blame you."

"I realize that, but I just wish I'd done more to stop it—dragged her off the horse or something. For that I feel I should be there."

Miles nodded, and both young men looked behind them. Sunny, triumphant and glowing after her victory, rode next to Holly's trap, chatting along as though she hadn't a care in the world.

As they all arrived at the house and trooped into the parlor, Sunny was a bit put out with her companions.

"You'd think someone had died the way you were acting," she commented just as they cleared the threshold of the room.

No one answered her, and Rand, Chelsea, and Brandon were glad to see them until they had a look at Sunny.

"Sunny." Chelsea was the first to comment, and did so with some concern. "What's happened to you?"

The younger girl was a mess. Her hair was in a riot around her face, and her riding habit was covered with dust. There was a smear of mud on her cheek, and sweat ran in a small trickle down her temple.

"I raced!" she answered Chelsea, her eyes sparkling with pleasure. "That idiot Cradwell said that nothing good ever came out of the Gallagher stables, so we had a wager."

Chelsea, who had done far worse in her day, and had not seen them on the ridge, leaned forward in her chair. She failed to notice that her brother was livid.

"Whom did you race? Jeremy?"

"Yes!"

"Did you win?"

"Chelsea!" Brandon's voice thundered in the room, and Chelsea settled back in her chair to circumspectly inspect her nails, as well as to work at not laughing.

A long-suffering look came over Sunny's face; Brandon clearly did not understand. "I had to uphold the honor of the Gallagher name. Jeremy said—"

"We saw you on the ridge," Rand put in quietly, looking and feeling quite pale now that he knew which horse he had seen and who had been riding it. "You were riding my horse without permission."

All amusement faded from Chelsea as she understood the severity of the circumstances. Barely holding himself in check, Brandon allowed Rand to handle the situation. After he had seen Sunny and realized who the rider of the black horse had been, Brandon's anger mingled with fear.

"You will not ride Lady or any other horse for a week, Sunny," Rand said quietly. "Now go and get cleaned up."

Sunny glared at her brother in fury. "You're only saying that because Brandon is here, and you know if you don't punish me, he'll have a proper fit. I was defending the Gallagher name, I tell you!"

"No name is worth your life," Rand continued with more calm than he felt. "And I dare say, if Brandon had his way, you'd lose riding privileges for a month and get a sound thrashing to boot."

Sunny's furious eyes swept the room until they rested momentarily on Brandon's own angry gaze. Her chin went into the air, and she left the room in a swirl of chestnut hair.

No one spoke for some minutes, but Miles turned to find Rand's eyes on him. The younger man's hands went into the air in a pleading move.

"Don't say it, Dad. You don't know Sunny at all if you think we could have stopped her. She was gone from the Cradwells' before we even came out of the house. I could have come for you, but it would have been over by the time we got back."

"Where was Hank Cradwell?" Brandon wanted to know.

Jordan spoke this time. "He's very much like his son; he would have thought it a good joke."

They quieted again, and everyone became aware of Holly's muffled sobs. "I tried to stop her," she cried, "but she wouldn't listen. I was so scared. All I could do was pray."

Rand sat down next to his daughter and put a loving arm around her. "You're not responsible for Sunny's actions, and she's all right, so don't cry anymore. I'm going to talk with her later and see if I can get through to her."

The young people went their separate ways then, and Rand gave his wife a loving, if not reproving, look, his hand reaching to stroke her cheek before he walked her to the door. She wanted to check on Sunny.

Brandon spent some time wondering how he would be able to talk with Sunny about her finances without mentioning the race.

Thirty-Seven

SUNNY SAT OPPOSITE RAND'S DESK and stared at the back of the paper in Brandon's hand. It was one of her expense sheets. Brandon had brought the last several months' reports with him, but he had asked for her new one, and now he was studying it and leaving her to sit.

"If you're going to take this long," she finally spoke impatiently, "I'll go and come back."

"Stay where you are, Sunny." The paper never moved, and the voice behind it was maddeningly calm.

Sunny, who had finally settled down after the incident in the parlor, began to boil all over again. She had really thought Brandon would be far too busy to spend time on her finances, but here he was, poring over her records as though he hadn't a care in the world.

Brandon needs a family of his own, Sunny concluded silently. *A wife and at least four kids, maybe six. Then he wouldn't have time to nose into my affairs. After all, the money is mine. What does he care what I spend? Yes indeed, marriage would be perfect. You need a wife, Brandon.*

The paper dipped slightly; Brandon's dark eyes met Sunny's over the top.

"Sunny?" Brandon's brows had lifted, and his voice was soft— too soft. Sunny realized she had uttered the last sentence aloud. "Would you mind repeating that?"

"I'd rather not."

The paper was laid on the desk. "I'd rather you did."

215

Sunny sighed and saw no hope for it. "I was just thinking that if you had a wife, you wouldn't have time to bother me about my money."

Brandon tried not to laugh at the comical look on her face. To Sunny's annoyance, he raised the paper again as though she hadn't spoken. With ill-concealed impatience, she shifted around in her chair and waited once again. She had decided to leave without permission when the paper lowered for the last time.

"What is this entry for riding boots? It must be an error. Twenty-three pounds? How many pair did you buy?"

"Just one," Sunny said with a shrug.

"I thought you were never going to marry?"

Sunny blinked at him in confusion. "I'm not."

"Well, the way you're going through money, you'll be broke in five years and in desperate need of a rich husband to support you."

It wasn't quite as bad as all that, but Brandon did not know how to get through to her.

"You're just saying that," Sunny accused, but her voice was uncertain.

Brandon stared at her young face, and when he spoke, his voice held all the love he felt for her. "You're right; I am. But your spending is rather excessive, and I'm worried about you."

Sunny's heart would have needed to be made of marble not to respond to the love his eyes displayed. She nodded reluctantly and gave him a small smile. He joined her on the far side of the desk then, and they looked over her spending together. He pointed out some areas where she needed to show a good deal more discretion, and when Sunny had questions, he answered them with just the right words to help her understand.

When the business was settled, Sunny thanked him graciously and they moved to the davenport to talk about the family and the London social season. It felt like old times.

Holly's "coming out" the following spring was the central topic, and Sunny was quite excited about all that would go on. Brandon allowed his head to fall against the back of the davenport, his long legs stretched before him as he spoke.

"It's hard to believe how old you and Holly are now. She's the first of the granddaughters to come out. It's at times like these when I really miss my grandfather." Brandon, his eyes on the ceiling, did not see Sunny's body stiffen.

"I can tell how much you must miss him." Her voice went cold without warning, and Brandon lifted his head and frowned in surprise at her. When he saw that she was about to rise, he put a hand on her arm.

"What did you mean by that, Sunny?"

Sunny pulled her arm free and stood. "In my country a man does not bury his grandfather one day and seek a wife the next." Sunny knew that wasn't the truth, but she was angry. She headed for the door, but Brandon was there first, reaching over her head to push the portal shut as she tried the handle. Without turning back to him, Sunny spoke.

"Move your hand; I wish to leave."

"We need to talk."

"No."

Brandon ignored this and began to speak. "I think you've been unfair, but you probably know that. I do not care to be told that I've feigned my mourning."

Sunny turned then, surprised at his words.

"I loved my grandfather, and I do not believe my seeing Dinah has blasphemed his memory. But then that's not what this is really about, is it, Sunny?"

She moved from the door then, her movements nearly panicked. "I don't care to discuss it." Brandon watched her go to the window. Had there been another exit in the room, she would have bolted. He stayed by the door and began to speak softly to her back.

"You can't understand how we can go on living a normal life after saying goodbye to a man we loved so well, can you? I miss my Papa, more than I can say, but I know where my grandfather is. I know I'll see him again someday."

"You can't know that." Sunny turned back to him, her eyes fierce, her hands clenched at her sides.

"Yes, Sunny, I can." Brandon's voice was so gentle that it brought tears to her eyes, but she would not break down. His heart melted at the sight of those tears.

"You fight, sweetheart. You fight against what we believe in with all of our hearts. You admired Papa, and I know you admire Rand and me and all of us, but you refuse to face why we're different; you refuse to face the Person who has made the difference."

"But I'm a good person too," Sunny interjected.

"Be that as it may," Brandon's voice was still tender, "your goodness counts for nothing outside of Jesus Christ. It won't save you from a lost eternity, separation from God, and having to live in torment forever."

Brandon could see he had upset her. She looked distraught.

"Sunny," he called her name softly. "Turn to Him now, Sunny, and He can help you through this pain and confusion."

He watched with a good deal of hurt as she gave a small shake of her head and composed herself once again. He couldn't help but think that if he felt pain, God must be in agony.

Oh, God, he prayed in his heart. *She won't let go of her pride. She needs You so much. Help me to keep loving her, and please, Father, break down the wall around her heart.*

When Sunny was back in control of herself, she once again approached the door where Brandon still stood.

"I'm sorry. What I said about you and Dinah was wrong. I've met Dinah Hadley, and she's a lovely person. If she's the one, Brandon, I hope you'll be very happy." She hugged him then, and Brandon's arms went gladly around her.

He was still hugging her when he spoke. "Promise you'll come to me, Sunny, if you need to talk about Grandfather."

Sunny looked up into his face. "I will, but I don't think I'm going to change my mind."

"If you're that confident," Brandon told her, "then it won't bother you if I tell you I'll be praying that you will indeed."

Sunny looked at those raised brows and determined eyes and smiled a little. She didn't know that Brandon caught the extreme uncertainty lingering in the lovely depths of her violet eyes.

Thirty-Eight

"Pardon me, your Grace."

"Yes, Parks?" Brandon looked up from the massive desk in his study.

"Your nephew is here and wishes to speak with you."

"Miles?" Brandon was surprised.

"Yes, sir. When he found you were working, he asked me not to disturb you, but he looks a bit upset and I thought—"

"Send him in," Brandon said easily and rose from the desk to greet him.

"If this isn't a good time, Uncle Brandon," Miles spoke by way of greeting, "I can come back."

"This is fine, Miles. Come, have a seat."

Miles sat in a plush chair by the fire but did not relax. Brandon sat opposite him and watched him for just a moment. He was so like Rand in appearance that it was uncanny, but today there was a look of near desperation about him; he looked younger than his 19 years. Brandon wondered if maybe he hadn't quarreled with his family.

It then occurred to him that Miles should be in school. Brandon was only seven years older than his nephew, but suddenly he felt much older and had to keep from asking Miles why, in early November, he was out of school.

"I suppose you're wondering why I'm here," Miles began.

"Well, I must admit to some curiosity."

"I've come to ask you a question, and I don't know how."

Brandon felt surprise at this. There had never been any hesitancy between them before, and he wasn't certain what to think.

"This might be easier if you were still at sea. I mean, I think it would. I don't want you to think I'm taking advantage of your title."

"You should know better than most, Miles, that the title is just that, a title. Outside of some added responsibilities, little has changed since I became the duke." Brandon's smile became rather wry. "I dare say any pull I might have had before I stopped sailing is still with me today."

Miles laughed a little and relaxed some.

"Let's have it, Miles," Brandon suddenly said, and saw that those were just the words the younger man needed to hear.

"I want to go to sea." All at once Miles' eyes were alight with excitement, and quite abruptly all hesitation fell away. "I've been doing some extra studying at school, studies on a nautical theme, and I want to go to sea; no, I *need* to go to sea. If I can't, I just don't know what I'll do. I don't want to sail my own ship, but over the next three or four years I want to sail with every craft on the water so I can someday build ships of my own."

If Brandon had had more warning of Miles's appearance, he might have dreamt up a number of reasons for the younger man's visit. But this would not have been one of them. That he'd thought through his idea was quite clear, but Brandon had to have an answer to the first question that came to mind.

"Do your parents know about this?"

Miles shook his head reluctantly and stared into the fire.

"Why, Miles? You've never been hesitant to go to them before. At least I'd never thought you were."

"Oh, Brandon," Miles rose and paced the room, talking to the floor at large. "This is so much bigger than anything I've ever wanted. I think I've been a good son, and I know my parents want whatever I want, but I can just see Mum's face when I tell her I want to go to sea—that I'll be gone for months or years at a time to who knows where."

Miles turned back to him, his heart in his fine brown eyes. "I was hoping that if you would agree to help me—I mean, help me find the right ship to start on—you would also go with me to break the idea to my parents.

"I've prayed about it for a long time, and I know I tend to underestimate God. He could be working in Mother's heart right now, somehow preparing her for what I'm going to say. I'm not afraid to go to them on my own, but I think my father has always assumed I'd help in the mills. I don't know what Mum thinks. I wouldn't be gone forever, but, well—"

Miles seemed to run out of words at that point and dropped back heavily into the chair. He stared pensively into the fire, so it took a few moments for him to see that his uncle was smiling at him. Miles blinked in surprise at the look.

"I think it's a great plan, Miles. And you're right about underestimating God; we all do. You've taken it a step further, however. You've underestimated the very people who want your happiness above all else." Brandon paused to let this sink in. "You don't have anything to fear from your parents, Miles. I can assure you of that."

"So you'll help me?"

"Of course. If your parents are dead set against this, I'll not come between you; but if you want to go to sea, I know several men who would welcome you to their crews."

Brandon laughed when Miles shot out of his chair with excitement. He looked 15 all over again as he nearly danced around the room in glee.

"So you'll come with me and tell them? Today?"

"Today?" Brandon looked comically overwhelmed. "What about school?"

"Oh, I'm all done," Miles spoke offhandedly, his mind distinctly on other things.

"Done?"

Intent on studying a ship in a bottle that sat on the mantel, Miles didn't hear him.

"Miles," Brandon's penetrating voice finally got through. "Come back on land and explain to me why you're not in school."

"Oh," Miles turned to him. "My teachers knew I wanted to finish early, so I've worked extra hard and already taken my examination. Even if my parents say no, there is no reason to go back to school."

Brandon was very impressed. He'd never thought of Miles as lazy, but this was a drive that Brandon had not witnessed before.

"So you'll come with me?"

"Yes," Brandon answered without hesitation. He pulled a watch from his pocket and studied it. "Let's have some lunch and then we'll leave for Willows' End."

"Great," Miles said, his voice breathless with excitement. "Thanks, Brandon."

"You're welcome, Miles. You know I'll do all I can."

With the closing of 1846, Sunny's birthday and the holidays passed as they never had before. As the family gathered, no one could help but look around and know that it would never be quite the same again.

Much to the family's delight, Brandon had spoken to Dinah's father, and the anticipation of her presence as Brandon's wife for Christmas the following year was a deep joy. On the other hand, the fact that Miles was headed to sea just after the first of the year put a slight damper on the spirits of all concerned. They realized he might not be home for Christmas for years to come.

Miles was sensitive to everyone's feelings, but his excitement over leaving could not be masked. His parents had given their full support to the endeavor, and although he knew there was great work ahead for him, at the moment he was stepping on a cloud.

Mid-January came much too swiftly, and when the seventeenth arrived, Chelsea opted to stay at their London house, Heather at her side, rather than say goodbye to Miles at the ship. Rand, Jordan, Sunny, Holly, Foster, and the twins all saw Miles to the docks and stood as a group when the *Gypsy* pulled from the berth. The young people all agreed that they would miss him, but as the ship sailed away they also thought it a most wonderful adventure. Only Jordan noticed how quiet Rand was on the ride back to the house.

That night, Chelsea broke down. She had waited until she and Rand were in their room for the night. Rand sat by Chelsea's prone form on the bed, his arms around her, feeling very helpless as his wife cried.

They had both met the captain of the ship and believed him to be an honorable man, but suddenly they asked themselves where the years had gone. Their firstborn was 19 years old and headed into a life of which they had no part. They were excited for their son, but that didn't stop the pain of separation, and for this reason Chelsea sobbed.

When her tears were spent Rand and Chelsea spent the next hour praying for their son and reading Scripture about God's tender care. Rand read from Psalm 91, verses 2, 3, and 4, where the Scripture spoke of how trustworthy God is: "I will say of the Lord, he is my refuge and my fortress, my God; in him will I trust. Surely he shall deliver thee from the snare of the fowler, and from the noisome pestilence. He shall cover thee with his feathers, and under his wings shalt thou trust; his truth shall be thy shield and buckler."

Greatly comforted by the words, Chelsea entrusted Miles to God's care each and every time she felt her worry coming on. Surprisingly they had a good night's sleep, and they returned to Willows' End in the morning.

Heather had been thrilled to see them and in fact wished they could have stayed longer in town, but any loneliness she might have felt was alleviated by the appearance of Dinah Hadley. Dinah needed to begin work on her trousseau, and she arrived with Brandon and her stepmother just two days later.

Brandon stayed for supper and had a delightful evening. The twins were allowed to stay up and entertain the adults with their latest piece on the piano. The evening passed much too quickly for the engaged couple, and it was with a heavy heart that Dinah walked Brandon to the door.

"It was a lovely evening, wasn't it, Brandon?"

"Lovely," he whispered never taking his eyes off her face.

Dinah smiled and Brandon pulled her into a small alcove off the entryway and into his arms. When Dinah could speak again, she laughed with tenderness.

"So my kisses make you laugh." Brandon tried to sound indignant, but could only manage contentment.

"No. I was just thinking of what Heather said Sunny's latest plans were."

To Dinah's surprise, she felt Brandon's arms stiffen.

"You're upset," she stated quietly.

"Yes, I am. She just turned 16, a time when most young women should be settling down a bit, but she's still running from one escapade to the next."

"But Brandon," Dinah's voice was kind. "Teaching some of the village children to read is a wonderful idea."

"I guess it is," Brandon replied, relaxing some, "but as I said, I wish she wasn't so frantic to always keep busy."

"I think you worry too much," Dinah remarked amiably.

Brandon looked down into her face and wondered how he could be worrying about Sunny when he was holding his future wife in his arms. He kissed her then until they were both breathless, and it was with great regret that they parted. The promise of seeing each other in the morning, and the way Brandon whispered his love for Dinah as he left, made the wait a sufferable chore for both of them.

≈ *Thirty-Nine* ≈

RAND STEELED HIMSELF for the next event. He didn't know when or where it would happen, but the very way his sister walked and moved told him she was cooking up yet another scheme.

Surprisingly enough, the incident with the horse race had made them closer than ever. Rand had waited until Brandon was gone and all was quiet that evening. He'd gone to Sunny's room, and even though she was already in bed, they had talked for the better part of two hours.

It had taken some time for her to see that the very fact she had ridden Jackson without permission needed to be dealt with. Sunny was under the impression that since she wasn't hurt and the horse wasn't injured, and she had won the race to boot, all was just fine. The fact that rules had been broken and an unnecessary risk had been taken did not seem to matter to her.

Rand did not leave the room until they did matter. He explained in a logical voice why she was wrong, and after much talk and some genuine soul-searching, Sunny had admitted she'd been out of line. Rand hated to do it, but he had even increased her punishment. In the week that she was restricted from riding, she was to sit with the dictionary for two hours each day and find words that pertained to obedience.

Other than the word "obey," Sunny discovered such related terms as "compliance," "submit," "yield," "duty," "respect," and "loyalty." After finding the words, she was to write out a detailed

225

definition and even use the word in a sentence. At the end of the week, Rand asked her for the list. At the bottom he wrote one word and handed it back to her.

"Why did you write the word 'love' on my list, Rand?" Sunny had wanted to know.

Rand chose his words carefully. "I believe love is the only motivation that's going to prompt you to follow our rules. It is my hope that your love for Chelsea and me will prod you into making the correct choice, even when you don't want to. You know we'll love you no matter what, but we hope that in return your love for us will be evident in the way you honor us with your obedience."

Rand found that his words did just the trick. Sunny's eyes misted over, and she gave him a fierce hug. "I'm sorry, Rand," she whispered in his ear, and this time it was more heartfelt than ever before.

Months had passed since that time. Miles was gone, and his absence was painful. For a few weeks Sunny had worked almost every day to teach a handful of village children how to read. Holly was all aflutter about her coming out, and in the midst of this, with the weather very cold, Rand waited with trepidation.

"Has Sunny said anything to you about any new schemes?"

Chelsea chuckled. "No, Rand. You ask me that every night, and it's always no. I can't understand why you're worried. She always comes to us now, and when you stop and think about it, it's never been anything too outrageous."

Rand punched his pillow into a more comfortable position and stayed quiet. He was nowhere near as optimistic as his spouse. Sunny was not depressed as she had been in the past winters, but Rand was sure that was only because she was dreaming of a new plan to drive him into an early grave. He prayed himself to sleep, but felt very faithless. It was too much to hope that they might make spring without Sunny falling into more trouble.

"Jordan!" Sunny cried his name and ran to greet him on this unexpected visit. "Why are you home?"

"Oh, I had some business that needed my attention, so I thought I'd take time to drop in."

Jordan was finished with school; however, his father had an estate some three hours away and preferred for him to live there to manage it. Jordan did not mention to Sunny that he had come home to ask his father one more time if he could live at home. All his dreams about how close he would be to Sunny when he finished school went up in a puff of smoke when his father told Jordan where he needed to work.

He had always tried to honor his parents, but this time Jordan had been sorely tempted to leave home, propose to Sunny, and disappear with her to the far ends of the earth. Instead, he prayed and waited. He also worked hard, and even though he missed Sunny so much it hurt, he stayed on and did a fine job. In fact, his father was so pleased that when they had talked, he had given him some hope. It seemed that Jordan would be needed at home all that summer, and when the fall came they would reevaluate the situation.

"So how long are you here?"

"Just until Monday, but I'll be working here all summer."

"That's wonderful!"

"What's wonderful?" Holly wanted to know as she went to hug Jordan.

"Jordan will be home this summer."

"Now we only need Miles," Holly sighed, accepting the tea Sunny passed to her.

Chelsea joined the young people, and when they were just finishing, Jordan remembered a favor he wished to ask of Holly. Holly was more than compliant and rose to go and find the book he was looking for.

"Good old Holly," Jordan commented as she was leaving. "She's always a pal."

Holly didn't turn on these words, but Sunny was seated in such a way that she could see her niece's face as she left the room. What she saw so alarmed her that for a moment Sunny could not school her features.

"Why, Sunny," Chelsea commented when she spotted her distressed look. "Whatever is the matter?"

Sunny gave a small laugh and tried to sound normal. "Oh, nothing really. Maybe the sandwich didn't agree with me."

Sunny's hand trembled as she reached to smooth her hair, but no one noticed and, thankfully, Holly's departure had caused her to miss the entire exchange.

Jordan stayed for another hour, and during that time Holly behaved so normally that Sunny began to wonder if she had imagined the whole thing. By bedtime, Sunny had convinced herself of this very fact, but sleep would not come. She tossed and turned for what felt like hours before finally leaving her bed and going down the hall to Holly's door.

There was no answer to her knock, and Sunny was certain that Holly was asleep. She was about to go in anyway when a voice startled her from the rear.

"Now what are you up to at this time of the night?"

"Oh, Boots dear," Sunny said with a hand to her pounding chest. "I need to talk with Holly."

"Why, love," she spoke affectionately, "I'm sure she's asleep, just as you ought to be."

"But I've got to talk with her."

"Would you like me to get your brother? If you're upset, you know you can go to him."

"No," Sunny was adamant. "It's Holly I must see."

Mrs. Boots could see no help for it, so she opened the door and crossed silently into the room. The noise they had made in the hallway, however slight, was enough to awaken Holly. Upon seeing this, Mrs. Boots turned back to Sunny.

"Well, we've certainly woken her, but you are not to be in here long. You'll not be able to stand up in the morning after this little midnight jaunt. I'll be back shortly to check on you." With that she made her way quietly to the door and then to the downstairs study to tell Lord Randolph that the girls were awake.

"What's the matter, Sunny?" Understandably, Holly was looking for answers. She'd been awakened from a deep sleep only to sit and listen to Mrs. Boots as she said the most cryptic things to Sunny.

"I need to talk with you, Holly. Can I light the lantern?"

By way of answer Sunny heard Holly removing the chimney. Within moments the bed was bathed in a soft glow. Holly pushed herself up against the head, and Sunny sat on the edge. Sunny's mind raced with how to begin. She studied Holly and wondered if there was anyone in the world who was half as lovely. She knew of no one else who had hair as dark as a crow's wing, or whose complexion was like that of a rose petal. Her eyes were dark and expressive, and her figure was lovely and full.

Sunny thought Holly must be every man's ideal, but as much as Sunny wanted to tell her, the words would not come. Instead she suddenly blurted out the only question that had been on her mind.

"You're in love with him, aren't you?"

Holly saw how easy it would be to pretend, but instead her whole body slumped in defeat. Sunny would hate her now.

"Yes, I am, and I'm sorry."

"You're sorry? Why would *you* be sorry? I'm sorry I never knew. I'm sorry that I'm always taking all his time and controlling the conversation."

"You don't hate me, Sunny?" Holly's voice was filled with wonder.

"Why would I hate you?"

"Sunny," Holly became very still. "Aren't you in love with Jordan?"

"Of course I love Jordan, just like I love Miles. Holly, you know I'm not going to be married."

Holly burst into tears. Sunny came closer and put her arms around her, which caused Holly to sob all the harder. Her voice shook when she spoke, but Sunny caught every word.

"All this time I thought you loved him. I thought you were just waiting until you were older to say anything. I've hated myself for caring so much, but I've loved Jordan for years, and he just thinks of me as a little sister.

"I know he'll marry someday, and I'll have to go away because I won't be able to stand seeing him with someone else. Until tonight," Holly added as she'd begun to calm, "I thought that someone else would be you. Please don't tell him, Sunny, please. I'll do anything, but please don't tell him."

"I won't; I won't," Sunny assured her, "but you could, Holly. You could talk with him. Maybe he loves you too, and if you were to tell him, he would feel like he could declare his own love."

Holly studied Sunny's face in the lamplight and could have cried all over again.

She's serious, Holly thought to herself. *She really doesn't know. We're all such grand pretenders. I'm eating my heart out over Jordan, and he practically worships Sunny with his gaze. She can't even see it's there.*

"I don't think that would work," Holly said slowly. "But that's all right, just as long as you're not upset with me."

"Of course not. I just can't believe how blind and insensitive I've been."

The girls talked until all was well between them. They were sleepy, but closer than ever when at last they went to bed. Mrs. Boots came to check on them some minutes later, this time with Rand on her heels, only to find both girls in Holly's bed, heads nearly touching and fast asleep.

Forty

THE DUKE AND HIS FUTURE DUCHESS RODE THEIR HORSES at a leisurely pace and talked about their life together. So eager was he to be married to the woman he loved and have her settled at Bracken that Brandon was beginning to count the weeks.

The park in London where they rode was not nearly as private as they would have liked, but in any other place they would have to be chaperoned. That morning Dinah had finally selected the style and fabric for her gown, and even though Brandon could see she was dying to tell him, she had kept silent. He was now in the midst of teasing her, but still she wouldn't say.

"Let me guess. It's covered with tiny pearls and has a very long train."

"Do you wish my dress was covered with little pearls, Brandon?" Dinah's voice was very unsure, and Brandon shouted with laughter. Her very look and voice told him exactly how her dress did *not* look.

"You're terrible, Brandon," she said as she caught onto his game. "It's supposed to be a surprise."

"You mean bad luck and all that?"

"You know I don't believe in luck, but it is tradition for the groom to be surprised."

"Is it also tradition to be married on your late mother's birthday?"

"Oh, Brandon, I know," Dinah's voice was a sigh. "When father suggested it, it sounded so thoughtful and tender, but I didn't think about the fact that it would be months away."

"I'm sorry I mentioned it." Brandon's tender smile accompanied his apology.

They had already talked it out, and he shouldn't have brought it up again. In any event, it was just three months away now, 86 days to be exact, and then the business of chaperons and separate homes would all be a thing of the past.

Chelsea knew that her face was going to give her away in a moment. She had spent so much time telling Rand not to worry, and now Sunny had finally confided in her. Rand was going to explode when he found out, or worse yet, grow very, very quiet.

Chelsea shrugged. There was no help for it at this point, so she might as well get it over with. She took a deep breath, hoping he would be too busy to talk with her, and entered Rand's study.

His "hello, love" was not what she wanted to hear at the moment.

"Are you busy, Rand?"

"Come in."

Just as Chelsea had feared, Rand immediately read something in her face. He watched in silence as she took the chair opposite his desk and tried to smile. Rand smiled back in genuine amusement.

"You might as well give all, love, because I know something is amiss."

Chelsea's smile dropped, and her shoulders slumped. "Oh, Randolph, you must try to stay calm."

"Randolph, eh? As bad as all that?"

"Yes, and Sunny is already asleep, so you mustn't wake her."

Rand's frame tensed. "What has she done?"

"She wants a job at the mill."

"The mill? One of our mills?"

"Yes," Chelsea said softly.

"Well, it's out of the question." Rand's voice held a note of finality.

"It's already done."

"*What?*" Rand came out of his chair so fast he nearly tipped it over.

"She disguised herself, dressed in near rags, and pulled her hair back. She went to the big mill under a false name, and Johnson gave her work. I knew she was going to the village, but I didn't see her when she left; she only told me about it when she got home."

Praying and trying to stay calm, Rand sat down very slowly. "Did she give a reason for wanting to do this?"

"Yes. She said she'd never really shown much interest in your work with all the sheep and the mills, and she wanted to know how it was for the workers. She was too tired to eat, and I didn't get suspicious until Mrs. Boots said she had taken a bath and gone to bed. When I asked Sunny, she told me everything."

"Well at least she's got it out of her system."

"She hasn't. She plans on returning in the morning. The workers could not say enough about you, and she rather enjoyed the work on the looms even though it was long and backbreaking. She wants to finish out the week."

"Do you know what will happen if she's discovered? I'll have a walkout on my hands. They'll think she's there to spy. Chelsea, I've got to stop her."

"Well, I think you can, but you'll have to talk with her in the morning. I just checked on her, and she's out cold. She's probably never worked a day so hard in all her life."

Rand stared in amazement at his sister. Had he not known it was her, he would never have guessed. Like so many worn at the mill, her dress was shapeless and nondescript. Only a small section of her hair showed at the front of her scarf, and even her face looked darker and rougher. When Rand drew near, she squinted, effectively masking the shade of her eyes. Not until she grinned at him did his shock fall away. She had blackened one front tooth.

Rand turned away from her to hide a smile and to think. He'd wanted to talk with her before she dressed, but she begged him to wait. He'd called through the door that she was not to get dressed for the mill because the plans were off, but she had only put him off. Now, an hour later, he could actually see how she'd gotten away with it the day before.

Rand turned back, and his eyes traveled to her shoddy gloves and old scuffed boots. He was afraid to ask where she'd gotten everything.

"Please, Rand," Sunny spoke into his silence. "I was hoping to go all week, but please just let me go this one last day."

"When is this going to stop, Sunny?" The question came softly. "I feel as though I've encouraged you to keep running and searching when I know I have the answer for you."

Sunny looked away, not wanting to face the meaning of his words.

"Do you understand the problems I would face if you were discovered?"

"I won't be, and what if I told you this would be the last escapade?"

"I think you've said that before."

Sunny thought she might have too, so she fell quiet.

"All right," Rand said after a moment. "You can go, but I'll be around today, all day. And I'll hear no more of this Sunny, ever. You are to stay away from the mills from now on. We won't speak of this or mention it to anyone. I'll sit down with Johnson tomorrow and try to explain why you're not coming back."

Sunny threw her arms around Rand. He hugged her back, but his heart wasn't in it. When was it going to stop?

Thirteen hours later, in order to protect her disguise, Sunny walked back home from her day at the mill. Satisfied she had worked hard, Sunny found herself mentally thanking Rand for saying she could not return. How did they do it? How did the women from the village work those looms day in and day out?

Sunny's thoughts caused her attention to wander, and without warning, her foot caught in a hole and she fell. She wasn't hurt really, just too weary to rise. It was growing quite dark and the temptation to lie there and go to sleep was almost more than she could take.

She did fight the feeling, however, and just as she stumbled to her feet, a rider came down the road, headed away from Willows' End. He pulled alongside her and dismounted before she could move on. Even in the darkening gloom she recognized Brandon.

"Are you all right, miss?"

"I thought you were in London." Sunny spoke without thought and immediately knew her mistake. She took a step back and turned to run, but Brandon's hand captured her wrist. Sunny struggled, but it was like fighting against a padded manacle.

"What are you doing dressed like this?" Brandon's voice was furious.

"Let me go."

"Does Rand know where you are?"

"Yes! Now let me go." She tugged harder, but Brandon was not about to release her. He was still trying to puzzle together why she was out here when Rand's carriage came up the road.

Understanding the scene in a moment as he alighted from the carriage, Rand spoke softly.

"You can let her go, Hawk."

Brandon was swift to comply.

"Get in the carriage, Sunny."

Brandon waited until she'd taken a few steps toward the rig before turning back to the older man. "So you did know about this?"

"Yes, she worked at the mill, but now it's all over. She assured me no one would recognize her, and they didn't. We're not speaking of it to anyone else, and I've told her there will be no repeat performance."

Brandon had a few more questions, and Rand found himself telling him most of the story. The younger man left as soon as Rand was finished, and Rand could see that he had been dissatisfied. Rand hoped that he had handled it well and that Brandon would be accepting of something over which he had no control. He also wondered if maybe he should take over Sunny's finances himself. Perhaps it was too much of a burden for Brandon. Rand knew he had made mistakes as a parent, but he also knew that Brandon could be much too hard on Sunny.

"What could he be thinking?" Brandon stormed at his mother and his fiancée that evening. Hours had passed, and he was still upset.

"You should have seen her. Anything could have happened."

"I'm sure Rand was aware of the possible dangers, Brandon." His mother's voice was calm. "You did say his coach was right behind her, and he is an experienced parent. I think he's handled Sunny very well." Andrea could see that her son wasn't listening, and she fell silent. She had never seen him like this and wasn't quite sure what to think. Her gaze flicked to Dinah, and Andrea was concerned over the look she saw on her face.

Andrea didn't know that Dinah *had* seen Brandon like this before. She had seen it nearly every time Sunny's name was mentioned.

Forty-One

HOLLY SAT BY SUNNY'S BED, staring at her flushed face and listening to her slightly labored breathing. Feeling totally responsible for her illness, Rand had sat by the bed continuously, until he'd fallen into exhausted sleep in his chair. Chelsea had urged him to bed, and Holly had taken his place. She had been motionless since early that morning, silently praying for Sunny.

Sunny had contracted a cold at the mill that had worsened as each day passed. By the week's end, her chest heaved for air, and her body burned with fever. The doctor was summoned at once, and his prompt diagnosis had been pneumonia. It had peaked a few days ago, and the doctor said the worst had passed, but Sunny was still very weak, sleeping 18 of each 24 hours, and not able to sit up or feed herself.

Holly thought she looked like a pale skeleton, and fresh tears sprang to her eyes when she remembered how frightened she had been that Sunny might be slipping into eternity before her very eyes. Holly had begged God to spare Sunny and to give her a chance to speak with Sunny about Christ.

It had taken this painful time for Holly to see that she had been very timid where Sunny and Christ were concerned. She knew that her parents had talked to Sunny about God's Son, and Sunny always listened when her father read from his Bible, but Holly knew well that she had been remiss in her own efforts and prayers to introduce Sunny to the Savior.

Now Holly's reserve was at an end. God had indeed spared Sunny, and when her aunt was once again in full health, Holly would no longer be silent about her Lord. She knew that most people thought her mind was filled with little except piano lessons and the latest fashions, but she knew exactly from whom her salvation came, and worked daily to trust the God who saved her. She knew she wasn't perfect, but she also knew she wasn't frantic, as her aunt seemed to be much of the time.

"How is she?"

Chelsea had come in quietly and gently slipped her arm around her weary daughter. Each had taken her turn at Sunny's bedside, but Rand and Holly were by far the more emotionally upset over her illness.

Mother and daughter exchanged a few words in which Chelsea convinced Holly to eat and get some rest. The older woman saw her daughter to the door and then took up her chair, praying as she did that the lively Sunny they loved so well would soon return to their lives.

Ten days later, Sunny sat on the edge of the bed, knowing she was not supposed to be up at all. The day before, she had finally talked Mrs. Boots into allowing her a bath. She would have liked another long soak today, but she knew she would have to be content with a covert walk around the room while everyone thought she was napping.

She had been at the window, enjoying the sunny view of the outdoors, when the door opened and closed quietly. Since she did not want to appear as guilty as she was, Sunny did not turn from the window. She stood waiting to hear Mrs. Boots scold her or Holly ask whether she wanted to listen to her read.

Her ploy worked. Thinking he would find her asleep, Brandon thought Sunny looked quite healthy. Her robe settled nicely around her, and her hair fell to her waist in dark waves.

"I'd been led to believe that you were still sick in bed; it's good to see you up and around." His voice was light and friendly, and Sunny felt a mix of emotions: She was delighted to see him, but not pleased that he should see her in such a weakened condition.

She had already begun to tremble a little from her exertion, but managed to turn with some grace and smile at him. Brandon smiled in return and started toward her. The smile, however, abruptly died as he crossed the large expanse of room and saw just how pale and thin she had become. He also swiftly took in the fact that she was balancing herself with a hand to the wall.

"Sunny," Brandon's voice was full of concern. "Are you supposed to be out of bed?"

"No," she admitted, looking much younger than he'd ever seen her.

"Can you make it back?" Brandon wasn't sure why he asked. In the past he would have kept silent and taken her back.

"Of course." She decided not to tell him how weak she was really feeling. "Why don't you give me a minute and then come back in? I'll get settled back on the bed, and we can visit then."

Tempted to argue since she looked quite frail, Brandon kept still for a moment and then turned to leave. Long before he reached the door, however, he turned back to check on her once again.

Sunny, who had closed her eyes the moment Brandon turned away, knew that any moment now her legs were going to give way. She was surprised that they had held her as long as they had. With all that was in her, she fought to stay upright, but there was now a rushing sound in her head, and she groped for the wall with her other hand.

"Brandon," she called weakly, suddenly hoping that he was still in the room. "Please—"

He was immediately there, his arms around her. She was lifted carefully and borne easily to the bed. Brandon's stomach clenched at how gaunt she looked and light she felt. He knew that after such an illness, even her skin would be tender, so with the greatest of attention he placed her on the bed. When the bed covers were tucked gently around her, Brandon moved a chair close, sat down, and leaned near to her face.

"I wanted to see out the window," Sunny admitted softly. "Now I'm so tired, I don't care."

"You could have asked someone for help."

Sunny's head moved restlessly on the pillow. "They all would have said no and scolded me about wanting to be up. I'm so weary of this bed." Her eyes closed with these words, and Brandon smiled gently into her sleeping face, a smile that changed to a frown of concern over the way she had tried to send him away.

"You're as proud as the day I met you," he whispered. "Will you ever let go of that pride, Sunny?"

Sunny's slumber did not allow her to hear his question, but then Brandon remembered that Sunny had called to him.

Maybe there is hope. This time Brandon spoke in his heart to the Lord. *Maybe she is starting to see her need for help.*

Brandon stayed for another ten minutes, praying for Sunny's physical well-being. He also confessed his own sin of pushing her away in the past, of making her feel that she must meet his standard in order to be loved by him.

The sudden image of her on the road in a peasant dress kindled anew his anger with her and her endless restlessness. Brandon found himself having to stay where he was, continuing his talk with the Lord until finally he had confessed all his anger and sin and totally surrendered Sunny to God.

"My, but that's a serious look," Sunny commented to her niece as she joined her under the trees that lined the courtyard at Willows' End.

It was a beautiful June day, and Sunny was completely back on her feet. She slept longer than before the illness, but her color was back, and she had nicely filled out again to look like her old self.

She and Holly had become closer than ever during her recovery, but Holly had never once talked to Sunny about what was burdening her heart. Today was the day.

"I do feel serious today, Sunny, and I hope you'll hear me out."

The younger girl looked rather taken aback, but stayed silent. Holly settled herself down before Sunny and opened a book. Sunny instantly saw it was Holly's Bible.

"I was really frightened when you were sick," Holly began softly. "You were so pale and weak, and I was scared when I watched you struggle for breath. I was afraid you would die, and when I felt like that I prayed. I asked God to spare you because I realized something awful—I'd never talked to you about my Lord."

Sunny shifted uncomfortably, not sure she liked the direction of this conversation. "You believe like your folks do, right?" Sunny said this hoping that Holly would simply agree and drop the whole discussion.

"Yes, but I don't base my belief on my parents' convictions; I base it on the Bible." Holly lifted the book and read. "This is from 1 John 2, verses 1 and 2. 'My little children, these things write I unto you, that ye sin not. And if any man sin, we have an advocate with the Father, Jesus Christ the righteous. And he is the propitiation for our sins, and not for our sins only, but also for the sins of the whole world.'

"I've heard you tell Mummy that Jesus Christ isn't God, but it says here that He's righteous, and I know He couldn't be righteous, utterly sinless, unless He is God." Holly became a little excited, and anything Sunny might have said was put aside in the light of a rather adamant Holly.

"He died to save us, a horrid death on the cross," she went on passionately. "And your unbelief is like a slap in the face to Him. You run all over trying to hide from what you know must be true but are too full of pride to accept."

Holly was really worked up now, and Sunny was hurt by her words. Still, she said nothing.

"I know people think I'm featherheaded, but I've got a peace and contentment that you can't even grasp. Now this last time—you snuck off to the mill and came home so tired that your body couldn't even fight the cold you caught. *You almost died, Sunny,*" Holly nearly shouted at her. "And then where would you have been? I'll tell you where—in hell—separated from God forever!"

Holly's chest heaved for a moment, and she continued a bit more softly. "I didn't think it was possible for a person to care like I do about you. I love my parents, but you're so dear to me, Sunny, that I can't even express it. I know that you think we go into our graves and sleep for all time, but you're wrong. When we die we must face God as our Savior or our Judge."

"And what if you're wrong?" Sunny interrupted, her voice subdued.

"Then I have nothing to lose. I'll just sleep forever in my grave," Holly spoke calmly, prepared for the question. "On the other hand, if I'm right, and I believe I am, you've got everything to lose."

The two stared at each other for long minutes, and then Sunny watched as Holly's eyes filled with tears. "Have you really heard anything I've said to you, Sunny? Have you heard anything *anyone* has said to you since you came to England? Or are you going to be off on another flight-of-fancy in the next few weeks? Chasing after some dream that can't bring you lasting joy or fulfillment because the only One who can do that is God's Son."

If Holly hoped Sunny would repent of her sins on the spot, she was to be disappointed. Holly went on to tell Sunny that she would love her no matter what, but that in the future she was not going to be timid about her faith. If Sunny wanted to talk, she would know that Holly was there.

Sunny thanked her for explaining and made her way to the house and then to her room, where she sat in a chair, deep in thought, for nearly an hour. After supper she returned to her room as soon as she ate. Again she sat, and would have continued to do so, but Mrs. Boots and Christie came along, clucking over her not being ready for bed.

Staying quiet because she saw that her mistress was preoccupied, Christie brushed Sunny's hair out. Christie left her sitting in a chair once again, the bedside lantern turned high. Not until the door closed did Sunny show any sign of life.

Taking the lantern with her, she rose and went to her dresser. In the top drawer were her treasures: the box from the emir; the rope star Kyle had given her on the ship, three years ago already; letters from Miles, Brandon, and Heather; and on the bottom, the Bible Rand had given her for her birthday last year. She lifted it out, and in doing so, her eyes landed once more on the jewel box.

"If Holly is right, then we're all lost, Indira and Rashad—all of us." Sunny stood in the dim room and looked up. She knew that Rand, Chelsea, and all the family bowed their heads when they prayed, but Sunny wanted to look upward.

"I've never even tried to talk with You because I don't believe You're there, but now I'm not sure. I'm afraid You are there, and that You're angry because I've been so willful."

Feeling quite foolish for speaking into the air, Sunny stopped for a moment. But something compelled her to go on. "Holly said I would have everything to lose if she is right, but how can I know? Brandon is so sure he's going to see the duke. I can see the peace in his eyes when he talks of it, but I just don't know if I can force a belief that simply isn't there."

Sunny fell silent then and looked back at the Bible. She had never read Genesis as the duke had suggested. She knew something of the Bible's account of creation, but her memory was vague. Moving the lantern again, this time back by the bed, Sunny settled down to read. She opened to the first page and read, "In the beginning God created the heaven and the earth...."

Sunny read for the next four hours. She pored over the pages of Scripture. Noah, Abraham, Lot, Sarah, Isaac, Esau, Jacob, and Joseph all leapt off the pages at her. They were people whom God loved and were created by Him, and when they loved and obeyed Him in return, He showered them with blessings, even amid the harsh times.

Sunny was most taken with Joseph. Finally, in the last chapter of Genesis, when she thought he would have his revenge on his brothers for the awful things they had done, he offered them forgiveness. Joseph believed that God used his brothers' treachery so he would be in the place where he could best serve God.

And what about Ahmad Khan's deceit? Sunny found herself asking. *Would I offer him forgiveness? What if his actions were God's way of bringing me to Him? No one in Darhabar would have told me what Holly did today, or what Rand and Brandon have been saying for years. O God,* Sunny tried to pray again. *I don't know how to believe. I mean, what if You're really there and all this time I've—*

Tears streamed down Sunny's face, and she thought her heart would break as all her doubts continued to mount within her. She knew it was very late, but she had to see Holly. She had to tell her she couldn't believe even though she now wanted to do so. Without bothering with her robe, she raced from her room and down the hall.

Sunny wrenched the door open without knocking, and Holly sat up with a start. The room was black, but Sunny's voice told Holly in an instant that she was upset.

"I don't know how, Holly," Sunny cried. "All this time I've run away and now there's nothing there. I want to know your God, but I don't know how." Sunny sobbed harshly into her hands while Holly lit the lantern and came to her. She put her arms around the other girl and held her close.

"Come over to the bed," Holly coaxed. "We can talk over there."

Sunny was willing to be led, and they'd just settled against the headboard when Chelsea's shadow fell over the bed. She carried her own lantern and placed it on the floor before leaning against Holly's footboard.

"Everything you said today was true," Sunny cried. "I've never wanted to admit that I was afraid to die and that I am filled with pride. I read the entire book of Genesis just now. I thought I might be like Joseph, who believed God's hand had been in control at all time, but when I tried to pray, I just didn't know how. I just—"

Sunny couldn't go on, and her family let her cry. She sobbed for some minutes, and when she began to calm, Chelsea's loving voice came through to her.

"I think you need to ask God to help you believe, Sunny. There isn't anyone who wants you to believe more than He does, and I know He's just waiting to hear the sound of your voice."

"But Chelsea, I didn't believe for so long, and I don't think He wants me now."

"You couldn't be more wrong, love. God is so patient. He longs for you to turn to Him, and I promise you, you'll not be rejected."

Sunny looked at Chelsea and then at Holly, who still had an arm around her. She lifted her face to the ceiling, her eyes young and earnest as she spoke.

"I want to know You're there. I'm sorry I've been so stubborn and blind to Your presence. I know I sin, and I want to believe that I can have eternal life." Sunny hesitated, and when she spoke again her voice was filled with wonder.

"Your Son, Your holy Son provided the way, and I want to know Him. Rand said He died for me before I was even born, and I want to believe that, God. I have so many doubts and questions, but I can't go on my own any longer. Please help me believe; please help me to find You."

With a little help from Holly, Sunny placed her life in God's hands. She confessed her need for a Savior and asked Him to be her Lord. Just as Chelsea had stated, Sunny asked God to help her believe, and believe she did. After she prayed, the three of them read in the book of John where Christ was hung on a cross for the sins of all men.

Tears streamed down the faces of all three women as they discussed the magnitude of this love God showed to all mankind. Sunny read the words with new insight and love. Her heart filled with questions and joy.

It was in the wee hours of the morning that Chelsea and Sunny went back to their own beds, but that didn't stop Chelsea from waking Rand and telling him of Sunny's decision. His strong arms trembled as they hugged her, and tired as they were, Chelsea and Rand took a few moments to pray and thank God for His saving love.

When Chelsea had fallen asleep, Rand slipped from the bed and made his way to Sunny's room. He placed his lantern on her nightstand and stared at her as she slept. He knelt next to the bed, and it was some moments before he even felt the tears that rolled down his face.

O heavenly Father, Rand prayed in his heart. *Thank You for making her Your own. Thank You for Your patience and all-encompassing love. You are so faithful, Lord. I knew such happiness when she came back from Darhabar, but nothing compares to this joy, Lord. Thank You, Father; thank You, Lord.*

Rand's heart was too full to go on, but it didn't matter. A moment later he saw that Sunny's eyes were open and she was smiling at him. They moved simultaneously, and in an instant Sunny was wrapped in Rand's embrace. It was tempting to talk for hours, but Rand kept it brief.

"Welcome to the family, Sunny."

"Oh, Rand," Sunny breathed. "It's real. Jesus Christ really is God's Son, and He loved me enough to die for me." Sunny could not continue.

After another great hug, Rand pressed a gentle kiss to his sister's brow and rose from the bed. With a promise that they would talk in the morning, he left her to once again find her rest.

It was very late before Sunny woke the next morning. Someone had opened her curtains, and without rising from the bed, Sunny prayed as a new child of God.

"O God," Sunny spoke softly in the quiet room, not knowing what else to say. "Thank You," she finally managed, so overcome with peace over this renewing of her life. For long minutes she simply lay and thought about her life. She reflected on her restless spirit and the emptiness she had always known. And then with peaceful ease, her mind moved to the night before. She contemplated how all the emptiness had been swept away, to be replaced by God and the knowledge of His love for her.

When Sunny did rise, it was with a delight and purpose such as she'd never experienced before. After she had learned that she could be financially free her entire life, she had been relieved. Now, however, she was a new creature in Christ and was just beginning to understand the true meaning of freedom.

Forty-Two

IN THE HOURS AND DAYS TO FOLLOW, Sunny constantly pored over her Bible. Unlike other times in her life when she ran from one whimsical pursuit to the next, she knew that Jesus Christ was there to stay.

Both Rand and Chelsea warned her that she might not always be excited to read her Bible and pray. "But whenever you feel that way," Rand told her, "those are the first things you should do. If you don't feel like praying, pray. If you don't feel like studying your Bible, get reading."

Sunny, in her newfound standing as a child of God, could not imagine such a feeling. She was like a sponge these days, taking in every word. Although she had never before been excited when Rand led the family in Bible study on Sunday nights, Sunny was now bursting with thoughts and questions.

As she studied on her own, the book of Hebrews swiftly became a favorite of hers. In the thirteenth chapter, Sunny found a verse she felt God had written just for her. It said, "Let your manner of life be without covetousness, and be content with such things as ye have; for he hath said, I will never leave thee, nor forsake thee."

This verse became so dear to Sunny that it was the first she memorized. Years of searching and emptiness were wiped away as Christ filled her with joy and contentment. Rand, Chelsea, and Holly were all a tremendous help as Sunny discovered more about God and His Son every day.

Not everyone in the family was doing as well as Sunny in her brand-new life, however. It was at this same time, when Sunny felt more alive than ever before, that Brandon felt as if his own life were coming apart at the seams.

The Duke of Briscoe, who felt as though all he did lately was sit at his desk working over the estate accounts, was glad to have Parks interrupt him. He was even more pleased when it was with the news that Dinah had come to call.

"To what do I owe this wonderful surprise?" Brandon asked as he moved to approach her when she came in the door, but the look on her face caused him to hesitate.

"Dinah, what is it?"

She didn't answer, but stood looking at him, her heart in her eyes. Brandon covered the distance between them and enveloped her in his arms. Dinah did nothing to resist him. It was going to make it all the harder later, but she selfishly wanted this one last embrace. After a moment, Brandon tried to kiss her, but Dinah drew away. That he was confused by her actions was clear, but Dinah moved to the window so she wouldn't have to look at the pain in his eyes. She looked outside for a moment and then turned to face Brandon.

"I can't marry you, Brandon." Dinah's voice was low, and Brandon waited for her to smile in teasing. "It's not fair of me to wait until a month before the wedding, but our union won't work, and I think if you'll consider what I'm saying, you'll agree."

Brandon had never been so stunned in all his life. He was so surprised he couldn't speak, but if he had been able to talk, he would have told Dinah that he didn't understand, and wouldn't understand; not now and not ever.

"I guess I've surprised you, and I owe you an explanation. Would you like to hear it?"

Numb, Brandon nodded. Dinah sat down by the cold fireplace, and Brandon took a chair opposite her.

"Is there someone else?" Brandon suddenly asked.

"Oh, no, Brandon." Dinah was so distressed at such a thought, she didn't notice that Brandon had relaxed a little. She went on in a bit of a rush. "Brandon, I think you're in love with Sunny. I know she's young, but I think that deep inside, you love her."

Brandon stared at her again, waiting for her to laugh, and

instead had the wildest urge to laugh himself, partly with relief and partly with astonishment that she was serious. He moved from his chair then and came down on one knee next to Dinah. He took her hand tenderly within his own and spoke with love in his eyes.

"Dinah, I do love Sunny, she is very special to me. But it's not the same type of love I have for you. You and I are going to be husband and wife, and I—"

"No, we're not, Brandon," Dinah cut him off, forcing herself to pull her hand away from his touch. "I love you, and I believe you love me, and if you could show me a fraction of the passion that you show when Sunny's name is merely mentioned, I might not be sitting here right now. I know this is painful for us both, but it's for the best."

"Dinah," Brandon's voice pleaded with her. "Don't do this."

"I'm sorry." The words came as though wrenched from her. "But I won't marry you. I've prayed and agonized over this for weeks, Brandon, and there is no other way. I'm not saying you should run off and propose to Sunny, but at some point you need to face what you feel for her."

"Dinah," Brandon began to know frustration, "she's like a sister to me."

Dinah's small hands came up to frame his face, her eyes filled with love. "I can understand why you feel that way, what with her age and the tie through Rand and Chelsea, but, Brandon, it's simply not so. She's *not* your sister, and it's time you stop telling yourself that lie."

Brandon was again without words. He was still on his knee when Dinah rose.

"I'll say goodbye now, Brandon. I'm sorry my decision seemed so abrupt. I will of course take the blame for everything. I'll ask my father to put a notice in the paper."

"Dinah, please, I know we could work this out." Brandon tried one last plea.

Dinah shook her head, and he watched as she moved to the door. Turning, she gave herself one last look at his beloved face before walking away.

Brandon couldn't move for some time after the door closed, but he realized that they each needed some time alone. He thought he would wait two days to see if she would reconsider.

Telling himself that he had to make her understand, Brandon

went back to his desk to stare unseeingly at his work.

When he went to call on her two days later, it was too late. Dinah's stepmother told Brandon that Dinah had gone to visit a friend in the south of France. They didn't know when she planned to return.

Forty-Three

"OH, MILES," SUNNY CALLED FROM LADY'S BACK, her breath showing white in the cold January air. "Where are you taking me?"

"Haven't you ever been this direction?" His voice held a smile.

"No, I guess I haven't. Are we still on Gallagher land?"

"Sure. This is the west quarter. It's beautiful, isn't it?"

"Mmm, yes." Sunny spoke with contentment as they topped a rise and sat looking out on the lovely valley below. A light covering of snow powdered the land, showing every dip and hollow. The trees were old and huge, and Sunny was captivated at the variety. She let her eyes drink in the scene until they swung back to her nephew. He was grinning at her.

"Why are you smiling?"

Miles shrugged. "It's just nice to be home. Part of me wishes I wasn't leaving in a week."

"We sure missed you at Christmas."

"I missed you too, but the things I've learned and seen have been worth every lonely moment."

Miles went on to tell her of the places he had been and ideas he had for starting his own ship-building company. Sunny was captivated.

"I've prayed for you, Miles," Sunny said when he paused, and Miles' eyes looked a bit moist.

"You don't know how glad I am to hear that. I've prayed for you also." He wanted to say more, but Sunny was pulling her glove off and searching in one of the fingers. She drew forth a small piece of paper and handed it to him.

"I gave everyone a Bible verse this year, and this one is yours. Like I said, I missed you, but it's rather nice to give it to you now."

Miles unfolded the paper. The verse Sunny had inscribed was Isaiah 64:8: "But now, O Lord, thou art our father; we are the clay, and thou our potter, and we all are the work of thy hand."

"Rand has been teaching me about keeping verses in their context," Sunny said shyly. "That is, I understand that some promises are for Israel. I must admit that I'm not certain if that verse applies to believers today, but when I read it I thought of you and your willingness to be what God's wants you to be—your desire to be molded by Him."

Miles was so moved he couldn't speak for some moments. He sat looking off across the acreage, thanking God that Sunny's spirit was so gentle.

"Thank you, Sunny," he finally managed.

"Is that a house over there?"

"What?" Miles laughed at the change in topics.

"Way over there, see? I think I see a home."

"That would be Ravenscroft, Grandmama Sunny's home. Want to see it?"

By way of an answer, Sunny grinned and heeled Lady into motion. They raced down to the floor of the valley and made their way smoothly in the direction of the house. Grandmama Sunny's home came into view as they circled a group of trees, and Sunny reined Lady rather sharply in her surprise at having come up to the Ravenscroft gate so suddenly.

The beautiful two-story sandstone with graceful alcoves and dormered windows was quite simply the loveliest manor house she had ever seen. Sunny rode Lady up the drive and then dismounted in the forecourt. Feeling the frozen ground beneath her feet, she walked all the way around the old house as though in a trance. In truth, she was praying.

O Father, her heart whispered. *It's so lovely, and it lets me know my grandmother just a bit.* Sunny's thoughts stopped then as she thought of something so wonderful she could barely think.

I want to live here, Lord, her mind raced on. *I want to have a home of my own. Please help me to be patient. Help me to trust You for this.*

"What's going on behind that delighted face?" Miles asked her suddenly. They had come full circle and were now nearly back where they had begun. This was no small home.

"Oh, many things," she admitted. "I wish I'd known Grand-mama Sunny. I mean, everyone speaks so lovingly of her, and it would be wonderful to have a grandmother of my own."

"You'll see her again someday, you know."

"Oh, Miles, I'd forgotten about that," she grinned at him. "Thank you."

"It is a wonderful house isn't it?" Miles went on. "Do you realize how centrally it's located? The village is about 15 minutes that direction," Miles pointed to the east. "Willows' End and Bracken are both within 20-minute rides."

"It's wonderful, and do you know what I just thought? I think it might be mine." Sunny's smile was nearly off her face.

"Yours?"

"Yes. Brandon told me years ago that Grandmama Sunny had left me nearly everything."

"Hey," Miles spoke with delight. "I'll bet you're right. I wonder whether it has slipped Father's mind or whether he'd rather you didn't know."

Miles' voice had grown very dry on this last note, and Sunny laughed with amusement. She was still laughing as they remounted and made their way home.

"Well, you're certainly right; it is yours," Rand told Sunny over dinner. "And you're also right about my forgetting to tell you. It was built in the sixteenth century, and your grandmother lived there until the day she died. We'll have to go back and have a look inside. I must say that it holds some pretty wonderful memories for me."

"I hate to throw water on those memories," Chelsea intervened. "But a certain young lady is coming out later this year, and we've got a lot to do before we even think of Ravenscroft."

Sunny gave a long-suffering groan and began her old argument, but Chelsea stopped her with a laugh.

"It's not going to work. You *are* coming out and you *will do* it properly."

"Holly dreaded her debut. She was sick for days before," Sunny reasoned.

"But I survived," Holly chimed in.

"You're supposed to be on my side, Holly. Tell your mother that no girl should ever have to go through all that."

"I thought it was a real learning experience," Holly said innocently, and the table roared at Sunny's howl.

A month later Holly and Sunny practised for Sunny's coming out. All the debutantes for that year were to go to the palace together. As each girl's turn came, she was to stand alone before the queen, curtsy low, and receive a brief word of approval. Sunny was still dreading the event.

"No, no, Sunny," Holly told her as they worked in the upstairs salon. "You bow with your head down."

"But then I won't be able to see her. What's the point of finally being in the same room with the queen only to have to look at the floor?"

Sunny's look was so comical that Holly collapsed in a chair with a fit of giggles.

"It sounds like a lot of work is getting done in here." Rand spoke from the doorway of the gallery.

"In a few weeks' time I must go before the queen and make a fool of myself, and all Holly can do is laugh."

"And all Sunny can do is make jokes," Holly put in.

"Well, I think you're going to do fine. Chelsea lived through it and so did Holly. I can't see any reason for you to be upset."

"But Rand," Sunny tried her last tack, "the whole point is to introduce me to suitable men for marriage. I'm not getting married, so why all the fuss and expense?"

"I guess because it's tradition," he said logically.

"You're also hoping I'll change my mind."

"Actually," Rand admitted, "I'm not. If you don't care to marry, I won't force you. On the other hand, it's a state I highly recommend, and if you do find the man God wants you to spend your life with, I'll be thrilled."

Sunny could hardly argue with that, so she and Holly continued their practice. Rand saw that he was not needed and headed toward the door. Sunny's voice stopped him.

"Did Brandon get my invitation?"

"I believe so. Chelsea told me she sent one to Bracken as well as London."

"He's still in London?" Holly wanted to know.

"I'm afraid so," Rand answered cryptically, leaving the girls to stare at one another after he had gone.

Brandon stared across the candlelit table at his rather harsh-looking, dark-haired companion, and wondered when he would stop comparing all women to Dinah.

She wasn't on his heart constantly anymore, but then that was because he had finally taken her advice. He had faced the fact that Sunny was not his sister, and in so doing, saw that he had been keeping Sunny from his mind by dwelling on Dinah.

After admitting this to himself, Brandon found he had several options. He could see more of Sunny, to prove one way or the other if she was in his heart the way Dinah had said, or he could put the whole business from his mind as being ridiculous. He found he could do neither.

The thought of courting Sunny and seeing a look of revulsion cross her face over having a man who was like a brother to her acting in such a way was more than he could take. He decided to put her from his mind, but found that impossible as well. He'd moved into his London town house and immersed himself in his work. He hadn't been to Bracken or Willows' End for weeks.

He had learned of Sunny's salvation just days after Dinah's departure. Thrusting his pain aside, Brandon had gone to see her, but that was before he had worked Dinah from his mind. Even though he praised God that Sunny was now a sister in Christ, at the time he could only see Dinah everywhere he looked.

Now today, an invitation to Sunny's coming-out ball had arrived. Brandon, who had been struggling terribly with his prayer life, found himself pleading with God for answers.

He recognized that the first thing to be done was to face matters and stop hiding in his work. He must also get back to Bracken. Staying in London and avoiding the country, where he would certainly see Sunny, had to cease.

At times he was angry with Dinah. His life had seemed so well ordered. Then she was gone, and he had found himself without a wife, as well as uncomfortable around a little sister he loved dearly.

"She's not your sister," Brandon reminded himself quietly.

"Who's not your sister?" his dinner companion asked crossly. "Honestly, Brandon, I don't think you've heard a word I've said."

"I apologize, Leslie. My mind was wandering."

"Well," she said, still in a huff. "The Marks are over there, and I must speak to Karen. It is to be hoped that when I return, you'll be in better spirits."

Brandon watched her stalk across the crowded restaurant, knowing he would cut the evening short. *I've not been trusting You, Lord,* he prayed, even as he nodded absently to some passing diners. *But I need guidance so badly. I honestly can't see Sunny and me as a couple. But Dinah was right, Lord, I've got to examine my feelings. I still hurt over her rejection, and I've never felt like this before. My focus has been only on my pain and not on You. Help me, Lord, to start again, and to glorify You in my life.*

Forty ~ Four

"I ACTUALLY SURVIVED IT, HOLLY," Sunny said with glee. "I didn't faint *or* trip and fall into the queen's lap."

Holly laughed and hugged her for the fifth time. "Now you only have to get through the dance."

Sunny shrugged. "That'll be a breeze. It's only people we know and—" Sunny stopped at Holly's look. "It will be a breeze, won't it, Holly?"

"Well, actually," the older girl admitted, "you feel just a bit like a cow for sale on the open market."

"Are you serious?"

"Yes. Every eligible male from 18 to 80 will be downstairs to look you over."

Sunny's face showed her chagrin and then new understanding. "That's why you keep getting marriage offers from complete strangers."

"I'm afraid so, but I think you'll do fine. You tender the most wonderful look when someone's advances are improper. I call it your 'empress' look."

"What do I look like?" Sunny, who had been totally unaware that she'd ever done such a thing, was captivated.

Holly tried to emulate her, and Rand and Chelsea entered to find both girls nearly hysterical.

"Now just look at you both," Chelsea remonstrated as she fussed with the lace on Sunny's dress. "You're so flushed, it looks as though you've been drinking."

The girls laughed all over at this, and Rand joined them. "You're

257

a big help, Rand," she scolded him, fighting her own mirth. "Now this is Sunny's big night, and it's almost time to go downstairs."

The family worked at controlling themselves, and within moments Sunny found herself alone. She took a deep breath and prayed. "O heavenly Father, this is not something I'm excited about, but so much work has been done and I want to please Chelsea and Rand. Please help me to honor You tonight with what I do and say. And please, Lord," she added. "Please let me see a few friendly faces."

Sunny had prayed at some length before she suddenly realized she had lost track of time. Walking from her bedroom into the hall, she looked down the wide staircase and saw Rand anxiously looking up. Her fears were confirmed—she had kept them waiting. He smiled tenderly though, his heart swelling with love at the sight of her, and Sunny returned the smile and began her walk down to the dance.

Christie had pulled Sunny's hair up and piled it high atop her head. Her slim white throat was adorned with the amethyst necklace she had found in the jewel box from Darhabar; the matching earrings glistened on her lobes. Her gown was a deep purple with a tiered skirt. The neckline was rounded and frothed with cream-colored lace. The same lace hung in gentle folds from her wrists and over her hands. The tiers in the skirt were also lined with lace. When Chelsea had first seen it, she had commented that Madam Angelica had once again outdone herself. As with all her creations, the gown was perfect in style and color.

Traditionally, the father of the debutante started the dancing with his daughter, but Rand, as Sunny's oldest brother, was more than happy to fill in. He swung Sunny onto the floor in time to a waltz. Chelsea stood on the sidelines, biting her lip to keep from crying. Several minutes into the dance, Rand and Sunny were joined on the floor by other couples. Within moments they were surrounded by the crowd.

"Well, I'd say you're a success."

"I don't know if I like all of this, Rand," Sunny admitted in a small voice. "You're not going to believe this, but I just realized why Holly keeps getting marriage offers."

"Ah, yes," Rand spoke softly as they continued to dance. "You'll be amazed at how many offers come from men you've not even met."

"But why?"

For the first time, Rand realized how their living in the country had sheltered her. "Because you're beautiful, titled, and wealthy."

"Are there really so many men who would marry a woman they didn't even know?"

"Most would, my sweet...I'm afraid most would."

They finished the waltz in silence, and Rand ushered Sunny back to the edge of the floor. He had barely released her when she was converged upon by admirers. Sunny was gracious to the crowd of some 20 young men surrounding her, but as Holly had stated, she had a way of looking at a man that told him when he had pushed too far.

At least six young men were vying for her immediate attention when a familiar face appeared on the fringe. Sunny looked up into Jordan's beautiful blue eyes and gave him a special smile. Many a heart turned over with roaring jealousy when they saw that private smile, and some hearts turned to anger when Jordan extended a hand and Sunny moved toward him without being asked.

"I asked the Lord to send me a friendly face or two," Sunny remarked, smiling at him as they waltzed. "I believe the saying 'you're a sight for sore eyes' would be appropriate right now."

Jordan laughed. "I could say the same about you, Sunny. You've never looked lovelier."

"Thank you, kind sir," she replied primly. "I fear if this pace keeps up for the remainder of the evening, however, I'm going to greatly resemble a damp cloth."

"I sincerely doubt that," Jordan told her, and could see by the face she pulled that she did not believe him. The dance with Sunny was over much too soon for Jordan, and only the knowledge that he was somewhat special in her eyes kept him from walking across the floor and cutting in on her next dance partner.

Jordan glanced away from Sunny's progress when someone jostled his arm. He brushed at his sleeve and in so doing, caught sight of Holly, lovely in a rose-colored silk gown, talking with a few other girls. He hadn't danced with her all evening or told her how pretty she looked. As Jordan moved toward her, he was also faintly aware of the fact that she must miss Miles on a night like this, and told himself that the least he could do was fill in for her brother.

"Excuse me." Jordan's manner was most urbane. "I wonder if I might interrupt you ladies in order to claim Miss Gallagher for a dance."

The others in the group dimpled at him, and his own smile was charming as he swept Holly away.

"Do you miss Miles?" Jordan asked after a moment.

"Yes," Holly said inadequately, knowing that he wouldn't understand why his nearness made it so difficult to speak. To Holly he was by far and away the most captivating man at the ball. She had seen the look on his face when he had danced with Sunny in his arms, but even though she longed to be the one on the receiving end of that look, she wasn't vexed with either of them. Sunny would keep her secret for life, and Jordan simply couldn't see past the end of his well-shaped nose.

"I failed to tell you when I came in earlier that you look wonderful tonight."

"Thank you," Holly said shortly, wanting to pinch herself for her tongue-tied response.

"Have you heard from Miles?" she finally managed.

"Not for a month at least. Have you?"

"Last week I think it was. He said that you had written to him about some land you wanted to purchase."

"The Bailey land. The deal is almost closed."

"A good buy, was it?"

"Definitely," Jordan replied with some pride. "I know a good thing when I see it."

Holly, quite angry all of a sudden, stopped on the floor so abruptly that Jordan nearly stumbled.

"Jordan Townsend, you wouldn't know a good thing if it bit you on the nose," she said in soft anger.

It was a relief to hear the music die down on that note. Holly knew she had done the unforgivable; they were both embarrassed. But at the moment she couldn't stand near him for another second. With as much dignity as she could muster, Holly swept off the floor. Her Uncle Douglas was there to dance the next dance with her, and she was spared, at least for the moment, having to face the man she loved.

Sunny tipped her head back to look up at Dexter, and he grinned.

"You'll hurt your neck that way."

Sunny shook her head. "How does Judith stand it?"

"Why, she's madly in love with me," Dex said with a cheeky smile on his handsome face. "And when you're in love, what's a little height difference, give or take a foot? Actually, you've no reason to complain—you're quite tall."

"Compared to Judith I am, but next to you and Brandon I'm a stubby thing."

Dexter glanced down at her slim, graceful carriage and slowly shook his head. "You might not be up here with me, but by no stretch of the imagination would anyone label you stubby."

The tempo of the music increased, and Sunny was not able to make a reply. In fact she was completely out of breath when the dance ended and she found herself back next to Chelsea.

"Well, you're certainly having a horrid time," Chelsea teased.

"Oh, it's been lovely," Sunny returned, her eyes alight with happiness. "Thank you for all the hard work, Chelsea, and for pushing me to keep going when I wanted to quit."

Chelsea chuckled over the image her words evoked. Sunny had hated dance lessons and had begged with all her heart to get out of them. Rand had been insistent, however, and it had obviously paid off. Chelsea watched with a small smile as she saw Jordan claiming Sunny yet again.

"Oh, Jordan—"

"I hope you'll pardon me," a deep voice cut in before Sunny and Jordan could exchange another word or even take the floor. "I'm late, and I've not danced with the guest of honor. You will excuse us, Jordan?"

"Of course, my lord," the younger man replied and stood quietly as he watched the Duke of Briscoe swing Sunny onto the floor.

"Hello," she smiled up at him. Brandon beamed in return.

"I'm sorry I'm late. How are things going? Did you see the queen?"

"I did!" Sunny told him triumphantly, "and got a 'very nice, my dear.' I think she says that to everyone, but I was so relieved to have it over, I didn't care."

"I knew you could do it."

"Did you? I wasn't too awfully sure of myself. I've missed seeing you around Willows' End, Brandon," Sunny said, quickly changing the subject. "How have you been?" The last question was offered in such a way that Brandon knew she was speaking of Dinah.

"I'm well, thank you," he told her kindly. "It hasn't been without its difficult moments, but God's comfort is more than abundant."

Sunny gave him such a serene smile that Brandon felt something move within him. He was doing it again, comparing his companion with Dinah, only this time something was remarkably different. This time his companion measured up.

He had realized some weeks ago that his love for Dinah had drastically waned, but she was still the godly example he held up whenever he considered getting serious again. Until tonight, when he danced with Sunny, he thought he'd never find her equal.

"You've grown rather quiet," she commented softly.

"You've grown, period," Brandon said smoothly, "into one of the most beautiful women in London."

"Thank you, Brandon. I've heard that and similar comments all evening, but coming from you, someone who has been like a brother to me, it's somehow very special."

Brandon hid his disappointment at being referred to as a brother. "It's rather hard to reconcile the little ragamuffin I took aboard my ship a few years ago with the woman you are today."

"Well," Sunny spoke sincerely. "We can thank God for that."

Brandon smiled and refrained from arguing. The memory of that ragamuffin was very dear to him, and even though she'd had much growing up to do, Brandon had loved her at first sight, loved her as a sister. Now it was happening all over again, only this time the love was different, no less deep, but far more intimate. The new Sunny, this older, grown-up Sunny, was more captivating to him than any woman he had ever met. Even Dinah.

As the dance ended and he was forced to turn her over to another partner, Brandon realized that the seemingly impossible had happened. The little girl had grown up, and even though just a month ago Brandon could not imagine them as husband and wife, he now found himself struggling with how delightful she had been to hold.

The gaunt woman he had lifted into bed following her illness weeks ago was a distant memory. The Sunny in his arms tonight had been all woman, soft and lovely, and Brandon felt as though a precious jewel had been wrenched away from him as he'd watched her dance away with another man.

"Has something happened, Hawk?" Rand's voice came quietly for his ears alone.

Brandon was glad for his company, but the emotions raging inside him were in such a turmoil, he didn't know where to begin. "Something has happened," he admitted finally, "but I'm not sure you'd understand."

Rand was quiet for just an instant. "I've always known there was something very special between you and Sunny. If you're thinking I would object to you because of your age or for any other reason, you couldn't be more wrong. I think you'll find I'm a most understanding man, if in fact you have fallen in love with my sister."

Brandon looked at Rand with such profound relief that the older man nearly laughed.

"Come by tomorrow. We're staying here in town for at least a week. Sunny is sure to have a slew of callers, but you and I can sequester ourselves in the den."

The dinner bell sounded on those words, and both men went off in search of their dinner partners. Rand anticipated a few minutes with his wife. Brandon, who prayed as he tracked down Sunny, found himself a bit nervous that he might do or say something tonight that would spoil this evening for her.

Jordan was doing some praying of his own as he walked a delightful young lady by the name of Roxane Carley into dinner. Holly was supposed to be on his arm, but a last-minute change of dinner partners had occurred. Jordan, who had been counting on this time to talk with Holly, found himself keenly disappointed.

An hour later, his own dinner companions felt the same way. Jordan had spent the entire meal watching Holly some three tables away, talking and laughing with the men on either side of her.

Forty-Five

"IT SMELLS LIKE A BOWER IN HERE," Rand commented as he joined Chelsea in the morning room.

"Indeed it does," she agreed with him. They both looked around the large room overflowing with flowers for the Lady Sunny Gallagher.

"Has Holly seen these?"

"Yes. And if by that question you're asking if she's jealous, nothing could be further from her mind. You know the only proposal she's interested in."

"Well, we can praise God then, because his isn't here." Rand spoke as his hands sorted through the morning post. "Everyone else in London has written for Sunny's hand, however. They're calling her the 'Jewel of London.' Here's one you might find interesting," Rand noted as he made himself comfortable in a chair.

"From whom?"

"Lord Lindley."

"_Lord Lindley!_ Rand, he's 60 if he's a day."

"He's 57 according to his letter," Rand stated calmly. "Here's what he has to say: 'I realize my suit may come as a surprise to Sunny, and she may consider my age a hindrance, but regardless of my age I wish her to be a wife in every sense. I believe she would enjoy her position as the Duchess of Colton.' "

"Who else?" Chelsea asked, knowing she was now forever past surprises.

264

"Lord Kenmore, Percival Cromery, Cecil Jamieson—"

"Foster's brother?" Chelsea interjected.

"Yes. I'm sure it has something to do with the fact that Foster and Heather are out of town, and Foster is not around to discourage him."

"He's cared for her since before she moved to Willows' End. That's a lot of years to carry a torch."

"How about Lord Lindley? He writes on to say that he met Sunny in December of 1844 while she was riding with Brandon in the park. That was just days after she arrived."

Husband and wife stared at one another. There didn't seem to be much to say.

"Are you going to tell her?"

"I'll have to."

"When?"

As if on cue, Sunny and Holly chose that moment to arrive home from shopping.

"No time like the present," Rand said under his breath and rose as the girls came in.

"Chelsea!" Sunny spoke in surprise, and her sister-in-law watched as her adorable nose wrinkled in offense. "Why in the world would you put all of these flowers in the same room? Couldn't you spread them around the house a bit?"

"There are more in your room." Chelsea's voice was droll. "And more still in the upstairs salon."

Sunny sat down on the settee and stared around her. "This is what you were talking about, isn't it, Holly? Total strangers sending flowers and proposing."

"This is it. Has Sunny received proposals, Papa?"

"Oh, Holly," Sunny laughed. "Certainly not yet. I—" She stopped when Rand held the letters in the air.

"Who are they?" she wanted to know.

Rand began to read the letters. Sunny, listening intently, had a comment for every one.

"Oh, I remember him."

"You're not serious!"

"Not Cecil!"

"He has no chin."

"He was nice."

"I've never heard of him."

"His hand kept stroking my waist!"

"He promised me the moon. He really did."

"He stepped on my foot, twice."

"Who?"

"I think his hair was fake."

Holly had her face in a pillow to stop her laughter, and Chelsea was thinking that if Sunny kept it up, she wouldn't be able to contain her own mirth. Rand had more to read, but a caller was announced. Sunny stood in a panic, thinking it was more flowers being delivered or someone coming to declare himself. She sagged in relief when Brandon's frame filled the doorway.

"Oh, Brandon, I'm so glad it's you and not someone else coming to propose," Sunny told him bluntly.

"As bad as all that?" Brandon managed to keep his voice light.

"Yes. I wish they would all understand that I plan never to marry."

Brandon arranged a smile on his face and gave everyone a brief greeting, but he felt as relieved as Sunny did when Rand almost immediately suggested that they head into the study.

❧ ❧ ❧

"I don't know when it happened exactly. When Dinah first mentioned it, I was so flabbergasted I nearly laughed in her face. But since then I've thought about Sunny off and on, and then last night when we danced...

"Oh, Rand," Brandon shook his head. "I sound like a lovesick schoolboy. You heard what she said." Brandon pointed toward the door. "After all these years, she still doesn't want to be married."

"She's never been in love, so of course she would feel that way," Rand offered compassionately.

"What about young Townsend? They certainly seem interested in each other."

"I believe *he* is, but Sunny thinks of him only as a friend."

"It seems that we have something in common."

Rand studied Brandon's face as he weighed his next words. He didn't want to give him false hope, but Rand believed that Brandon meant more to Sunny than either one of them realized.

"Would you have considered loving Sunny if Dinah hadn't planted the idea in your head?"

"I don't believe so, no."

Rand didn't say anything, and Brandon turned to him, his look intense.

"Are you thinking—"

"I don't know." Rand cut him off before his hopes could rise. "I know how she cares for you, however, and that she's very young.... Maybe given time..." Rand let the sentence hang, and Brandon nodded. He certainly couldn't ask for more than that.

"Thanks, Rand."

"No thanks needed. I've shared with Chelsea, and we're both praying for you."

"What did Chelsea say when you told her?"

"That it was about time."

Brandon was so surprised he blinked in stupefaction.

"And she agrees with me," Rand added. "She thinks Sunny has probably loved you for years."

"You realize that she's loved him for years."

"Who has, Aunt Lucy?" Holly wanted to know.

"Why, Queen Victoria, my dear. She's loved Albert for years," the elderly aunt replied, and Holly wondered how their conversation had moved from Aunt Lucy's flower garden to her bunions and then on to the queen and prince consort.

"Now, Sunny," she turned to the younger girl. "How was the ball? I wish I could have been there, but I don't like evenings on the town; they fluster me. I remember when I was young—"

Aunt Lucy was off again, and she failed to notice that she had given Sunny no chance to answer the question. The girls had been invited to tea just that morning, and even though they both wanted to see some friends, they knew that this would be their last chance to visit with their beloved aunt before heading back to Willows' End.

"Have you accepted a proposal?"

Sunny, whose mind had begun to drift, came back to the present with a jolt.

"No," she said a bit too vehemently. "That is," her voice was softer now, "I haven't really had time." Sunny knew the last thing she should tell Aunt Lucy was that she didn't plan on marrying.

For once Aunt Lucy was quiet. Sunny began to look uncomfortable, and Holly smoothly filled in the breach by asking Aunt Lucy how she liked living in London.

"Well, you know I do, my dear. But I so love the country. I would dearly love to live where you can hear the birds singing in the morning and listen to the creatures of the night as you fall asleep. London is so busy and noisy at times."

Sunny and Holly couldn't have agreed more. They were both eager to return, and in their opinion tomorrow could not come soon enough. Brandon was to go back with them, as was Andrea. In fact, Andrea was to come for them any time now. She had needed to shop and passed up the offer of tea with the promise that she would see Aunt Lucy another time.

Andrea did arrive just after they had finished their tea, and with little fuss or bother ushered the girls into her waiting coach.

"Are you girls ready for tomorrow?" Andrea asked when they were settled inside. They were headed to Andrea's for the night. Her mansion overlooked the Thames.

"Yes," Holly told her fervently. "It might be a bit strange without Mummy and Dad, but I know we'll have fun." Holly suddenly looked very worried. "They might be away for a few weeks. You will stay until they return, won't you, Grandmama?"

"Of course I will. Your parents need a rest, and the north country is so lovely. We'll have a splendid time, and you won't even miss them."

They finished the ride in silence, Andrea thinking how delightful it would be to stay at Willows' End with the girls, and the girls thinking that they would like to be anywhere but London.

Forty ~ Six

BRANDON SHIFTED CAREFULLY AGAINST THE SEAT, so as not to wake Sunny where she slept against his shoulder. For the first half of the journey, Brandon, Andrea, Holly, and Sunny had shared a coach, but then Brandon had stopped the coaches so he could stretch his legs. He also had wanted to move to his own carriage to put some distance between him and the woman he loved. He realized now that he'd wasted his time, since Sunny felt sure he would be lonely and moved to ride with him.

She shifted, and the smell of her hair rose to assail his senses. Brandon wondered just how long he could keep up the big brother act, when all he wanted, whenever she was near him, was to crush her in his arms.

You'll keep it up, he told himself firmly, *just as long as you need to, or you'll destroy everything between you. Please, Lord,* his heart went on, *please give me strength to wait for her. Show her, Lord, that I am a man, a man who would cherish her for all my years.*

Brandon's prayers and the rocking of the carriage finally got to him. He had asked everyone to be ready early that morning, and now the dawn departure was starting to catch up with him. With his mind picturing how Sunny would look surrounded by several dark-haired children, Brandon fell asleep.

The drive to Ravenscroft came into view, and Sunny smiled. She had ridden out by herself this time, not something that was usually encouraged, but she'd felt an urgent need to be alone. Rand had said they would come sometime and go through the house, but with her coming out, his plan had never materialized.

Sunny walked around the neglected courtyard and knew she didn't have to go inside. From the placement of the windows, she could imagine the interior. She sat on the low stone wall that surrounded the base of a tree and prayed, Lady's reins hanging from her fingers.

Sunny asked God to give her this house and to let it be a place of peace and caring. She asked Him to prepare Rand and Chelsea's heart before she talked with them.

"I'll not go against their wishes, Lord," she said as she stepped up on the wall and boosted herself back into the saddle. "If I don't have Rand and Chelsea's approval, I'll let the matter drop and rest in You."

It was with some regret that Sunny rode away from the house; partly because Rand and Chelsea would not be home for another two weeks, and partly because the few times she was near Ravenscroft, she felt as if she'd come home.

"Well, Jordan," Andrea greeted him kindly as she entered the small salon, "what a delightful surprise."

"Good morning. I hope I'm not coming at a bad time." Jordan gave her a tentative smile that left Andrea confused. She didn't think he had ever been hesitant to come to Willows' End.

"Your timing is just fine, but I'm afraid Sunny isn't here. She went riding."

"Actually, I'm here to see Holly."

"Oh, I'll have her sent down. Do make yourself comfortable."

Jordan was anything but comfortable as he waited. Holly had been so heavily on his mind since the night of the ball that he had thought he would go crazy thinking about her. Why it had taken until that morning for him to realize he could go and talk with her was a mystery to him. But here he was at last, and for some reason, unaccountably nervous.

"Sunny isn't here." Holly's voice sounded from near the door.

Jordan spun away from studying a picture he had seen a hundred times before and frowned as Holly's words registered.

"I didn't come to see Sunny. I came to see you."

"Binks said as much, but I was sure he was mistaken."

"No, he wasn't. I came to see you," Jordan repeated.

"Why?" Holly asked bluntly, leaving Jordan thoroughly nonplussed.

"Can't I come to visit you?" he finally asked.

"You never have before." Holly's voice had been very kind through this entire exchange, but Jordan knew something was amiss. Holly simply didn't talk to him this way. She had always been thrilled to see him, making him feel at home and as though his very presence had brightened her day.

"Would you like to go for a ride?" Jordan tried a change of subject.

"I don't like to ride," Holly told him, her voice showing her hurt that he couldn't remember even that.

"I'm sorry...I forgot. A walk then." Jordan was not to be put off. "It's a beautiful day."

Now it was Holly's turn to frown. "Jordan, if you want to wait for Sunny, you don't have to entertain me while you do so."

"I'm not here for Sunny," Jordan replied, thinking this was the oddest conversation he had ever had. "I came to see you. I've done something to hurt you, and I'd like to take a walk so we can discuss it." It felt so good to have all of this said that Jordan let out a gusty sigh.

Holly couldn't help smiling. Jordan took it as an olive branch.

"Please walk with me for a while?"

"All right," Holly agreed, albeit unwillingly. "My music teacher comes today, so I can't be gone long." Holly knew it was an excuse and wondered if Jordan saw through it.

With a somber nod Jordan agreed, and they headed out the door. It was a beautiful day just as Jordan had stated, and for a time they walked in complete silence.

"Have you heard from Miles?" Jordan suddenly asked, and Holly wondered, a bit testily, how many times they were going to play this scene.

"You know, Jordan," she stopped suddenly and spoke with some annoyance. "I've come to realize that our only links are Sunny and Miles. If neither one of them existed, you wouldn't care if you ever saw me again. So I think it might be better to stop pretending. You needn't worry about anything you might have said or done to me, because I'm fine." It was not the complete truth, but Holly knew that given time, she would be fine. In fact, she felt better just having said it.

Holly took Jordan's silence as agreement. Turning, she started back toward the house. She was surprised speechless when his hand shot out and captured her wrist. With a gentle but determined move he brought her back to stand directly in front of him.

"That isn't true," he stated with more force than Holly had ever heard from him.

"Yes it is." Holly's voice was equally firm. "You're just denying it to spare my feelings, and there's really no need."

Jordan's hands were on her upper arms now, and he drew her even closer. He bent his head until his face was very near to her own and then spoke.

"I don't know where you've picked up such a ridiculous idea, but it isn't true. And—" he cut her off when she opened her mouth to speak, "if you tell me that's not true, you're calling me a liar. I wouldn't care to hear that from you."

"What would you care to hear from me?" Holly tried to keep her voice light, so Jordan would not know the way his touch had affected her.

Jordan's eyes searched her hair and features. Her hair was raven black and pulled into an elegant chignon at the back of her head. Her eyes were wide and dark, and her skin looked like the first rose of a spring day. Added to all of this, Jordan thought she was the most compassionate, kindhearted woman he'd ever known. Her sweetness was something he had always admired in her. Suddenly he couldn't remember what she had asked him.

"This hasn't gone the way I'd hoped it would. I don't have any more answers about what's happened between us than when I arrived, but I have to leave for London. I will tell you this however, we *will* talk. My father has business for me, and I don't know how long I'll be away. It could be weeks, but when I return—"

Jordan lost track of his own thoughts when he realized how soft her arms felt beneath his hands. His eyes followed the movements of his own fingers as they lightly stroked the skin above Holly's elbows.

"Your skin is so soft, Holly," Jordan whispered as though to himself. "Why have I never noticed how soft your skin is?"

Jordan's glance flickered back to Holly's face, and the unreadable look she sported made him drop his hands as though he'd been burned. Holly felt bereft at the loss of his touch.

"I'll see you when I get back," Jordan's voice was now stiff. Holly didn't move a muscle as she watched his tall, lean form walk away. Only minutes passed before she heard the beat of his horse's hooves as he rode from the stable yard.

Her hands came to her arms then, touching herself in the place where his hands had lain. Holly's heart could have easily left reality and gone into dreams over the words Jordan had said, and the look she'd seen in his eyes, but she swiftly reined in her thoughts.

He's in love with Sunny, she reminded herself, *and all the hoping in the world is not going to change a thing. If you let your heart stray, you'll only hurt more than you do right now.*

≈ Forty-Seven ≈

SUNNY AND HOLLY LISTENED WITH RAPT ATTENTION to Rand and Chelsea's details of their trip. They had gone north to stay with old family friends, Lord Philip and Lady Denise Briton, whose hospitality and estate size worked together to allow one to lose oneself figuratively, sometimes literally. Rand and Chelsea had slept late, enjoyed leisurely teas, gone horseback riding, and wandered the area in restful peace and comfort. The Britons were often away from home, but hospitality was always extended at their front door.

Rand and Chelsea looked very relaxed when they returned, and didn't appear to want to move an inch from the upstairs salon, not even when Binks announced that Holly had a visitor. Sunny was not at all sorry to have Rand and Chelsea to herself for a moment, and as she began to pace just a bit, they both stared at her.

"Did something happen that upset you while we were gone?" Chelsea wanted to know.

"Not really, but I want to talk to you, and I don't know how to start."

Rand felt a bit alarmed. If he didn't know better he would have said she was planning yet another scheme. Sunny had done nothing of the sort since she'd come to Christ, and even though she was as lively and fun-loving as ever, the frantic search for happiness was gone. Rand hoped it would stay that way.

"Actually, it's about my birthday present," Sunny finally said.

Rand found himself relaxing; birthday gifts he could handle.

"Your birthday *is* coming up," Chelsea encouraged her. "Did you have something special in mind?"

"Yes," Sunny answered with a smile. "I wish for your blessing, because I want to move into Ravenscroft."

If Sunny had told them she had eloped while they had been away, she couldn't have shocked them more.

"If I don't have your blessing, I won't go, but I hope you'll hear me out." Sunny waited for her brother's nod before continuing.

"I fell in love with Ravenscroft the first time I saw it, and I think it would suit me very well. I probably feel that way because Grandmama Sunny and I are alike. I can't really explain it beyond that, except to say that Ravenscroft has utterly captured my fancy."

Sunny's eyes were shining with such peace and warmth that Rand and Chelsea could only stare at her. Chelsea knew at that moment that she had never really faced the fact that Sunny and Holly would move away someday. There were several points Chelsea could have raised in argument, but she didn't really believe any of them herself. Rand, being the logical person that he was, spoke his very valid thoughts.

"You can't live at Ravenscroft alone, Sunny." Rand's voice was regretful, and Chelsea knew he wanted to grant Sunny's request. "Even if you've a passel of servants around, you *cannot*, at 18 years old, go off and live alone."

"I've given that quite a bit of thought," Sunny told him, still very much willing to bow to his judgment. "And if it's all right with you, I'll write Aunt Lucy and ask her to live with me. She's a bit eccentric, but I do care for her. She and I have written to each other often, and the last time Holly and I were with her, she told us how much she would love to live in the country."

Rand nodded slowly in thought. Aunt Lucy was the last person who would have come to his mind, but in some ways she was perfect for Sunny. In other ways...well, for the moment Rand's mind refused to think on it.

"Write Aunt Lucy, Sunny, and see what she has to say. We'll keep this quiet for the time being, but we'll definitely move as far in that direction as we can go."

Rand earned a huge hug from his sister and watched quietly as she dashed from the room. He stared at the closed portal until he felt his wife's eyes on him.

"I never really thought she'd move away."

"Oh, Rand, I was just thinking that myself. I'm awfully glad I came home so rested, or I'd be bursting into tears."

Rand stared at the drops pooling swiftly in her eyes. "It looks like it's going to happen anyway."

"I think you're right," Chelsea said with a sob. Thinking he might very well cry himself, Rand pulled her against his chest.

Sunny wasted no time in writing to Aunt Lucy, and everyone was a little surprised at how swiftly the plans moved. Sunny's birthday passed in a flurry of preparation, for she was determined to be at Ravenscroft by Christmas. Brandon heard of her plans and came one afternoon. He saw Rand first, and the older man could see that the young duke was barely holding his temper in check.

"Aunt Lucy has the sense of a peahen, Rand. How in the world are they going to do on their own out there?"

"I don't have many reservations, Hawk, and the ones I do have, I've discussed with Sunny. Remember, they're not headed off into the hills." Rand's voice was dry on that note. "They're very near the village and only 20 minutes from here or Bracken. Lucy is bringing a very loyal staff with her, and I've just hired a man who will go to Ravenscroft as head of housekeeping. He also understands that he is to keep a careful eye on things, especially Sunny and Aunt Lucy."

"I still don't like it," Brandon said firmly.

"What don't you like?"

Both men turned to find Sunny in the doorway of the study. In her preoccupation she hadn't realized anyone was inside and had opened the door without knocking. Brandon looked at her, his brows low, and when Sunny caught his look, she stiffened. She knew in that instant to what Brandon had been referring. He watched as her chin came into the air and she worked at controlling her own temper. She opted for retreat.

"I need a book, but I can come back later."

"Don't go," Brandon said when she would have backed out of the room. "I want to have a word with you."

"If by having a word," Sunny told him directly, "you mean to tell me how foolish it is to move from Willows' End, then you can hold your tongue. I don't want to hear it."

"Is that right?" Brandon's voice had become smooth.

"Yes, it is."

"Well, I *am* going to have my say, Sunny, so you might as well come in and sit down."

Sunny did as she was bade, barely aware of Rand's heading for the door. He prayed that Brandon would not dig himself in too deeply and left them on their own.

"Aunt Lucy is a dear," Brandon began without preamble and worked at keeping his voice level. "But she is also very absentminded."

"What does that have to do with our living together?" Sunny wanted to know.

"It's not just Aunt Lucy; it's the entire situation. You haven't pulled one of your schemes in a long time and..." Brandon went on relentlessly telling her why he was opposed to the move. Sunny was left with no doubts that he was very much against it. In his mind Sunny was much too independent, and this move was only encouraging her to be more so. It took some time for him to see that she was just as upset as he was.

Brandon brought his tirade to an abrupt halt. How in the world had he actually thought to reach her by scolding her? Her eyes were shooting purple sparks, and Brandon knew that he'd lost her for the moment. Before he could make amends, she stood, her gestures very final.

"I can see that some things never change." Sunny's hurt over his words had turned to fiery wrath. "I'm still a child in your eyes, a baby sister to be exact. You're very used to getting your way, Brandon, but this time you're about to be disappointed. I *am* moving to Ravenscroft, whether you like it or not."

She swept from the room on those words, and Brandon was left alone, calling himself every class of fool. He decided against searching her out right then and walked to the stables with a thoughtful heart. His ride back to Bracken was made while talking over his dilemma with the Lord.

"So when is the big move?" Jordan asked Sunny on his return from London, as he tried not to look across the room at Holly. The three of them had been talking, and between Sunny and himself all was fine. Holly, on the other hand, was a different person.

She was kind, but there was no spontaneity left within her. She seemed to measure every word before speaking, and Jordan felt something akin to grief over the changes he saw. He couldn't help but wonder if the changes were on account of him. He rather hoped to get her alone and find out, but Sunny, in her excitement, failed to notice any underlying signs of strain.

"Aunt Lucy is coming next week, the day after I go," Sunny chattered on. "I'm still sorting and packing. I can't believe how much I like to save things. I found treasures I hadn't seen in years."

Jordan listened with only half an ear. He chanced a glance in Holly's direction, but she didn't notice. He was very relieved when Wilson, the man Rand had hired to go with Sunny to Ravenscroft, interrupted them, asking for Sunny's assistance. Jordan saw it as an opportunity to talk with Holly, but turned to find her slipping out of the room. He was fast on her heels, but not fast enough—the entry-way was empty. He wondered how she could disappear so swiftly and understood how deliberate such a move had been on her part.

Jordan could still hear Wilson speaking with Sunny, so he decided not to disturb them. With rather slow steps and a heavy heart Jordan made his way to the stables. He would have been greatly encouraged if he had chanced to look up toward Holly's bedroom window. He would have caught her watching his departure with studied concentration.

Wilson exited after just a few minutes of conversation with his mistress, and Sunny stood staring down at the place where he had stood. She was still deciding if she liked the man. His clean-shaven, nondescript face was familiar somehow, but Sunny was certain she had never seen him before. He was always the soul of respect, and she had to admit that his help in going to Ravenscroft had been invaluable, but the feeling that he watched her constantly was always at the edge of Sunny's mind. She never actually caught him in the act, but nevertheless the feeling lingered.

She glanced down at the papers and fabrics he had handed her, and in an instant all thoughts of discomfort evaporated. They were swatches from the curtains, wallpaper, and bed hangings to her bedroom, the last room to be renovated and redecorated. Sunny suddenly found herself wishing that Aunt Lucy were coming before next week.

Calm down, she told herself. *You're to be content right where you are. After all, you've only a few days to wait before you can call Ravenscroft your home.*

Part Four

THE LADY OF RAVENSCROFT

Forty-Eight

"I CAN'T UNDERSTAND WHY IT UPSETS YOU SO MUCH." Sunny was remembering Rand's calm words.

"He treats me like a child," Sunny had insisted, but Rand had not looked convinced.

"From what you told me, he only voiced the same concerns I did, and you had no problem taking it from me."

You had no problem taking it from me.

The words echoed in Sunny's mind again and again. It had been a poorly planned conversation, occurring the day before she moved from Willows' End. The exchange had put something of a blot on her departure, but when Rand asked her if she had heard from Brandon since that day in the library, all her old anger bubbled to the surface.

Now, sleep eluding her, she lay in her bed at Ravenscroft and recounted the entire conversation in her mind.

"Why, Sunny? Why does it make you so furious when Brandon treats you like a child? Chelsea and I do often enough, but you never react like this."

"I don't know," Sunny admitted. "I guess I'd like him to see me as a woman, but every time we're together I do something he disapproves of, or I end up looking like a child."

"I disagree. I don't think you act any differently around Brandon than anyone else, but for some reason, you can't handle his reaction to you."

"You're getting at something, Rand." Sunny was very alert and slightly suspicious.

"I guess I am."

Neither one of them spoke for some minutes, and Sunny, knowing that Rand had accurately read her, decided there was no point in holding her secret any longer.

"It's not going to change a thing to say it aloud, but it is as you suspect—I've loved Brandon for as long as I can remember. But as I said, my admitting it changes nothing. He sees me as little more than a sister, and a young one at that."

"You've never said anything or let on in any way." Even though Rand had suspected that Sunny's love for Brandon was more than familial, he was quite surprised at her admission.

"No, I guess I haven't. I'm learning to share my feelings, but it doesn't come easily for me. Please don't misunderstand me, Rand. I wasn't devastated when his engagement to Dinah was announced, but something in me hurt and I couldn't figure out what it was. I was very upset for Brandon when they dissolved their engagement, but at the same time, I couldn't believe the relief inside of me. Knowing that he was so hurt, I felt deep guilt over my relief."

Sunny could not know that she had shocked Rand into silence. He had hoped that his questions would spur her to examine her feelings, but he was not prepared for just how much she had already done this.

"Should he ever find out, Rand," Sunny went on resignedly, "it would destroy all we've shared through the years. I love Brandon like I love no one else, but I love him enough *not* to have him. Does that make sense to you? I love him enough to let him be my big brother for all time. I had been dealing fairly well with all of this before I accepted Jesus Christ, but afterward, when I felt at the end of my tether, Christ gave me the strength to carry on.

"I have no expectations for the future, but one thing I know won't change: My love for Brandon gives him a power of which he is unaware—the power to hurt me. His opinion means so much. That's why I react the way I do. I don't always escape without sin, but God is getting me beyond that, and He's always waiting to hear my voice when Brandon and I have had a confrontation."

Sunny did not know that her every word, even the tone of her voice, confirmed to Rand his decision to let her move. She had truly become a godly, wise young woman; a woman who accepted her situation and trusted God when she knew pain.

As he hugged his precious sister, Rand realized he could change everything for her and Brandon with just a few well-placed words. As soon as the thought surfaced, another one followed, and that was that he must allow Brandon and Sunny to work this out for themselves. Feelings were tender things, and knowing the way Brandon felt, Rand was certain he would someday make himself understood.

For the present, however, Sunny was losing a night's sleep because of worry and pain. Rising from her bed, Sunny lit the lantern and turned in her Bible to the Psalms. She loved the verses in Psalm 119, especially verses 57 through 64, and began reading them softly to herself:

"Thou art my portion, O Lord; I have said that I would keep thy words. I entreated thy favor with my whole heart; be merciful unto me according to thy word. I thought on my ways, and turned my feet unto thy testimonies. I made haste, and delayed not to keep thy commandments. The bands of the wicked have robbed me, but I have not forgotten thy law. At midnight I will rise to give thanks unto thee because of thy righteous judgments. I am a companion of all them who fear thee, and of them that keep thy precepts. The earth, O Lord, is full of thy mercy; teach me thy statutes."

Sunny smiled ironically at the verse that spoke of midnight. "I'm not awake at this time of night to give You praise, Lord, as I should, but I'm up to fret and hurt. Please comfort my heart. Thank You for Your mercy, Your lovingkindness. I feel relieved that Brandon will be away and not at Willows' End for Christmas. But I can't live my life that way. Change me, Lord. Pour Your grace upon me and help me to trust You for the future."

Sunny closed her Bible and blew the lantern out. She settled back against her pillows and continued to pray. It was still some minutes, but in time she prayed herself into peaceful sleep.

"How did you sleep, my dear?" Aunt Lucy asked over breakfast.

"Actually I was a bit wakeful. How was your night?"

As sometimes was the case, Aunt Lucy was quite lucid this morning. She ignored the question about herself, her face showing greater concern for Sunny's welfare.

"Was it a worry of some kind, my dear? If there is something I can do, you know I'd be more than happy."

"Thank you, Aunt Lucy," Sunny replied sincerely. She had truly come to care for this woman in the few weeks they had lived together. "But I'm fine. I'll lie down this afternoon if I'm feeling weary."

"A very sensible idea, my dear. Tildy and I are going to work on my papers. I've decided to write a book."

"A book?" Sunny stopped with her fork halfway to her mouth.

"Yes, a book." Aunt Lucy looked triumphant. "I've led an interesting life, and I think it only fair, since I've been so blessed, that I share my adventures on paper with any and all."

Thinking what a wonderful winter project writing a book would be for her, Sunny smiled. It had been on her mind that Aunt Lucy might feel a bit shut in until spring, but this was going to be perfect.

"I've also decided to stay here Christmas Day." Aunt Lucy held up a hand before Sunny could protest. "I know you're expecting me, but I'll be more comfortable here. If Milton were still alive, I would make the effort to go to Bracken, but Tildy and I will be very happy right where we are."

Sunny could see that she had made up her mind, so she let the matter rest. In fact it would have done little good to try to discuss it. Aunt Lucy and Tildy closeted themselves in Lucy's bedroom right after breakfast, and Sunny didn't see them the rest of the morning.

"Do you know that for the longest time I fancied myself in love with you?"

Sunny could only stare at Jordan as he quietly bared his heart. He had arrived less than an hour ago to see Sunny's new home. She had shown him around with the excitement of new ownership, but it didn't take long to see that his heart was not really with her. Sunny had wisely waited until tea, when Jordan was relaxed and sitting in her lovely front parlor, before questioning him about what was wrong. His answers flabbergasted her.

"Have you ever had something or someone right under your nose, and not been able to see it?" Jordan went on, almost to himself. Sunny wondered what he was talking about.

"I mean, Holly is my best friend's sister. She's always been the sister I've never had." Jordan noticed Sunny's puzzled look then, and smiled a bit sheepishly.

"I have a confession to make to you, Sunny. I only came over here today because I wanted to go to Willows' End, but I knew I couldn't take any more of Holly's indifference toward me."

"You're in love with her then?"

"Yes, but I no more than recognized it than she got all cold and prickly with me. I don't know what happened. It doesn't matter, though," Jordan went on vehemently. "If it takes years I'm going to win her heart. I'm going to show her I can be far more than a big brother to her."

"I don't think it will take years." Sunny spoke softly, and even though his heart was filled with Holly, something in Sunny's voice made Jordan pause.

"What did you mean by that?"

Sunny bit her lip and turned her gaze out the window. She would never give Holly's secret away, and now she deeply regretted her words. Jordan was sure to press her, and they might quarrel. When Sunny remained silent, Jordan began to warm to his subject.

"She cares for me, doesn't she, Sunny?" His very being radiated hope over the question. "She cares for me and is hiding behind her indifference, isn't she?"

Sunny was stubbornly silent, but Jordan was now quite sure of himself. She couldn't stop a smile when he nearly jumped to his feet and began to pace the room.

"Sunny, Sunny, Sunny. Do you realize what this means? I thought it would be years, but now!" Jordan let the sentence hang as he plopped down next to her on the davenport. His arm stretching along the davenport behind her, he leaned very close, and smiled into her eyes.

"You're wonderful, do you know that?" Jordan felt as if he'd been set free.

"I haven't said a word, Jordan," she reminded him.

"You didn't need to."

Sunny could only shake her head and laugh softly when Jordan dropped a light kiss on her nose. Thinking he was such a dear friend, she smiled up into his eyes and knew that he and Holly were going to be very happy.

Unfortunately Brandon chose that moment to come in unannounced. To him, the interplay on the sofa was not one that would be shared by good friends, but by a couple who were involved far beyond friendship. In fact, if she was carrying on with Jordan, he wondered how she could be so lax as to not even close the door.

In the moments before Sunny saw him, Brandon realized that he had never had opportunity to see her around other men. What if she had turned into a flirt and a tease? Brandon's feelings were so mixed that when Sunny finally saw him, he just stared at her a moment.

"Well, come in, Brandon," she repeated twice.

Brandon did so, but felt his worst fears confirmed when she didn't appear uncomfortable after being caught in a near embrace.

"Thank you." He worked quickly to school his features as he took a seat.

"I have to be leaving," Jordan said softly, having noticed the duke's unease and wanting some time alone to plan his visit to Holly.

"Don't run off on my account," Brandon told him.

"No, no," Jordan said with a smile. "I've been here awhile."

Brandon nodded and couldn't stop the thought, *and what have you and Sunny been doing in that time?* He was ashamed of his own thoughts, and was thankful that Sunny, in her move to see Jordan to the door, did not notice.

How ironic, Brandon's mind went on while he was still alone, his pride stung to the core. *I come to tell Sunny how I feel, and that I want to see more of her, and find young Townsend here. I guess I should be thankful I found out before making a fool of myself.*

"Well, now," Sunny spoke with very real delight when she came back into the room. "May I give you a tour?" Her voice and face turned a bit hesitant, and Brandon remembered the words they'd had over her move to Ravenscroft. At the moment, her vulnerability melted his heart, and he knew he would have to put his feelings aside. He stood with a ready smile.

Forty-Nine

"I MUST SAY I'M VERY IMPRESSED, SUNNY."

Sunny beamed but didn't speak. Brandon's approval meant so much to her. They had come full circle, toured the house and the grounds, and were now back in the parlor.

"Where is Aunt Lucy today?" Brandon asked as they settled on opposite ends of the davenport and Sunny rang for tea.

Sunny's eyes sparkled with merriment, her face so lovely and radiant that Brandon convinced himself that she was completely innocent of his every wicked thought.

"She's sequestered in her room writing a book."

"You're not serious," Brandon said with a smile.

"Indeed I am. She told me this morning. Actually, I think it's a great project. I'm rather proud of her for trying."

"Well, at least it will keep her busy. Do you miss Willows' End?" Brandon asked suddenly.

"Yes. Holly especially. She's such great fun. Although," Sunny added dryly, "I won't miss her having male visitors and my having to hide because I'd rather not see them. She would always tease me when they left and call me a wanton." Sunny chuckled softly at the memory, but Brandon didn't share her mirth. Jealousy riding high, he spoke without thought.

"Holly might not find it so amusing if she'd seen your behavior with Jordan a short time ago. Have you become a wanton, Sunny?"

The smile slowly died on Sunny's face. The look on Brandon's made her feel very cold inside.

Where the question had come from, Brandon could not at the moment tell, but it had suddenly popped out. He wanted to pull his own tongue out when he saw the look in Sunny's eyes. Any amends he might have attempted were cut short by her terse voice.

"I can see why you would say that, Brandon." Sunny's voice dripped with sarcasm. "After all, I flirt with every man I meet. Oh, and then there's the way I'm always pretending to be faint, or to have a lash in my eye so I can press myself against you and you can look into my eyes. Aside from all of that, I'm sure you've noticed the way I stayed in London as long as I could, simply dying to be the belle of every ball."

This said, Sunny stood. Trembling with pain and anger, she marched toward the door with head high, and was on the threshold when Brandon's voice stopped her.

"Sunny," he spoke.

She stopped but did not turn.

"I'm sorry."

She heard the agony in his voice, but still did not turn. "Thank you, Brandon," she replied after a moment. "I think it would be best if you left now." Again she hesitated. "I never thought I'd say this, but I think I'm rather glad you're going to be away at Christmas."

Brandon watched helplessly as she went through the door. He had gone to the threshold and watched her run up the wide staircase. He'd felt terrible for days over their last encounter. This time he wondered if either of them would ever get over it.

Jordan stepped quietly inside the music room at Willows' End and leaned against the door. He had specifically asked Chelsea not to have him announced.

Now he stood motionless and studied Holly's lovely profile as she bent sternly over the keys of the grand piano and played Beethoven's Sonata No. 14. Jordan felt mesmerized by the sound. Holly's fingers never missed a key, nor her foot, the beat.

Jordan was thankful for her concentration, since she didn't notice him until she had finished the last note. He had mentally prepared himself for her reaction, but it still hurt to see the dismay in her eyes when she spotted him.

"Jordan," Holly said rather inanely, as she folded her hands tightly in her lap. She stayed on the piano bench with an effort as he pushed away from the door and approached. Holly watched as Jordan moved to the piano and leaned nonchalantly against it.

"Are you going to ask me to sit down?" Jordan wanted to know, telling himself that he was not going to let Holly put him off this time.

"All right," Holly spoke reluctantly, and then bolted from the bench when he moved to sit down next to her. It was now Holly's turn to stand by the piano, as she watched Jordan make himself comfortable in the middle of the bench.

Holly told herself that her heart simply couldn't take seeing him again. She had talked with her mother and felt better, but now she planned to unburden herself to Miles when he came again, hoping for some advice about his best friend. In the meantime, she knew she wasn't doing well at all.

For the moment, Jordan allowed her the distance and spoke with studied ease as his hands lightly touched the keys. His eyes, however, were not on the keyboard; they were considering Holly.

"How were your Christmas and New Year's?"

"Fine," Holly answered carefully and wondered at the unfamiliar gleam in Jordan's eye. It was almost as though he were laughing at her, but she must be mistaken.

"I'm glad to hear it. Tell me, Holly, have you ever wondered at the fact that you and I have never kissed?"

"*What?*" Holly nearly shouted at him, sure that she had misunderstood.

"Well, it's a perfectly normal thing to think." Jordan was as calm as if he'd been discussing the season's rainfall. "I mean we've spent hours together over the years, and it's not as if we find each other repulsive." Jordan had shifted to one side of the piano bench and was studying Holly with a roguish eye. Holly moved to put more space between them; in fact, she moved to put the piano between them.

"I don't know what's come over you, Jordan, but I think you had better leave." Holly hated how breathless she sounded, but she couldn't seem to help it.

"No," he said easily as he came off the bench. "I'm too curious to leave."

"Curious?" Holly felt a bit inquisitive herself.

"About what it would be like to kiss you." Jordan started toward her.

Holly's eyes widened, and she moved completely around the piano, talking as she went.

"Now you stop this, Jordan Townsend," she admonished him. "You're in love with Sunny, and you've got no business kissing me or anyone else."

"In love with Sunny?" Jordan sounded amused, as he calmly stalked her. "Who told you that?"

"No one told me. I, unlike some people, have eyes in my head."

"Ah, yes," Jordan was now back standing in front of the bench where he'd begun, looking tenderly over the top of the piano at Holly. "I believe it was the night of Sunny's coming-out ball," he continued. "You told me I wouldn't know a good thing if it bit me on the nose. You were right, my love," Jordan added gently as he sat down once again.

"Come over here, Holly." His voice was still as soft, but it was a command. Holly, always obedient, moved toward him dutifully, but then stopped short.

"I can just as easily come to you," Jordan went on. "In fact, if I have to climb right over the top of this piano, I will. I'm rather hoping, however, that you'll want to come over here, as much as I want you to."

Holly was uncertain, but she allowed herself to approach him nonetheless. Jordan moved to one side of the bench, and Holly sat next to him. As soon as she came near enough, Jordan turned slightly and reached for her hands.

"Never has anyone or anything confused me like you have. I didn't know if I was coming or going," he admitted. "It wasn't until you spoke to me at the ball like you did that I realized what I'd been missing."

"Sunny—" Holly began.

"Is a good friend. I care for her deeply, but she's not the woman I want to marry. Not even when I thought I was in love with Sunny did I feel for her as I do for you."

"You'll change your mind," Holly began.

"No, I won't," Jordan stopped her gently. "I want to marry the sweetest woman in all of England. I want to marry a black-haired woman with skin as soft as rose petals and eyes so dark and lovely I could get lost in them."

Tears pooled in Holly's eyes. "Do you have any idea how long I've cared for you?" she asked softly, suddenly sounding very weary.

Jordan's answer was to pull on her hands until she was close enough to kiss. Jordan's lips gently touched her own for just an instant. Holly's sigh was so heartfelt that Jordan kissed her again, this time, his arms going around her, and with all the love he felt inside.

"I want to be married right away," Jordan told her when he could speak. "In fact I want to talk with your father today. Any objections?"

Holly's answer was to kiss him again. Jordan smiled when she broke the kiss. "That's what I love, Holly, a woman who knows a good thing when she sees it."

"Sunny," Aunt Lucy called. "Have you seen my little jewel box? The one I keep by my bed?"

"Why, Aunt Lucy," Sunny replied. "I wouldn't touch your things."

"Oh, I know, my dear, but I know I put it there, and now it's missing."

"I'm sure it will turn up," Sunny said rather indulgently. This wasn't the first thing Aunt Lucy had misplaced, and as Sunny had said, everything always turned up. The elderly woman went back to her papers then, and Sunny was given a few moments of quiet thought.

Since moving to Ravenscroft, she had misplaced a few things herself, and they too, always turned up. But it wasn't like her to do that, and for a moment Sunny wondered at her staff. She hated to doubt them—it felt very disloyal—but she couldn't seem to help herself. Some of them had come with Aunt Lucy and had been with her for years, but one maid, Tina, had been recently hired. She had worked for Heather, and when she had found out that Aunt Lucy was moving to the country, had asked to be replaced at the Jamiesons'.

And then of course there was Wilson. Sunny was still not comfortable with him. She had even talked with Rand, who had admitted that he had asked Wilson to keep an eye on her. At the time it seemed to explain the feeling that someone was listening outside the door and the sense of being watched, but then recently something else had happened.

Wilson had come up missing one morning when Sunny needed him. When she questioned the staff, no one knew where he 'iad gone. He had shown up in just a few hours and had a very valid explanation for leaving, but Sunny had been disturbed. She told him if it happened again, he'd be dismissed. He was quite apologetic, but Sunny was not comforted.

And then there was Phipps. He worked in the stables, and Sunny was always a bit alarmed over how willing he was to ride with her. He was not a young man, nor did he make improper advances in any way, but his protection of her seemed a bit excessive.

Sunny let out a soft sigh. Maybe she wasn't cut out to be the mistress of her own home. Chelsea and Heather had made it look so easy. Since Aunt Lucy was still quiet, she began to pray.

Lord, if there is something unsafe here at Ravenscroft, please show me. Help me to be discerning. If You want me to go back to Willows' End, I'll go. I love my home here, but something just isn't quite right.

"Excuse me, my lady," Wilson interrupted from the door. "Lady Holly is here to see you."

"Thank you, Wilson," she said softly and made an instantaneous decision. Holly's wedding, scheduled for April 20, 1849, was just ten days away. After all the celebrations calmed down, she would speak to Rand.

"Hello," Holly called as she entered and nearly danced across the sunlit salon. Sunny rose to hug her and then turned her to face Aunt Lucy.

"Aunt Lucy," she said with a gleam in her eye. "Don't you think that Holly looks a bit ill these days? I mean, she has no color in her face at all, and her eyes have such a listless look about them."

Aunt Lucy, who never caught a joke the first time, studied Holly's radiant countenance with a serious expression.

"Well," Aunt Lucy spoke hesitantly. "She does look rather flushed." She stopped at Sunny's low chuckle.

"Oh, you dear girls," she beamed at them. "I never know when you're making a joke."

The younger girls laughed then and took the davenport. They sat with heads close together and talked about the wedding to come. Aunt Lucy listened with half an ear and didn't interrupt. She remembered well how it felt to be young, and the way she felt at her own coming out.

"I must put that in my book," she said decisively as she stood. "Tildy," she called as she exited the room, not bothering to bid the girls goodbye.

"How do you like living with Aunt Lucy?" Holly wanted to know when the older woman had left.

"I really like it. If I need to think, and she's rattling on, I just tell her. Some days she's quite clearheaded and others she's not. Strangely enough, she seems to be aware of what a chatterbox she can be and isn't the least offended if I ask her to stop. The only cloud—" Sunny hesitated.

"What were you going to say?" Holly urged her.

Sunny, wanting to confide in someone about the servants, explained briefly and then asked Holly to be praying with her. "It might not be anything, and I don't want to overreact. I'm going to talk with your father after the wedding."

"Why don't we pray right now?" Holly suggested, and they did just that. They sat together for an hour, covering subjects far wider than Ravenscroft as they lifted loved ones near and far to the Lord.

Fifty

Sunny had never seen or even imagined a bride as beautiful as Holly Gallagher. She was a vision of loveliness in a snow-white gown and a veil that streamed out for yards behind her. Sunny, who couldn't take her eyes off Holly, didn't realize the vision she herself made in a deep rose gown. Her hair was piled atop her head and little curls fell around her neck and forehead.

As maid of honor, Sunny was to be the last to come down the aisle ahead of Rand and Holly. She waited in a room by herself this time, and found she was more nervous than when she had stood up at Dexter and Judith's wedding. Sunny's nerves had been affecting Holly, so Rand had found his sister a small room where she could be alone to wait and pray.

Brandon seemed to know he was needed and sought out Sunny while guests were being seated. They'd had little contact since he had been to Ravenscroft, but when he showed up to keep her company, she was much relieved to see him. Keeping his feelings for her at bay, Brandon carried on an effortless conversation, and even managed to make Sunny smile and forget her nerves.

"Have you seen Mother?" he asked kindly.

"No."

"Well, I think she looks especially lovely, but since the first of her grandchildren is being married, she's somewhat tearful."

"She is?" Sunny was very concerned, not ever having seen Andrea break down and cry. "Is she all right? Maybe I should go to her."

"Well," Brandon smiled to himself at how selfless she was. Sunny had quickly forgotten the long walk she must make up the aisle. "I believe she's already seated, but do find her at the dance. I know she'd enjoy talking with you. Did I tell you how lovely you look?" Brandon's tone was just as conversational with this change in subject, but Sunny's entire demeanor altered.

"Do I really Brandon?"

"Yes." He was surprised at her question. "Did you think otherwise?"

"It's not that," Sunny admitted, her cheeks heating slightly.

"What is it?" Brandon prompted her gently.

Sunny hesitated for just an instant, studying the floor as she answered. "I just value your opinion, that's all."

Brandon's long-fingered hand was gentle as it captured her jaw and brought her gaze to his own. His fingers were tender as they stretched up onto the soft skin of her cheeks.

"I'm glad to hear that. And since I am now aware, allow me to alter my first choice of words. Utterly captivating is a much more accurate description for the way you look." His eyes were loving, and Sunny could not tear her gaze away.

"And please allow me to apologize once more," he went on in soft regret, "for my unforgivable question while in your home. I can't think what caused me to act in such a fashion, or to speak to you that way, but I've deeply regretted it ever since."

"Thank you, Brandon." This second apology meant more than she could say. Again their eyes held, and Sunny thought her heart would melt with the love she felt.

I would make you a wonderful wife, she said in her heart, hoping beyond hope that he would someday see past the calm face she always presented, and also hoping that someday she too would be able to share her feelings.

Brandon did see something, but he wasn't sure of the source. He opened his mouth to speak, but someone knocked on the door.

"That's your cue," Brandon told her, moving his hand slowly from her face and taking a step back.

Sunny's thoughts were such a jumble that she moved past him without a word. In just moments Brandon was forgotten. Sunny caught sight of the crowd and took her place at the rear of the church, her heart again thumping with fear.

❧ ❧ ❧

Jordan led his bride onto the dance floor in cadence to the first waltz. Sunny stood watching them and worked to control her tears. She thought they made the most beautiful couple in the world. The love she saw in Jordan's eyes as he looked into Holly's face made something painful squeeze around her heart.

Jordan had said that Holly looked at him as a big brother and that he was going to change all of that. Sunny couldn't help but hope that someone else might be feeling the same way. Brandon, unnoticed by Sunny, was feeling just that, as he stood to the side of her and surreptitiously studied her face.

Does she regret that it's Holly who's married and not her? Brandon asked the question of himself, now knowing that Sunny was not in love with Jordan. Through various conversations Brandon had learned that the very day he had seen Sunny with Jordan was the day Jordan had come to tell Sunny of his love for Holly. Brandon felt agony all over again at how he had judged her. He now watched as Foster claimed Sunny for a dance and found himself wishing he had asked her first.

"You're scaring them away, do you know that?"

"Who, Mother?" Brandon feigned innocence, his eyes still on Sunny.

Andrea was not fooled. "The several young men who were interested in dancing with Sunny. Your scowl was so fierce it even scared me."

Brandon chuckled softly, but sobered on his mother's next words.

"If you're not going to claim her, Brandon, give her a chance to love someone else."

"You make it sound as though she loves me now."

"Indeed. I believe she does." Andrea watched Sunny and Foster's progress on the floor as well.

Brandon looked at his parent for the first time. Her face was a study in confidence. Still, Brandon slowly shook his head.

"I would act within the hour if I believed that were true, but I'm afraid I see no evidence."

Andrea could only nod. He was right. Sunny was a master at

hiding her feelings. However, Andrea believed that Sunny wouldn't be hiding her feelings if Brandon would only reveal his. Suddenly she smiled to herself. Milton had asked her years ago if she would wish to marry again.

No, my sweet matchmaking father-in-law, she thought to herself. *The Lord has made me most content just as I am.*

"Where are my manners?" Brandon's voice broke into her thoughts. "Mother, may I have this dance?"

Andrea beamed up at her oldest son and allowed him to swing her onto the floor for a minuet. The dance took all his concentration, or Brandon might have noticed the way Rand had captured Sunny and was talking to her in an alcove just off the dance floor.

"I don't want to overreact. That's why I didn't come to you right away."

"And you say that it's Wilson, Tina, and one of the stable hands?"

"Yes, but there's more to it than that, Rand. I always felt protected at Willows' End, but never spied upon. Now at Ravenscroft I hear noises in the hall, but no one is there. I feel eyes on me, but no one appears to be watching. My room feels as though it's been invaded at times, but nothing is ever missing. A few times I thought I misplaced something, only to have it turn up a day later." Sunny shrugged, suddenly uncomfortable with how near to tears she felt.

"I don't want to cry at Holly's wedding" was all she said, and her brother understood completely. His voice was no longer tender, but became extremely businesslike.

"I'll be coming by just as soon as we head home. I'll do some checking and have a look around. I think we should return to the dance, but before we go I need to tell you that I trust Wilson. Call it gut instinct if you will, but I think he'll do all right by you."

Rand's voice, as well as his words, rescued Sunny, and within moments they returned to the dance floor.

"Chelsea?" Sunny called from the doorway of the bedroom, hoping she was not asleep.

"You can come in, Sunny," Chelsea answered from the bed, "but if you're looking for Rand, he's still downstairs."

Sunny shook her head and slowly approached the bed; she climbed onto the foot, her feet tucked beneath her.

"It was a beautiful wedding, wasn't it?"

"Yes, indeed," Chelsea agreed, and waited for the real reason Sunny had sought her out at this hour of the night.

"Whenever a new woman would come into the harem," Sunny began, "she would be prepared, bathed, and groomed for her first night with the emir. It didn't matter how she had come to be there, as a slave or as the daughter of another household; she was always terrified. All the women went willingly to the emir's chambers after the first night, but they were very frightened that first time."

Chelsea, a bit in shock over Sunny's words, watched as tears puddled in her eyes. "I can't stand the thought, Chelsea," she finally sobbed. "I can't stand the thought that Holly will be frightened tonight. I know Jordan is a wonderful man, but I can't stand the thought that she'll be afraid."

Chelsea's arms opened, and Sunny climbed high onto the bed to be held. She was 18 years old, but tonight she felt about ten. Chelsea pressed a large handkerchief into her hands, and Sunny didn't notice that Rand had joined them. Chelsea waited a moment for the harsh sobs to abate, and then began to speak calmly.

"First of all, you're exhausted, and everything always looks worse when you're tired. Second, you couldn't be more right about Jordan; he is a wonderful man. But there is something else I want you to consider. Have you thought about how scared Jordan might be tonight?"

Sunny's head came off Chelsea's pillow, and she stared at the older woman in the lantern light. Rand was in the dark, sitting in a chair on the other side of the bed. He smiled at the look on Sunny's face.

"Sunny." Chelsea spoke gently as she brushed the tangle of hair from the younger girl's face. "Rand and I both saved ourselves for marriage. Neither one of us came to our marriage bed with experience, but Sunny, that's just the way God wants it. I won't tell you that we weren't a little nervous, but we loved each other, desired each other, and knew we were married in the sight of God and with His blessing. No relationship is perfect, but because we've always worked to please each other above ourselves, we've enjoyed the physical side of our marriage for years."

"Oh, Chelsea," Sunny was sobbing again. No one had ever explained it that way, and Sunny was so relieved that all she could do was cry. Chelsea knew it was time to get this girl into bed. They moved down the hall toward Sunny's room, Chelsea's arm around her, still talking softly. Chelsea bent low over Sunny's bed to kiss her goodnight and told her to sleep as late as she wanted in the morning.

Sunny had drifted off before Chelsea could get out the door, and Chelsea was glad to return to her own bed. She herself was more weary than she had ever been in her life, and with Rand's arms around her, she felt sleep coming swiftly to claim her. Rand's whispered words, telling her he thought she was wonderful, sent her into slumber with a smile on her face.

Fifty-One

BRANDON AND SUNNY RODE IN COMPANIONABLE SILENCE on the ridge between Ravenscroft and Bracken. They had been to visit the ruins of Hawkings Crest. Hawkings Crest, as Brandon explained, had been the home of his early ancestors, a mighty fortress built in the mid-1400's.

Brandon told Sunny that he actually had a document from King Henry VIII, commanding Bracken of Hawkings Crest to marry a daughter from a neighboring castle. Knowing this made the name of Brandon's home all the more special.

As they rode, they talked of many things, and Sunny's heart was nearly singing with how well they were getting along. After more than an hour with nothing but gentle words between them, Sunny found herself confiding in Brandon about the goings-on at Ravenscroft.

She was able to tell him that Rand had come on the scene after the wedding, and in a few weeks' time had dismissed Phipps, the stable hand, and given word to the staff that they were all on notice. Rand, not willing to take any chances, had even told Aunt Lucy's staff. It had taken some days to calm ruffled feathers.

After feeling secure for many days, Sunny was once again growing uncomfortable. Convinced that it had nothing to do with Ravenscroft or the people there, Sunny admitted she would move back to Willows' End without delay if she could uncover evidence that she truly was in danger.

"I don't understand you," Brandon said after she'd told all, thinking this uneasiness was the perfect reason to move back to Willows' End.

"Well, I think all of this has something to do with me, not the house or even the staff. I don't know why, but if I go back to Willows' End, I'll always feel as if I've left a job undone."

"In the light of your safety, I think that's a small price to pay." Brandon's voice had become very formal.

Sunny sighed. They were sitting beneath a huge willow. Their horses were tethered nearby, and they were leaning back against the tree, their shoulders just touching.

"You're going to get angry, aren't you, Brandon?"

"Not if you go back to Willows' End."

Again Sunny sighed. "It's gotten so that I can't tell you anything anymore, Brandon. What's happened to us? You disapprove of everything I do."

"No, I don't." He spoke softly, regretting the way he had made her feel. "But what you've told me is very alarming, and I can't stand the thought of your being hurt. Why don't you live with Heather and Foster for a time, or Mother? That would give you a nice break, just until Rand and I can make sure all is well."

"I won't do that because Ravenscroft is my home, and I don't know that I'm in any serious danger," Sunny told him calmly. "Whatever is going on, I want to see it through."

Now it was Brandon's turn to sigh. He had to stop treating her like a child. She had trusted him with this confidence, and he must now trust her decision, as well as God's care of her. It went against his own judgment, but he had begun to wonder if he could even trust his own reasoning where Sunny was concerned.

Brandon turned away from his thoughts and glanced over to find Sunny, her face near his own, studying him intently. His look seemed to tell her he would not argue, and the pleasure Brandon saw on her face made him act without thinking. With a move so gentle that Sunny never felt threatened, Brandon brushed her lips with his own.

He was a fool to think that one kiss would be enough and a moment later his lips had claimed hers again, this time with a good deal more insistency. Brandon raised his head seconds later to find Sunny's face frozen in shock. Regret knifed through him so deeply that a look of near-revulsion crossed his face.

"Why did you do that?" Sunny's voice was stiff, having misinterpreted his look.

Brandon came awkwardly to his feet. "I'm sorry, Sunny. It won't happen again."

The ride back to Ravenscroft was made in silent agony, and Sunny was never so glad to see her own room. Without a care for the dust on her clothing or boots, she lay across her bed and cried herself into exhaustion.

Three hours later, Sunny sat with a cold cloth on her eyes as Christie brushed her hair. Not wanting to deal with Aunt Lucy's questions at supper, she was trying to erase the signs of her tears.

There was a knock on the door just as Sunny was being buttoned into a fresh day dress. Wilson entered and informed Sunny she had a visitor; she assumed it was Brandon.

"I don't really care to see anyone, Wilson. Thank whoever it is and tell him another time."

Wilson hesitated.

"Is there some problem, Wilson?" Sunny had a headache, and her voice was a bit sharp.

"No, my lady," Wilson's said apologetically. "But it's Lord Miles, my lady, and I know he is most anxious to see you."

Sunny's eyes slid closed. "Thank you, Wilson; of course I'll see him. Tell him I'll be right down."

The door shut, and Christie spoke softly. "You don't like Wilson, do you, my lady?"

Sunny's head turned sharply at her impertinence, and Christie looked swiftly at the floor. "I'm sorry, my lady. It won't happen again."

Sunny was sorry she felt so ill-tempered. "It's all right, Christie. Why did you ask that?"

The personal maid shrugged and looked hesitant.

"Go on. You can tell me," Sunny urged.

"I don't care for him any more than you do. I saw him peeking into your jewel box one day. He told me he was fixing the latch, but I pack your jewel box for you every time you travel, and I've never seen it broken."

Sunny trembled just a little. She thanked Christie and dismissed her, needing a few moments to be alone. Rand had been so sure of

Wilson. Dare she approach the man? Her thoughts were such a muddle that for the moment she forgot about her guest. With measured tread she moved to the jewel box, took it from the dresser, and placed it in the large drawer in the bottom of her desk. It was never out of place when she was home, and she hoped such an action would not draw attention to her newfound knowledge.

As she finally went down to meet Miles, she remembered that Rand was on a trip. Just before opening the door to the salon, Sunny prayed and made an instant decision not to say anything to anyone until Rand returned.

Miles Gallagher was tanned and gorgeous, and Sunny could only stare at him where he stood near the mantel.

"Have I grown another head?"

Sunny laughed. "No, you just look so wonderful and older and—" Sunny faltered for more words.

Miles smiled and the two met in the middle of the room and shared a great hug. Sunny held his hand as she led him to the davenport. When they were seated, she repeated herself.

"I've missed you, and you look just wonderful."

It was Miles' turn to chuckle. "I missed you too, but if I can be very honest, you look a bit drained."

Sunny looked indignant. "Of all the nerve, Miles Gallagher, telling a lady she doesn't look well!"

Miles only stared at her, and Sunny's bluster and fuss seeped from her.

"I have a headache," she admitted.

"You don't normally get headaches, if I recall. Are you coming down with something?"

Of all the things they could have discussed—Miles' sailing, Holly's wedding, or Sunny's move—Sunny found herself unburdening to Miles about Brandon. Miles listened attentively, catching more than Sunny was saying, but not giving anything away. He had, on his last voyage, met someone himself, and knew very well the signs of love.

Sunny was sharing things about Brandon that Miles did not recognize. Brandon was the kind of uncle whose level head and wisdom had always impressed him. This Brandon was a man acting without thought, letting his fears destroy his judgment—this Brandon was a man in love. Brandon had allowed his regard for Sunny's safety to come between him and the woman he loved.

It was not surprising that Sunny couldn't see any of this. Her head and heart were equally as confused, and she was hurting as much as Miles suspected Brandon was.

Miles stayed for several hours, and he and Sunny talked about everything under the sun. Sunny was thrilled to know of Miles' new love and from his description, thought she sounded like a wonderful woman. Miles planned to visit Jordan and Holly soon, and Sunny found herself wishing she could join him.

When Miles finally took his leave, Sunny's headache remained, but she felt much better. Aunt Lucy did not come down from her room until just before dinner, and after eating, Sunny was feeling almost like herself.

Since she knew the next few days before Rand came home were going to be spent in watchful silence, Sunny decided to go to bed early. Unfortunately Brandon's presence was announced just as Sunny told Aunt Lucy she was going to take a walk in the garden.

"Well, you go ahead, dear. The night air will do you good; it will help you sleep. I'll keep Brandon company until you return."

Feeling very much a coward, Sunny thanked her gratefully and fled. The lights of the parlor allowed Sunny to see exactly when Brandon came in and sat opposite his aunt.

Before she began to move among the flowers, she stood watching him for a moment, asking herself why she did not want to think about the reason he must have come back or the kiss he had given her that afternoon.

Fifty-Two

BRANDON'S FOOT TAPPED SOFTY ON THE RUG, but Aunt Lucy didn't notice. She was telling Brandon about the chapter she had written that day, a lengthy subject detailing her days in America. Brandon wondered if her excited chatter would ever stop.

He glanced toward the French doors that opened at the far end of the parlor. One stood open, allowing the night air to cool the room, but not allowing him to see past the darkness where he knew Sunny to be.

With an effort he forced his attention back to Aunt Lucy and hoped he was nodding in all the right places. He had decided that afternoon that nothing Sunny or he could say to each other would make him more miserable than he was now. He knew he had to see her. It had been an effort to wait until that night, and all the way over he had prayed she would speak to him.

It had been most discouraging to have Aunt Lucy say that she was in the garden. Brandon had reluctantly taken a chair. He told himself he was not going to wait much longer. Only five minutes to be exact, and then he was going to excuse himself and go out to find her.

As it was, the scream, short and muffled, came only moments after Brandon made his resolve. Without one word to the still-talking Lucy, he was out of his chair and bolting for the open door.

307

Sunny had done very little walking once she passed over the threshold into the garden. The giant shrubs were a comfort to her, and she loved to gaze at their silhouettes in the moonlight. She did stroll some, but when the attack came, she was standing completely still, gazing at the stars and praying.

Sunny heard the shuffle of feet just a moment too late. A hand was clamped firmly over her mouth and she was borne to the ground. She began to struggle in earnest as the tearing of cloth came to her ears, and all at once the night air touched her legs, back, and shoulders.

Sunny fought with everything that was in her, trying desperately to free her mouth, but there seemed to be hands all over her.

"Where is it?" a voice demanded.

"I can't find it," another answered.

When Sunny felt hands moving on her legs she bit the hand over her mouth. She was able to get out one desperate yell before she was stifled again.

As quickly as the attackers had come, they were gone. Sunny lay where they left her, every part of her trembling in fear and shock. Even when she heard more footsteps, she could not make herself move. Someone was there now, calling her name and touching her shoulder. Sunny scrambled back away from the hand as fast as she could move.

"Don't touch me," she sobbed, and then she saw a crowd and heard Brandon telling someone to bring a blanket. It was in his hands before she could blink. He spoke softly as he approached.

"You're going to get cold if we don't cover you. Let me put the blanket around you and then we'll go in and send for Chelsea. You'd like to see Chelsea wouldn't you?"

"I don't want anyone to touch me."

"I won't, but we need to keep you warm."

She tried to move away when he came closer, but she was trembling so much she was out of strength. She flinched and shrunk away from him as best she could, but he kept his word, and she felt only the blanket as it surrounded her.

"I'm going to lift you now," he was saying as he carefully covered her.

"No Brandon, no. Please—" Sunny begged him but he ignored her and lifted her in his arms.

Sunny told herself to fight, but the feel of him and the smell of his coat made her sob. Her tears approached hysterics as she clung to him. Brandon cradled her tenderly against his chest all the way upstairs to her bedroom.

"Where are you putting me?" Sunny cried suddenly when she felt the mattress beneath her.

"Your own bed. It's the best place for you right now." He tried to reason with her, but she was struggling to keep him near. "Sunny, what is it?"

"Don't leave me," she cried, clutching at him frantically. "I know you're angry, Brandon, but please don't leave me until Chelsea comes. Please, Brandon. I know we've had words, but I need you here."

"Shhh," he hushed her gently and stayed close enough so she could touch him. She was trembling violently, and her trembling, along with her words, made him feel as if someone had thrust a knife into his side.

"I won't go," he told her softly and pressed a kiss on her brow, his hand covering the trembling one that clung to his shirt. "I won't ever leave if you don't want me to. Chelsea has been sent for and so has the doctor."

Brandon kept up a steady flow of talk, but Sunny heard little of it. Some of the shock was lessened and her mind, terrorized as it was, was trying to work through the attack. She remembered that the men had immediately ripped her clothing and searched her. And their voices, their accents, were so familiar. Thirteen years ago...

Sunny's mind stopped there. What she was thinking was just too impossible for words. Could she really trust her own ears when she had been so terrified? Before she could work it through, she heard Chelsea's voice. She thought she might be able to hold her tears even with seeing her, but then Rand's face came into view. He had been in London on business, and Sunny had forced herself not to yearn for someone who couldn't be there. The sight of him standing at the foot of her bed as Chelsea's arms surrounded her was more than she could take. Blackness came crowding in.

"Actually, I'm quite pleased that she slept through the entire examination," the doctor told Brandon and Rand. "There are scratches on her, as though she was searched by someone with long fingernails," he said thoughtfully, "but other than the area around her mouth, she's not even bruised."

Rand was so weak with relief that he couldn't even stand. Brandon saw the doctor to the door and rejoined his brother-in-law. Neither one spoke for a few moments and when Chelsea came in the door, Brandon rose in alarm.

"Who's with Sunny?"

"Tildy," Chelsea told him calmly and watched as he slumped back down.

"This is all my fault," Rand spoke raggedly.

"No, Rand," Chelsea began, but her husband shook his head.

Just after the doctor had come, Rand had called the entire staff to search the grounds for the intruders, but they had found nothing. Brandon sent two groomsmen to the village to summon the constable.

When all were gathered, Tildy stepped forth to tell Rand that Wilson, Tina, and Sunny's long-time maid, Christie, were all missing.

Rand's heart, already in agony over the night's events, plummeted. He'd been so sure about Wilson, and when he had found out that Tina had been a maid at Heather's, he had reassured Sunny on that end too. Christie was a mystery to everyone.

Now Rand sat fingering Sunny's ruined dress. It had been slashed repeatedly. What had they been searching for? He began to pray.

"I've been formulating some plans," Brandon stated, breaking into Rand's thoughts. "When Sunny wakes up, I don't want you to say anything to her. I'm leaving for London tonight—"

Brandon went on to outline his plan in a soft voice, Rand's and Chelsea's heads bent close to his own.

"She won't like it," Chelsea said when he was through.

"But it's the best thing to do," Rand interjected. "I wish I'd thought of it." Rand praised God that Brandon was stepping in.

"I realize Sunny won't be too happy, but I'm not about to have her sit around here and wait for the next attack," Brandon said as he stood. "I'll be back in two days, possibly less. Tell Sunny I'll explain everything later."

Brandon took his leave, and Rand and Chelsea went upstairs. Chelsea climbed into bed next to Sunny, who never stirred, and Rand made himself comfortable on the daybed by the window, his gun beneath his pillow. Surprisingly, all slept through the night. The turmoil didn't begin again until Brandon returned.

Fifty ~ Three

"I WON'T GO," SUNNY TOLD BRANDON, only to be ignored.

"Chelsea, get someone in here to pack Sunny's trunk. We're leaving in one hour."

Sunny gritted her teeth in frustration when Chelsea moved to do as he bade. She turned from the door to find Brandon studying her.

"I tried asking you, Sunny, but you wouldn't budge." Brandon's voice was soft, but Sunny caught the underlying hint of steel. "You *are* leaving Ravenscroft today. I know you're not feeling at your best, and I wish you liked the idea more, but even if you hate me forever, I'm going to see you safely away from here."

All of Sunny's anger drained away. "I don't hate you," she responded. "But you're treating me as if I have no mind at all. I really don't think they'll come back. They obviously know that whatever they're searching for is not here—" she stopped when she could see he was not listening.

"Brandon!" Sunny spoke in frustration. "I'm not an idiot!"

He came to her then and put his hands on her arms. "I know you're not an idiot." His voice was deep and passionate. "What you are, is someone very dear to me, someone I plan on protecting from whomever is out there, and even from herself if necessary."

Brandon's hands moved to frame her face. He bent low and pressed his lips against her forehead.

"We are leaving here in one hour," he whispered, holding her eyes with his own. "Unless you want to leave this house in your robe, you had better get dressed, Sunny."

He was out her bedroom door before she could reply. Chelsea had come in on his departure, and Sunny could only stare at her. It felt as if the whole world had joined forces against her.

What Sunny didn't realize was how much Chelsea had missed this Brandon. This was the Brandon who had sailed without hesitation to Darhabar to bring Rand's sister home. This was the Brandon who captained his own ship with skill and success, and then stepped with confidence into the title of Duke of Briscoe upon their grandfather's death.

This was the Brandon who had been missing since Dinah walked away from him and he had realized his love for Sunny. Chelsea didn't know what was to happen next, but the real Brandon had returned, and in that she took great comfort. She also knew that Brandon's words had been wise: England was no longer safe; not until they found out who was trying to harm Sunny.

The ride to London, all three hours of it, was made in almost complete silence. Sunny asked once where they were going, only to be told by Brandon that he would explain everything as soon as he was able. She saw that she was going to have to be content with that. Even though she was not angry, she was not in the mood to converse either.

Brandon was just as glad for the silence. He praised God that Dallas Knight had been in port, and more than willing to help out, when Brandon had ridden to London two days earlier. He prayed that since that time, Dallas had found enough time to take care of every need.

The carriage lurched into a hole in the next moment, and Brandon heard his pistols move where they were concealed beneath the seat. His eyes flew to Sunny, but she was lost in thought, and Brandon knew she hadn't noticed. Even so, Brandon continued to watch her.

This was no arduous task. Considering she hadn't wanted to leave, she was as beautifully turned out as ever in a navy traveling suit and matching hat. Smiling, he saw Grandmama Sunny's ring on her finger. Sunny noticed, and Brandon watched her brows raise in question.

"I was just thinking about the night I gave you that ring," he confessed.

Sunny brought her right hand up for inspection. She smiled at the memory too and thought once again how dear the ring had been to her all these years. Unfortunately, the smile was short-lived. When she again turned to look out the window, she told herself that Brandon only smiled because he still saw her as that little 14-year-old girl.

Dallas watched the Hawkesbury coach stop on the dock. His ship rocked easily beneath his wide-legged stance, and his brows raised in surprise when the door opened and first Brandon, and then a woman, stepped down.

Why, Dallas was asking himself, had he been under the impression that Brandon was bringing a young girl on board for protection? As they drew near, Dallas could see that he couldn't have been more mistaken. She was very definitely a woman, and a beauty at that. Dallas' eyes lingered on her a moment, and he nodded briefly when her eyes met his. Watching her as she moved, Dallas realized she hadn't spoken a word.

Sunny walked away from the men and stood near the rigging. Brandon had watched the interplay, and Dallas found the older man's eyes on him when he looked back.

Brandon smiled at him suddenly and was rewarded with a white-toothed grin. The men were alike in height and build, but Dallas' skin was deeply tanned from his days at sea. With dark wavy brown hair and crystal blue eyes, Dallas looked as much like a pirate as anyone could imagine. His pants and knee-high boots were black, and his shirt was dazzling white with billowing sleeves and an open neckline. He even sported a small gold hoop in one ear.

"I'd forgotten what a handsome scoundrel you were, Dallas," Brandon admitted grudgingly.

Dallas' grin only widened.

"Whatever you do," Brandon spoke again, this time only half joking, "don't let her fall for you. I don't think I could handle that."

Dallas' chuckle was low as he watched Brandon walk away. "The Grand Duke," as Dallas teasingly called him, was as charming as they came and had never been troubled with females. The two men had always agreed that God would provide the perfect mates someday, and in the meantime, there was no use worrying or asking for trouble.

Dallas' gaze flicked back to the woman. Obviously Brandon's worry- and trouble-free days were over. It looked as though "trouble" had come in the form of a slim, chestnut-haired beauty with deep amethyst eyes.

By the time Sunny sat down to supper that night, she was nearly out on her feet. She was hungry, but when Brandon sat down across from her and urged her to eat, she knew she couldn't take anymore. It took a moment for Brandon to see that she was staring at him and hadn't touched her plate.

"Eat up, Sunny," he told her.

"I want to know what's going on," she stated resolutely, her voice soft.

"As soon as we eat," Brandon replied, thinking he had never seen her look so drained.

Sunny didn't move a muscle; she hardly even blinked. Her hands were folded sedately in her lap, but she told herself that she wouldn't do another thing until she knew why she was on this ship.

Brandon easily read all of this on her face and put his fork next to his plate.

"I've known Dallas Knight since my sailing days. He's an American who trades in our waters. I'd trust him with my life; yours too. When you were attacked, I contacted him and told him I had to get someone out of England quickly. I really didn't feel I had a choice, Sunny. I know my actions seem highhanded, but on land anyone can be hiding in the next room and listening to every word.

"Dallas was more than willing to help, and handpicked this crew. Every man on the ship would protect you with his own life. You're completely safe out on the sea."

"But where are we going?" Sunny was still confused.

"We're not sailing anywhere in particular, if that's what you mean. Tomorrow at midday we're meeting another ship. One of my men will be on board, and we'll find out what the men I've hired in London have learned. I'm going to find out who wants you, or *what* they want, before I take you back home."

It all made such perfect sense now. Brandon's comment about others listening was the reason he wouldn't tell her before this time where they were headed. His taking her from Ravenscroft without servant or chaperon told her he was more concerned with her safety than with her reputation. With a tired nod and a soft thank-you, Sunny began to eat. Brandon left her to her thoughts.

She was drooping over her plate by the time she was finished, and Brandon quickly downed his coffee and left her alone for the night. Falling into bed fully dressed, Sunny slept until morning.

At noon the next day Sunny watched as a longboat rowed toward the ship, which had lifted anchor the night before and was now circling just beyond the mouth of the Thames. Two men were on the craft and one of them climbed the ladder and came onto the deck. Sunny watched at a distance as the man and Brandon talked. She saw Brandon scowl, and not sure she could watch anymore, turned away.

"He won't let anything harm you—do you realize that?"

Dallas had come up to Sunny and stood by her at the railing. She tried to smile at him, but it was more than she could manage.

"It's just struck me how many people, including Brandon, could be harmed because of me. That scares me quite a bit."

"But it's not because of you," Dallas spoke reasonably. "I know Hawk would be upset if he knew you felt that way."

Sunny sighed, her gaze still out to sea. She was quiet a moment, thinking that this was the first time she had spoken to the captain. She turned to Dallas, her back still to Brandon.

"I thank you for your words, Captain Knight, and would also like to say I'm sorry for the way I acted when I came aboard yesterday. I was quite rude, and I would now like to ask your forgiveness."

Dallas looked down into Sunny's captivating face and knew in an instant why Brandon would give his life for this woman.

"I took no offense," he stated compassionately. "I only hope you will be comfortable while on board. The *Zephyr* was not built with luxury in mind, but if you do need something, please ask."

"Thank you, Captain."

"Please call me Dallas."

Sunny smiled then, her first real smile since she had been attacked. Dallas returned the smile, nodded politely, and moved away.

Sunny's mind ran in all directions as she once again stood alone. She had prayed herself into a semblance of calm when Brandon appeared at her side.

"I have news, but I think we had better go below."

"Brandon, what is it?" Sunny clutched at his arm the way fear clutched at her chest.

Brandon was tempted to press her below, but with the fear he saw in her eyes, he felt it almost cruel to wait even a moment.

"Christie, your maid, has been found dead." Brandon spoke softly and watched as grief entered her eyes.

"How? Where?" Sunny whispered.

"She was found in a London alley, murdered, shot in the heart."

Brandon reached for her as he watched the color drain completely from her face.

"I'm not going to faint," she whispered, even as the ship seemed to tilt.

Brandon ignored this and lifted her into his arms. Sunny did feel quite weak, but was conscious all the way to her cabin, where she finally gave way to the tears gathering in her throat.

She sobbed against Brandon's broad chest until she was totally spent. He then lifted her onto the bunk, and Sunny slept before he could even cover her with the blanket.

Fifty-Four

"BE CAREFUL FOR NOTHING, but in everything by prayer and supplication with thanksgiving let your requests be made known unto God. And the peace of God, which passeth all understanding, shall keep your hearts and minds in Christ Jesus."

Sunny read the verses and sat very still on her bunk. Her Bible, open to the book of Philippians, lay in her lap. She had slept for nearly two hours and awakened with a roaring headache. The cook had brought her some tea, and now she was trying to deal with the ache she felt inside. It was greater than the one centered behind her eyes.

"Was Christie innocent in all of this, Lord?" Sunny spoke to the empty cabin. "Or did she make choices that led to her death?"

No answers were forthcoming, but Sunny continued to pray and give her anxiety to God. She confessed all known sin in her life, so as to be certain that her fellowship with God would be unhindered. Then Sunny found herself asking that whoever was out there would confront her.

"I'm not afraid for myself, Lord, and I want to see this settled. I know Brandon would not want me to take the risk, but Lord, let them come to my face. If it's my life they want, I would wish to know why. If it's something I possess, I'll gladly give it."

Sunny felt a tremendous lift of her spirits after her prayer. Her head still throbbed, but she knew that Brandon would be coming to fetch her for dinner very soon now, and she strongly suspected that, for the moment at least, food would be just the thing.

Sunny dozed off again for a time, but when Brandon knocked on her door, she was in a clean dress and her hair was brushed. By just looking at her, Brandon could see a significant change had taken place. He held his inquiry for the moment, since Dallas was expecting them in the small captain's dining room for dinner. He hoped, however, that before he took her back to her cabin, he would have a chance to question her.

"You actually jumped from the ship?" Dallas' face was a mask of shock as he stared at Sunny's quiet, serene features. She and Brandon exchanged a glance, and both laughed.

"You're giving away all my secrets, Brandon," Sunny told him softly, and again he simply chuckled.

Dinner, the men, and their light banter had been a balm to Sunny's heart as the evening progressed. They had piled her plate high, and then proceeded to make her laugh so much with stories of their days together on the same ship that she couldn't eat.

At one point Brandon had teased Sunny about jumping ship, and Dallas had wanted to know all. It hadn't been funny at the time, but the look on Dallas' face had been worth any embarrassment Sunny might have felt over the retelling.

"So how did you get back?" he now wanted to know.

"Well," Sunny answered, her eyes wide with innocence. "Brandon called to me to come back, and of course, being the compliant person that I am, I came immediately."

Brandon shouted with laughter on this, but Dallas hadn't been fooled in the first place.

"Let me guess," he said dryly. "He dragged you back, kicking and screaming."

"Actually," Brandon interjected, a smile lighting his handsome face, "she never did scream. She bit me, but never made a sound."

"Oh, Brandon." Sunny's lovely eyes now held alarm. "I'd forgotten all about that bite!"

Instead of teasing her for worrying about an incident that was years old, Brandon's gaze became very tender. He reached with one hand and stroked her cheek with the backs of his fingers. Sunny's smile was one of profound gratitude and caring as she looked into his eyes.

Dallas had not made a sound during this exchange, but Sunny suddenly remembered his presence. She stood so quickly that her chair scraped loudly against the wood floor.

"Don't go, Sunny," Brandon said softly, even reaching for her hand. Sunny evaded his touch.

"Actually, I'd planned on getting some fresh air." Sunny spoke these words to the tablecloth, her voice breathless with shame. "Thank you for supper, Dallas. I'm going up on deck now. I'll see you both later." She never once met either man's eyes, and they both watched as she fled. The room was quiet only a moment before Dallas spoke.

"Why in the world are you two hiding your love from each other?"

"It's not that easy, Dallas," Brandon told him with regret. "In her eyes, I'm only a brother."

Brandon ignored Dallas' snort of unbelief and stood. "I realize she has nothing to fear from your men, but I don't think she should be alone up there."

"I quite agree," Dallas said, having to refrain from offering to go topside himself and look after Sunny. Brandon looked miserable right then, and the last thing his old shipmate needed was to be teased.

Thinking how he'd been praying for a wife just days ago, Dallas sat still for some time after the room emptied. Suddenly the idea of *not* being in love didn't seem so bad to the young sea captain at all.

The light of the full moon bounced off the water, and Sunny felt mesmerized by the sight. The image of herself being manhandled and searched momentarily blocked her view of the water, and suddenly she trembled. Other than tenderness on her back where she lay on the ground, and a slight overall body ache, she had no physical side effects. Mentally, however, she was attacked all over again and at the strangest times, like now.

Why the remembrance should come in so strongly just then, Sunny could not guess. Deep in contemplation, Sunny didn't hear Brandon approach. She started violently, only to hear his soft, deep voice apologizing with great regret.

"Oh, Sunny, forgive me. I never dreamed you hadn't heard me. Are you all right?"

"Yes," she spoke softly. "I was just thinking; my mind was miles away." Sunny hoped he wouldn't ask for more than that. Now that he was near, her every sense was centered on him.

"It's beautiful out here, isn't it?" Brandon commented, his heart going to the first time they had met on the *Flying Surprise*, a ship very much like this one.

"Yes," Sunny agreed with him.

Brandon turned to lean against the railing, giving him a perfect view of Sunny's profile and just the right angle to observe the way the moonlight played off her hair. She was so lovely to look at, but Brandon was very aware of the beautiful person she was inside as well. He watched as she folded her arms over her chest and continued to stare out to sea.

"It's chilly out here," Brandon offered. "Maybe you should go below."

She didn't answer right away, and Brandon heard her sigh. "Some things never change, do they, Brandon?"

He was so surprised by this question he didn't answer.

"I'm still a child to you," Sunny went on. "So much of a child that I don't even know when I'm cold and should go inside out of the wind."

Brandon's hand grasped her upper arm, and he pulled her gently to stand before him.

"That's not true," he told her earnestly.

"Yes, Brandon, it is. All your actions toward me are those toward a little girl. You kissed me once, and it repulsed you. When will I be a woman in your eyes?" Sunny's voice was filled with regret and resignation.

Before Sunny could draw another breath, Brandon's head dipped and his lips captured her own. There was nothing rough or savage in his kiss or hold, but Sunny knew he was serious. She also felt as if she could melt into her shoes. After what seemed an eternity, Brandon raised his head. Disappointment knifed through Sunny when he did not speak of love.

"I haven't thought of you as a child for years, Sunny. Nothing about you repulses me, but if there is any doubt lingering in your mind, I'll gladly kiss you again."

"No," Sunny spoke breathlessly, tempted to say yes. Brandon released her, and she stepped back. "That won't be necessary."

Brandon's breath was as ragged as her own. "Whether or not you're cold, Sunny, I'd like you to go below."

"Yes, I'll do that," Sunny turned without another word and made her way to her cabin. She was quite aware of the way Brandon followed her and saw her safely into her room, which made it easier for her to hold her tears until her door was closed. By the time Sunny slept, she had convinced herself that Brandon still felt only friendship for her. The kiss had been used to make a point.

Sunny surprised herself by falling almost immediately to sleep. When she woke in the morning, she felt refreshed, and even though it was still dark out, she knew she'd had a full night's sleep. After lighting her lantern, she reached for her Bible, read for a time in the Psalms, and then spent some time in prayer. While telling the Lord again that she would prefer to meet her enemy face to face, Sunny suddenly had a clear recollection of the night in the garden.

"How could I have forgotten that?" Sunny spoke aloud even as she was throwing off the covers and reaching for her robe. Unmindful of her hair and attire, Sunny grabbed her lantern and dashed to the door and across the passageway to bang on Brandon's cabin door.

"Brandon," Sunny cried. "Brandon, I've remembered—"

The door was wrenched open to reveal a sleepy Brandon, who had come to life from a sound sleep to pull on his pants and a shirt in order to answer her summons.

"Are you all right?" he asked, his voice sharp-edged with concern.

"Yes. I'm sorry to scare you, but I forgot all about their voices. The men who attacked me at Ravenscroft had accents. They sounded as though they were from Darhabar."

Brandon could only stare at her, his mind racing in all directions. A sound reached out of the darkness as someone came below decks and approached. Brandon's arm went protectively around Sunny. She found herself huddled against his side, thinking she never wanted to move.

"It's me." Dallas' voice came from the gloom before he stepped into the dim light.

Brandon and Sunny both relaxed but didn't step apart.

"I'm glad to find you up." His voice was serious, and Brandon tensed once again. "We've been contacted, or I should say, Sunny has."

"When?" Sunny wanted to know.

"Just minutes ago." Dallas held out a scroll-like paper to Sunny, and both men watched her shaking hands as she opened it.

"Shani," the letter began. "I wish to come aboard your ship. I have information for you, and I have something I wish from you in return. If your flag flies at half-mast by noon on the fourteenth, I will consider myself welcome." It was signed, "Ahmad Khan, Ruler of Darhabar."

"The morning of the fourteenth," Sunny whispered mostly to herself. "That's today."

Fifty-Five

SUNNY PACED THE SMALL CONFINES OF HER CABIN while Brandon, sitting in the room's one chair, watched her.

"When you returned to see the emir, did he give any indication that he would someday see you again?"

"No. He was very smooth in manner, and I got the impression he was glad to be rid of me. He did question me about you, but when I said you were doing well, he seemed quite satisfied with that."

Sunny shook her head in bewilderment. "Do you suppose he had Christie murdered?"

"I don't know, Sunny." Brandon's voice was soft with regret as he watched the play of grief on her face.

"I wouldn't put it past him," she added with remorse. Brandon, who had been having the identical thought, stayed quiet.

"Come here, Sunny," Brandon finally said. Sunny sat on the edge of her bunk, and Brandon moved his chair close. "Let's take a few minutes and pray before he comes. Our God is sovereign. We need to stop fretting and put our trust in Him."

Sunny placed her hand in his when Brandon extended his fingers, and listened while he prayed. He thanked God for whatever His purpose was in these events and surrendered their wills to His.

Sunny knew God's peace as she prayed along with Brandon. It was easy to imagine his warm hand would feel much like that of the Savior's, large and reassuring, as she passed through these rough waters. They were still praying when Dallas knocked on the door, telling them that the emir was waiting in his cabin.

Brandon preceded Sunny into Dallas' cabin but did not speak to the emir. He stepped aside as soon as he saw that it was safe, allowing Sunny a full view of her one-time father. Sunny came slowly into the room, her gaze locked with Ahmad Khan's. Dallas, after stepping in behind her, shut the door.

"I have received an update on you every month you've been gone." He spoke, and his voice was just as she remembered. "Often the reports spoke of your beauty and grace. The words did not do you justice, Shani."

The name seemed to snap Sunny out of her trance, and she lifted her chin slightly.

"My name is Sunny Gallagher. You will not address me as Shani."

Had the interchange not been so serious, Brandon would have laughed. How had he entertained thoughts that Sunny might not be able to handle this situation? Brandon watched the emir bow to Sunny's wishes, his eyes alert for any surprises.

"Of course." The emir's voice was smooth, hiding his disappointment over Sunny's response to him. "If we could have a moment alone, I would like—"

"Wilson!" Sunny interrupted as her gaze moved to yet another man in the cabin. She missed the emir's frown over the interruption, his eyes narrowing in anger. His gaze swept the room and found both Brandon and Dallas watching him intently, their expressions giving nothing away. The emir's features smoothed, and he made himself listen patiently to Sunny and Wilson's conversation.

"You don't recognize me without my beard, do you, Sunny," Wilson commented, his voice more kind and personal than Sunny had ever heard it. "You hated me some days, especially when I made you study your English lesson when you wanted to be in the stables."

Sunny's mouth dropped open in a most unfeminine way. "Uncle Graham?" she whispered.

"You've not been out of my sight since you landed in London over four years ago," Wilson told her gently.

Disappointment knifed through Sunny. "So you have been the one reporting to Ahmad Khan?"

"No, that was your maid Tina. It became a little more difficult when you left the Jamiesons' for Willows' End, but she was still able to keep tabs. Then you moved to Ravenscroft and she moved with you, making reports infinitely more simple."

Sunny's gaze now swung back to the emir. "You will explain yourself," she commanded him.

"Orders, Sunny?" His voice was mocking, his eyes again glinting, this time with the light of a man who always gets his way. In Sunny's younger days this look would have sent her to the floor, instead her chin raised yet another fraction of an inch.

"There are no words to describe the hurt I felt when you sent me away, but that little girl is long gone. You no longer have the power to hurt me. In your letter you spoke of something you want from me. I have nothing, so I see no reason for you to stay."

"Where is the jewel box I gave you?" the emir asked without warning.

"Why?" Sunny demanded.

"Because the document that secures my position on the throne is inside."

"I have no such document."

"Bring it to me, and I will show you." The emir's calm was commendable, but Sunny was not fooled. He wanted the box with every fiber of his being; his eyes gave him away. Sunny silently praised God that she had taken it from her desk just before she left with Brandon.

Sunny's eyes went to Brandon, and he gave her a slight nod. Dallas stepped forward, and with whispered words, Sunny told him where he would find the box in her cabin. Sunny continued her interview when the door closed.

"You will tell me everything or not touch the box."

The emir was stubbornly silent until Dallas entered once again and shut the door. The sight of the box seemed to loosen his tongue.

"From early childhood you heard of Darhabar's centennial year and the Centennial Seal. Now, in six months' time, the centennial approaches. I am on the throne because at the last centennial, my grandfather held the document and the ring. There is a powerful family who wishes to usurp the throne. They will stop at nothing to gain the ring and document you possess. This is why I sent you away with the document and the seal, and why I have come." He spoke this as though it answered every question, but Sunny was not satisfied.

"It is unlike you to come in this way. Where is Ali? He usually does your dirty work." The emir's entire stance changed at Sunny's words, and he looked old and defeated.

"Ali is dead. As I said to you, they will stop at nothing."

"My maid Christie is dead," Sunny went on ruthlessly. "She was murdered in a London alley. It looks as though *you* will stop at nothing as well?"

"She was working for my enemy, as was Phipps—both bought by the lure of much gold. I had nothing to do with her death."

Sunny was not sure she believed him, but other questions crowded into her mind.

"But if she knew where the ring was, why did Christie not take the box years ago?"

"Christie knew nothing. Tina knew, but she had orders to report to me and only keep an eye on the box. When the attack came, she panicked and ran. She tried to find the box before she left, but you had moved it."

"The attack—" Sunny began, her face going quite pale.

"Was from my enemy," the emir told her, again masking his pain that she could find him capable of such an action against her.

"What about Wilson?"

"He also knew the contents of the box, but he had been misled and was not at Ravenscroft during the attack. His orders were to waylay the men, but they eluded him."

Sunny felt limp with all she was hearing and suddenly she was very sorry for the emir, whose whole life hinged on a seal ring and a piece of paper. Sunny turned slowly and took the box from Dallas. She stepped forward and handed it to the emir.

All in the room watched as the emir moved a piece of wood on the side of the box and then slid the entire base to the side. Just as he predicted, a piece of paper and the top portion of a seal ring rested inside. The compartment itself had been built around both objects, so they never gave hint of movement in their secure hiding place.

As the emir drew them forth, Sunny once again watched his demeanor change. As if the cares of the world had been lifted from his shoulders, his face glowed with an inner triumph. He unfolded the paper and read it, even as he tightly squeezed the ring in his fist.

"You have what you want," Sunny said softly. "I hope that I will not be followed, reported on, or bothered in any way, ever again."

Sunny was surprised at the vulnerable look that crossed the older man's features.

"May I have a word with you in private?" he asked. Sunny had never seen him so humble, but she was not comfortable with being alone with him.

"I think whatever you have to say can be said right now."

The emir nodded, looking hesitant, and then began. "I have long regretted the way I sent you from me. I knew that someday I would see you again, and this made the situation bearable. My oldest son will be ruler someday, and he has not yet wived. I wish for you to return with me and be his wife. You would be the most beautiful woman in all of Darhabar. There is no wish my son would not grant you. You would be treated as a queen for the rest of your years."

"You want me to return to Darhabar?" Sunny asked in stunned confusion, not really believing her ears.

"Yes," the emir stated quietly. "My ship is near. I wish you to leave with me today."

Fifty-Six

BRANDON WATCHED THE PLAY OF EMOTIONS on Sunny's face. To his eyes she actually appeared to be considering the idea.

"I need to speak with you, Sunny." Brandon spoke for the first time.

Sunny barely heard him as she stared at Ahmad Khan.

"Sunny," Brandon repeated himself, this time taking her arm. "I would have a word with you."

He did not allow her to object or ignore him this time, but with his hand holding her arm, moved out into the passageway to stand in front of her cabin.

"You're not really considering going with him, are you?" Brandon demanded.

"He just took me by surprise." Sunny spoke as if in a daze, not even looking at Brandon.

She suddenly found herself in his hands. Brandon's fingers were grasping her upper arms and holding her nearly against him.

"You can't go. Do you hear me, Sunny? You *can't* go."

Sunny looked into Brandon's face for the first time. He looked desperate.

"Why, Brandon?" Sunny's voice was whisper soft. "Why can't I leave?"

"Because you can't," he stated emphatically.

"Why?" Sunny pressed him.

Brandon hesitated only a moment, before saying words that

329

sounded as though they'd been wrenched from him.

"Because I love you." Brandon had to hold back from telling her that he had loved her for years and always would.

Sunny wanted nothing more than to throw her arms around him, but the emir's face came to mind, and Sunny knew she had a job to complete.

When Brandon could read nothing in her expression, he slowly released her. Sunny, knowing that if she looked at him she would burst into tears, moved away from his touch and back to Dallas' cabin. Knowing that he would physically detain Sunny if she tried to leave with the emir, Brandon waited outside the door.

Only minutes passed before Ahmad Khan and Wilson exited the cabin. Wilson glanced at Brandon's strained features, but the emir did nothing as they moved topside. Brandon would have gone to the cabin, but the door opened then and Dallas emerged.

"She wants to be alone," Dallas told him.

"What did he say to her?"

Dallas shook his head. "A pack of lies, but I could tell they hurt."

Dallas moved to go on deck then and Brandon, after a brief glance at the cabin door, followed him.

"I regretted my offer the moment you left the cabin," the emir had said. "I can see now that you would never again fit into the royal household. You obviously no longer know your place. Blinded by your beauty, I momentarily thought you would make a suitable queen."

Sunny knew the words should have no effect on her, but she had been stung. When she had heard the footsteps leave in the companionway, Sunny had left Dallas' cabin for the security of her own. She'd prayed and cried, and after a time, slept.

When she woke and looked out, it was to find it growing dark outside and the ship already docked in London. They had never been out of sight of land, so this shouldn't have surprised her. With sudden and painful remembrance, Sunny thought of the words she had forced Brandon to say.

You're a fool, Sunny Gallagher, she told herself. *Why did you do such a thing? What kind of love declaration is it when you have to force it out of the man? He certainly couldn't have meant it the way you wanted him to.*

Sunny told herself she was not going to torture herself any longer. She washed her face, brushed her hair, and went in search of Brandon. Better to face him in embarrassment than to wonder and wait. Unbelievable pain assailed her when Dallas told her he was gone. He'd had some things to take care of and would be back soon. Sunny moved wordlessly toward her cabin to pack.

When Sunny returned some 45 minutes later and asked Dallas to have someone bring her trunk topside, he knew his attempts to detain her would be a waste of effort.

"Sunny," he said kindly. "Please wait for Brandon."

"He told you to have me wait?"

"Well, no," the sea captain began. "But he just left, and I know—"

"I need to go home, Dallas. Please see to my trunk."

"I won't," Dallas decided. "You need to wait."

"Then I'll go without it," Sunny said, starting for the gangplank. Dallas, seeing no help for it, had her trunk retrieved and followed her.

"Please help me find a carriage, Lord," he heard her mumble as they moved toward the dock. She walked along, ignoring the astonished looks of the sailors around her, and stopped abruptly when a carriage drove up and Wilson suddenly appeared before her.

"I've a carriage for you, my lady," he stated softly, his eyes not betraying the tear of emotions within.

"More reports, Wilson?" Sunny asked with regret.

"Never again, my lady. I followed the emir's orders because I feared whom he might entrust with the job. And now today, as always, I would gladly lay down my life for yours."

Sunny's eyes held Wilson's as she tried, in her exhaustion, to read the man. He never blinked or looked ashamed, and Sunny was certain she would know his honesty by his eyes.

"How did the emir feel about your decision?"

"It was nothing new to him. He's known all along I would stay in England and keep watch over you like I've done for over four years."

Sunny was so awash with relief that he was now an ally and not an enemy that she nearly cried. Rand had been right about this man all along. Sunny couldn't look at Wilson any longer, so she looked at the carriage instead.

"This is Rand's carriage, isn't it?"

"Yes, my lady. I've seen him and asked if I could borrow it to wait for you."

"I want to go home," she told Wilson softly, not really having heard his words. "Home to Ravenscroft."

"As you wish, my lady," Wilson said, opening the door.

"Sunny," Dallas tried again. "If you'll just give Brandon a little more time."

"My reputation will be in shreds as it is, Dallas," she spoke softly, "and I simply can't stay here any longer. Thank you for all you've done."

Dallas watched Sunny disappear into the interior, helplessness washing over him. Brandon had said he would be very brief, and Dallas had no clue as to how to contact him. Now Sunny was leaving, and nothing had been resolved. Dallas knew as he went back on board that he could pray for them. Beyond that, however, he could not get involved.

Halfway to Ravenscroft, Sunny told Wilson she would rather go to Willows' End. They pulled along the willow-lined drive very early the next morning, Sunny having completely forgotten that Rand and Chelsea were not there. She was relieved however, to see lights downstairs in the library windows. And she was equally glad to see Miles, since she was nearly out on her feet and terribly disappointed that her brother wasn't there.

"They're in London, aren't they?" Sunny sounded like a lost girl. "Wilson had their coach and said as much, but I never grasped that they were right there."

Miles, very glad that he had been unable to sleep, wondered with pain for his aunt and what she'd been through in the last few days. Gently, he made her feel at home.

"What did you want to see Papa about, Sunny? Maybe I can help."

"I want to go away for a time, Miles. I need something of a rest, and even though I'm looking forward to going back to Ravenscroft in safety, I feel the need to get away."

"There's something else going on here, isn't there, Sunny? You don't have to tell me, but I think you might feel better if you did."

Sunny looked into his kind eyes for just a moment before bursting into tears and telling all. Miles was furious over the things the emir said to Sunny and sincerely shocked that Brandon would leave her on the ship. Even though he believed that Brandon had been totally honest when he said he loved Sunny, he could understand her hurt.

The hours passed as Miles, much as Dallas had, tried to talk Sunny out of leaving. But when he saw how determined she was, he decided to lend her his aid. They went together to Ravenscroft. Miles watched Sunny, tired as she was, wake the household and take control.

"Aunt Lucy," Sunny told her aunt calmly, finding her surprisingly lucid for being awakened at such an early hour, "I'm going away for a few weeks."

"Alone, my dear?" Aunt Lucy looked uncertain.

"Yes," Sunny told her.

"Where is Brandon?"

"I don't know, but this doesn't concern him." Sunny's voice was final.

"But, my dear, you've had such a traumatic few days. Maybe I should go with you."

Sunny thought how little help Aunt Lucy had been after she had been attacked. The entire affair had upset her so, she'd taken to her bed.

"No, Aunt Lucy," Sunny's voice was gentle. "I wish to be alone."

"Oh, oh my," Aunt Lucy nearly flapped like a chicken. "Well then, take Tildy."

"Tildy will not want to leave you—"

"On the contrary," Aunt Lucy interrupted. "Tildy thinks the world of you, and she'd be only too happy to go. Isn't that right, Tildy?"

"Of course, my lady," the elderly servant spoke calmly. "I'll go and see to Lady Sunny's packing."

"Thank you, Tildy," Sunny responded, feeling very relieved that Aunt Lucy had insisted.

"Now," Sunny turned back to her. "I want to tell you where I'm going, but I want you to keep it to yourself. I'll have Wilson and Tildy with me, so I'll be perfectly safe."

"Oh, oh my," Aunt Lucy did flap then, her head shaking in fierce denial, and her elbows going back and forth at her sides like wings. "But it won't work, my dear. Brandon or Rand will come and give me one look, and I'll tell all."

Sunny opened her mouth to deny it, but then closed it with a snap. The old girl was right. She was no match for Brandon or Rand.

"You're right," Sunny told her. "I'll just go, and see you when I return in about a month's time."

It wasn't what Aunt Lucy wanted to hear, but she could see Sunny had made up her mind. Within an hour, Sunny was in her own carriage, Tildy seated across from her. Packed with fresh clothes, her trunk was stowed in the rear. The coachman and Wilson sat up top. Miles stood at the door of the carriage, his tender feelings for her written all over his face.

"Are you sure you're not running away?"

"I'm sure, Miles. I just need some time to think. I really *can* live with the fact that Brandon and I are never going to be anything more than friends, but I just need some time. You'll keep my secret?"

"You know better than to ask," he admonished her. "I'll see you in about a month, and believe me, you'll love Lord and Lady Briton."

With these words the door was shut, and Miles watched as the carriage lurched onto the road. Inside, Sunny sat looking out the window, but that didn't last long. Within three miles, she was sound asleep.

Fifty-Seven

IN A RARE SHOW OF DARING, Aunt Lucy stayed in her room, refusing to come down when she was told that Rand and Brandon had arrived.

It was much later that same day, and Lucy had done nothing but fret and stew over Sunny's departure. With a fierceness she didn't know she possessed, she took Sunny's side. She didn't care what Rand and Brandon did or said to her, she would never tell a soul where her dear Sunny had gone.

Some of Lucy's thunder was stolen when she remembered she didn't know where Sunny was. She made up for this, however, by staying in her room and ignoring the announcement. If she didn't come downstairs, Rand and Brandon would simply have to go away. She shifted in her chair and went back to the book she was reading, looking forward to the time when she could tell Tildy about the way she had championed Sunny.

Aunt Lucy completely underestimated Brandon's need to find the woman he loved. She was shocked speechless when there was a knock on her door and Rand's voice sounded in the hall.

"Please get dressed if there's a need, Aunt Lucy. Brandon and I are coming in."

The older woman gasped and stared in surprise at the door that opened just minutes later.

"Aunt Lucy," Rand's voice was gentle. "Are you coming down, or do we come in?" When the old woman stayed mute, Rand opened the door completely and he and Brandon entered.

"Where is she, Aunt Lucy? The maid downstairs said she was here and gone. Now tell us where Sunny is."

"I can't." Aunt Lucy was shaking with fear, but her heart was resolute. "Sunny didn't tell me, but if I did know, I still wouldn't tell. She wanted to be alone, and I for one respect her wish."

"She gave no hint at all?" Brandon's voice was deeper than Rand's, and Lucy was immediately reminded of a powerful young man she had secretly loved many years ago. She always melted at the sound of that voice, and although she held onto her resolve, she felt shaken.

"She didn't say. I trust her, and I trust Miles. If he was helping—"

"Miles was here?" Rand asked in astonishment, and Lucy could have pulled her own tongue out.

With a movement born of desperation, the older woman shifted in her chair and gave both men the cold shoulder. She was so angry with herself *and* with them that she could hardly think straight. She was surprised nearly witless when both men suddenly came toward her. They bent simultaneously to place a kiss on each withered cheek.

"I love you, Aunt Lucy," she heard Brandon say. She stared at their backs as they exited her bedroom with fast, long-legged strides.

"Miles talked about going to see Jordan and Holly," Chelsea told her worried husband and her pacing brother. "I'm not sure where he is right now."

"I'll head to Jordan's then," Brandon said. "I'll stop here on my way back out to tell you what I learn."

The words were no more out of Brandon's mouth than Miles entered the room. He looked slightly uncomfortable, but he had decided when he watched Sunny's carriage pull away that no one was going to bully him.

"Miles," his father asked, cutting right to the point. "Do you know where Sunny has gone?"

"I know where she was planning to go," he said evasively and fell silent.

His uncle and parents all stared at him, waiting for him to go on, but Miles only stared back. He was beginning to grow angry that they were putting him in this position.

"I need to talk with Sunny," Brandon told him quietly.

"You should have thought of that before you left her alone on that ship."

Chelsea stifled a gasp, and Rand looked at his son as if he had taken leave of his senses.

"I had reasons for leaving that ship." Brandon's anger matched his nephew's. "But I do *not* feel I need to explain myself to my nephew."

"Suit yourself," Miles said and started for the door.

"Don't open that door!" Rand commanded sternly. When Miles turned back, he saw just how upset his father had become.

"I'm not sure what has made you turn on Brandon this way," his father said. "But I think you had better tell us where Sunny is, and now."

"Why?" Miles asked baldly. "So he can do more controlling? She feels like a puppet on a string where Brandon is concerned. She wants to be alone, and she's with faithful servants who'll see that she comes to no harm. Brandon has hurt her terribly, and uncle or not, I'll not betray Sunny's trust in me. She'll be here in a month; you can talk to her then."

Rand opened his mouth to rebuke Miles, but Brandon interrupted.

"You're right, Miles. I have handled things badly and hurt Sunny." His voice was soft now, and Miles saw the pain in his eyes. "That's why I must find her. I know you gave your word, but please, Miles, please forgive my anger with you and tell me where she's gone."

"She'll never speak to me again." Miles felt torn in two.

"Yes, Miles, she will, because before we come back, she's going to know exactly how I feel. If you can't tell me where she is, then please head me in the right direction."

Miles couldn't ignore the pain he saw in the older man's eyes.

"She's gone north," Miles admitted painfully, only to have his uncle approach and surround him with his long arms. He spoke when Miles returned the embrace.

"I'll explain everything to her, and please, Miles, just try and imagine how you'd feel to be kept from the woman you love."

Brandon released Miles and moved toward the door. He turned back, and Rand caught his eyes.

"I'd head toward the Britons' if I were you," the older man

advised. "I can't be certain, but I think it's a pretty good guess."

Brandon thanked him and slipped out the door. Miles would not look at his parents, and when he tried to leave, Chelsea's voice stopped him with the door partly open.

"I know you hurt, Miles, and you feel as though your father and uncle have ganged up on you when you were trying to do the right thing, but please stay. Please stay so we can talk."

Miles hesitated. He turned to look at his mother and then his father.

"Please, Miles," Rand added gently, and the younger man shut the door and came back into the room.

Fifty Eight

THE RIDE TO THE BRITONS' ESTATE WAS LONG, so the coach made several stops on the way. Sunny knew it was not the wisest decision on her part to travel with just a maid, but Tildy, Wilson, and her coachman, Kent, watched over her like fierce hens with a chick.

Sunny was beginning to think she would never reach the Britons' estate when the coach came to a final stop. Armed with the letter of introduction Miles had given her, Sunny approached the door. It seemed that Lord and Lady Briton were not at home, but their spinster daughter, Maretta, greeted Sunny as if she were a long-lost friend, immediately seeing her into a warm bath and bed.

She had slept for almost 15 hours when she woke to find Tildy hovering near.

"You've eaten so little, my lady. Please get up and try something. I swear you're wasting away."

Sunny hated the look of distress in the elder servant's eyes, so she rose to clean up and dress. She found, as she sat before the mirror so Tildy could fix her hair, that Tildy was right. In just two days' time, Sunny's cheeks had begun to have a hollow look about them. She examined her wrist and hands and thought they looked bonier too.

Never one to carry surplus flesh, the scant bit of food she'd had on Dallas' ship and the last two grueling days were beginning to take their toll.

Knowing this still did nothing for Sunny's appetite when a sumptuous tea was placed before her. She nibbled a bit, but with the emotional turmoil and sleeping until after noon, she felt disoriented and listless. Tildy held her tongue when she saw how little Sunny had eaten, but inwardly she fretted terribly over her mistress.

Since she planned to be out that day, Maretta had left word for Sunny to make herself at home. Simply loving the rambling old castle, built in the early 1600's, Sunny was only too happy to oblige. She had no desire to ride. Instead she roamed the grounds, watching the birds and praying, giving all her heart over to her heavenly Father.

Sunny lifted her heart in thanksgiving that the whole affair with the emir had come to an end. She didn't try to deny that his treatment of her hurt, but if she had been afraid that seeing him again would make her long for Darhabar, she was wrong.

Greedy and self-seeking, Ahmad Khan was a wicked man in many ways. Although Sunny grieved for his soul, she knew he would not have had a positive influence on her. Her only regret was that she hadn't asked after Indira.

The image of Brandon's handsome face interrupted Sunny's prayers. Her eyes closed in pain, and she again told God that she would need His strength, and His strength alone, to go on. She believed with all of her heart that she could live as a mere friend to Brandon. And as soon as she'd rested up for the encounter, she would see him and apologize for the way she had acted on ship.

"I'm sure he didn't mean it when he said 'I love you.' It's really too bad," she spoke softly to the empty library where she had finally wandered to read and rest. "I think I would have made him a wonderful wife."

Sunny prayed then that she would be able to handle Brandon's marriage someday, for it was sure to happen. Her Bible lay neglected in her lap as the sun flooding through the windows made Sunny feel drowsy. She fell asleep again, this time with a frown on her face as she pictured living at Ravenscroft, all alone, until she was Aunt Lucy's age.

An hour later Brandon quietly entered the Britons' library and stood looking at Sunny. He felt every muscle of his body tremble with relief and fatigue. Moving silently, he sat down in the chair across from hers and just stared. Her face was pale, her hair was coming down, and her body looked frightfully thin, but Brandon saw past all of this. She was still the most beautiful woman he had ever known.

Sorely tempted to join her in sleep, he fought the urge, certain she would awaken and be gone again before he could stop her. As it was, not many minutes passed before two groundsmen walked by, their voices floating through the window, and Sunny awakened. Brandon watched her head come up and her eyes blink at him as if she were seeing a vision.

A vision was exactly what Sunny thought she saw. She felt a bit tormented that Brandon was the vision, but then the vision moved and Sunny's heart plummeted to her toes.

"Oh no, Brandon," she whispered, and he had to force himself to stay where he was.

"I'm not ready to see you yet." Her voice held an edge of panic. "I'm really not ready. How did you find me?" she asked suddenly.

"Your eyes," he told her gently. "No one can forget your eyes. You made three stops on the way here, and each and every innkeeper told me a beautiful lady had been in, a lady with lavender eyes."

Sunny came out of her chair, her Bible dropping to the floor. Her fatigue and confusion made her movements clumsy as she moved to put her chair between them. Brandon moved to the edge of his own chair, but with great effort remained seated.

"I'm sorry for the way I acted on the ship, Brandon."

She sounded near to tears, and Brandon knew he wouldn't be able to take much more.

"Sunny," he began but she shook her head.

"It was just so silly of me to make you say that. I'm horribly embarrassed. I realize we'll only always be friends, and that's fine."

Brandon came to his feet then; he'd heard enough. Sunny saw the determined look in his eyes and backed away from him, but he moved toward her with resolve. He was thankful he had found her indoors since she was flat against the bookshelves before she stopped.

Brandon didn't touch her, but placed his hands on the shelves on either side of her and bent low to speak into her upturned face.

"Do you love me, Sunny?"

Great tears puddled in her eyes, and she shook her head yes. "I couldn't help myself," she said and gave a small hiccup.

Brandon's smile was tenderness itself. "I thought a lady always knew when a man was in love with her."

"But I forced you to say that. I—" Sunny protested, but stopped when Brandon smiled and shook his head.

"Oh, Brandon," Sunny whispered. "I've been in such pain."

"I'm sorry," he told her, still not moving to touch her. "Much of your pain is my fault. When I left the ship you were sound asleep. It never once occurred to me that you would wake before morning. I went to get Heather so you could leave the ship in the morning and salvage your reputation.

"I had no idea Rand and Chelsea were in London, or I would have sent them to you immediately. I also never dreamed that you would leave the ship so late at night."

"I didn't think about how dangerous that was until we were headed out of London," Sunny admitted. "If Wilson hadn't arrived, I'd have gone back on board with Dallas, but there he was when I felt like my world had fallen apart and I just—" Sunny shrugged helplessly, and Brandon filled the breach.

"There you were, loving me, thinking I didn't love you. You were also bruised over the emir's actions as well as my own. I've been highhanded and a fool at regular intervals. Can you ever forgive me, my love?"

"Oh, Brandon," Sunny spoke painfully. "Why couldn't I see how you felt? Why was I so blind to your true feelings?"

"I was equally blind to yours. Of course," Brandon added dryly, "you're a master at hiding your feelings, and I simply hid mine behind a mask of anger."

Sunny chuckled softly. "I'm certainly able to get under your skin." She looked doubtful then. "We will quarrel, you know."

"Why Sunny, you're acting as if we're going to be married." Brandon teased her with a smile.

He felt panic when she failed to return his smile, her lovely face frozen with uncertainty.

"We are going to be married, Sunny. Do you hear me?" At the moment he didn't care if he sounded high-handed or not.

"Yes," she still looked uncertain. "I hoped we would, but after Dinah, I wasn't sure how you would feel."

Brandon took her hand then and led her to the davenport. When they were seated, he spoke.

"I cared for Dinah very much, and I was tremendously hurt when she broke off with me, but I'm thankful for her because she was the one to tell me I loved you."

"Oh, Brandon, no," Sunny said. "I was the reason?"

"Yes. She believed I loved her, but not until your name was mentioned did she ever see even a fraction of the passion I had within me."

Sunny frowned again, and Brandon, watching her face so closely, questioned her.

"What is it, sweetheart?"

"Nothing really. It's just that I only see and hear your passion."

Brandon's brows flew to his hairline on this statement, and Sunny, to her credit, did not blush.

"Oh, Hawk," she went on, using his nickname for the first time. "Do I really have to ask? Will you please kiss me the way you did on board ship?"

Brandon gave a great laugh of relief then, even as he reached for Sunny. In truth he had been afraid of moving too fast. She was such a lovely fit in his arms, and Brandon wanted to laugh all over again that she'd had to ask.

Sunny, on the other hand, couldn't laugh or even think at that moment. Her senses swam as Brandon's lips held her own. When she could talk again, her voice was so content that Brandon could only smile.

"I'm so glad we're going to be more than friends."

Brandon laughed at the direction of her thoughts. "Friends," he said, "lovers, husband and wife, and Lord willing, mother and father."

"Ummm," Sunny sighed contentedly, only to have Brandon kiss her again.

Outside the door, Wilson found Tildy listening, her head tilted to hear every sound.

"Afraid he's going to eat her alive?" Wilson teased the old woman, who sniffed indignantly.

"They're not married; I ought to go in."

"Well do, by all means, but give them a few moments. They've just come together. Something tells me that when Lady Sunny comes out, she'll finally be ready to eat."

"That's right," Tildy straightened quickly. "I best see that cook has a decent meal prepared for my lady."

Wilson stood and chuckled at how easily she had been distracted.

His gaze swung to the closed door when he heard Sunny's light laugh. He wasn't worried about her being alone with Lord Brandon, because he was a man in love. And in Wilson's experience, there wasn't a more gentle creature in all the earth than a man in love.

Epilogue

November 1849

LADY ANDREA STOOD AT THE WINDOW of her bedroom at Bracken and watched Brandon and Sunny below. The Duke and Duchess of Briscoe had been home from their honeymoon, a European tour, for about two months and had asked her to come for a visit.

Andrea had arrived some 40 minutes ago, only to be told that the lord and lady had gone for a walk. She didn't know what noise had made her move to the window, but as she watched her son's and daughter-in-law's antics, she was certainly glad she had.

Sunny was moving around the base of a tree, and Brandon was stalking her. Even with the window shut she heard Sunny's laugh and laughed herself. A moment later Sunny called something to her new husband; Brandon roared and charged.

Andrea watched as Brandon swung Sunny up into his arms in a swirl of petticoats. When his lips came down on hers, Andrea let the curtain fall back into place.

Twenty minutes later Andrea sat next to Sunny on the davenport and listened to her animated account of their honeymoon. Andrea had been to all the places they had visited, and Sunny was thrilled to have such a captive audience.

From time to time Andrea's gaze would flicker to her son, who had said little during Sunny's monologue but was certainly enjoying himself. Brandon's eyes rarely left his lovely bride, and it was easy to see he found Sunny thoroughly captivating as her eyes sparkled with excitement and her soft laugh sounded in the room. The older woman watched with amusement when Sunny kicked her shoes off and tucked her feet beneath her.

When Andrea was able to get a word in, she informed them that Holly and Jordan were expecting. One would have thought the news was Sunny's own, so excited was she. Andrea and the newlyweds went on to speak of Miles' forthcoming marriage and the family's plans to be at Heather's for Foster's fortieth birthday party the next week.

Andrea's visit made Sunny feel ten years old all over again. In fact, she was still talking late that night when Brandon came into her room, dismissed her maid who had been brushing Sunny's hair, scooped Sunny up, and carried her to his own bed.

Minutes later Sunny sat before her husband on his huge bed and chattered as he brushed her thick chestnut curls.

"It's so lovely to have Andrea here. She's going to be a great-grandmother! Isn't that something? She doesn't look at all old. I can't wait to see Holly. Jordan must be thrilled. I hope she isn't feeling ill."

Sunny shifted so Brandon could better reach her hair and fell silent. Brandon, who had been enjoying Sunny's easy banter, wondered at her quiet.

"You've fallen awfully still," he said softly.

"I was just thinking about the past," she admitted.

"Want to share?"

Sunny gave a low laugh. "I was just thinking about the little 13-year-old girl who sat on the *Flying Surprise*, demanding a maid, while Captain Brandon Hawkesbury tried to brush her hair. I was so self-centered, wasn't I, Brandon?"

Sunny found herself hugged and hauled carefully backward to lay across Brandon's lap. His face was so close to her own that she could feel his warm breath on her cheek when he spoke.

"No, you weren't."

"Oh, Hawk," Sunny spoke, shaking her head in disbelief.

"You were young and frightened, and you melted my heart the first time I laid eyes on you," Brandon responded, ignoring her doubt.

"Is that true?" Sunny loved his words.

"Yes, and even though my love has grown into something entirely different from what is was in those days, one thing has never changed: My heart still melts every time I look at you."

"Oh, Hawk, I love you so," Sunny whispered as her hand at the back of his head brought his lips down to her own.

Rain had begun to fall against the windows of the master bedroom at Bracken, but the duke didn't hear the sound. Kyle had told him years ago that Sunny would lead some man on a merry chase. He'd also said that someday she would be a priceless jewel. Brandon knew that if he ever saw Kyle again, he would have to tell him he had been right on both counts.